Amanda Cockrell, writing as Damion Hunter, is the author of seven previous Roman novels: the four-volume series The Centurions, concluding with *The Border Wolves*; and *The Legions of the Mist* and its sequel *The Wall at the Edge of the World*. *Shadow of the Eagle* is the first in The Borderlands, a new Roman series. She grew up in Ojai, California, and developed a fascination with the Romans when a college friend gave her Rosemary Sutcliff's books to read. After a checkered career as a newspaper feature writer and a copywriter for a rock radio station, she taught literature and creative writing for many years at Hollins University in Roanoke, Virginia, where she now lives.

www.amandacockrell.com

Also by Amanda Cockrell writing as Damion Hunter

The Legions of the Mist
The Wall at the Edge of the World

The Centurions Trilogy

The Centurions
Barbarian Princess
The Emperor's Games
The Border Wolves

The Borderlands

Shadow of the Eagle
Empire's Edge
Birds of Prey

AMANDA COCKRELL WRITING AS
DAMION HUNTER
BIRDS OF PREY

CANELO

First published in the United Kingdom in 2024 by

Canelo
Unit 9, 5th Floor
Cargo Works, 1–2 Hatfields
London SE1 9PG
United Kingdom

Copyright © Damion Hunter 2024

The moral right of Damion Hunter to be identified as the creator of this work has been asserted in accordance with the Copyright, Designs and Patents Act, 1988.

All rights reserved. No part of this publication may be reproduced or transmitted in any form or by any means, electronic or mechanical, including photocopy, recording, or any information storage and retrieval system, without permission in writing from the publisher.

A CIP catalogue record for this book is available from the British Library.

Print ISBN 978 1 80436 579 3
Ebook ISBN 978 1 80436 581 6

This book is a work of fiction. Names, characters, businesses, organizations, places and events are either the product of the author's imagination or are used fictitiously. Any resemblance to actual persons, living or dead, events or locales is entirely coincidental.

Look for more great books at www.canelo.co

Printed and bound in Great Britain by Clays Ltd, Elcograf S.p.A.

For Tony

ORCADES

High Isle

CORNOVII

Castra Borea

CALEDONES

Castra Pinnata

EPIDII

Bodotria

Clota

HIBERNIA

Tara

BRIGANTES

Eburacum

BRITANNIA

MONA

Deva

Bryn Epona

Dragon's Head

ORDOVICES

DEMETAE

SILURES

ICENI

Octapitarum

Dinas Tomen Llanmelin

Isca Silurum

Porth Cerrig Venta Silurum

Londinium

Sabrina Cow's Inlet

Aquae Sulis

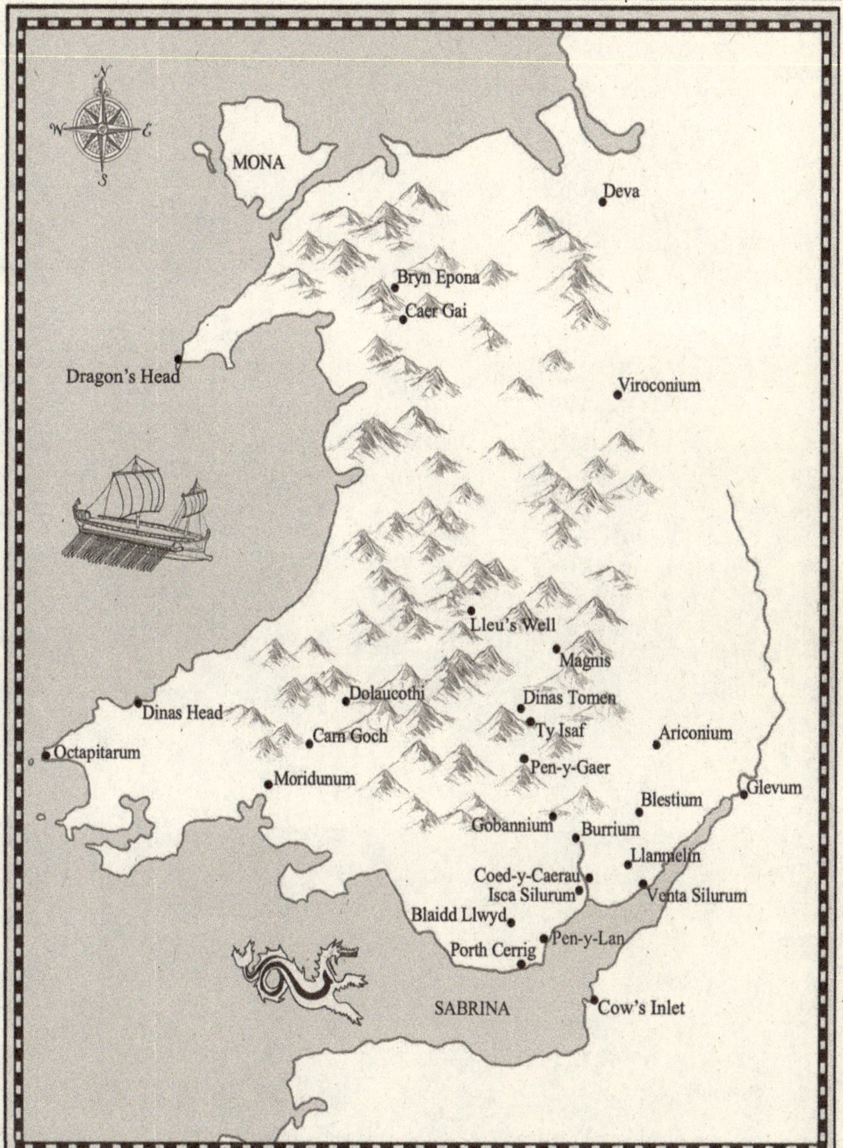
N
W
E
S
MONA
Deva
Bryn Epona
Caer Gai
Dragon's Head
Viroconium
Lleu's Well
Magnis
Dinas Head
Dolaucothi
Dinas Tomen
Ty Isaf
Ariconium
Octapitarum
Carn Goch
Pen-y-Gaer
Moridunum
Glevum
Blestium
Gobannium
Burrium
Llanmelin
Coed-y-Caerau
Isca Silurum
Venta Silurum
Blaidd Llwyd
Pen-y-Lan
Porth Cerrig
SABRINA
Cow's Inlet

Characters

Romans

Agricola Gnaeus Julius Agricola, former governor of Britain
Arvina Vitruvius Arvina, legate of the XX Valeria Victrix
Blaesus centurion of third century, First Cohort, II Augusta
Caecilius Aulus Caecilius, legate of II Augusta
Clio shopkeeper
Faustus Faustus Silvius Valerianus, primus pilus of the II Augusta
Gaia Valeriani (Guennola) Faustus's mother; deceased
Galerius primus pilus, XX Legion Valeria Victrix
Lucius Lucius Manlius the younger, son of Silvia
Lucullus Sallustius Lucullus, former governor of Britain; deceased
Lupinus prefect of the Fleet post at Moridunum
Manlius Lucius Manlius, husband of Silvia; deceased
Marcellinus tribune of II Augusta
Marcus Silvius Marcus Silvius Valerianus, father of Faustus; deceased
Marcus Silvius Minor Marcus Silvius Valerianus Minor, older brother of Faustus; deceased
Naso optio under Septimus, second century, First Cohort
Paullus Faustus's slave
Quintus third century optio, First Cohort, II Augusta
Rotri Aurelius Rotri, formerly of the border wolves, centurion in the XX Legion
Rufus Quinctilius Rufus, narrow-stripe tribune in XX Valeria Victrix

Septimus centurion of the second century, First Cohort, II Augusta
Silvia sister of Faustus
Terentius broad stripe tribune of the XX Valeria Victrix

Britons

Aedden king of the Silures
Badger Owl's sister at the sidhe of Blaidd Llwyd
Bendigeid king of the Silures before Aedden; deceased
Cadr a boatman
Curlew Old One of the sidhe of Llanmelin
Eirian Orkney woman, Faustus's wife
Fox Old One of the sidhe of Blaidd Llwyd
Fychan tinker
Gronwy chieftain of the Demetae
Guennola original name of Faustus's mother
Gwladus Dobunni woman hired to take care of Silvia
Gwydion Silure, king's captain and counselor
Heron Old One of the sidhe of Ty Isaf
Iodoc spear brother and driver of Gronwy
Iorwen sister of Loarn
Llamrei Silure, king's captain and counselor
Llew Silure, king's captain and counselor
Loarn new king of the Silures
Madog smuggler
Owl girl of the sidhe of Blaidd Llwyd
Plover Owl's sister at the sidhe of Blaidd Llwyd
Pwyll Silure, king's captain and counselor
Rail Owl's sister at the sidhe of Blaidd Llwyd
Rhodri Silure, king's captain and counselor
Salmon Curlew's brother, of the sidhe of Llanmelin
Teyrnon Chief Druid of the Silures
Thorn man of the sidhe of Blaidd Llwyd
Ula Ordovice lord

In Inis Fáil

Baine Queen of Inis Fáil
Cassan Tuathal's counselor
Dai Tuathal's counselor
Fiachra Tuathal's counselor
Owain Tuathal's counselor
Tuathal Techtmar High King of Inis Fáil

I. THE STAG

LATE SUMMER, 844 ab urbe condita, from the founding of the City, as the Romans count the years, in the tenth year of the Emperor Domitian.

As the Silures count them, in the thirteenth year since the peace with Rome.

"Aedden is dead."

Llamrei looked up at Loarn from the spearpoint she had been setting to a new shaft, her eyes wide and apprehensive. Aedden, who had ridden out to hunt on this bright midsummer day. "How?"

"In the same way as the old king." Loarn's face was nearly white, like bone against his dark hair.

Her stomach clenched. "That I do not believe."

"Not like that. But he rode onto a stag's horns, and it was not an accident."

Llamrei shivered, cold where before she had been contentedly soaking up the summer warmth. On the seaward side of Porth Cerrig, the cries of gulls echoed in a raucous chorus above the fishing boats coming in below the cliffs.

"Why?" she asked Loarn. But she knew.

"I don't know." Loarn's voice was anguished. But he knew, too. "In regret for the bargain he made maybe."

"*I* made that bargain, with the Roman governor," Llamrei said.

"Not that one. With the old king. Likely Aedden has felt his breath on his neck since."

Llamrei closed her eyes for a moment. "That was the old king's choice. I dressed him for his death, Loarn. And if you are right, this is Aedden's choice."

"Perhaps I am not right." Loarn stood uncertainly in the doorway, as if looking for a different door to go out of again. They were in the upper sleeping quarters of Porth Cerrig, in the chamber of the king's captains, strewn with hunting spears and pony bridles, half-mended boots, and the untidy leavings of meals. He was the youngest of them. He had been a boy when Bendigeid died, but he had watched with his mother's hand on his shoulder. It was a great thing to say that once you had seen a king-making, seen a king die in the old way that had not been done for generations. That day had sealed Aedden's right to the kingship in a way no other succession could have done, and persuaded the Romans to make a peace that did not include a puppet ruler of their choosing.

"Despite that Aedden is of the Royal House," Llamrei said, "he did not wish for the kingship. He took it for all our sakes." She wondered if he had been glad of the chance to hand it away again, even in death. If it had been in his mind over the last years. It must have been. The Roman governor in Britain had been executed on the emperor's orders two years since and he had not been replaced; Roman troops were taking ship for wars elsewhere. Aedden had taken advantage of Rome's distracted eye to rebuild some of their defenses and to stockpile grain and iron. But the act that had sealed Aedden to the kingship had sealed the Silures to the peace. A new king would free them of it.

"They are bringing him back," Loarn said. "Rhodri and Llew are with him. Pwyll and Gwydion are downstairs. I came ahead to tell you."

And see if I could find you a way out, Llamrei thought. "They will take him to Dinas Tomen," she said as gently as she could. Loarn looked like a horse balking at a gate. "You have some time yet."

"And if I say no?"

"Ask Teyrnon what will follow you if you do," Llamrei said.

"Teyrnon is older than the mountains," Loarn snapped. "He sees things no one else does."

"He is supposed to," Llamrei said. "And he is still here, although the Romans have outlawed the Druids. That should tell you something. Even I am afraid of Teyrnon."

Loarn sat down beside her on her bench, pushing aside the tangle of old bindings and the pot of oil she was rubbing into the new shaft. She moved her feet aside to make room for him. Llamrei had been captain and counselor to the old king and then to Aedden. Her hair was graying now, and like all the king's captains, cut at shoulder length and tied back with a red thong. She wore woolen shirt and breeches, and catskin-lined boots with an antler-handled knife sheathed in the right one. The spear mark tattooed on her breast was the same as theirs.

"You will take what is sent to you," Llamrei told him, "because you are of the Royal House of the Silures and it is your obligation as well as your right. Your sister became Goddess on earth when she was twelve because there was no other, and you will do this too."

"She has a son," Loarn said.

"Who is five years old." Llamrei stood. "I will put on a gown, as befits me to greet a king's body." She unfolded one from her clothes chest and stripped off her shirt and then her breeches, tugging the gown over her shoulders. The king's captains slept together and dressed together. That Llamrei was a woman had never made a difference. "I hear them," she said, buckling an enameled belt around the blue folds of her gown. "Come."

Loarn followed her down the stone steps and out to the landward gate. A little ripple ran through the ground as they reached the sea hold's outermost court, making them stumble and right themselves. Earthquakes were not unknown here – a small bucking of the earth – but they had become more frequent in the past year, and the Druids debated what that meant. It left everyone with a sense of coming upheaval. Llamrei heard a crash of crockery from the kitchen's open door.

The returning hunting party had been seen as soon as they came over the first rise on the track from the wooded hills to the west. The king's household crowded the gates. There was always someone on watch, and Loarn's appearance behind a lathered team had been warning enough that something would be behind him.

Aedden's body was laid in his chariot, his feet overhanging the car's floor, with Rhodri cradling the king's head in his lap. Llew and another man bore the stag that had killed him, with the king's blood on its antlers.

Loarn braced his shoulders, face still white. Then he walked to meet the chariot as it halted inside the gates, and laid his hand on the king's bloodied chest. The king mark on Aedden's forehead was stark against pallid skin. "Carry him with me," he said to Rhodri.

Together they lifted Aedden, and Llamrei took his hunting spear from the driver. Pwyll and Gwydion, white-faced, set up a bier in the great hall, laden with furs and blankets. They laid Aedden on it, and Llamrei set his spear beside him. Loarn knelt to scrub his fingers in the cold ashes of the hearth lest he inadvertently smear the king's blood on something.

Teyrnon Chief-Druid stood beside the bier. The gold sun wheel on his staff caught the last light spilling through the doorway. It lit his white gown and beard so that they glowed too. The king's household waited in silence for him to tell them what this meant.

Teyrnon looked a long time at the wound in Aedden's chest, blood already stiffening in the checked fabric of his shirt. He said, "The land begins to speak as Rome grows weaker. Each trembling in the earth is a word." He put a finger on the mark on the still forehead. "Now it has spoken to the king."

"The king of the Silures is dead."

Aulus Caecilius, legate of the Second Legion Augusta, looked from one of his senior officers to the next as they filed into the Principia. His barber was just departing with a kit under his arm and the remains of a midday meal lay spread on the desk in a litter of eggshells and empty wine cups, which the legate's slave was endeavoring to clear away without disturbing those summoned to his presence. They stood mostly in a ring around him, the broad-stripe tribune and the primus pilus occupying the only other chairs.

"How?" The primus pilus asked the obvious question.

"A hunting accident, Centurion Valerianus," Caecilius said. "He missed his kill, and the stag caught him up on its antlers."

Faustus's eyebrows went up.

"No one appears to have murdered him for the throne, if that's what you're thinking, but I'm concerned about what's likely to happen as a result." The legate reached for his wine cup before the slave could tidy it away. "Bring a jug and more cups."

"I was thinking of how he succeeded to the kingship in the first place," Faustus said.

Caecilius looked skeptical. "You told me that tale when we were both serving in the north; I had forgotten it. Just a campfire story on a boring night, yes?"

"Not really," said Lucanus, the Second Cohort centurion. "I've heard it too."

"Do you think he arranged it somehow?" the legate asked. "And if so, why?"

"I don't know," Lucanus said. "But there will be a new king now, who made no treaty with Rome."

Caecilius considered. He was new to this command and most of his officers had been in Isca Silurum longer than either he or the senior tribune, including Faustus Silvius Valerianus, the primus pilus, who was half Silure himself, which made him useful; and also possibly suspect, despite the fact that Caecilius's predecessor had asked to have him posted to Isca.

5

"What we do know," Caecilius said, "is that the Silures have been getting grain and military quality steel from somewhere. Grain that is not stored in the official warehouses as it should be, and steel that they should have no use for."

"Where is it coming from?" the tribune Marcellinus asked.

"An obvious source would be Gaul," Lucanus said. "But we keep an eye on what goes in and out of the ports there and grain sacks are hard to hide. Iron is heavy and hard to shift inconspicuously. My bet is on Hibernia."

"We have always had trade between Britain and the Gaels," Faustus said. "Grain isn't a usual commodity, but it's not interdicted."

"And iron?" Caecilius asked. "Valerianus, you have had some dealings with them. You were sent to help put the current High King on his throne and cement an alliance there. How likely is it that he would be willing to arm Rome's subjects?"

"Not quite an alliance," Faustus said carefully. "My position was entirely unofficial." He thought he would leave out mention of the hapless governor Lucullus, Caecilius's former commander, who had sent him to train Tuathal Techtmar's mercenaries for him.

"Would the king allow trade in iron?"

"He would allow trade in anything," Faustus said frankly, "including if by 'trade' you mean raiding. Raiding between West Britain and Hibernia has been a mutual occupation for centuries. If they have formalized it somewhat, that won't make any difference to him."

"Could he be persuaded to put a stop to it?"

"Not without military force, which he knows we don't have."

"I thought there was a friendship between you."

"Not that would help us here, sir. I like him, and I think he likes me, but it won't make any difference. It's to his advantage to have Rome too busy keeping Britain in hand to waste time with ambitions about Hibernia."

"He outlawed the men who came to fight in the north against his orders three years ago," Caecilius pointed out.

Marcellinus said, "I imagine that he sees a difference between attacking Rome on our territory and selling supplies to natives here who want to do so."

"That would be my guess," Faustus said. "He has a fair idea of exactly what would provoke the emperor to send an army to invade Hibernia. He won't risk that. Allowing smuggled grain and iron isn't enough of a provocation. If we were even sure that's where it's coming from."

"We don't know where they're landing it, either," Caecilius said. "There are little bays and inlets all along this cursed coast where a man who knows the waters can come in at night and meet a train of ponies to offload." He pulled a map from the desk drawer and jabbed a finger at the coastline, most of which had been derived from guesswork. "Our scouts have seen activity at Porth Cerrig and Dinas Tomen and at Carn Goch, but nothing substantial enough to be proof. And by the time we get there they've moved it."

"To go to Carn Goch you have to get by Moridunum," the Fourth Cohort commander said.

"You do, and they are."

"Carn Goch is a Demetae settlement," Lucanus said. Moridunum was a Demetae city as well – the old sea fort of Dun Mori – but Moridunum was the site of their tribal government and hence well under Rome's eye, and had a ship of the Fleet assigned to its harbor as well.

The legate's slave returned with a tray and cups in one hand and jugs of water and wine in the other. "I think you'll appreciate this," Caecilius said as cups were poured. "A small gift from the emperor himself. I thought I would share."

Caecilius had been a tribune on Governor Lucullus's staff and his posting to a legionary command was slightly premature in the ordinary way of things. Sallustius Lucullus had been implicated in a failed revolt in Germany and a great many heads had rolled, including the governor's. That Caecilius had not lost his too, argued a hand in suppressing any inclination that troops at Eburacum might have had to follow Lucullus down the same treasonous path.

Faustus noted that the emperor's gratitude had not extended to posting Caecilius outside of Britain, which had seen enough troops drawn off to make any lingering ambitions impossible. But it was very good wine.

"And will the Demetae follow the Silures into rebellion?" Lucanus asked, coming back around to the subject.

"If the Silures pressure them, it would be likely," Faustus said. "The Demetae and the Silures are kin, and the Demetae are not as numerous or as powerful."

"What about the Ordovices?" Marcellinus asked.

"I got a thorough lesson in West Britain tribal politics from my predecessor," Caecilius said, "and it made my head ache. Essentially, they all hate each other, but the Silures and the Ordovices hate each other more than others. They lost the last war because the old Silure king and Cadal of the Ordovices couldn't come to terms on alliance and spent most of their councils lying to each other."

"Useful for us," Marcellinus said. "That attitude should be fostered."

Lucanus said, "Cadal is older and probably wilier than he was then, but the garrison at Deva has reported no signs of trouble so far."

"May it stay that way," Marcellinus said. "Half their legion is in the north trying to shore up the mess at Eburacum."

No new governor had been appointed, and the emperor plainly had no intention of trusting another one yet, leaving the province under the nominal command of a procurator. Eburacum had been undermanned since vexillations of the Ninth Legion had been sent to the Rhenus, and worse, a few of its senior officers, although mercifully not the legate, had been involved along with Lucullus. The result had been grim. As a result, the Brigantes had become more of a nuisance than usual and the legate of the Ninth had asked for help.

"We move troops around like stones on a game board," Caecilius said. "Don't expect that to end soon, either, so we had best shift for ourselves." He took a swallow of the emperor's gift-wine and considered. "The other thing we don't know, among the many, is how they are paying for smuggled goods. There's some evidence that they're skimming from the mines at Luentinum." Skimming was always a problem at the mines, even with Roman overseers, and particularly hard to detect if the entire mine crew was in on it.

"River trade has slowed," Caecilius went on. "Which argues that there are boats slipping past our customs officials or being waylaid."

"To my mind, it's more urgent to solve the first problem," Marcellinus said. "Catch whoever is bringing in grain and iron, deal with them, and then worry about how it's paid for. I think it's safe to assume the grain is to tide them over a protracted war if their crops are destroyed. Julius Frontinus essentially starved them into submission the last time."

The legate's cup rattled on his desk, and he swore. "Not only does this cursed place rain all the time, now it quivers like a custard. Valerianus, is this normal?"

"Not entirely, sir," Faustus said. "It's not unknown but these feel as if it's building to something." The tremblings in the earth had gradually increased over the year he had been posted to Isca Silurum. The haruspex had examined a sheep's liver and failed to see anything useful in it. Sacrifices to Neptune had been made, but with little result.

"My worry is that it's likely the Silures are reading a message in it," Lucanus said.

"Something about heaving Romans into the ocean?" Marcellinus asked.

"I want to know how the smuggled grain and iron are getting in," the legate said, returning to a problem he could get a grip on. He looked at Marcellinus who looked at Faustus. A tribune *laticlavius* was nominally second in command of a legion but since he was most often posted only for a year, it was the primus pilus, commander of the First Cohort, who knew things.

"Can you pass for a native?" Marcellinus asked him.

"Not in the long term," Faustus said. "Not enough to go wandering about asking casual questions about smuggling if the border wolves couldn't manage it." The border wolves were the elite of the frontier scouts, known for their ability to go into enemy territory and return with their heads attached. "That line of inquiry generally ends badly even for natives." Faustus added. He studied the contents of his wine cup and considered the advisability of his next sentence. "I do know someone who might know someone, so to speak."

Caecilius ran his hands through his black hair, freshly cropped, and over his newly shaven chin. An example needed to be set for his officers, or they would all dissolve into barbarians. Valerianus, for instance, needed a haircut. "Thank you, Centurion, that is entirely unclear. Kindly elucidate."

"Sorry, sir. I know someone who might be receiving smuggled goods. This person might be inclined to be useful, but I would not like to expose this person to difficulties as a result."

"What goods precisely?" Caecilius inquired.

"Silk, sir. And eastern dyestuffs." He eyed the gold-bordered scarlet cloak that hung with the legate's cuirass and helmet from a rack in the corner.

"Silk? I am not a portoria agent. You may consider this person's secret safe with me."

"She keeps a shop in Aquae Sulis," Faustus said. "My sister has heard from some of the officers' wives that the prices are low enough to make the trip to Aquae worth their while."

Caecilius chuckled while his subordinates strove to look disinterested. Even a senior centurion's pay ordinarily stopped short of silk. "Thus the suspicion that she may be getting smuggled goods?"

"Yes, sir. She's a, er, enterprising sort and silk is lightweight and easily concealed and getting wet doesn't damage it. And the import taxes on luxury goods are high."

"And you think she would be helpful if you asked her?"

"I doubt she would know who's been supplying the Silures; I imagine her goods come through other channels. She might put me in touch with her supplier, and I do think he might know. People in that line tend to know their competition. It would have to be carefully done. I expect I'll have to bribe somebody."

"I am positive of it," Caecilius said. "How do you know this woman?"

"She used to live in the vicus. I was acquainted with her then."

"Selling silk in Isca?" No shops in the vicus ran to that kind of merchandise, or clientele.

Faustus gave up. "She used to be one of Abudia's girls," he said to hoots of laughter from the rest of the room. He flushed. "She came into some money. Tuathal Techtmar grew fond of her while he was in General Agricola's camp, and he promised her a gift if he became High King. I was the one who brought it to her."

"We may assume that you knew her at least as well as Tuathal Techtmar did," Caecilius said, "but you may leave out further details."

"Thank you, sir."

"Perhaps you might pay her a visit."

—

The journey to Aquae Sulis took two days along roads crowded with travelers bound for the healing waters there. Faustus had hired a carriage for his household and his wife Eirian hung out the window with his nephew Lucius beside her, observing it all. On the other seat Faustus's widowed sister Silvia sat with her maid Gwladus. Faustus and Paullus rode beside them; master and slave both watchful for any trouble on the road, the dog

Argos padding at the horses' heels like an enormous friendly wolf. It was not an inconspicuous journey, but Faustus had decided that it gave his mission verisimilitude. No spy in his right mind would take so many encumbrances with him on his ventures. And he had promised both his wife and sister to take them to Aquae Sulis months ago.

Silvia's dislike of Isca had waned in comparison with their stay on the northern frontier. Her son Lucius was entirely happy there, with the run of both the fortress and the vicus, the surrounding civilian settlement. And Eirian, daughter of the Orcades islands, was content anywhere there was water; although he knew she was hoping for a child, and that had not happened yet.

Only Faustus was discontented, unsure of place or purpose. Julius Agricola's conquest of the highlands, which Faustus had been so proudly a part of, had been almost entirely erased: an achievement for the history books, but otherwise ephemeral. Everything above the line between Clota Mouth and the Bodotria estuary had been abandoned, even Castra Pinnata, which was to have housed a legion: everything that would burn set on fire and everything else buried. Now Faustus felt as if the land in West Britain too wanted to shake him off, fling him from its hills like a dog shaking water. And yet, with that feeling, running braided with it, was an odd sense of belonging, whether it wanted him or no.

It was the thing his father had feared; something in the blood that would make him unsuited for the life he was born to. The old man's shade, which had pursued Faustus fussing ever since he had joined the army, had beaten about his ears all the way to Isca a year ago, and periodically appeared now to offer dire pronouncements. Faustus would have long ago decided he was mad if not for the fact that Paullus occasionally saw him too. Eirian had a sense of him now and then and Gwladus thought he was a cobweb and swept vigorously at the patch of wall beside the household gods. Only Silvia seemed oblivious to him, and she was the one who would have agreed with him. That their mother had been Silure was more a source of embarrassment to her than anything else. Their mother had become Roman with her manumission and marriage to their father; in Silvia's mind that erased all other identity. The territory, human or geographic, that Rome acquired became Roman.

Now in a place where Rome's hand and Roman identity had been long established, something was brewing. Patrols from Isca Silurum – and even occasionally from Deva – were being hit by ambush and strike-and-run attacks, arrows or slingstones from the trees. When one of the culprits was caught and killed, the Silures professed no recognition of him. Bandits, no doubt, they suggested. Faustus would see what Clio's supplier – if he could make contact with him – might tell him about that. Runners of contraband almost always found that it paid them to know things.

The most direct route to Aquae Sulis was by ship across the Sabrina estuary to Abona, and then by hired carriage. Eirian had balked at the carriage, and they had had one more conversation about how respectable Roman women – or unrespectable ones for that matter – did not ride horses. She knew that but it irked her.

"I will put on breeches," she suggested.

"They'll think you're my catamite. No."

She grinned at him and got in with an air of wifely obedience that was entirely manufactured. She seemed now resigned to watch the rolling green landscape unfolding and the blue loops of the river in the distance and speculate about other travelers with Lucius, who was twelve and specialized in imagination.

"That one," Lucius suggested, pointing to a large man on a mule, "has been bitten by an adder and his foot is horribly damaged and turning black and he's going to the waters for a cure."

"And that one." Eirian pointed to military courier bound in the other direction for the posting station at Abona. "He has a very important message for someone. What do you think it is?"

Lucius considered. "Sea monsters. There have been sea monsters sighted off the coast. They are headed for Isca."

Eirian looked at Silvia out of the corner of her eye. Silvia was inclined to think this game was frivolous and encouraged foolishness, but she seemed to be asleep, dark head sunk against the cushions despite the jolting of the carriage. "They will swim right up the river and eat the new tribune if they aren't stopped," Eirian said. "We will need a great hero for that."

"My uncle could stop them," Lucius said.

"Maybe."

Faustus reined in his horse beside the carriage window, and she blew him a kiss. Night was falling and he halted them at an inn where the Glevum road joined theirs. There was no point in inviting actual bandits.

In the morning they rode into Aquae Sulis and found another inn. Paullus took Lucius to the baths and the temple of Sulis Minerva, and Faustus escorted the women to the shopping district beside the temple. The hot mineral spring sacred to a Dobunni goddess was ancient but much of the temple complex was new, product of Roman prosperity. The streets were crowded with bathers arriving to take the waters, bathers protesting that their clothes had been stolen from the changing rooms, and bathers and others buying curse tablets from several vendors, on which their imprecations against thieves and faithless lovers could be inscribed, sealed with a nail, and dropped into the sacred spring for the assistance of the goddess. A warren of shops surrounded the temple complex, selling clothing, silver, jewelry, and kitchen ware, and crowded with shoppers whose slaves trailed behind them with their purchases.

Clio's shop sat on the lower floor of a two-story house with her living quarters above, cheek to cheek with the buildings on either side. Over the entrance a red awning proclaimed SILK

AND EGYPTIAN COTTON, with piles of brilliant goods displayed on tables beneath it. The interior was draped in whisper-thin gauze and an expensive rainbow of silks in deep cherry red, emerald, and the bright yellow of egg yolks that caught the light like a sunset. On a shelf behind the counter sat rows of stoppered glass jars of dyestuff.

Clio looked much as he remembered, a bit plumper and more prosperous, swathed in a bright blue gown and scarlet overgown pinned with gold and lapis lazuli pins. A pair of scissors hung from her girdle.

Her eyes widened when she saw him. "Faustus!"

She looked as if she might throw her arms around him, and he said hastily, "Let me present my wife and sister."

Clio became politely dignified. "Centurion Valerianus, it's very nice to see you."

Introductions were made and Faustus suggested that she bring out a few of her best lengths of fine wool and perhaps her more affordable silks. He would be extravagant in the Empire's service.

Clio called to someone at the back of the store and bustled about selecting goods. A maid came with an armful of other yardage. They piled them on the counter. "Pay attention to the front of the shop," Clio told the maid, before she said to Faustus, "Aquae is dreadful for the number of thieves about. It's because of all the visitors. They wander about gawking at the temple and the gardens and not watching their purses."

Silvia ran her fingers across a length of yellow silk.

"Not quite first quality, but an excellent buy for the price," Clio said. Faustus imagined that she had a fairly precise knowledge of what army pay would stretch to.

"This is lovely." Eirian stroked a folded piece of pale blue wool the color of sea water.

"See what you might like," Faustus said. "Within reason. Something for Gwladus, too," he added. Gwladus's man had been under Faustus's command when he died. It was hard to forget that. And he owed her doubly for putting up with Silvia.

"How are things in Isca?" Clio asked Faustus while the women unfolded various lengths of cloth, holding them to the light and against each other.

"Interesting," Faustus said. "I need to talk to whoever brings in your silk."

It was a stab in the dark and he could see it went home; Clio radiated suspicion.

"I'm not the tax man," he said. "And nor is my commander. But we do need information and I think your man might have some, of the secondhand sort."

"Faustus, this is my livelihood. I am entirely respectable in Aquae Sulis. Not even a business in the back. Why on earth did you bring your wife and sister? I had no idea you were married. You might have warned me. Why are you here?"

"I brought them because I promised them dress goods," he said, trying to untangle her questions. "I have no intention of overturning your respectability, which I can see is monumental. Or of setting customs agents on you. The opposite in fact. Your contacts are no good if they shut you down."

"What do you want to know? And I'm not admitting there's anything to know."

"I need to find out who's running grain and weapons into West Britain under our noses and selling it to the Silures."

"Not Cadr," Clio said firmly. "He wouldn't want any business with insurrection if that's what you're getting at."

"We have suspicions. And we'd like to stop it now. Did you know that Aedden of the Silures has died? Speared on a stag's antlers while hunting."

Clio's eyes widened again. "When?"

"A seven-day since. I'm surprised the news hasn't reached Aquae."

"It will. It will be on your heels. It's the doing of the gods when one of the horned ones takes a king. I don't want anything to do with this."

"They aren't your gods," Faustus protested. "Aren't you Greek?"

"That's just the name Abudia gave me. She thought it was high class. I was born in Gaul same as you."

He was embarrassed that she knew more about him than he did about her. He had never bothered. He wondered if any of her customers had bothered. "I'm sorry I never asked you that," he said.

"You had no reason to. But we both know the horned one, don't pretend you don't."

One of the old gods of Gaul and Britain. Old enough that his image, a dancing figure crowned with antlers, was painted on the walls of caves so old that no one knew who had lived in them.

"Then you will see the urgency of what we need to know," he said.

Clio folded her arms across her chest. "Persuade me, Faustus. I don't like this."

Faustus said, "You won't like it if there's a rebellion. A thing like this could spread to the Ordovices and the Demetae."

"This is Dobunni territory," Clio said. "They surrendered while Claudius Caesar was still on his way to Britain. They aren't going to join any rebellion."

"No," Faustus admitted. "But think how bad it will be for trade." He gestured at the shop. "The whole Roman military will be tied up fighting in West Britain instead of shopping here, and the patrols in the Sabrina Channel will be looking for anything suspicious, which will be your boatman Cadr. He'll have to start landing on the south coast and that will cost you. If he even can. Contraband runners have their territory. The southern coast is probably someone else's."

Clio frowned. "I've always liked you, Faustus. You were always kind to me, and the other girls. Not everyone was. And you didn't have to bring me the gold Tuathal sent. You could have kept it."

"I would not!" Faustus said, insulted.

"No, but some would. Girls in brothels don't have any recourse when someone cheats them." She looked around the shop. "Can you promise it won't come back to trouble me if I ask Cadr if he'll talk to you?"

"It won't come through me," Faustus said. "I'm hoping that Cadr can tell me who I ought to be looking at, and if he can I'll keep the source of my information private."

"Even from your superiors at Isca?"

"I told them I was going to see you."

Clio's expression darkened.

"They are uninterested in monitoring the import taxes paid on silk," Faustus said.

"Some of them are customers," she admitted. "So they should be."

"There you are then."

"And Cadr?"

"If Cadr will speak to me, I will keep his secrets."

Clio still looked troubled, but she said, "Very well. I will ask him. But it will take some time. I don't see him often, and he comes to me, not the other way round."

"I understand. But you will ask him? And send me a message when he agrees?"

"If he agrees."

"Remind him that he doesn't want more patrol craft in the channel."

"I won't need to," she said grimly. "I think he will probably talk to you."

Faustus glanced at Eirian and Silvia. They seemed to have made up their minds. He took Clio's hand and kissed her fingers. "Thank you. The legate thanks you. Rome thanks you. I think my ladies have made their choice from your splendid goods."

Clio took her hand back. "I will not be charmed, Faustus. You watch your back. Whoever Cadr tells you about is going to be someone dangerous."

II. DINAS TOMEN

The moon was almost full. Llamrei could see its light on the water although cloud cover made all the shadows murky. She dipped the branch with its tuft of straw into a clay jar of coals until it caught. When it was well alight she raised her arm, waved it once. A flash of light came back from the water and she stamped the straw out under her foot. The ponies wuffled restlessly in the salt grass behind her and she heard Rhodri whisper to them. A little breeze from the water below the headland carried a murmur of voices and Llamrei looked uneasily at the faint light that moved in the distance: the Roman watch at Dun Mori making its rounds.

By rights she should have been at Dinas Tomen, but this shipment could not be called back and some things did not wait even for the death of kings. She could see the boats drawn up on the beach now, three of them, the boatmen wading through the surf carrying crates between them. She whistled to Rhodri, and he started the ponies down the switchback path to the beach. Three Demetae men followed him.

They would leave this shipment at Carn Goch until Loarn had been made king, and then they would take the Demetae chief to Dinas Tomen with them. The Demetae might be unwilling allies but Gronwy would come to Dinas Tomen to see a new king of the Silures crowned and the old one laid in the earth. They had seen Bendigeid buried mostly to see that he didn't come up again, she thought. That had been a long time since, and no amount of wishing had ever brought him back to her. Not even at Samhain, when the veil between the worlds was thinnest. Bendigeid had gone to his death to buy them the time that had brought them to this night; Aedden to his because they no longer needed it. Kingship was a bargain, a debt owed to the tribe, not to be undone from the moment that Teyrnon Chief Druid put the king mark on his forehead. That was why Loarn had shied from it.

On the beach, the boatmen broke the crates open while Llamrei flinched at the sound, and Rhodri and the Demetae men separated their contents into the ponies' packs. Llamrei caught the glint of steel in the milky light. Sword blades, spear-points, the smooth curve of a helmet. Her people's smiths made fine weapons, but good iron was hard to come by under the Romans' eye.

The coin they had brought changed hands. The Silures did not mint their own silver but traded in coin from the Dobunni upriver. The boatman inspected it and the three small boats slipped back into the water.

Llamrei watched the laden ponies come back up the path, a small rattling of stones beneath their hooves the only sound, no more than a fox might have made. A hunting owl floated overhead and was gone. The night was still around them, the creatures of the wild hiding from the owl and the humans both. Still enough that the small crack of a twig in the stand of windblown trees – that bordered the sedge and salt grass – snapped her head around. The first pony's nose came up to the top of the track. Llamrei stared into the trees. She laid a hand on Rhodri's arm as he came level with her.

"What is it?"

"In the trees. Something."

Rhodri handed the pony's lead to one of the Demetae. "Take them that way." He pointed away from the trees. "And then back to the trail. Go slowly. We will catch up with you." He nodded to Llamrei and they crouched in the grass to watch, spears in hand.

When the string of ponies had gone some distance, a pair of figures slipped from the trees and moved after it. They didn't look back to see Rhodri and Llamrei hunting behind them.

The pair were almost on their quarry when the men finally heard them and turned, swords out. The faint light glimmered on helmeted heads, on shirts of mail over skirts of leather and short tight-fitting breeches. Romans, which was not a surprise.

There was no time to decide anything. If they killed a pair of Romans on Demetae territory, the chief of the Demetae would be angry. If they didn't, the Romans would know exactly where the boats came in.

Llamrei ran hard at the man on the right, spear braced in both hands. She had the advantage as long as she could stay out of his sword's range. He pulled his cloak from his shoulders, ripping the pin free, and swung its folds at her like a shield, trying to tangle the spearshaft. It caught the tip of her spear and she jerked it sideways trying to pull the cloak from his grip. It snarled in the heavy wool. She yanked at it again and tore the blade free before he could use it to pull her toward him. They circled each other. She was aware of Rhodri fighting with the other man but could give them no attention or take her eyes from the man before her. If the Demetae men had halted the ponies at the sound of the fighting they might come to help. Or might not. Demetae and Silures were entwined in a knot made half of kinship and half of old hatred, grievances built over the years on the imbalance of power between them.

If they didn't kill these men, they would run. The Romans weren't here to confiscate the weapons, they were here to see where they came from and where they went. Llamrei drove her spear hard at the Roman's chest and felt it nick his ring mail. He knocked the spearshaft to one side and tried again to entangle it in his cloak. She staggered back and feinted, waiting for an opening. When he raised his sword arm and swung the cloak with his left to block the feinted blow, she aimed her spear the other way and ran it under the sleeve of his mail into the armpit.

Blood poured out and he swayed for a moment. Then he turned and ran.

Llamrei went after him. The ground was rough with hummocks of salt grass and outcropping stone. She saw him stumble but he kept going with his sword in his left hand now, cloak abandoned. Blood loss would slow him, she hoped. She was closer, closing on him. He fell, picked himself up and kept running. She could hear Rhodri shouting behind her. Closer. A spear wouldn't go through mail on the back of a running man. She put the shaft between his legs, and he fell again. Before he could rise, she dove past the sword blade and pinned him to the ground with her body. The sword swung awkwardly at her head, and she caught his wrist and turned it hard. The blade fell from his grip, and she drew her belt knife and drove it into his throat.

She stayed kneeling over him, breathing hard, as Rhodri came up to her. He pulled her to her feet.

"Where is the other one?" she asked him.

"Dead," Rhodri said. He was bleeding from a cut on his forearm. She pulled the Roman's scarf from his neck and tied up Rhodri's arm. They picked the body up and carried it back across the salt grass to where the other one lay still, blood running from his mouth. With the weight of desperation Rhodri had driven his spear through the ring mail and the padded coat beneath it. A gaping hole showed where he had pulled it out again, the split rings crusted with drying blood.

"What do we do with them?"

"Take them to Carn Goch?"

"Gronwy would bar the gates. The last time he had Romans in Carn Goch they burned it."

"These are dead."

"And someone will be looking for them."

The string of ponies had halted ahead of them. Rhodri whistled to the Demetae leader.

He came grudgingly and looked at the dead Romans. "I'll not have them here at the foot of Dun Mori."

"Help us carry them then," Rhodri said. "Send the ponies to Carn Goch and you and one other come with us. Else we will leave them here."

"If you do the Romans will know where the boats come in," the man said.

"If we do, they will blame you," Llamrei said.

He shrugged then and called one of the others over. They stripped the dead Romans and added their steel to the shipment on the ponies' backs. Then they set off along the coast backwards from Dun Mori and Carn Goch both.

It took the better part of the remaining night to find a place that satisfied Llamrei and Rhodri, while the Demetae men grumbled under their breath. Finally Llamrei said, "Here," and they stopped at a cliff top above the wide flat beach where fishing boats from a village on the headland came ashore. They took each one by the arms and feet, swung them in a wide arc, and heaved them over. They tumbled through the air onto the sand among the fishing boats.

"They will blame the village," one of the Demetae said.

"They will not," Rhodri said. "Particularly not if the village buries them. Or takes them out to open water. They are not fools."

They began to make their way back in the dawn light, cross-country, avoiding the Roman roads for the old tracks worn by deer, and stopping to sleep in a farmer's house where the wife gave them bowls of stew and the best spot by the hearth. The Demetae land had healed somewhat in the years since the Romans had despoiled it, fields reclaimed and herds rebuilt, although much of the grain, wool, and hides went to the Romans in taxes. The ditches had been dug out again, and walls had been mended, and in the peace the Romans had let be. This was their last chance before the Romans turned every village into Dun Mori, Llamrei thought, round thatched houses torn away to make room for sharp-angled dwellings and temples to the Romans' gods and their government. Already the veterans were retiring where they had served, marrying and raising half-Roman children. The land would otherwise look the same, but it would not be.

Carn Goch, the Place of Red Stone, sat on a ridge above a broad river valley, a defensive hold along the western edge of the Silures' hunting runs. Since the Romans had taken Dun Mori it had become the chief's hall as well. The ponies were there ahead of them, their cargo unloaded and hidden.

"We are unwelcome," Rhodri said to Llamrei with a grin as Gronwy met them grudgingly and shouted at a slave to bring them food and beer.

Gronwy was annoyed by his men's report and by the delay. "You will find another place for the boats to come in," he said to Llamrei. Gronwy had been nine when the Romans had allowed him to become chief of the Demetae after the battle that killed his father and brothers. That Aedden and the Silure lords had treated him as a child had irked him, both then and now.

Llamrei shrugged. "We have used that mooring too often. When the new king is crowned, we will choose another and send someone to tell you."

Gronwy glowered at her. The peace that Aedden had made with Rome had kept the Silure land from the devastation the Demetae's had suffered; devastation that the Silures had sat back and watched. Aedden's captains marching lordlywise through his hold was an insult.

He was in no better mood in the morning as they made ready to meet the procession traveling from Porth Cerrig to Dinas Tomen. There was honor due to both old king and new however, and Gronwy was clad in his best, accompanied by Iodoc, the spear brother who was his driver. He sniffed at Llamrei's transformation: a gown of blue and brown checked wool, hair in a fall down her back, throat and arms ringed with gold. Her driver waited in her chariot, trading friendly insults with Rhodri's man. The chariot was red-painted, with silver-mounted trappings, the ponies' bridles bright with enamel.

Gronwy shouted to his driver and stepped up into his own chariot. He would go first, before the Silure lords, as was his right.

—

"And where are they?" Llew squinted into the distance past Pen-y-Gaer and saw nothing. "Something has gone wrong."

"They will come," Gwydion said, but he bit his lip. Llamrei and Rhodri should have been waiting for them here.

Two oxen pulled the wagon that carried Aedden's bier, decorated with yew and rowan branches, the ox harness hung with gold bells, their horns red-painted and capped with gold. Loarn's chariot followed it, Loarn's shoulders covered with a black-and-white cloak like a magpie, his shirt and breeches new, his boots new. A gold torque at his throat and gold armbands caught the light that spilled over the procession. The sky had cleared around a burning sun as if acknowledging the accession of a king. It had lit Teyrnon Chief Druid's white gown and beard and the gold sun wheel on his staff as he set off in a wagon with three younger Druids, going their own ways through the mountains out of the Romans' sight.

As many as had the ability followed the bier from Porth Cerrig, or joined on the way, to see the king-making. The road to Dinas Tomen was a four-day journey, slowed by the oxcart. Its first leg lay along the coast and upriver to Isca, where the Roman commander had sent his senior tribune to accompany them; out of respect, he said blandly. From Isca, they turned north along Roman-built roads topped with flat stone where each mile marker proclaimed the emperor's name and the distance from the road's beginning. Along the way the tribune inspected the road's surface and made notes on his tablet; Silures with Roman overseers had laid it, and maintenance was the tribe's responsibility.

The Roman garrisons at Burrium and then Gobannium came out to watch the Silure lords ride by. "We are a show for them," Llew muttered, but it was as well to keep the Romans' attention on their procession and not on any other travelers.

The garrison at Pen-y-Gaer was equally interested, lining the sentry walk along the wall to stare. It was at Pen-y-Gaer that Llamrei and Rhodri were to have joined them, escorting the Demetae's young chief. They had not.

"I understood that the chieftain of the Demetae was to meet us," the tribune, Marcellinus, said now, inconveniently. Marcellinus too was very splendid, in a silvered cuirass and greaves, and a helmet with a scarlet crest.

Gwydion, who spoke Latin, having been young enough to learn it when the Romans came, answered him. "The Chieftain of the Demetae no doubt has business to slow him, being not our vassal." In practicality that was exactly what Gronwy was, and Gwydion hoped his annoyance at that was the source of the delay.

"We will wait overnight for them," Loarn said. He also spoke Latin, as did Llamrei and the other captains save Llew, who had never been willing to learn more than a word or two, and that grudgingly.

"As you wish, King," Marcellinus said.

"I am not king," Loarn told him. "The king lies on that wagon."

Gwydion thought that if he were Loarn he would not take that name before he had to, either. Kingship was a burden, a stone pinning the king to the land. Some men wanted kingship for the power of it, certainly, but those men made bad kings. The Druids knew which men they were and where the Druids had power something happened to those men before they could be crowned. Loarn would take the crown not for power but because he had to, the same way that Aedden had.

They camped for the night outside the garrison's stone-and-turf walls. Their fires spread across the slope below the fort and the nearest village brought beer and roasted meat to the travelers by way of welcoming the king home.

"Something is wrong," Loarn said quietly to Llew and Gwydion when the tribune was safely in his tent. "Or Gronwy has made trouble."

"That in itself would be something gone wrong," Llew said.

"The Roman is still asking where they are," Gwydion said. "And getting the same answer as before, which he doesn't like."

"They will come tomorrow," Loarn said abruptly, "trouble or no," and Gwydion wondered if he actually knew, in the way that the captains had seen that Aedden sometimes knew things. Aedden's captains and now Loarn's, unless he chose new. Loarn who had been one of them and now suddenly was not.

—

In the morning six chariots came along the road from Circutio in the west. Gwydion recognized Gronwy's muscular shoulders and red ponies with relief, and saw Llamrei and Rhodri behind him, trailed by Gronwy's councilors.

"We regret our late arrival," Llamrei said formally to Loarn. She took in the presence of the tribune. "We stopped to mend a broken axle on the road."

"Ill luck," the tribune commented.

From Pen-y-Gaer the way diverged from the Roman road to a track that wound into the high mountains, slopes going russet with autumn. Behind the bright sun was the chill of winter coming; the air overhead was full of birds bound for southern roosting places on aerial roads, which somehow the young ones knew already. Even the otters that poked their whiskered faces above the riverbanks looked unusually purposeful.

By midday they came to the long green bulk of Ty Isaf, the Lower House, the ancient grave mound that gave its name to Dinas Tomen, the Fort above the Mound. Ty Isaf was still a holy place and the little dark people who were the last remnants of their kind frequented it, considering themselves to be the children of Ty Isaf although they didn't live there and probably had no memory of who had been buried there when they had still been kings in the land. It was screened by trees that grew up onto the top of the mound and the procession gave it a wide berth. Despite the old blood that ran in most of their veins, Silures were children of the Sun Lord, and were somewhat afraid of the magic the little hill people made under the sod of Ty Isaf.

Beyond it, Dinas Tomen crowned a spur jutting from the main mass of the Black Mountains. A banked chariot-way switchbacked up the steep slope, and at the third turn there were men to meet them: Teyrnon Chief-Druid and his pupils, in plain gowns with mistletoe in their hands.

"Priests of the Sun Lord," Llamrei explained to the tribune. "The one you call Sol."

The tribune nodded. Every people had priests. Distinguishing which might be Druids among them was not his task just now. His task was seeing where the damned iron was coming from.

The priests tied red thongs to the oxen's headstalls and led them up the track to the gate in the southwest wall. Dinas Tomen was built in stair-stepping courtyards, sheep and cattle pens and then pony sheds and dairy, round huts, women's house, kitchens, and storerooms. The great hall sat at the top, where Aedden's bier would rest until the next day. Then they would carry him down the track again and lay him in a barrow at the foot of the hill with the kings who had come before him.

The villages in the shadow of Dinas Tomen gathered throughout the afternoon and at nightfall a feast was laid in the great hall, with cups of mead and plates of roasted meat set before the bier. The Druids had treated the body so that it remained undecayed. But it looked empty, the king mark on Aedden's forehead stark against gray skin, the dark hair beneath the red gold crown lank and dusty looking.

Gronwy and Iodoc gave Aedden and Loarn both a perfunctory homage and sat feasting well away from the Silure lords. The Roman tribune sat by himself. Llamrei kept an uneasy eye on them all, and on Loarn, who drank from his cup and held it out to be filled again, and then again. After a while Llamrei and Teyrnon spoke to him, and he nodded and left the hall. "Give him something to make him sleep," Llamrei said.

"No."

"He will chew himself into rags by morning."

"That is what he is supposed to do." Teyrnon's voice suggested clearly that she not argue. "He is no king if he does not."

—

The sky was still clear as the sun rose, but the air had seemingly frozen overnight. The courtyard was rimed with frost when they carried the old king back down the track. Iorwen, who was the body of the Goddess on earth and sister of Loarn, led the women of the royal house ahead of the bier, strewing the path with flowers, such as could be found in autumn, and wild grasses. The priests followed, bundled in bearskin mantles. The sound of pipes and chanting came from those waiting for them beside the newly dug grave, a thin wailing that hung in the air.

Llamrei and Rhodri led a pair of black ponies pulling Aedden's empty chariot. At the foot of the track they unhitched the chariot and maneuvered it down an earthen ramp into the grave. Pwyll and Gwydion piled it with the grave goods: bronze vessels, a jug of blue and green Roman glass, silver plates and cups. Then they lowered the bier into the ground beside it. Loarn, no longer one of them, stood aside; looking, Llamrei thought, as if he would prefer to be the one going into the earth. They laid Aedden's sword beside him on the bier in its scabbard of red leather, and his hunting spear with a new collar of kite's feathers, and over him a blanket of fox skins. The gold torque at his throat showed above the fox skins and his hands were folded on their fur, ringed with gold and stones that seemed as drained of their color as his face.

Teyrnon came forward, clutching his bearskin around him against the icy air, and raised his arms to the sky, giving back to the Sun Lord what had been lent to them this while. He bent and took from the still head the red-gold crown.

Marcellinus watched politely from a distance as they began to backfill the grave. Gronwy stood arms folded and scowling. Llamrei saw the tribune take note, wondering no doubt how delicate the Demetae alliance might be, and how easily undermined.

When it was done and each of Aedden's captains but Loarn had taken a turn to push the cold earth back in, they set a cairn of stones on top. Iorwen and the other women laid the last of their flowers and grass around it, a reminder that the Goddess too was in all things: that all that died would be reborn in some new fashion as barley resprouted from seed.

Loarn stood for a long time looking at the piled stones until Teyrnon took him by the arm and they set out again up the track to Dinas Tomen.

In the upper court, the captains laid nine fires in a circle around a cleared space before the great hall. Llamrei was grim and closed-mouthed and the rest kept their distance until Rhodri put a hand on her shoulder.

"There will be no death between the fires this time," he said gently. "Aedden chose his way so that Loarn was not forced to it."

"He may need to be," Llamrei said grimly. "I dressed him, Rhodri, and I walked him to his death. Aedden nearly balked. Loarn should be grateful and instead he is in the hall getting drunk."

Rhodri was silent. Bendigeid had been the only man Llamrei had ever gone to for the asking. All others were of her choosing, Rhodri included. Only Bendigeid had touched whatever was at her core. "Teyrnon is with him," he said now of Loarn. "He will make sure he can still stand at nightfall."

"Loarn is of the royal line," Llamrei said. "Almost the last. None of the rest of us are but Iorwen's boy and he's a child.

Aedden should have married," she added angrily. "If we do not shift the Romans out of our land now, they will only grow more acquisitive until *they* break the treaty they made, and there are roads and toll booths and temples to their state gods and more taxes and a Roman official everywhere, like weevils in the grain."

"So we break it first," Rhodri said, half laughing. "Loarn will be well enough. But watch the tribune. He has a nose like a ferret. I found him poking it in the storehouses."

"He won't find anything," Llamrei said. Iorwen had put their stockpile in the outer chamber of Ty Isaf. They would have to shift it soon because the little dark people did not take kindly to the presence of iron in their holy places, but Iorwen had a bit more sidhe blood than most and they had a tenuous understanding. The iron could stay until the tribune left.

—

A festival mood hung over the crowd that gathered as night fell. This king-making meant renewed life for the tribe, and new promise of a fight with Rome; bought by Aedden when he had bared his breast to the stag's horns. Those who had followed the procession from Porth Cerrig mingled with men from the mountain villages, children perched on their shoulders, women carrying gifts of bread and apples. Gronwy had demanded a place of honor and been given a chair to sit in, his men behind him. Chanting and the wild music of pipes rose again from the lower courts and a thrumming of drums somewhere in the distance kept pace with it. The chanting came nearer: nine women with Iorwen at their head in white gowns, and catskin cloaks against the cold. Teyrnon stood between the first fire and the ninth, his face tiger-striped with shadow as the fires blazed up one after the other around the ring. It was the equinox when light and dark were balanced, one of the eight hinge points of the year, a propitious night, the sky overhead clear as black glass but for the milky stream of the great star road spilling across it. The hall and the other buildings of the upper court were shadows beyond the fire ring.

The crowd drew apart to let the women pass into the circle. Hands reached out to touch the catskins and the twigs of mistletoe that hung from their girdles, absorb the luck of a king-making. To the other side, Loarn's captains came, weaponless, stalks of wheat in the empty scabbards at their belts. They circled the fires, crossing paths in an ancient pattern, first fire to sixth, sixth to second, second to seventh, dropping wheat and mistletoe into the flames as they went. The high, thin music of the pipes and the distant drumming rose up with the flame and then stilled as the fire-gift blackened to ash.

Marcellinus watched with interest. He had heard of the crowning of Aedden after a ritual battle and the death of the king before him, from Centurion Valerianus who had had it from someone who was there. Supposedly, that had always been the way of things centuries ago, when the Mother goddess was paramount and the queen chose each new king. That notion made Marcellinus's skin crawl. Lleu Sun Lord was brother to the Roman's Sol and the goddess's power much diminished if not gone entirely, and that was a far better way to organize things in Marcellinus's opinion. Also in Marcellinus's opinion the Britons still gave their women far too much authority. He had taken Llamrei for a man at first.

A shiver of anticipation ran through the crowd. Teyrnon stood in the center of the fires and Loarn walked to him out of the darkness, naked but for the king mark daubed in red on his forehead. A king was the physical embodiment of the land, and so a king must be whole and show at his crowning that he came unblemished. Below the paint, his face wore the patterns of the Silure royal house and his chest a faded spiral: the spear mark of king's captains. His hair was loose over his shoulders. Teyrnon put a thumb to the still-wet paint. He pressed it to Loarn's chest and belly, leaving smudges that looked almost black in the firelight. Then he lifted the cap of the Horse Lord, a red stallion's crest with a gold sun wheel between its ears. Loarn bent his head to it, a final capitulation.

Teyrnon settled the cap and knotted its thongs into Loarn's dark hair. Then he wove the red gold crown that had been Aedden's and Bendigeid's before him through the red mane and forelock.

—

Loarn swayed as the crowd shouted their acclamation and the distant drumming began again: the people of the hills acknowledging a new king in Dinas Tomen. He could feel the presence of the red horse's cap – worn only on the night that a new king was made – like a living thing. He was cold to the bone and grateful when Llamrei came with a woolen cloak and wrapped him in it. Pwyll handed him a pair of fur boots and he pushed his freezing feet into them. Gwydion put a cup of hot mead in his hand. Tomorrow, Teyrnon would wash the king mark from his forehead and prick it into the skin with blue dye instead. But the thing was already done. There was no going back. There had never been. He was Loarn, lord of the Silures and that would not leave him as long as he lived.

His vision shimmered, and he thought at first it was his own exhaustion until a gasp of fear and wonder rose all around him. He turned to the north where Llamrei was staring, her hand to her mouth, at a sky blazing with green light.

The murmuring stilled to silent awe while the green veil flickered above them, the trees on the skyline black against dancing waves of green that shaded to red higher in the sky, bowing, turning, undulating like waves or the wings of great birds. Loarn lifted his face to them. Some vast unreadable message was written in those lights. That it came for him he had no doubt. He stared at the overwhelming, terrifying beauty of that emerald light burning in the air.

Llamrei saw the tribune gaping at the sky. "The Dancers are come to greet the new king in Dinas Tomen," she told him.

He turned to her uneasily, suspicious. "What is it? Some forbidden Druids' magic?"

"Certainly," Llamrei said in a voice that meant *you are a fool*. "No doubt it will strike your armies dead if you do not leave Britain."

"If you could have done that, you would have," Marcellinus said.

"We would," she admitted.

"Not magic, then?"

"It is the Dancers. Do you not see them where you are from? Rome is too far south, I suppose."

"What are they?"

"They come in winter when it's very cold and the sky is clear. It's rare to see them here. They come more often farther north, or on Mona. Maybe it is the holy women there that summon them."

"Someone told me about lights in the sky, I remember now," the tribune said. "An officer's wife in Isca, a woman from the northern islands. I put it down to women's fancy."

"Perhaps you should stop doing that," Llamrei said.

Marcellinus raised his eyebrows. The dancing green shimmer reflected in his helmet and cuirass. "Perhaps. Do all your women dress as men?"

"No. We are all trained and those who wish to join the spear band may, but most do not since it is not possible to marry if we do."

"And you have never wished to marry?"

"No," she said shortly. "Nor is it your business."

"I apologize. I am curious about your ways."

"We are not exhibits in a collection of curiosities. Do you wish an escort for your journey south?"

He raised his eyebrows again. "Will I need one?"

"No. You have been the king's guest. Not even the most reckless would offer you harm. But you had best be on the road soon. Just to be certain."

The Dancers flared in the sky all night, and most stayed to watch and ponder what sign they gave. Dinas Tomen was still asleep when Loarn woke at daybreak to dress and set the king's crown on his head. Teyrnon had put away the red horse's cap where the sacred things of the tribe were kept, but Loarn could still feel it on his scalp. The crown itself felt as if he would have a headache soon, but this morning's journey required formality. In the dimness of the great hall, he passed a tumble of hounds, boys fostered in the king's hall, puddled in sleep like puppies before the banked hearth. A slave woman came to stir the embers up and prodded the boys awake with her foot. "Go and fetch wood."

He was about to tell her to wake Iorwen, when Iorwen came from her sleeping chamber, yawning and pulling a thick woolen cloak around her. The hall was cold and where they were bound colder still. In the pony shed he harnessed his team and hitched them to his chariot, waving away his driver who came tumbling from his bed when he saw that the king was awake. Loarn took Iorwen up beside him and they drove alone down the track to Ty Isaf while the sun crept up the sky.

The long mound was overgrown with trees and sod whose grass was turning winter brown. A false entrance on the north face led nowhere, while others to east and west had been blocked up long ago, maybe as soon as the ancient ones had been laid there. The southern opening was narrow and low enough that even the little dark folk crept through it cautiously; Iorwen had had to promise a gold ring apiece to the three boys who had helped her offload the weapons and set them inside. No one, not even the people of the hills, knew what ancient kings lay in the inner chambers so long closed up, but Ty Isaf reeked of power and old magic and the boys had come out white-faced. It would likely cost her another gold ring to get them back in to drag it all out.

Loarn tethered the ponies and they sat together to wait beside the curbstone of the southern entrance. They would be expected. The dark people and the Silures had a relationship that ran from enmity to occasional intermarriage, mostly enmity. Despite that, a new king made his respects to the Old One of Ty Isaf. Even Aedden had done so after Bendigeid had laid waste to their dwelling in a fury because they had betrayed him. Matters had healed somewhat since then, when Iorwen became Goddess on earth.

It was not long before a small figure appeared from the scrub of rowan and thorn on top of the mound. He bowed his head to Loarn and then to Iorwen. "The Old One sends to say she will speak to the king of the Silures."

He was no taller than a ten-year-old and wore a woolen shirt and a kilt of catskins, his feet bare even in the cold. His black hair was braided with red beads, brown face and arms tattooed in the way of the Silures but in ancient patterns mysterious to their eyes. "The royal woman might enter our house," he added, "but not the king, so the Old One will come to you."

"The Old One does us great honor," Loarn said. Iorwen and Loarn were half-siblings, the sidhe blood on Iorwen's side. No full-blooded Silure would be allowed inside a sidhe, nor would wish to go there.

The small man didn't say anything else. He simply waited, frozen into immobility until Loarn wasn't sure he actually still saw him. Then, two more men appeared on the edge of the trees. Between them they carried a chair with a woman seated on its cushions: Heron, the Old One of the sidhe of Ty Isaf. She wore a necklace of owl's talons with blue beads between them, a gown of dark checked wool, and a rug of wolfskin over her lap. She was ancient, her gray hair thin as mist, the bones of her face and hands stark under the skin. Her eyes though were bright as lake water and shrewd as a crow's. The men set her chair down and she inspected Loarn.

"So a new king is made in Dinas Tomen," she said after looking him up and down. "And profanes our holy place with iron." Iron had come with the Sun People, iron to break bronze, a conqueror's metal, wrong and unclean. The dagger blade at Loarn's belt was a mark of the abyss between them.

"That was my doing, grandmother," Iorwen said. Grandmother was a courtesy term; the relationships of the little dark people were convoluted. "We made agreement on it, you and I."

Heron sniffed. "So we did. But the last time my house agreed to aid the Sun People because the one who asked was also one of ours, we were lied to."

"That was long ago," Iorwen said.

"We do not forget. And it is profane, nonetheless. It must be gone by night."

"It will be."

"And you will leave the cow you promised. You can tether her here and be glad if that is the only price. There is always a price. For us, for you, for the king."

"I am grateful to the Old One," Loarn said.

"We do not permit this for your sake," Heron snapped, "but because the Romans are Sun People also and somewhat worse, with their straight roads and their new cities and their leveling of forest for farms. If we must choose between you, we will take your kind."

"The Dancers came last night," Iorwen said.

Heron nodded. "We saw them."

"Do you know what they mean?"

"The Dancers are not human and speak no language except light. But they are the second sign, after the tremors in the earth. Thus, there is a third coming."

"Do you know what?" Loarn asked. He didn't doubt her. He had been thinking it himself and Teyrnon had said so too.

Things came in threes. Three good things, or three ill ones. Or three whose meaning became clear only later. But three. Three was the number of legs that kept a stool from tipping, the number of men who could arbitrate a dispute.

Heron shrugged her thin shoulders. "It is cold, king. I will go home now. My sons will come tonight to be certain that the iron is gone. These signs are for your kind, not ours. Just remember, king, that there is a price for everything."

III. LLANMELIN

The fortress of Isca Silurum dominated the landscape, an unavoidable reminder of Rome's hand. It sat on a wide bend of the Isca River behind a ditch and earthen ramparts reinforced with oak piles. Wooden towers connected by a sentry walk stood on either side of the four gates and at intervals between them. The old Silure stronghold on the hill to the north was empty and beginning to be overgrown, abandoned since construction of the fortress had begun. Instead, the vicus had grown in size and respectability to resemble a small city, its graves already lining the roads around it. Within the fortress walls, centered on the great four-columned tetrapylon that rose where the Via Praetoria crossed the Via Principalis, were barracks, baths and granaries; the Principia; the Praetorium, home of the legate; and smaller houses for senior officers, including the cohort commanders.

Grander even than the great tetrapylon were the baths. The Roman legionary felt that baths were second only to regular meals and Julius Frontinus, governor of Britain at Isca's founding and engineer of waterworks, had given his passion free rein in the Isca baths. The vaulted ceiling covered exercise yard, changing room, and hot, warm, and cold pools. In the courtyard a dolphin-headed fountain cascaded from a nymphaeum down marble steps at the shallow end of a swimming pool. Eirian was wide-eyed at it and at the equal grandeur of the civic baths outside the fort walls.

After the wilds of the northern frontier, Faustus's household had settled gratefully into their quarters, arranged around a courtyard and small garden, with kitchen, latrine, and stables on two wings, bed chambers, dining room, office and atrium on the others, and partly heated like the baths by a hypocaust beneath the tiled floor.

The fort and its outskirts were in constant motion. The wharf along the river was busy with cargo ships and the patrol craft of the Fleet. Something was perpetually being built or rebuilt: the original structures of the fort gradually replaced with stone, an arena under construction west of the fort to house games, mock battle exercises, gladiatorial shows, and the traveling theater troupes that sometimes visited. Because the arena impinged on the civic baths, new ones were being installed to the south.

All of this construction was the work of the legion, from molding roof tiles and drainpipe to digging the hypocaust chamber for the baths. On his return from Aquae Sulis, Faustus's cohort came up in rotation for work on the arena foundation.

"I don't see why *you* have to dig in the mud," Silvia said when he returned late for dinner, dripping brown muck. "You're their commander."

"A commander has to be able to do what his men do," Lucius volunteered.

"Indeed he does," Faustus said, while Silvia glared at him. Lucius's fascination with the army was a sore point between them. Silvia considered that Faustus encouraged Lucius in it, while Faustus was aware that Lucius didn't need any encouragement.

"Go and get clean," Eirian said. "You're dripping on the floor Gwladus just washed. Paullus will keep dinner hot."

He kissed her gingerly, shed his muddy tunic in their chamber and took a flask of oil and a strigil to the baths. He wouldn't have admitted it to Silvia or Lucius, but his back ached like someone had run a hot poker up his spine. A spine not nearly as young as it had been when he was first posted to Britain. That time seemed inordinately long ago.

He soaked in the hot pool until his back unkinked and then went home to a late dinner and an early bedtime. Paullus had removed the filthy tunic and taken his muddy boots away as well. "Turn over," Eirian said. "I'll rub your back. You aren't still twenty. Silvia has a point."

"I'm not ancient either," Faustus protested.

"Not yet." She pushed the base of her thumb into his shoulder muscles, and he grunted. "Shift a little bit. There. How do you actually know that woman with the silk shop?" There had been no message yet from Clio and Eirian could not have helped noting his restlessness and the number of times he had inquired if one had been delivered.

"None of your business," he said into the pillows, laughing.

"I thought so. I don't care. I liked her. Don't get her into trouble."

"I'm not going to, Eyes-and-Ears. You really aren't supposed to know about this."

"But I do, because you told me. I won't tell anyone else."

"That's why I told you." Perhaps he shouldn't have, but since he had married Eirian, it had been a relief to have someone to tell things to, things that he couldn't explain to Silvia or Lucius. Eirian was a keeper of secrets. She'd proved that. He turned over and reached for her. "Rub something else," he suggested.

She was about to when the bed quivered and they felt the floor sway beneath it. As Faustus sat up it settled but while he waited to see if it would do it again, they heard shouting in the street outside. He stood reluctantly and pulled on the clean tunic and undertunic that Paullus had laid out, and then his boots and cloak.

Silvia appeared in the corridor with a lamp in her hand. "I wasn't asleep yet," she said hastily when Faustus eyed the lamp. Since the ground had begun to shake periodically there had been orders that any flame that could be tipped over should be put out at night. "What's happening?"

"I don't know," Faustus said. "Neptune turning over in his bed, no doubt. But there's Typhon's own row going on outside."

41

The shouting was louder now, not angry but more of the *Come and see* variety.

Silvia followed him to the door with Eirian and the rest of the household behind her. In the street a growing jumble of people, legionaries and their officers, slaves and households wakened by the noise, called to each other and poured toward the western gate.

"I imagine something has fallen down finally," Faustus said. "I'm going to have a look."

"We will stay," Silvia said firmly, grabbing Lucius by the shoulder as he tried to slide by her.

At the Dextra gate, a centurion of the Seventh Cohort – which had watch that night – pointed to a ring of torches and lanterns in the half-dug foundation of the arena. "We were just giving a check to the works," he told Faustus, "because of commander's orders to make sure supplies don't walk off."

"What happened?"

The legate strode past them, headed for the arena with his cloak over his night clothes. Two slaves and a Principia optio hurried after him with lanterns.

"There's a sinkhole where work stopped today," the centurion said. "Crispus fell right in, opened under his feet. More like a crack than a hole, but wide enough. They just now got him out. But it shoved up some kind of old idol or something. I had that from the man sent to fetch the legate."

Tribune Marcellinus pushed past them now, heading for the arena. Faustus followed and a hastily posted pair of sentries let him through when they recognized him. Someone, presumably Crispus since he was covered with mud, was being checked by a medic, and the legate and tribune were standing over the rift in the ground, watching as a crew began bracing the sides with timber. Faustus could see what they were trying to get out, a stone shape protruding from the earth, perhaps two-thirds of it still buried. The edges of dressed stones showed to either side: a vault maybe, Faustus thought, an old one, something that might have shifted with the shaking of the ground. They pulled the statue farther from the earth and a face like a great cat's looked back at him from the stone.

The legate spotted him. "Valerianus! What was the state of these works this afternoon?"

"Perfectly normal, sir. No sign of upheaval." He stared at the stone.

"What is that thing? It looks like some sort of god."

Faustus thought so too. An ancient one.

"Maybe we should rebury it, sir," the optio suggested. A rain of dirt and pebbles slithered down again past the timber braces as if the thing was trying to pull the earth back over itself.

Caecilius shook his head. "We can't leave it under the arena floor."

Any unexpected happening, any injury, the legion would put down to the old god under the sand, until no one would set foot in it, Faustus thought. No, they couldn't leave it.

"Have you dug up anything else?" Marcellinus asked him.

"Nothing like this," Faustus said. "But this spot has been inhabited for centuries. Centuries of centuries. We've found bits of pottery and a few coins, even a shoe. And yesterday, flint points. My nephew added them to his collection."

The men in the trench began to ease the stone cautiously from the earth's grip amid shouts of "Careful!" and "Put another brace in!" The ground was soggy with recent rain and the ancient vault had air pockets that made subsidence likely. They didn't need a legionary swallowed by the old god as they pulled him free. Crispus had been close enough.

A nursery story came back to Faustus as the whiskered face emerged, protruding from the greater part of a stone the size of a man's torso. Twined around the tufted ears were vines and what might be antlers. "Old Cat," he murmured.

"Who?"

"It was a nursery tale," Faustus said. "Of the sort my father didn't approve, being likely to fill my head with nonsense. Something my mother told me."

"If this is what the earth has been trying to spit out," Caecilius said, "the Silures may take it as a sign."

"They will," Marcellinus said. "You didn't see those lights in the sky. They tried to act as if great blazing green fires in the air were perfectly normal, but you could see they were adding it up."

"They are normal, strictly speaking," Faustus said. "I saw them in the Orcades."

"These people called them the Dancers," Marcellinus said, "and between that and the earthquakes, this makes three signs and signs usually point in the direction someone already wants to go."

"Is there any chance of keeping this quiet?" Faustus asked.

Caecilius snorted. "Not a butterfly's chance in winter." Too many people had seen the thing already and gossip spread through the ranks and outward from there like windblown seed.

"What do we do with it, then?" Faustus asked.

"We finish digging it up and put it out of sight. Then we… you, find out what it is." It was starting to drizzle again and Caecilius said, "Get a cover over this hole before it fills up."

While the crew pounded supports into the wet ground and laid a sheet of sailcloth over it, Faustus said, "You have more faith in my mother's ancestry than it warrants, sir, with respect. Being half-blood isn't being native born. I'd be more inclined to ask Aurelius Rotri. He's with the Twentieth and he was born here, British mother like me, but different circumstances." *Not war spoils bought in a slave market, for instance.*

"Silure?"

"Well, no. Atrebate, I think."

"Everyone has told me the Silures aren't like anyone else, including you. All you need do is look at them."

That was true enough. Most of the tribes were tall and fair- or fox-haired. The Silures were small, dark-haired, and they were usually at odds with everyone, except perhaps for the Demetae, who were their kin and afraid of them. "There is old blood in the Silures," Faustus said. "Besides everything else."

"The little people in the hills?" the legate asked and Marcellinus looked interested. "Will they know this thing?"

"Maybe," Faustus said. Probably.

"What are they?" Marcellinus asked.

"The ones who were here before the Silures," Faustus said. "They don't like the Silures, but they don't like us either. They have excellent reasons," he added.

"Go and ask them what this cat god is," the legate said. "And this time please don't tell me that you don't know how to find them."

Faustus sighed. "I can find the ones near Llanmelin." The previous legate had obviously told him so. "A load of grain would help. They are always hungry."

"Very well." Caecilius told the optio, "Give him a chit for the granary." To Faustus he said, "How have these people survived?"

"By staying out of sight," Faustus said. "Plenty of people don't believe in them at all. And maybe by making the others a little afraid of them."

"Are you sure now that these raids on our patrols are not partly their doing? We're missing two men from Moridunum now."

"Positive." Faustus said. "They won't touch iron. You'd be finding little bronze arrowheads in someone's neck. Every man we've caught has been Silure whether they admit it or no."

"Mmmm. Could you take me to meet with their headman?"

"They don't have one, sir," Faustus said. He tried not to sound horrified. "The Old One is always a woman. If I had you with me, we'd never see them. We smell of iron."

Caecilius looked thoughtful. "I *could* ask why they are friendly with you then."

"It was when I was first posted here. One of them was a mine slave at Dolaucothi and ran off on my watch."

"Loss of the Empire's property. I trust they docked you?"

"At any rate he was grateful," Faustus said, "although I assure you it was unintentional." Salmon had recognized his people's bloodline in Faustus. Faustus still didn't know how although the hill people had noses like dogs. He didn't say that. Sometimes he thought Caecilius already regarded him as one step removed from a wattle-and-daub round house.

"All right, Centurion, take a load of grain and go see them. Find out what this thing is. Then I'll decide what to do about it."

"Yes, sir." Faustus thought of Curlew, now the Old One, who still loved apples. He would buy her some apples.

As they watched, the men in the ground heaved the stone up over the lip of the hole. It lay face up to the misting rain, round eyes staring. Two of their fellows reached down to pull the excavators up after it. "Is there anything else down there?" Caecilius asked.

"Just the stone that made the vault," one of the legionaries said. He was mud-smeared from helmet to boots.

Caecilius asked Faustus, "How much deeper does the foundation go?"

"Not much," Faustus said. "Another handspan before we can set the footers. If it ever stops raining."

"Well put some concrete down that vault when you do. Not much comes up through concrete."

—

In the morning Faustus took his chit to the granary, bought a bag of apples in the vicus, and sorted out an escort from his cohort: Septimus, centurion of the second century, and sixteen of his men.

"We've unearthed some ancient stone god," he told Septimus. "Or the earthquake has. No one knows what it is, and we don't like to ask the Silures."

"Not without knowing the answer already, sir, I wouldn't," Septimus said. "You think the little dark ones will know? What's it look like?"

"It's got a cat face," Faustus said, "And I don't know, but they know most things."

"They're like smoke," Septimus said. "Here and then not here. It's a good thing they took a fancy to you."

Septimus had been Faustus's optio, and then a junior centurion of the Ninth Cohort promoted from the ranks on Faustus's say-so. When Faustus took command of the First as primus pilus he had promptly poached him from the Ninth to that commander's annoyance. What Septimus might or might not suspect regarding Faustus's relationship with the people of the hills he knew better than to ask.

Silvia and the rest of Faustus's household came to see him off on the road toward Venta Silurum, the market town that was the official center of Silure government. Well before Venta the track would branch northeastward into wilder country where the strange small people Silvia had never seen and to whom their great-grandmother had belonged, so Faustus said, lived in houses dug into the hillsides. Silvia had spent a good deal of effort in not believing in them, but it was getting harder.

"I wish I could go with Uncle," Lucius said now, for probably the tenth time that morning and Silvia said wearily one more time, "I won't allow that, and neither would he."

Lucius frowned at her, and Silvia said half-heartedly, "Go and read your lesson."

She felt as restless as Lucius, as if something was beginning to surface unwanted in her too. Old Silvius Valerianus had considered his wife's British blood a taint that had been painted over with a new identity upon her manumission and marriage to himself. If he could have scrubbed off the tattooed tribal mark between her breasts he would have. Silvia discounted it when thinking of their ancestry: two hundred years of respectable, well-born provincial gentry. Then Faustus had told her that their mother had a grandmother from the little dark people and that was harder to paint over, no matter how determined she was or how often she declared that she wished to know nothing about them, how often she made him promise not to tell Lucius, how often she stared rebelliously into a mirror. That Lucius looked like his father was a relief to her.

Faustus had tried once to take her with him to see the Old One who had told him this, and she had refused. He hadn't tried again; Eirian said that friendship with the little hill people was a delicate matter.

"Are there folk like that in the Orcades?" she asked Eirian, coming at the matter sideways while they walked home, herding Lucius ahead of them to an appointment with his tutor. Eirian had clan marks too, on her breast and upper arms. Eirian was also small, but muscular and solid-looking, with hair the pale brown of a moth's wing. Silvia and Faustus had their mother's dark hair. Most Romans were dark; that didn't mean anything.

"They like not to be seen," Eirian said. "But, yes. It was always a good idea to leave them something to eat."

Silvia was silent until Lucius had been sent off to bedevil the scholar who was attempting to instill in him the principles of geometry and a fluency in Greek. Then she said quietly, as they took up spindle and distaff in the atrium, "I have always done what I was supposed to, and thought as I was told to. And this is what it has brought me."

"This?" Eirian asked gently. The house was quiet. Paullus and Argos had gone to Llanmelin and Gwladus was in the vicus shopping for supper.

"Britain." Silvia jerked at the spun thread, and it snapped. Her spindle clattered to the floor, and she left it there. "I couldn't imagine anything worse when I had to come here, almost worse than my husband dying. Manlius said my mother's people were something we did not discuss. He didn't like his friends knowing. Now they all do, of course."

Eirian spent a few moments carefully arranging the wool on her distaff. She scooted her chair a little closer to the brazier that warmed the atrium. She retied her shoelace. Finally, she said, "Did you love him?"

"Of course," Silvia said. "I mean…"

"You were told to and so you did?"

"I liked being married. I liked having a house of my own." She looked despairingly around the atrium, a tidy, pleasant room in the Roman style, lacking only the central pool and open skylight, since West Britain's constant rain made those impractical. The walls were painted with a vista of sea creatures frolicking in green waves while women on the shore admired them. A niche held her household gods, small silver statues of the Lares, protectors of the family. Those at least hadn't been sold when she paid her husband's debts. No one would ask that. It would bring ill luck to have someone else's ancestors. They were still with her, but it wasn't her house.

"It must be trying to live with your brother. And then with me," Eirian said. "Particularly since you were here first." She seemed to be attempting to think of something useful to offer. "Have you thought of marrying again?"

Marriage was the obvious solution. The only one, actually. Although prospects on the frontier were lacking and Faustus hadn't the connections or the money to find her a match at home in Gaul.

"It seemed to me that Centurion Galerius found you attractive when he visited us," Eirian suggested. "I liked him."

"A brother in the legions is bad enough," Silvia said.

"Galerius is primus pilus with the Twentieth," Eirian said. "That's a very good post. Are you afraid of losing your man again? That's understandable, we all worry." She paused because Faustus had come close in the north. "I can't think of anything worse. Still, and I don't mean to be unkind, but your husband wasn't in the army, and he…"

"Died anyway," Silvia said. "It isn't that. People die. Father says… said… that our family had no business with empire-making or in the legions that support it. He was very proud of our position, and he disapproved of people who got involved in political life in Rome. Father had the money for equestrian rank – until he lost it – but he thought buying status was unworthy."

"Do you think so too?" Eirian asked her. "Or are you just hearing your father's voice in your head?"

Silvia picked up her spindle and began to tease a new strand onto it. "Of course I am. I told you I was brought up to. You did not heed your father's opinion?" Eirian in the gown and mantle they had bought in Aquae Sulis overlaid Silvia's memory of the woman who had ridden into Faustus's fort in ragged shirt and breeches. She looked dutiful now at her distaff, someone who would have heeded a father's wisdom.

"I didn't ask for his opinion. I knew what it was anyway."

Apparently not.

"And went to pilot a ship for men you'd never met before?" Silvia had never understood what would make a woman do a thing like that, although she knew that Eirian had been gossiped over in her village because of a mother who was supposed to have been some sort of seal woman. That was just uneducated superstition. More upsetting to Silvia was that the men had been frontier scouts with dangerous business and Eirian had known that when she went with them. It made Silvia feel somehow like one of the women on the atrium wall, stranded on the shoreline while merfolk frolicked in the water.

"It was an adventure," Eirian said.

And had had something to do with Faustus, Silvia knew. Faustus had spent a winter in Eirian's islands and made love to her and left. Eirian didn't seem to resent that. They had simply mended the situation after finding each other again by happenstance. What would it be like to be a person like that, Silvia wondered. She said, "I have never had an adventure."

"Maybe you need one."

"I have done what I was told. I told you that."

"Maybe you should stop."

Silvia laid the spindle down again. "Here is Gwladus with supper," she said, relieved to be able to back out of the conversation she had started. "I'll go see what she's planning." Dinner was something she knew what to do with.

—

From Isca to Llanmelin was a day's march. The way branched north past the sentry camp at Coed-y-Caerau to follow a wooded ridge where the hazel, birch and oak were turning autumn brown and gold, the rowans and guelder-rose heavy with berries. The trails that criss-crossed beneath them became more visible as the understory died back. Most were deer tracks, others worn by hunters from Coed-y-Caerau, some no doubt by the small hill people, although generally they left no trace or used the deer trails. Small streams ran through the wet leaves and rock, fed by springs that bubbled up and trickled down the hillsides to join the rivers that laced the landscape, and eventually the great tidal estuary of the Sabrina. Faustus had first come to these woods in the year of his posting to Britain. He had always liked the Silure Hills, except for the occasional felled tree in the road or a trench cut across the path and overlaid with branches. Since the peace with Aedden such events had been rare, but now they went cautiously again. The woods felt welcoming despite that. He could hear a thrush somewhere. It went silent as they passed and then took up its song again. The trees murmured overhead, voices he couldn't quite make out, and probably only his imagination. For all that, the woods seemed to have something to tell him. This was his mother's country. He wished he knew where she had lived. And her grandmother, the woman from a sidhe? Curlew's predecessor as Old One had said she was not one of theirs. Maybe Ty Isaf, Faustus thought. Tribune Marcellinus had said that place gave him the horrors.

They came to Llanmelin at evening when the setting sun glowed on the red sandstone along the remains of its western wall. Llanmelin was old, said to be the burial site of ancient kings, and like the hillfort behind Isca Silurum, it had been abandoned when the Romans began to build at Isca. Now the walls, demolished by Roman troops, were grown over with moss and grass that crept between the stones. The thatched roofs had fallen in, saplings sprouting through them and jackdaws' nests in the rafters. Curlew's people didn't actually live at Llanmelin but like the people of Ty Isaf, took their house's name from the nearest place that had one.

Faustus's men unloaded the cart and piled the grain and apples under a roof that was still marginally intact. Someone would come for it once they had gone. The people of the hills would have seen them coming hours ago; no doubt they had been watched for most of their journey. He left his men cooking their dinner in the falling dusk and stripped himself of iron: armor, helmet, sword, and belt knife. Paullus had made camp bread and Faustus gnawed it as he walked down Llanmelin Hill to the grove of old oaks that stood at its foot. At the grove's center a spring rose out of a cleft in a rocky outcrop and fell into a stone bowl carved from the living rock below it. Faustus put a coin in the water and a white stone that he had saved because he thought the Goddess might like it. Curlew's people gave their worship to the Mother in her oldest form and this was one of her places.

It was almost full dark when Salmon appeared at his side. He was small and brown-skinned like all his people, but the scar of an old slave collar had left a white patch on his throat. "I could have been a wolf and eaten you as you slept," he said.

Faustus laughed. "If you were a wolf, I would have heard you. And I would have seen you if it wasn't dark."

"You are learning," Salmon admitted. "Come. The Old One wants to see you."

Faustus got to his feet. "And I her. And not only for friendship's sake. I have a thing to show her."

Salmon looked interested but he didn't ask questions and Faustus followed him into the scrub brush and bracken. The moon was waxing, a few days from full, and they went along a route that Faustus could almost recognize but schooled himself not to. The people of the hills were vulnerable to those who could find their dwellings. Best that not even he knew for certain.

When they came to it though he recognized the shape of the hillside and the wind-bent hawthorn that grew on top, black limbs stark against a bright, star-washed sky. He saw the door behind the thorn scrub with relief. The earthquakes had worried him although the hill people no doubt knew where the faults lay and avoided them in their excavations. The door was low, barely high enough for Salmon, so that Faustus had to bend to enter. Inside, in the dim peat-smelling chamber, he could stand, just barely. He didn't though. He went to the woman sitting by the peat fire and knelt.

"It gives me much pleasure to see you again, Old One." The title was an honorific, unconnected to actual age.

"And I you, Faustus." Curlew was still young, inheritor of her grandmother's or great-grandmother's position as matriarch of her people. Her black hair was braided with her namesake's speckled feathers and her face and arms were marked with an intricate pattern like vines. Faustus had tried to follow the twining path of those vines before and always lost himself somewhere in them. She smiled at him. "How is your household?"

"I am married now," Faustus said. "To a woman I found in the Orcades, and lost, and found again."

"The seal islands." Curlew cocked her head at him, considering that. "She is a long way from them here. Are there children yet?"

"She wishes for children, but they haven't come."

"And your sister? Does she still fear us?"

"She fears the knowledge of you," Faustus said. "It means we are not what she thought we were."

"But your wife doesn't?"

"My wife thinks a friendship with the people of the hills is lucky. On the whole."

Curlew nodded. "The people of the islands have left hand kinships of their own. Tell your wife to be patient. Those with outland kin can be slow to breed. Salmon says you have brought us grain."

"Apples, too," Faustus said.

"Apples!" She smiled, suddenly the child he had met thirteen years before when she had come looking for her brother at the Dolaucothi mines.

"And a question."

Another woman emerged from a corridor that went deeper into the hillside. She brought a tray of cups, something warm and tasting of herbs that Faustus had never been able to identify. Curlew was silent as he drank gratefully; the chamber was chilly despite the fire whose smoke drifted up through a gap in the roof to emerge on the hilltop.

"I will tell you the answer if I know it," Curlew said when the other woman had gone, "and the telling is not forbidden."

Faustus sat back and fished in the pouch at his belt for a wooden tablet. One of his men, who had an artistic talent usually given to rude portraits of his commanders, had studied the stone god and drawn its likeness. Faustus held it out to her. Salmon came to look over her shoulder and gave a short indrawn hiss of breath.

"Where did you see this?" Curlew asked.

"It's carved stone. It was buried in a vault where we are digging the foundation for a new arena."

"And you dug it up?" Salmon said. It wasn't so much a question as a statement of alarm.

"It dug itself up," Faustus said. "The last shaking in the ground pushed it up. We need to know what it is."

Curlew held the tablet on her palm. The enigmatic cat's face looked back at them. "Cath Mawr," she said.

Great Cat. "Who is that? Is he one of your gods? Or of the Silures?"

"He isn't ours or theirs. He just is."

"My mother called him Old Cat, I think," Faustus said, remembering the nursery tale again.

Curlew nodded. "He is very old. As old as the stone dances."

Bits of memory came back, his mother's soft voice soothing him to sleep, often enough after a beating. Old Cat *was* the land, the soft furred hills and the fanged mountains, the whiskers of bracken and the green pools of his eyes. Faustus could imagine the rolling of the ground these past months as Old Cat stretching, paws spread. He asked Curlew, "What will the Silures take it to mean that he comes out of the ground now?"

"To welcome the new king, no doubt," Curlew said derisively, "as they think all things align to themselves."

"The Dancers came to greet the new king," Faustus said.

"Indeed, the Old One of Ty Isaf told me that," Curlew said. The people of the hills had ways of communicating with each other that Faustus never quite understood.

"My commander is worried that this stone god makes a third sign for anyone inclined to read matters in that way."

"No doubt, and no doubt the Silures are most inclined," Curlew said, echoing Marcellinus.

"And your opinion, Old One?"

"Cath Mawr does not care who rules. We and they, and you too, Faustus, are only fleas in his fur. The other gods, even the Mother, give their attention to their people. Old Cat has no people."

"What should we do with him?"

Curlew thought for a moment. "Put him somewhere that is not under a roof. Somewhere the rain can fall on him, and the sun and snow."

"I will tell my commander." It was a very unsatisfactory answer, but gods were generally unsatisfactory. Faustus bowed his head to her and rose.

"Thank you for the grain and apples," she said. "Salmon will take you back to your people again."

The moon silvered the bracken and the tangles of elder and buckthorn as they walked back along a path that Faustus thought he could see now, glimmering like a silver thread. When he had first come to the house in the hillside, his fears had been the stuff of rumor – that he would emerge to find his horse a pile of bones, the land transformed, his people long dead. Now he was fearful *for* the little people of the hills, not of them.

"Take me by another way next time," he told Salmon. "I am learning this one."

"Then you will have to decide what you will do with that knowledge," Salmon said. "If we did not trust you, we would not bring you here."

Too many men had trusted him, Faustus thought, and died under his command. That was the way of the army, but each death felt like a debt owed. When Salmon parted from him, slipping into the silvery night, he made his way up Llanmelin Hill in the moonlight. Except for the sentries, the camp was asleep, fires banked. Paullus was snoring in their tent with Argos at his feet. Restless, Faustus walked the perimeter, tracing the outlines of the old defensive wall, now half buried in bramble. Septimus, on watch, saluted him as he passed. He was used to the commander pacing about at night. You never knew where he'd turn up, which was a good thing to remember for anyone with a mind on mischief.

An ashen figure formed itself out of the moonlight. "One day you'll go in there and not come out," it said.

Faustus glared at it. "I've come out so far."

His father looked grave, a pale morose face, translucent in the moonlight, like a tracing on glass. "A taint in the blood. If I had known, I would not have married her."

"She might have been happier for it," Faustus said levelly, slapping a mental hand down on his temper before it could escape. Shouting at his father's shade had never achieved anything but more shouting.

"That seems unlikely," Silvius Valerianus said. "The life I gave her was far better than the one she had in this dismal country, let alone afterward."

"Has it occurred to you that the life she had in 'this dismal country' was the life she was born to, and the life she wanted?"

"No," his father said. "It's never occurred to the emperor either or you wouldn't be here."

"The emperor isn't interested in making the Britons happier," Faustus said. "He is interested in having more provinces."

"Precisely. Tell me how that differs from my marriage."

"I can't," Faustus said helplessly. The benefits of Roman technology and civilization were the wrapping on a less palatable gift, and he knew it. "You had your own little empire on the farm, and you and he are not that different."

"Yet you serve him and insult me."

"I serve Rome," Faustus said uncomfortably. "Vespasian wore the purple when I joined."

"For which he fought a bloody civil war, until he was the only one standing," Silvius Valerianus said disgustedly. "Had I not good reason for keeping to our farm?"

"I don't know," Faustus said. "Maybe."

"I did what I was brought up to do," the shade said fretfully, and disappeared.

IV. DIPLOMACY

Faustus returned to Isca to find Eirian chattily entertaining Centurion Galerius of the Twentieth Valeria Victrix, a lanky frame occupying a chair by the brazier and dripping on the tile; it was raining again, had started midway into the journey home.

Galerius unfolded himself when he saw Faustus and clapped an arm across his shoulders. "Your wife invited me to dinner. Have you taught Paullus how to cook yet?"

"Minimally," Faustus said. "We rise in the world and have a housekeeper who can actually cook."

"Where did you acquire such a treasure? And will you sell her?"

"She's not a slave. You met her when you were here last. Gwladus. She lost her man in the north and of course they weren't properly married so they wouldn't even give her his back pay."

"Miserable rule," Galerius said, "not allowing them to marry. Doesn't apply to officers, of course." He looked sideways at Silvia sitting uncomfortably beside Eirian.

"Galerius has come to confer with your legate," Eirian said, squelching that conversational direction. "And cadge dinner invitations. Paullus came home with a jar of oysters."

Galerius was Faustus's oldest friend in the legions and Eirian had been prepared from the beginning to like him if only for that. Now she treated him like a sibling. "My brothers were pigs," she had said on adopting him. "I'll take this one."

"Where did Paullus get oysters?" Faustus asked.

Eirian said, "Reissued. I hope he didn't mean it literally, since it's oysters." *Reissued* generally meant *don't ask where it came from.* "I'm afraid they may be from the legate's cold house." Caecilius was notable for possessing an expensive cook and an extensive larder.

Galerius grinned. "Oysters don't keep, anyway. Someone would have poisoned himself if they weren't eaten soon. Paullus is a treasure."

"What are we having besides oysters?" Faustus asked.

"Lamb. If the dog hasn't snatched it," Silvia said. "Gwladus chased him three times around the kitchen for it earlier and now he's tied up or should be. I expect there's a tooth mark or so on it, but she's going to roast it."

"We'll pretend we don't know that," Galerius said solemnly and Silvia smiled. She actually liked Galerius. His only fault lay in being in the army. And possibly being too much like her brother. He was tall with a pleasant bony face and a shock of dun-colored hair. He wore a silvered parade cuirass, no doubt in honor of his visit with the legate; his helmet, adorned with a primus pilus's crest of feathers, sat on a chair.

"Is there news from Deva?" Faustus asked. With Vitruvius Arvina, the Twentieth's legate, in Eburacum with half the legion, Galerius and the legion's broad-stripe tribune were the de facto commanders.

"Nothing solid," Galerius said. "Tribune Terentius has acquired an extra air of authority in Arvina's absence. There are rumors of overtures being made by the Silures to the Ordovices. Cadal is denying any such thing, and it may be true. Or they may have done so, and he told them to jump in the Styx. The old hatred between the Silures and the Ordovices is only occasionally overcome by hating us more."

"Or Cadal may be sitting in Bryn Epona thinking up ways to put a spear up Rome's ass on a permanent basis," Faustus said. "What do the scouts say?"

"They can't find anything solid, either. They don't think the grain and iron Caecilius is worried about is coming through

Ordovice territory. Aurelius Rotri wanted to go feral and nose about and Terentius squashed that on the grounds that if he's known to the northern tribes it's not safe to assume he won't be recognized by the southern ones, which I doubt. Terentius just thinks Rotri lacks discipline and wants him shaven and brought up to standard."

"Nor is Rotri ever going to be happy in a uniform," Eirian said. Rotri had been one of the border wolves with whom she had fled her islands. That venture had nearly gotten them all killed and as it was they had lost Rotri's partner. Eirian felt oddly maternal about Rotri, now restlessly posted back to his home legion.

"Rotri serves Rome," Galerius said.

She nodded. That was what Faustus said about orders he didn't like. Liking didn't matter.

—

In the morning, both men brought their reports to Caecilius, Galerius giving his opinion at the end of his that the Ordovices were waiting to see which way the wind blew.

"Have you ever encountered this thing?" Caecilius asked him. For the time being the cat-faced god resided in the Principia where it made the junior officers nervous. Caecilius too probably but he refused to acknowledge it.

Galerius studied the whiskered face and half torso that emerged from the stone as if still in the process of unearthing itself. "Not as such. There are local gods all over the place but nothing like this one that I've heard of. A god with no people? Then who in Jupiter's name thought him up?"

Caecilius listened to the rain now sheeting off the Principia roof. "This damn island thought him up. Or he thought *it* up."

That struck Faustus as possible. The *genius loci* of a place was more the place itself than an inhabitant.

"Very well. Find it a spot near where we unearthed it and make it an altar," Caecilius told Faustus. "Let the Silures know we respect it."

"Yes, sir. Brick? And should there be an inscription?"

"The Legate Aulus Caecilius placed this altar here to scare the shit out of his legion," Galerius suggested.

"*Dedicated to Cath Mawr*," Caecilius said, "however you spell that, *Aulus Caecilius of the Second Augusta set this up*." He nodded at the scribe who had been busily taking notes. The scribe handed the tablet to Faustus. "Brick, with a stone top and the plaque on the front."

"Yes, sir." Faustus saluted. Galerius began to follow him out.

"Don't go just yet, Centurion," Caecilius said to Galerius. "We are going to practice diplomacy. Formal recognition of this new king is required for both manners and intimidation. I expect you to remain at Isca while we do so to let the Silures understand that we still have a presence in their neighbors' territory."

"Indeed, sir." Galerius saluted.

—

The legate's plans for diplomacy were elaborate.

"He's ordered up a state banquet," Galerius informed Faustus while Faustus supervised the building of a brick pillar for Cath Mawr under a dripping awning. "The Silures will instantly become tractable in the face of an empire that can produce a swan baked inside a peacock."

"He just wants a good look at Loarn. And for Loarn to have a good look at us. Where would he get a peacock?" Faustus eyed the squat brick pillar in progress. "That's out of true. Drop a line and you'll see."

"And a pastry boat," Galerius said as the crew pulled off the top level, scraping away the wet mortar. "I left out the boat."

"He sent the invitation around this morning," Faustus said. "More of a command, actually. All cohort officers, with a few presentable juniors and auxiliary prefects. I am to bring my wife and sister."

Galerius crouched under the awning. "It appears that Loarn has gone back to Porth Cerrig. A courier took the invitation there, for him and such of his lords as he chooses to bring. There isn't a queen, I understand. What will he do with the swan if Loarn tells the courier to stick his invitation in his ass?"

"He won't," Faustus said. "Anyone who can deal with the Demetae and Cadal, who all hate him, can make use of a state dinner with us." He eyed the brickwork. "Much better. One more layer and then leave it to cure. If it ever does." He looked disapprovingly at the drizzling sky. "This thing has to be up by the legate's big show, so you'd better put a tent over it. This isn't enough cover if it really rains."

"Is that cat thing still in the Principia, sir?" the crew leader asked.

"Yes, and I imagine the legate wants it not to be there, so that's another reason to get on with it. I'm told it doesn't like to be under a roof."

The legionary opened his mouth to ask him who had told him that before the answer appeared to come to him. There were rumors about the primus pilus and the little hill people, some of them wild enough to be obviously false to anyone with a brain, but some of them possibly true. What was known was that he didn't take kindly to discussion of them.

"When you've got it under wraps, get into your marching kit," Faustus told him. "The legate intends to parade the legion to impress the king of the Silures and we're going to drill this afternoon so that if anyone falls over his pilum in front of the reviewing stand, it won't be my cohort."

—

The rest of the week was occupied with practice drill for the entire legion, polishing of parade kit and weapons, and uncovering their scarlet shields to touch up the winged lightning and

Capricorn badge of the Second Augusta. Galerius, who had no responsibilities other than to sit on the reviewing stand with the legate and the new king, occupied himself with playing *latrunculi* with Lucius.

"You're beating me half the time now," he said approvingly.

"Uncle Faustus plays with me," Lucius said. "And Septimus, and some of the men. Uncle says never play with the frontier scouts," he added.

"Uncle is quite right," Galerius said. He slid a sideways glance at Silvia. "Don't throw dice with them either. That's even more important."

"Lucius is not throwing dice with anyone," Silvia said firmly. "Particularly not the soldiers. Please don't encourage his following them about."

"I won't if you'll stop acting as if we all have fleas," Galerius said.

"Silvia," Eirian said before she could snap at him, "show me how to drape my gown the way you said the empress does. It keeps getting twisted somehow."

"Come in your room then," Silvia said agreeably. "It's very pretty when you get it pinned. Of course, the fashion may have changed by now, and I was never actually at court, but this is what my husband's cousins showed me."

Eirian pulled off her plain gown and slipped the seawater blue folds of the new one over her head. "When I try it, it always looks like something's nesting in it."

"This is how it's done," Silvia said, deftly pleating the cloth between her fingers. She pushed the pin home. "And don't think I don't know what you're trying to do."

"Well, I really did want to know," Eirian said, unrepentant. "I've never been to a banquet like this before, just the legate's dinners. And I've felt out of place enough at those."

"Do you still?" A few of the other wives had been cool, whispering audibly about unwise marriages.

"Not as much now. I watched you and did what you did. Also, Faustus outranks most of their husbands. When I realized that, it helped. Some of them are nice."

"Those are the wives who actually want to be here," Silvia said. "The ones who thrive on following the legion. The snooty ones are the ones like me, I'm afraid."

"Who don't want to be here," Eirian said. "But you've always been nice to me."

"I'm not sure I was at first," Silvia said. "I wasn't being nice to anyone, to be fair."

"You could start being nice to Galerius."

"I am nice to him," Silvia said indignantly. "But I'm not going to marry him, if that's what you mean by nice."

"Show me how to do my hair, then. I want to make Faustus proud."

Silvia took a comb and studied Eirian's hair. "From now on, I am not going to do something just because the paterfamilias tells me to," she muttered. "And I learned *that* from you." She pulled the pale knot out of its pins. "Let's try a double band and curls. I have some blue silk ribbon that will set that off."

After a reasonably successful experiment with the curling tongs, Silvia brought out her box of face paint. Eirian had resisted paint until now, but Silvia showed her how to use a touch on cheeks, lips, and eyelids: "Just enough to be fashionable but not tasteless."

"It looks lovely on you, but I keep thinking of that tribune's wife who visited last year," Eirian said, examining herself in the mirror. "Faustus would go into a decline if he saw me like that. He said she looked like a theater mask."

"That is how you *don't* do it."

"What do you think kept her hair up?" The tribune's wife had worn the beehive of curls made popular by the empress.

"Glue," Silvia said. "That was a wig. Didn't you wonder where she got red hair?"

They pooled their jewelry, trading dress pins and eardrops, and felt pleased with the results. Despite the uncertainty of the political situation, the parade drill and the banquet promised more entertainment than anything since they had come to Isca.

"What do you think the Silure women will wear?" Silvia asked Eirian.

"A lot of gold," Eirian said. "They all will. And bright colors." Bright dye was expensive, another way to show wealth. "If any women are coming. I don't know that they will. The king isn't married. One of his captains is a woman though. Tribune Marcellinus told me. I don't think he approved."

"I hope she comes," Silvia said. "I would like to see a woman who can make Tribune Marcellinus pay attention to her. He treats me like Faustus's pet."

"Perhaps I should mention the difference between Tribune Marcellinus and Centurion Galerius," Eirian said.

"Perhaps you shouldn't."

The parade drill and banquet were held in Venta Silurum. Caecilius had no intention of inviting the Silures into Isca Fortress to take note of its defenses. Nor would the Silure king have allowed himself to be trapped behind its walls.

The rain obligingly stopped, and Sol gave them one of those pure, clear autumn days when everything seemed just a little brighter, a little sharper, a little more imminent, something important waiting to happen. A flock of crows, aware that marching soldiers often meant corpses, gathered at a distance to watch from the yellow branches of an ash tree. "You're going to be disappointed," Faustus told them.

The drill field was marked out by stakes alongside the red and gold vexilla of the Second Augusta. Both Tribune Marcellinus and Centurion Galerius were in attendance, seated on the reviewing stand with the legate. Loarn, new king of the Silures, sat beside his sister Iorwen, who was high priestess of her tribe or something close to that, the human habitation of the Goddess on earth. Five of the king's captains accompanied them, including the woman. They wore brightly checkered breeches and fine leather boots, throats and arms encircled – as Eirian had predicted – with gold. Their heavy cloaks were lined with fox fur or sheep's wool. The Roman officers' wives, allotted seats at the edges of the platform, peered around each other to stare at them.

Faustus was resplendent in a silvered cuirass strung with all his medals, including the new gilded version of the grass crown earned in the north. The sun reflected from the legion arrayed behind him as they saluted the reviewing stand, rank upon rank of polished steel and scarlet parade crests.

Faustus lifted a hand, his cornicen put the trumpet to his mouth, and the square melted seamlessly into an arc. At each call, they changed formation. Six ranks and then nine, opening down the center to surround an invisible enemy, drawing together in a pig's head wedge to drive through the same unseen ranks; each maneuver flawless, shields locked or overhead, pila upright or leveled. To Eirian it always looked as if they would tangle themselves, lose count, the formation collapsing in on itself, but they never did. It was for this precision that Faustus drilled his cohort in all weather, the discipline that had kept his desperate auxiliaries together in the north and held off five times their number. He had lost two-thirds of them in doing it. That was where the grass crown had come from, and she knew that he nearly wept every time he looked at it.

At the end of their drill the cohorts reformed into parade ranks and presented themselves to the legate with a crashing salute, four thousand fists to plated chests. Then they spread out to ring the parade ground while the cavalry took their place.

Two hundred and fifty riders – there should have been three hundred – were adorned in the elaborate sports armor brought out only for cavalry games. Their helmets, crested with bright feathers, bore molded curls or horns and silvered human faces that allowed only small slits for vision, and they carried shields painted with scenes from famous battles. Their troop horses, two hands taller than native ponies, wore bridles fitted with gilded eye guards, and gleaming coats of scale that covered breast and flanks. Lucius, sitting with his mother, transferred his allegiance immediately to the cavalry.

Two teams with wooden spears wove through each other's lines in close formation, tapping shields with the light lances, wheeling, coming about again in a different pattern, long red and blue standards streaming behind them. They crossed and re-crossed, splitting down the middle, forming again, each hoofbeat precisely placed, riders with no peripheral vision trusting completely to their mounts and the drill. It was another gaudy imitation of war, but it said plainly what the men and horses executing those maneuvers were capable of in earnest, what meal they could leave for the carrion crows if they wished.

—

The legate's banquet was laid in the Venta basilica, arranged in Roman fashion amid the red sandstone columns of its great hall. Couches wide enough for two people and each were set on the geometric mosaic of the floor, their heads facing a long table on which Caecilius's slaves, and others borrowed from his officers, placed and removed dishes as they were sampled, and filled silver cups from pitchers of wine and water to each diner's preference. There was no peacock, but a roasted goose sailed majestically on a pastry boat in an ocean of custard at the center of the table, and servers passed trays with balls of spiced lamb and dormice in lettuce leaves.

Caecilius's cook, in a burst of ambition, had proposed a temple to Jupiter made of fish paste and cheese but it had been decided against when Faustus suggested as tactfully as possible that the Britons usually liked their food to look like food. What they made of the goose on its custard sea he wasn't certain, but the slaves expertly dismembered it and offered slices and dollops of custard to each diner; the legate had provided spoons at each place in case guests did not bring their own.

The Silure delegation reclined somewhat uncomfortably on their couches, that not being a British habit. Except for one, they spoke Latin in varying degrees of fluency and attempted polite conversation over the meal with the Romans opposite them. The exception confined himself to eating and looking as if he wished to be elsewhere.

The king mark, newly tattooed on Loarn's forehead, stood out from skin that was still slightly reddened from the marking. He shared his couch with his sister Iorwen, with Llamrei and the other captains to either side of them. Caecilius and Tribune Marcellinus were opposite with Faustus and Eirian on their left, then Silvia and Galerius. Silvia's annoyance at sharing a couch with Galerius was tempered by the chance to get a good look at the Silures. Loarn was worth looking at, Faustus admitted. Under the red-gold crown his hair fell over his shoulders, cut at the length that his captains wore theirs, a reminder that he had been one of them until Aedden's death. His shirt was checkered blue and green wool, and his hands heavy with gold rings. Below the king mark were the older patterns of the Silure royal house. His sister wore a heavy gold collar and a thin gold fillet in dark hair that fell to her waist. A petal-shaped line of blue tattooing showed above the neck of a gown dyed sunset yellow and trimmed with bright stitching. The Silures stood out like a flock of multicolored birds against a sea of Roman military scarlet.

"I hope your ride from Porth Cerrig was pleasant," Caecilius said as the wine cups were filled. "The weather is fair for a change, no doubt in your honor. A welcome from Jupiter himself."

"Possibly," Loarn said. "Or from the stone god whose altar we saw as we rode past your fort."

"Perhaps so," Caecilius admitted. "I wondered whether you had seen him."

"We saw him. Where did you come by so ancient a thing?"

"He came to us. He unearthed himself with the last tremor."

"And you built him an altar?"

"We knew him to be yours, king," Caecilius said. "And thus gave him honor."

"He is," Iorwen said. "And he is not. Cath Mawr is the land's. I would be careful of him if I were you."

"Ah. It was Centurion Valerianus who found him." Caecilius nodded at Faustus. "I wondered if it was because he is kin to your people."

Loarn raised dark eyebrows. "Kin to us?"

Caecilius rarely said anything he hadn't thought through first. But why he had decided to tell them this, Faustus wasn't sure. It was possible he was just digging, to see what happened. "My mother was Silure," he said, because an answer seemed required. "She was taken captive when Claudius Caesar was emperor. My father bought her to keep house."

"And married her?" Llamrei asked.

"Yes," Faustus told her. "I wouldn't be eligible for the army, else."

"Is she still living?" Loarn asked.

"She died over a dozen years ago." Paullus came by with a tray of the little fattened dormice that were considered a delicacy. Faustus took one, thinking about what he should or shouldn't tell Loarn.

Llamrei cocked her head, studying him. She looked unnervingly like a raven when she did that. A raven in a deep green gown. She had put on women's clothing for the banquet. "Do you resemble her?"

"Not so much as my sister does." Faustus glanced at Silvia who gave Llamrei and the king each a respectful nod.

"You are very alike," Loarn said, studying Silvia. "And you are kin to us? What was your mother called?"

"Gaia," Silvia told him.

"Our father named her that," Faustus said. It had irritated him when he was old enough to think about it. Silvius Valerianus might as well have called her Woman. Gaia was the default name for any female. *Where you are Gaius, I am Gaia* was the marriage vow. It meant all men, all women.

"And her true name?" Iorwen asked him.

"Guennola," Faustus said. It wouldn't matter with her long dead, but she deserved that at least.

There was a small silence, he thought. Llamrei said, "We are glad to know her fate," so quickly that it was hard to tell.

"How came you to follow your brother to Britain?" Loarn asked Silvia.

Silvia set down the ball of lamb she had been nibbling. "I was widowed," she said, "and my husband left me nothing but my son. So we are come to be a burden to my brother."

"Certainly not a burden," Faustus said. "You know that I am glad to have you both."

"You have a son?" Llamrei asked.

"Lucius. He's only twelve." Too young for adult banquets. Lucius had been sent back to Isca with Gwladus, under protest, when the rest of the legion returned to quarters.

"Britain bids you welcome," Loarn told Silvia. "It is a great thing to have our own come home."

Llamrei and Iorwen both gave him a swift look and then returned their attention to their plates.

"Did you know our mother?" Silvia asked.

"No," Llamrei said abruptly. "It was a long time ago, that war."

"And you and she were very young," Loarn said to Llamrei. "War either erases memory or cements it." He took a piece of the roast goose on the end of his knife and bit into it.

"And you were not born," Llamrei said.

Iorwen said to Faustus, "Tell us how you found Cath Mawr. I am thinking it is important that he has come out of the earth just now."

"I didn't really find him," Faustus said. "The stone surfaced after the last tremor where my men had been digging. I doubt he came intentionally to me."

"I would not be certain," Iorwen said. "You knew him."

"Only from my mother," Faustus said. "Only nursery tales. She called him Old Cat."

"Still, he has come to the one who would know him. I will ask the Goddess what that means."

Llamrei said, "When the Goddess on earth has deciphered that message, the king must hear it." She spoke a little more forcefully than Faustus expected, and he saw that she was not watching Iorwen, but Loarn, who was watching Silvia.

Faustus too noted where the king's eyes kept landing as the banquet proceeded with a patina of root vegetables from the legate's personal garden, three roast sucking pigs, hare in sauce, and oysters with lovage and honey.

Eirian held her cup up to be refilled as a slave passed with the pitchers. Her sleeve fell away to show the edges of blue clan marks on pale skin.

Iorwen asked, "Are you British also, lady?"

"Cornovii," Eirian said. "From the Orcades."

Iorwen studied her. "The sea people. You are a very long way from home."

"Home is with my husband's legion." Eirian scraped her spoon through the sauce on her plate and waited to see where the conversation was going.

"Your children will be three parts British," Iorwen said. "The sea people are ours despite all." She looked at Faustus. "You may wish to rule us, but we will absorb you."

"We have no children as yet," Faustus said, refusing to rise to that bait.

"When you do, Centurion, remember what I said."

The banquet ended with sweet wine cake and stuffed dates. The Britons ate hungrily and drank freely, and mostly appeared to be enjoying themselves. But Faustus doubted that they were swayed to abandon any plans for insurrection by the elegance of the legate's table. And Loarn kept looking at Silvia.

At the end the legate rose to offer his guests a formal goodnight. "As representative of the emperor Caesar Domitianus

Augustus, I tender Rome's good wishes to you, lord of the Silures, on your accession to the kingship. May the peace and friendship born of the treaty with Aedden ap Culwych continue to benefit both Rome and Britain."

"Aedden ap Culwych was a man of honor even in death," Loarn said.

Caecilius's expression indicated that he found that response lacking, but he said, "May the gods give you safe journey back to Porth Cerrig, King."

—

The Silures had been given lodging in Venta's best inn, with the legate politely housing his own party in less luxurious quarters. The beds were reasonably free of fleas but not of lumps and Silvia rose before the rest, enjoying the sensation of having nothing in particular to do – Lucius was with Gwladus at Isca, and so were her spindle and distaff, along with any urge to wash the bed linens or clean out the oven. The inn had a small garden that let onto a wheel-rutted path that skirted the foggy woods beyond yesterday's parade ground before it joined the Isca road. She pulled her mantle around her against the early morning chill and set out for a solitary walk.

The sky was just pearling above the tree line and the birds singing the morning up. The crows that had watched the parade drill were gleaning someone's grain field on the other side of the path, industrious black shapes in the mist busy about the business of being crows. What on earth was she going to do? Manlius dying had upended her life, but somehow she felt less and less that if some god gave her the chance, she would buy him back again – go down into the Underworld like Orpheus to bring him out. Orpheus had looked back and lost his Eurydice, and more and more Silvia suspected that Orpheus had just changed his mind. No doubt she had loved Manlius as she had been instructed to, but less and less did she want him back. What she did want was entirely another question.

Silvia heard footsteps on the path behind her and turned to see, of all people, the Silures' new king.

"Forgive me if I startled you, lady." He wore traveling clothes of plain brown wool and heavy wolfskin boots.

"Good morning," Silvia said. "I don't know what to call you," she added.

"Loarn," he said. "I am Loarn ap Alwyn, but no one calls me that except when they set the crown on my head at Dinas Tomen. And you?"

She realized that no one had told him her name last night. She was Faustus's sister; that encapsulated her whole identity now that she wasn't Manlius's wife. "Silvia."

"Only Silvia?" Her brother had three names.

"Just Silvia. Roman girls have their father's name. If I had sisters, they would be Silvia too." She felt an irritable urge to be something more now.

"That sounds most confusing." Loarn had looked solemn all last night and now he smiled suddenly. Manlius had been ruddy faced and tall, always clean-shaven, brown hair cropped Roman fashion to less than a finger's length. The king of the Silures wore his dark hair long about his shoulders, his upper lip adorned with a luxuriant mustache. Beneath the king mark on his brow, older patterns marked his cheeks. He was taller than she but not by much. He fell into step beside her.

"Daughters in the same family are given different cognomina," she told him. "Or just Silvia Prima and Silvia Secunda." She had never been given a second name as there had been no need to distinguish her from anyone else.

"What does your brother call you?"

"He used to call me Goat's Butt when we were small," she said, and he laughed. "Now he calls me Silvia."

"I called Iorwen Pig Face," he said. "Until she became Goddess on earth. Then I thought I had best stop."

"What is the Goddess on earth?"

"She becomes the vessel for the Goddess, so that the Goddess may speak through her. It is always someone of the royal house and it is for life."

"That sounds frightening." A close connection to any god was frightening, let alone allowing one to inhabit you.

"It is," Loarn said. "But it fell to her because there was no one else. As the kingship fell to me."

"Did you not want it?" Silvia asked.

"It did not matter. We were the last of the royal house in any line, after... after the ones lost in the wars."

The mist had lifted as they walked. The sun was beginning to come over the trees and their shadow dappled the path, crossing and recrossing the rutted ghosts of old wagon wheels. The trees' image flickered across Loarn's face too so that it was hard to read his expression.

"My father was very angry when my brother asked to join the army," Silvia said. "He was supposed to run our farm because he was the last boy. Our older brother drowned when we were young, so Faustus was the heir whether he wanted to be or not."

"But he defied him?" Loarn asked.

"Not until after Father died," Silvia said. "Faustus was nineteen that year and so restless. I don't know what he would have done if Father had lived."

"Was the farm more important than what its children wanted for themselves?"

"Father thought it was," Silvia said. "And I did, too. Now I don't know."

"Would you like to see your mother's land?" Loarn asked. "The land I was given whether I would or no?"

"We are in it, aren't we?"

"Not this." He waved his hand dismissively at the Roman walls and tiled roofs of Venta Silurum, the broad expanse of the forum with the shadow columns of the basilica slanting across it.

"My brother says he will take me to Deva," Silvia said.

"That is the Ordovices' country, not hers. You should come to Porth Cerrig."

"I don't think my brother would let me." She was positive he wouldn't.

"It seems unreasonable that he should see your mother's land while you cannot."

"He sees it from the head of a patrol column," she pointed out.

"Indeed," Loarn said.

They had come nearly to the where the path joined the Isca road. "We should turn back," Silvia said. "He will worry."

She was answered by hoofbeats and the rattle of chariot wheels. Llamrei was behind a pair of black ponies, in breeches again and heavy boots like Loarn's. "The centurion is looking for his sister!" she snapped.

V. THE EMPIRE RUNS ON IRON

Llamrei waited until they had returned to Porth Cerrig to shout at Loarn. She found him sitting at a table in the great hall, sorting tally sticks that recorded the numbers of the horse herd, and the Demetae's herds, at least according to Gronwy who was probably lying. She leaned her spear against the wall and spread her cloak open to soak up the fire's heat. It was drizzling rain again outside. She stamped muddy boots on the hearth.

"You are a fool."

"I am the king, Llamrei. Do not lecture me." He didn't need to ask what she was talking about.

"That woman is a danger to you."

"She is not. And now you have made me lose count." He slapped the tally down on the table hard enough that the stack of them slid off the edge. The small hound attending him jumped up from his place beside the king's chair. So did the slave tending the fire. Both scrambled to gather them up.

"Go away somewhere else," Llamrei told them, and they put the tallies on the table and hurried out while Loarn glared at her. She turned back to him. "You are mad if you think she isn't dangerous. Llew says you are going to the Samhain fires at Isca."

"They are my people too at that village. Best they know me."

"I would believe that if I didn't think it was to see the woman."

"Believe what you will. This is not your business."

"She was raised by Romans. They will try to use her. If you don't believe me, ask Llew. Or Rhodri."

"I remember. I was not that young a child."

"Then you endanger your kingship to follow your cock!" Llamrei knew she was pushing her right to question the king past its limits.

Loarn took up the tallies again. "The Romans don't know what she is. If I am to be king, I will have the woman I want."

"Is the crown so great a burden?"

"Ask Aedden," Loarn said, recounting the tally sticks.

"The others are worried too," she said softly. "They all heard the talk at the legate's table." Except for Llew, the only one who didn't speak Latin, wouldn't learn it, regarded it as something tainted. But Pwyll had told him and Llew had threatened to leave the king's service over it. Llamrei didn't think he would take it that far, but Llew's spear brother had died the winter of the treaty of a sickness made worse by starvation. The Romans were to blame for that. He would give no welcome to a half-Roman woman, and particularly not this one.

"Aedden chose not to marry," Loarn said. "And thus put the crown on my head. Do any of them wish to wear it?"

Llamrei didn't answer. She doubted it, although it didn't matter. None of them were of the royal house except Loarn and Iorwen; her child was his presumptive heir. If none were left it would mean war over the kingship. The Druids would try to bend the matter toward a peaceful transfer to another house, but they would not be able to. There would always be more than one who wanted it – until they had it. And no doubt the Romans would try to have a hand. It would be better if Loarn married, for the sake of a royal house with a solid succession. Just not to this woman. Loarn had ever wanted what he couldn't have and not the thing that he must.

"Where is Iorwen?" she asked. Iorwen had seen. Iorwen had closed herself in the queen's wing, which belonged to her as royal woman of the Silures unless and until there was a queen, communing with the Goddess over a fire and a bowl of rainwater.

"She has gone back to her holding to bring in the cattle for the winter," Loarn said. "Her husband will be needing her."

"What did she say?"

"That the Goddess spoke to her," Loarn said.

Llamrei clicked her teeth, aggravated. "And what was the message?"

"She wouldn't tell me."

Llamrei felt as if she were arguing with a bog, where the answer to every question simply sank into the water before it could be heard.

"Teyrnon is here," Loarn offered. "The cold at Dinas Tomen makes his bones ache. Do you go and ask him, for the good it will do you."

Llamrei snapped her teeth again. The Druids never told a king what he should do. They merely looked at the night sky and told him what the stars said. If the Chief Druid was troubled by the stars' prediction, he would tell no one but Loarn.

—

"I said you would get nowhere with him," Rhodri told her. He was gnawing the last of a rib bone with the other captains, drinking and arguing over their evening meal – although mostly in a fair mood. Gwydion had taken out his harp and was running his fingers along it. In the wet air outside the sea hold gulls flapped and squawked as the fishing boats came in while the deep mournful lowing of dairy cattle coming to be milked came from the lower courts. With the new king crowned, Porth Cerrig settled to its usual business.

"Best leave the king to his own affairs," Gwydion suggested.

"The love affairs of kings are notorious for dangerous outcomes," Pwyll said, "to those who stick their noses in them."

"She's a danger and her boy is a danger," Llew said. "I don't like it." He scrubbed his mouth and gray mustache with his fist and drank sloppily from his cup, splattering mead across the table.

"You don't like most things," Gwydion said. "And you are drunk, which is not the best condition in which to discuss the king's affairs. Go and sleep."

Llew stood, pushing his chair backwards and balling his hands into fists. "I swore to serve him when he was crowned." He steadied himself on his feet amid the detritus of bones and discarded cloaks and bits of harness, and the hunting dogs that were asleep among it. "I will do so whether he likes it or no, or leave him. And you are a green puppy who ought to heed your elders."

"I was fostered as the old king's hound in the old king's household," Gwydion said evenly. "Do not be telling me about your great age and wisdom."

Rhodri got up from his place at the table and put a hand on Llew's shoulder. "You and I were puppies once too, and had our own opinions."

"Likely she won't have him," Gwydion said.

Pwyll took a piece of meat from the platter on the table. "Most likely the brother will have something to say as well."

"The brother is married to a Cornovii woman," Llew said. "I saw her."

"From the Orcades," Gwydion said. "They are all half seal in those islands. That's not the same."

"If you'd learn Latin, Llew, you'd have heard her say she follows her husband's legion," Pwyll said, chewing. "The Romans may marry out, but they don't let their women do so."

"I've no need to learn Latin, and nor should you," Llew growled, "the Silures being a free people. And the Romans will try to use her."

"They will," Rhodri admitted. "But you'll not stop them. Best instead to stop the talk about it and it may be they won't learn more than they have."

"The brother talks to the little dark people," Gwydion said, "and now we know why. They know. Worry about the brother instead."

Two days after the legate's diplomatic overture to the new Silure king, Faustus's cohort drew duty for the patrol that circled northeast from Burrium to the iron mines in the forested valleys above Blestium to Ariconium and back through open country to Burrium again. Detachments from the auxiliary forts that dotted the Silure Hills patrolled regularly, but Caecilius liked the legion's presence to be known and periodically sent a cohort detachment out in strength to make that point.

"I want an official eye on the iron works too," Caecilius said. "We can't have anything walking off, and it will if the overseers are asleep under a tree." Diversion of ore from the mines was always a problem but diversion of iron by the Silures could not be allowed.

Faustus decided on the first century, which was under his direct command, and the third, under Centurion Blaesus. That would leave Septimus in command of the cohort to help get on with the arena and with luck get the floor over the foundation before it filled up with water or any more ancient gods.

He announced the assignment to his family over dinner. Galerius, who had been dining with them nightly and was now somewhat overdue at Deva, said reluctantly, "I had best be on the road, too. Mithras knows what Terentius has done while I'm gone."

"Declared himself emperor, no doubt," Faustus said. The tribune, who considered himself an expert in military strategy and everything else, had been a source of annoyance to Galerius since his arrival at Deva.

"I'll go with you as far as Ariconium," Galerius said. "It's as quick a road as any and I'd like to see the mines. The Ordovices extract copper and lead under our oversight. I should probably be paying more attention to those works, if I had more than half a legion to go on with."

"That's more than ten days on the road," Eirian said. "Will you take Paullus?"

"I'd like to, if you don't need him."

"Will you take me?" Lucius asked.

"Certainly not," Faustus and Silvia said in unison.

"If I'm to go with the centurion," Paullus said, "they'll need you here."

Lucius rolled his eyes. "I know when I'm being condescended to, you know."

"I know when you're being rude," Silvia said.

Being rude was not allowed, particularly not to slaves or anyone else who couldn't be rude back. Lucius nodded. "All right. But I do wish I could go somewhere."

"You went to Venta," Silvia said. "And don't drown your food in garum."

"I wasn't allowed to stay for dinner with the king," Lucius said, ignoring the last instruction and pouring a lake of fish sauce over his turnips.

"You saw the cavalry games," Eirian pointed out. "They were *much* better than dinner with the king."

"I'm going to join the cavalry when I'm grown."

"You are not," Silvia said, and glared at Faustus. She held him personally responsible for Lucius's interest in the army.

"He has six years to go," Faustus said. "I am not going to argue this with either one of you for the next six years." He stood. "Paullus, leave the washing up to Gwladus and help me find my spare tunic."

"He knows where his tunic is," Silvia said, tight-lipped as Faustus left the room.

"Of course he does," Eirian said.

—

In the morning, the patrol paraded outside the barracks, debating under its collective breath the misery of carrying forty libra on the end of a pole against that of digging in a mud hole where primeval demons popped out at you. Besides weapons, helmet, and shield, an infantryman on the march carried cook pot, spade, spare clothes, and rations slung from the end of his pole. Only the tents rode on mule back.

"Shut it!" Blaesus snapped, and they muttered into silence.

Faustus, Galerius, and Centurion Blaesus were mounted, the privilege of rank, with their gear on spare horses. Like the rest of the legion and the British garrisons in general, the cohort was under strength. Two centuries amounted to a hundred and thirty-two men, twenty-eight short of full, and only two of the missing were in hospital. The rest simply didn't exist. Galerius had come down from Deva with a small escort and they trailed grumbling behind the column with the mules and their commander's considerable baggage. He had made them carry their own gear so as not to taunt Faustus's men.

The road followed the Isca valley on the west bank of the river between low, rocky hills. Beyond the cleared stretch on either side, forests of oak and ash covered the land in waves of autumn rust and yellow, the morning mist below them blanketing the lower ground.

"My first patrol in Britain was to Burrium," Faustus said, reining Arion, his troop horse, alongside Galerius. "Two days here and I had no idea what I was doing."

"I remember," Galerius said. "No one does at first. I didn't, and the Eagles were my family business."

"And do you now?" Faustus asked him.

Galerius shrugged. "I serve Rome."

At midday they reached Burrium, where iron ore was sent to be smelted. Once built to house the Twentieth Legion in the early days of the occupation, Burrium was still a military installation, and the work was done by an auxiliary cohort assigned there. Ore came in from the mines by wagon, and left beaten into ingots. The slag heap that resulted was reused as road fill.

A black cloud hung over the furnaces and a blackened crew were pulling the iron bloom from the bottom. The commander showed Faustus elaborate records going back to Agricola's day and it appeared clear that if any diversion was taking place, it was either slight or being done at the mines, not at Burrium.

"Or downriver," Galerius said, eyeing the crew loading ingots onto a barge at the dock. "Iron ore's bulky to move easily and they'd need the furnace to smelt it."

"There are iron works at Dinas Tomen," Faustus said, "although it's conspicuous to process ore in quantity there. But if it's going missing down river, someone's in on it to alter the bill of lading. *If* this is where they're getting it." Maybe by the time they got to Isca again there would be a message from Clio. Finished weapons were far more useful than iron ingots. If the Silures had a good source of those, skimming ore from the mines would be a supplementary endeavor.

They rested for the night at Burrium, which offered a bath house and a chance to sleep dry in the unoccupied section of the old barracks. Faustus spent most of the night going over the iron works records in his head, looking for gaps and getting so tangled in them that he got a headache and gave up. He wondered if the headache came from the iron itself. Salmon always said that he could smell iron, and at Burrium Faustus believed him. The air stank of it. He half expected his father's shade to make an appearance. It was the kind of restless night that often produced the old man. But maybe ghosts didn't like iron either since nothing appeared but a large moth courting death at the oil lamp. Faustus blew it out and tried to sleep again.

—

The mist came down again in the morning, blanketing everything. The calls of migrating geese, invisible in the white sky overhead, sounded like voices from the Otherworld. The road they traveled had been leveled and banked for wheeled traffic, but was covered only with gravel rather than stone. The dry tufted clumps of grass going to seed that struggled up through the gravel were nearly all they could see besides their feet. Faustus wondered what else the mist might hide, but that was the reason he had brought two centuries on what should be a routine patrol.

At mid-morning the haze that obscured their way began to burn off, showing a confluence of silver rivers below wooded hills, a third river joining them beside the timber-walled fort whose garrison oversaw the iron mines.

The Blestium commander welcomed them with the statement that wherever the damned natives were getting iron it wasn't on his watch.

"Certainly not," Faustus agreed. "We're mostly here to remind them of that, a show of force if you will. We're as undermanned as you are," he added sympathetically, "but we keep up appearances."

"And so we serve the Empire," the Blestium centurion said. "Which runs on iron." It was the iron mines of the provinces that kept Rome in power – iron for armor, iron for weapons. As much as Roman discipline, steel was the thing that turned the tide of battle against greater numbers with lesser armaments.

The commander offered space on the small drill field for the patrol to pitch their tents, and use of the bath house, and took Faustus, Galerius, and Blaesus off for a tour of the mines. Here extraction was mainly above ground where surface ore was plentiful, product of old upheavals that had opened underground caves to the air, or within the remaining caves. The road, barely wide enough for wagons, led through thick stands of trees, oak, beech, and hazel, and wriggled its way between outcroppings of moss-covered rock. The forest looked as if a god's hand had thrown down a great pile of jumbled stone and covered it over with a blanket of fern and lichen. The unpaved road was rutted by the iron-bound wheels of ore carts. It ended at the mine works, where paths led from the outcropping rock to a central clearing on ground that was only level in relation to the undulating landscape around it.

They tied their horses to the upright of an open shed beside an ore heap and a sluice diverted from a small stream. Workers with carts emerged from a cave mouth that opened at shoulder height into a slanted rock face.

"We can sink a shaft if a promising vein goes underground," the commander told Faustus, "but it often diminishes with depth. Mainly we stick to the surface or natural caves like this one."

The sun had dropped to a greenish dusk and now suddenly hundreds of little wings flitted past them from the cave. Galerius put his hands instinctively to his head, which was wearing a helmet. He took them down again, embarrassed.

"Our badge ought to be a bat," the commander said. "The men got used to them fast when they realized they're a sign there's good airflow."

"Are the workers all your own men?" Faustus asked him.

"All of them," the commander said. "We tried free Silures. We tried Silure slaves. All the sneaking beasts take too much watching."

At the Dolaucothi gold mines, the Silures had done the mining and the Romans the overseeing, but that had changed on Caecilius's orders. Apparently, it had here, too.

They found the same tight watch on the other mines and at the iron works at Ariconium. Galerius parted from them there, taking the road north and then east to Magnis to connect with the Deva road.

"Tell Silvia I improve the longer she knows me," he told Faustus as he mounted.

"My sister has crotchet about the army," Faustus said. "You know that. But I will tell her."

Galerius gave him a mock salute and rode away. Faustus looked after him wistfully. Galerius was his oldest friend, in Britain or anywhere truthfully. Galerius had taken Faustus under his wing as a very junior officer, advised him, sympathized with him, and got drunk with him. He wished he could give him Silvia, since that was what Galerius seemed to want.

Faustus's patrol headed in the opposite direction to circle westward through valleys dotted with small Silure farms and an occasional village, working their way down toward Burrium again. It was two weeks from Samhain, one of the great hinge points of the year when a man who stood still and listened could sense the world changing while he stood there. The geese filled the sky, and Faustus could hear the calls of curlews bound coastward to their winter roosts. The last of the summer grass had gone brown, tufted with seed heads. A fox slipped through it with some small animal in its mouth.

The fox saw them and doubled back as Paullus told Argos, "Leave be!" Anything resembling a dog, no matter how remotely, held Paullus's affection. "They're all stocking the larder for winter," he said.

"Voles are beginning to look tempting," Faustus said. They had been living mainly on army biscuit, a flat bread that never went stale because it was rock hard already, and half-burned camp bread. He had been reluctant to let anyone venture out to hunt, remembering the ambushes and strike-and-run attacks on other patrols. At the farms they passed they were informed curtly that there was nought to sell: "Barely enough to keep ourselves through the winter, with taxes to pay to Rome." To have conscripted a pig anyway would be more bad blood than the pork was worth. They had a bit more than a day's march to Burrium and a half day after that to Isca. They could stand army biscuit that long.

In open country, Faustus kept scouts ahead of the column and began to have the sense of something watching them, a feeling he had not had before. Toward Samhain the veil between this world and the next grew thin, and maybe the sense of eyes in the trees came from that but it was strong.

They halted for the night along a river, tributary of the one that ran past Blestium to the east, and dug a small marching camp, defended by ditch and turf wall. The sense that something followed them did not leave him and Faustus ordered a double guard. In the morning, he rearranged the column, put the baggage mules and spare horses in the center with Paullus and Centurion Blaesus's slave. Paullus objected. He was used to trailing beside the centurion, in the companionship of long service.

"If something's coming, I want you out of it," Faustus said. "And I mean well out of it. If it goes bad, take the horse and run. I've freed you in my will and I don't want you ending up with an iron collar in Porth Cerrig instead." In truth he would have freed Paullus any time he asked, but Paullus liked the army and as a freedman his only option would have been the auxiliaries, without the luxuries of a centurion's tent.

The column moved on, Paullus grumbling and Faustus's neck itching with the growing sense of being tracked. He thought the horses could smell it too. Arion was nervy, his usually complacent demeanor turned to eye-rolling temper. He bit Centurion Blaesus's horse and shied at a grouse whirring up from the grass.

Faustus eyed a copse of trees that had been let grow back too thickly near the road – the army made a point of clearing its ways of trees and scrub to a distance that gave warning of anyone launching an attack from their shadows. Just here there was little else in the way of woods; the forest had been cut for tilling and cattle graze. A flock of starlings gleaning a grain field beside the copse took to the air at their arrival and he relaxed. If anything human had invaded those woods, the birds would not have been there.

Beyond the shorn fields and the woods was a small village ringed by a wooden fence, its gates open in the quiet afternoon sun for the cattle that would be coming in soon. The stillness that hung over it seemed bucolic to Faustus at first and only when a slingstone smacked into his helmet, just off enough in its aim not to break his skull, did he realize the significance of that silence when there should have been shouts of children fetching cattle home, women talking across the lines of washing in the yard, men at work on the pile of new roof thatch.

"Down packs! Form up!" Another drill rehearsed so often it was second nature – stack carrying poles and packs orderly in the center of the column, up shields and make a wall around it.

Another burst of slingstones whined through the air to hit curved rectangular shields locked tightly together overhead. The Silures poured through the gates of the silent village behind a curtain of spearpoints. Faustus shouted an order and a rain of pila hit them and then another from his second rank. A few went down and were pulled away by their companions, but the rest kept coming.

The Silures were outnumbered and must have realized it, their intent uncertain, but there was no time to sort that out, only to keep his century in formation, signaling to his trumpeter and to Blaesus to push them to the left, keep them from retreating through the open gates again, hold them in the open. Three spearmen hurled themselves at him at the same time, and he saw that they were mobbing Blaesus, too. A spear thrust made him tuck his head below his shield before he rose to block another man's thrust at his ribs, lifting the oncoming spear upward on his shield. He drove the point of his sword under it, but the angle was wrong, and he felt the point turn on the leather hauberk of the spearman. He drew it back to strike again while two of his century wedged themselves beside him. Blaesus's men had surrounded him as well when it became clear that their attackers were going for the officers. Ordinary legionaries wore their helmet crests only on parade; the scarlet crosswise crest of a centurion made him instantly identifiable.

Barricaded behind their heavy shields, Faustus's line pushed into the Britons' ranks past spear range to close quarters where the wicked Roman short sword was most effective. Faustus slammed his shield into a tattooed attacker, this one bare chested, his torso splashed with blue and ochre paint. The blow knocked him backwards and Faustus pounced before he could rise, to drive his sword into the man's throat while he beat at Faustus with a shield that laid Faustus's leg open with its bronze bound edge.

The Britons kept moving backward, staying out of the Romans' sword range as much as possible while swarming around the officers. Faustus saw Blaesus go down and two of his men leap to pull him from the battle, while a knot of Silure spearmen came at him again.

He shouted, "Third century to me!" and Blaesus's signifer raised the century standard beside that of the first.

"Push them!" Faustus was furiously angry now. His patrol was too strong to take on with anything but a concerted attack with twice the men the Silures had, and the Silures could have seen that. He had no idea what they were playing at but to lose a good commander for a useless provocation was infuriating. Had Loarn ordered this? Or had the village acted on its own, angry over taxes and seeing an opportunity to make that clear?

The patrol was pushing them hard now and the Silures were beginning to run. A final spear went past Faustus's ear, thrown in retreat by a man who now took to his heels. Faustus turned to look at the wreckage of the column. Blaesus and two other wounded had been carried to the baggage and propped up while the field medics worked on them. Torn between pursuing the fleeing Silures and leaving his wounded unprotected, Faustus called his men back.

"Go into that damned village and rout out everyone you find!" he told them.

When they came back to report the village deserted, he swore. "Where are they then? That wasn't women and babies who went after us."

"Are we sure it was even men from this village?" Blaesus asked between gasps as the field medic unbuckled his lorica to get at the wound that ran from his collar bone down underneath the plate.

"The centurion should be still," the medic said grimly while blood welled up out of it.

"We should set fire to the place," Blaesus's optio said.

"Look for a wagon," Faustus said. "We'll get our wounded to Burrium and then we'll see."

There proved to be a wagon inside an empty barn but nothing to pull it. Faustus ordered his spare horse and Blaesus's hitched to it. Cloaks and packs were piled in the wagon bed to soften the journey and Blaesus's slave climbed in to sit with his master's head cradled in his lap. Two other wounded legionaries lay beside him.

The Silures had taken their few dead with them in their flight except for one. The man that Faustus had killed lay spreadeagled in bloody grass, the gaping scarlet wound in his throat coagulating.

"Put him across the village gateway," Faustus said. A pair of crows had already lit on the gatepost.

"Put him in their well," Blaesus's optio said.

"No. Move out!"

The horses protested the indignity of the wagon by trying to kick in the front boards until Paullus went to their heads and led them, talking to them as the driverless wagon rolled down the road toward Burrium. By the time they got to Burrium and a surgeon, one of the men was dead and Blaesus was still bleeding steadily, his face the color of milk. He died in the Burrium surgery that night.

"You lost two men, including a promising officer." The legate's face was grim.

"Yes, sir." Faustus stood at attention, helmet under his arm. "The third man is in hospital, but he may not live."

Caecilius tapped his fingers on his desk, a surface littered with papyrus and stacks of wax and wooden tablets. Faustus's report on the mines lay on top. The legate regarded the piles with irritation. "I might actually command the legion if I wasn't reading reports." He looked at Faustus. "I'm not blaming you."

Faustus decided that he probably meant that. He could always blame himself of course, and had been, ever since Burrium. "Thank you, sir. About Blaesus... They were going for the officers. They nearly got me." He had been chewing over the *why* of that, also since Burrium. "There's something I don't understand about that, but I can't figure it."

"No doubt they imagine we fall apart when a centurion goes down, same as them." The Britons mainly followed their local lords into battle rather than one overall commander. Rome had long learned that taking out the minor lords could destabilize the whole war band.

"Unless it was only another strike-and-run to annoy us," Faustus said doubtfully. "The thing is, they've fought us long enough to know taking out the centurion doesn't unravel the whole line."

"Well, we can't have this. They went too far, and these raids have gone on too long. I wouldn't be surprised if it wasn't some kind of statement about Aedden's treaty. Young Loarn was marvelously evasive. That village needs to be made an example of."

"I'm not sure the village was involved, sir," Faustus said uncomfortably. "It was deserted, not even livestock. It looked as if the war party that went for us had driven them out beforehand."

"They went to lie low so they wouldn't be blamed, more like."

"I don't know, sir."

"You don't need to know," Caecilius said. "You need to take your cohort back and tear that village down to the ground and burn it. The whole cohort this time."

Faustus tried to think of some argument that would carry weight. He had lost two men, and he was furiously angry. But he wasn't certain the village was the target for his fury. *I don't like that* was all he could think of and that stepped over the line into insubordination. Caecilius seemed to read his thoughts.

"You serve Rome, Centurion."

VI. THE BLUE-EYED BROOCH

Even undermanned, the First Cohort was a double and numbered more than seven hundred men, a sea of steel and scarlet coming up the valley, inexorable as fire in grass. The village had ample warning of their coming.

Faustus ordered helmets on and shields up, but no one approached. He was praying desperately that the inhabitants had fled again when he saw the village headman waiting for them in the gateway where they had laid a corpse five days ago. The man was well into middle age, hair and mustache gone gray, and he leaned on a staff. He must have known why they were coming but he stood stubbornly at the gate and waited for Faustus to come to him.

Faustus leaned down from Arion's back. He wore his short sword on one side, a long cavalry sword on the other. His shield hung from the saddle ready to hand. The helmet's rim shadowed his face, cutting a dark bar across cheeks and nose. "Take your people out of here. I will give you one hour."

The gray-haired man glared up at him. "This is our home. We had nothing to do with that." He pointed to what looked like a fresh grave outside the fence. A cairn of stones sat messily atop it, not a tribute but only a jumble of rock to keep the wolves away.

"You gave over your village to let them hide," Faustus said.

The headman's mouth tightened. "We had no choice. When the lords come with orders, we obey or suffer for it."

"What lords?"

The headman shrugged. "I did not know them."

"Don't lie to me!" Faustus snapped.

The headman's mouth tightened. "Men of the king's most likely. Men with good horses and weapons, and threats to burn us out if we did not let them in. I did not ask their names."

Faustus knew he was unlikely to pry more from him. "And so you gave over to them while they attacked a Roman patrol against the treaty. What did you think would happen for that?"

"That the Romans would come for us when they had beaten off the lord's men," the man said. "And thus, we hid until both took their wounded and left."

"And you were thinking we would not return?"

"We hoped you might think the village abandoned," the man said wearily now, anger overlaid with despair. "It is no easy thing when our lords battle yours and we are caught between."

"All the same," Faustus said, "I have my orders." He could see people gathered in a crowd behind the headman, women with babies on their hips, a small girl leading a goat on a rope. He thought of them picking through the devastation he was going to leave, and thought also of Blaesus, who was to have been married in the winter. He said, "You have an hour to get your people out, and what you can take with you."

—

"Where will they go?" Septimus asked as they watched the women and children streaming through the gate, driving cattle and a flock of sheep ahead of them.

"To other villages likely," Faustus said. Other villages that were already stretched thin with winter coming.

The headman boosted a woman that Faustus thought must be his wife into a chariot and set two children up behind her. She took the reins. "Go with her, you damned fool," he muttered.

"Will their men stay to fight us?" Septimus asked unhappily.

"You like to fight," Faustus reminded him.

"Not like this. Still, I suppose we can't expect them to just give over. I wouldn't, anyway." He fiddled with the latch that buckled his shield to his saddle, loosening it.

"Pericles said that was the problem with ruling an empire," Faustus said.

"Old Greek, wasn't he?" Septimus checked the spear lashed to his saddle on the other side. "What problem?"

"You can't let go of it once you've taken it."

"I hadn't thought of it like that," Septimus said.

"I expect the emperor has."

"I wouldn't be emperor for anything. Life expectancy seems a bit better in the legions, if you ask me."

Faustus gave a bark of laughter. He sobered again as they watched the evacuees crowding the gate. There were no men among them. "They're going to fight us," he said morosely.

"I wouldn't even be legate, if it comes to that," Septimus said. "And give orders like this one."

Faustus looked at the sun. Their time was up. No more people spilled through the gate and the village had gone as silent as if it were truly deserted. "Just remember Blaesus," he said. "It will help if you keep your mind on him."

The timber fence around the village was no more than a discouragement for wolves and solitary wanderers. It would not even need siege weapons to take it down when a rope with six men on the end would do. At Faustus's signal the third century rushed the gate in tortoise formation, shielding a dozen of Blaesus's avenging legionaries as they pulled the posts down with rope and ax. A rain of spears from inside the fence clattered against the roof of their shields.

"You can't stop us!" Faustus shouted. "Give way and we will only burn it."

A slingstone answered him from someone on the byre roof. "Fire it!"

The trumpeter lifted his horn. A stack of pitch-dipped arrows waited in the baggage wagon with a pot of coals, and they flared up like beacons as the archers drew their bows. Streaks of fire shot across the fence into roof thatch while at another trumpet call more men formed a wedge and drove it headlong into the battered gate. The defenders in the gate fell backward, fighting with the fury and desperation of men who have already given themselves to death.

Faustus rode over dying bodies and through the gate. Flames were already rising from the byre roof and the round houses that ringed the open yard. In the blacksmith's hut, they scattered the embers of the forge everywhere that something might catch alight. The men of the village formed a desperate spear band, plainly with no intent but to kill Romans until they were killed themselves.

One ran at Faustus, spear gone, howling, swinging a long sword with a strength born of hopeless fury. Faustus spun Arion to put his shield side into the blow and slashed at a bare ribcage with the cavalry sword. It bit deep, cutting across the old blue of tribal tattooing with a line of red that welled up and flowed the way Blaesus's blood had. The gash on Faustus's calf still stung, and he kept the image of Blaesus in his mind as he struck again and again and the man went down under Arion's hooves and another took his place, to be run through the throat with someone's spear. Faustus saw Septimus on the other end of the spear, dismounted, sword gone, driving it into the body on the ground until it stilled.

The defenders were fewer now, the cohort ranging through the houses with torches, taking what they could find and firing the thatch and the withy screens that partitioned the inner rooms. Blaesus's optio led the third century in the rout with a ferocity that made Faustus think he needed a new centurion as quickly as possible. They had been close, and Blaesus's death had left his second-in-command raw with anguish. That was a recipe for lethal mistakes.

The sky was black with billowing smoke now, and the air on the ground choking with ash. As Faustus watched, the roof of the village hall came down into the wreckage of its first story. A pig left behind ran squealing through the fire. Arion was beginning to dance under him, afraid of the flames. Faustus dismounted as most of his officers already had, and slapped him on the rump, pointing him at the ruined gates and the baggage wagons. A last defender staggered through the smoke and ran at him: the village headman, covered in ash as gray as his hair, spear in hand, cursing Faustus, cursing all the Romans.

"Curse those that brought you to this!" Faustus shouted at him.

"The Morrigan take them, too! May her birds eat their eyes and yours!" He flung himself at Faustus and Faustus brought his shield up and ducked his head against the fury of the blow. It went past his ear and the man stumbled forward with the force of it, onto Faustus's sword. The flames rose everywhere, sending smoke and showers of sparks into the darkened air.

—

They camped for the night outside the ruined village, watching as smoke filled the sky and then drifted away until there were only embers glowing red in the charred remains of houses. There were no dead among Faustus's avenging cohort and only a few with minor wounds, cleaned and bound up by the cohort's field medic. Paullus set up Faustus's tent and made him a supper of camp bread and dried beef. The smell of the bread in camp ovens overlaid the scent of burned thatch and Faustus was grateful they would be away before the bodies began to call the carrion birds down through the wreckage. Someone began to sing, one of the songs the legions marched to. The voice was insistent and after a while the rest took it up, raggedly at first. Septimus sat down in the grass beside Faustus.

"They're nervy now," he said, listening to the voices in the dark. "They'd get drunk if they could, and it's as well they can't."

"It was ugly," Faustus said shortly.

"It was. What was it you said about that Greek?"

"Pericles. According to Thucydides, he was talking about the hatred of the conquered for the conqueror, and the danger of letting loose your hold on them once you have them. *Your empire is now like a tyranny: it may have been wrong to take it; it is certainly dangerous to let it go.*"

"And when was he passing that advice around?"

"When Athens was still the great power in the world, not long after the fall of the kings at Rome. We were no doubt too busy with that to pay attention."

Septimus was silent for a while. Argos came out of the tent and sniffed at Faustus's leavings and Septimus ruffled his fur. He said, "Blaesus's century needs a new commander."

"I saw that, too," Faustus said.

"I'm grateful for the promotion and the pay," Septimus said, "but there are times, look you, when it seems simpler to follow another man's orders."

"Depends on which man," Faustus said.

"True. Mithras knows, there's always someone upwards of you, giving orders, and someone downwards that you've got to give orders to, so I suppose it doesn't matter so much where you are on the ladder."

Septimus in a philosophical mood was something new. Faustus said, "I won't get a replacement for Blaesus. New junior officers are all being sent to the Rhenus and the Danuvius. Would Quintus do if he had some leave first, do you think?" Quintus was Blaesus's optio.

"I don't know. I wouldn't trust him right now around civilians."

Faustus sighed. "He won't like it if I promote someone over his head."

"That's why you have the legate do it," Septimus said, standing up. "Good night, commander. I'll have a look-in on Quintus before I turn in."

A scutter of dry leaves went by on a little twist of wind and Faustus lay back in the dry grass, hands behind his head, watching the sweep of the Via Lactea flowing overhead through an inky sky. He wasn't surprised to see his father's shade materialize out of the milky shimmer. The old man had a habit of coming when Faustus most doubted himself.

"Does the farm you abandoned, our land you abandoned, seem somewhat more attractive to you tonight?" Silvius Valerianus asked. The starlight reflected from his pale hair. Argos thumped his tail, and the shade ran an insubstantial hand across his head. The old man had always preferred dogs to his children.

"Because I don't like what I just had to do?" Faustus inquired. "I didn't like what you wanted me to do either."

"If you remember, it was I who required you to read Thucydides. That might have been a warning."

"It might have," Faustus admitted. "Do you know, I think I have spoken more to you since you died than before."

"I saw no need for idle conversation."

"Just orders."

"I was paterfamilias. Now you are. Do something about your sister."

Faustus sat up. "I'm trying to. Unfortunately, you made her hate the army enough to reject the most suitable prospect she has, and the only one who doesn't care that she hasn't any money."

"You must get her and my grandson out of Britain."

"They wouldn't be here, and I would be most grateful for it, if *you* hadn't married her to a wastrel like Manlius with expensive hobbies above his income!"

"I was mistaken in Manlius," the shade admitted. "And in his uncles who refused their duty to your sister. Your mother's people..." he said, and then stopped.

"What about them?"

"I'm afraid of them."

"You're already dead. Why won't you go wherever you're supposed to?"

"I want to," the shade said fretfully.

98

The singers in the firelit camp had begun a new verse, led by Quintus, an old and vicious paean to the slaughter of the Iceni following their rebellion some thirty years ago. It was an excellent marching song but tonight Faustus found it made his skin crawl. "I am going to put a stop to that," he told the shade.

"Be quiet!" he bellowed. His parade ground voice roared across the camp, and they fell silent, looking uneasily at the commander's furious figure backlit by the flames of his campfire. Something pale and insubstantial hovered behind him.

"Hecate," someone whispered. "What is that?"

"It'll come for you in your sleep if you don't shut up," Septimus said. "Now!"

Faustus sat back down and then knelt, head bowed. "Mithras, god of soldiers, tell me what to do," he whispered.

"Foreign gods!" the shade snapped. "Where is your respect for the gods of Rome?"

Faustus didn't answer. Jupiter Optimus Maximus received his prayers every morning at the standards, with Juno and Minerva and Mars Ultor. Mithras, adopted by many in the legions, was a private worship, a pact between man and god for redemption and healing. The Mithraeum at Isca had been built in Julius Frontinus's day and saw steady worship among the men of the Second Augusta. Faustus shut his father's voice out of his head and listened to catch the drifting thought that might be the god's response. None came. He had half hoped that Mithras would tell him that he had only to do his duty, to serve, to follow his orders as the legate followed his. It should have been that straightforward.

"It never is," the shade said, despite the fact that Faustus had not spoken aloud.

"Get out of my head! You never wanted to know what I thought when you were alive!"

The shade dissipated, fading into the milky steam of stars.

—

The cohort returned to Isca on the day before Samhain. The vicus was stirring with excitement at news that the new king of the Silures would come for the Samhain fire. Households in the hills that usually lit their own fires came instead to Isca to see the king. The stack laid by the river was larger than usual, with room for cattle to be driven past for the luck of the king's presence.

Loarn and his captains arrived at midday on Samhain eve, a cavalcade of impressive finery – brightly painted chariots with silver mounts, ponies fitted with enameled headstalls, drivers and passengers brighter yet in scarlet and blue, green and yellow, gold at their throats and wrists. They drew rein outside a tavern inn, where Rhodri tossed the tavern keeper a handful of Dobunni silver and ordered any other travelers to find lodging elsewhere. Small hounds leapt from the chariots to unhitch the ponies.

Gwladus, shopping for fish in the vicus, saw their arrival and came back to report that they were very fine indeed. She had been impressed with the new king. "Dark like all the Silures, but if a raven was human that would be him. The tavern keeper saw me and gave me this," she added, handing a small wooden tablet to Silvia. "To save him a trip up to the fort, he said."

Silvia opened it and smiled. "In Latin," she said. "He's had someone write this for him. I'm flattered."

"He?" Faustus asked suspiciously.

"Loarn. He said I was to call him that. Apparently, he isn't as angry as I would be over the way you and that woman came roaring after us when we were talking at Venta."

"What does he say?" Faustus asked. "Communicating with the king of the Silures is not something you may do privately. It is a matter for the legate."

"He says he will be at the fire tonight and would like to wish me well," Silvia said stiffly. She handed Faustus the tablet. "You may take that to the legate if you wish. Alternatively, you may stick it in your behind." She stalked off and Eirian broke into laughter.

"I don't like this," Faustus said.

"And the more you try to stop her, the more stubborn she will grow," Eirian told him. "If he wants to court her a little, let him. It's unlikely that it's serious but I also doubt he will do anything to harm her."

"We still don't know who sent that ambush. And he knows about the village we burned. I don't trust him."

"No," Eirian agreed. She winced, hoping he wouldn't see. Her belly ached. She had begun to bleed again that morning despite her prayers to both the Mother and Juno Lucina. "No doubt all will proceed as it should," she said, as much to herself as to Faustus. He snorted and picked up his helmet.

—

Silvia took enough time dressing and having Gwladus arrange and rearrange her hair to make Faustus uneasy about her intentions, if not Loarn's. When he escorted the family to the bonfire at dusk to watch as the first spark was kindled, the vicus was mostly dark, fires quenched to await the Samhain need-fire, although the fort itself was well alight, torches on the sentry walk casting pools of light along the walls. Sellers of beer and pies threaded through the crowd with their wares, and those gathered to watch the fire spark were in a festival mood. The whooping that rose when dry tinder leapt into flame was partly beer and partly relief that things that rode the Samhain wind were barricaded outside the human habitations for another year.

Herdsmen driving cattle toward the fire stopped to duck their heads as they passed the new arena and the old god on his plinth. Offerings had begun to appear at its base: bunches of autumn seed heads, bits of red cloth, a polished green stone. They stared at the king's party, keeping a respectful distance, but Loarn didn't seem to mind when a small boy ran up, touched the hem of his cloak and darted away; the kingship held powers of healing and protection.

Faustus's family arrived as the first flames rose. Loarn smiled when he saw Silvia, left his captains, and made his way through the crowd while more hands reached out to touch the king's cloak.

"Stay with your uncle," Silvia told Lucius. She detached herself from her family, ignoring Faustus's glare, and went to meet Loarn. It was full dark now, the sky overhead thick with curdled cloud lit by the rising moon above them.

"The Goddess's greeting to you on this Samhain night," Loarn said. Samhain belonged to the Mother, as Lughnasa did to the Sun Lord.

"And to you, King." The Goddess of the Silures was not after all so different from the Bona Dea, who watched over the fertility of women and the land. To govern rebirth in spring was also to order the dying of autumn.

"Have you given thought to my offer to show you your mother's land?" he asked her.

Silvia smiled. "I have. My brother has not, nor will he."

"How if I gave your brother assurance that no harm would come to you?"

"Despite his having burned your village? I do know about that."

"Despite that. I would bring Llamrei with me so that there would be a woman at your side, and you could bring your maid if you wished. I would show you Porth Cerrig, and the green valleys that bred your Silure half."

"Llamrei does not like me," Silvia said.

"No," Loarn admitted, adding after a moment, "Llamrei is not king."

The firelight made dancing patterns on his dark face and the king mark on his forehead. Gwladus was right when she spoke of ravens. He was beautiful in a way that Silvia thought men rarely were. Certainly in a way that Manlius had not been. The fire shone on his dark hair and the mustache that made her wonder what it would be like to kiss him. Roman men were clean-shaven, hairiness the mark of a barbarian. Manlius's barber had shaved him every morning. Loarn took her hand in his and a spark like the first one of the need-fire ran up her arm. She wanted him, she realized with surprise. She had never wanted Manlius, only done her duty and if she wanted more, tended to it herself.

"You may speak to my brother," she said, "and he will no doubt speak to the legate. I don't know what they will say."

"They will want to send their soldiers with you."

"They will, I expect."

"And I will not have them in Porth Cerrig so that must be negotiated. You are going to be a great deal of trouble."

She laughed. "Then why go to so much trouble?"

"I want you," he said, and she knew that he meant it.

A pair of small boys ran past them with torches kindled from the flames to relight cold hearths. It was full dark now and he drew her a bit farther from the firelight, into the shadows of trees that lined the river past the docks and bridge. His white and black cloak blended with the tree shadow like patches of winter snow between stones. He put his hands on her shoulders and when she didn't pull away, he drew the cloak around them both. He put his lips against her throat.

"Your people will be looking for you," she whispered.

"They know when not to."

"And mine."

"We won't stay long." He kissed her and she gave into it with her whole body. The mustache was less bristly than she would have thought, soft like the face of some wild creature. She could feel him hard against her, feel herself responding, shivering. Then he unwound his cloak from about them and took her hand again. "Tell your brother that I could have done you ill tonight and I did not."

She might have let him.

"I will take you back to him now. And when spring comes, I will show you your mother's country."

Faustus kept his temper in check until they were home again and Gwladus had brought in their dinner. Silvia took the Lares from their niche and set them on the dining table, a ritual at every family meal. Lucius sprawled on his couch, full of sausages, apples in pastry and whatever else the vendors had been selling.

"If you're not hungry, Lucius, you may be excused," Silvia said, suspecting a row was coming. "Paullus will play rota with you."

"He's past rota," Faustus said. "He's teaching Paullus latrunculi, which I never could." He was aware that Paullus was also teaching Lucius to throw dice, but he didn't mention that. He had no intention of giving Silvia ammunition to hurl back at him.

"Lucius has a logical mind," Silvia said as Lucius departed. She glanced at Eirian, who was serenely eating the stewed hare that Gwladus had set before them. She had the look of someone who intended to keep her opinions to herself when the battle began. Silvia said, "I have been invited to see the west country."

"No."

Silvia glared at her brother. "I am an adult and a widow. I am capable of my own decisions."

"I am paterfamilias," Faustus said. "You are under my protection."

"Don't try to sound like Father."

"You can't go haring off into the countryside with the Silure king and no escort. Did he say you could bring an escort?"

"Of course not," Silvia said. "Nor would you let him loose here in the fort with his men."

"And you can't throw a rock in the works when we are trying to avoid a revolt. I don't even know if he ordered the attack on us."

"He says not."

"I lost a good officer. If you go off with him and I can't get you out again we have a diplomatic crisis of the sort that generally ends with siege weapons."

"He won't hurt me." Silvia smiled into her wine cup in a way that made the hair rise on the back of Faustus's neck.

"You don't know what he will do. For Venus's sake, if you want a man, marry Galerius. Do you realize what a fine hostage you would make?"

"You wanted me to know Mother's people," she said.

"And you behaved as if they were all diseased goatherds. Now you're seduced by a romantic delusion. Stick with your own kind." He pointed at the silver figures of the Lares, representatives of generations of their ancestors.

Silvia's eyes slid toward Eirian. Eirian went on placidly eating stew.

"That's different," Faustus said. "I told you that any doings with the king of the Silures are a matter for the legate, not something you may conduct privately. Last night will be the end of that!"

Silvia dipped her spoon in her bowl. "This needs parsley. Have you spoken to the legate?"

"No. I'm oddly reluctant to mention that my sister is trying to create a diplomatic incident."

"Perhaps you should. You brought me to Britain, Faustus. You wanted me to know my mother's people. I intend to."

"I did not bring you to Britain. You arrived when your spendthrift husband keeled over – no doubt from the weight of his debts – and his family packed you off to me."

"Manlius died of a fever!" Silvia snapped. "You are making things up."

"So are you."

"*You* rejected every offer of a suitable wife, from Father and Manlius both."

"The child with fits or some hideous affliction that no one would be specific about, that Manlius dredged up?" Faustus asked acidly. "Stay with the subject at hand, please."

105

"I am." Silvia's expression was stubborn, eyes narrowed. "My point is that you married the person you wanted. You have no moral standing to prevent me from doing the same."

"You intend to *marry* him?"

"I don't know," Silvia said stiffly.

"I will be surprised if he intends to marry you."

"That's my business."

"It is not."

"Perhaps a little bit," Eirian murmured.

They both turned toward her.

"You will have to go to the legate," Eirian said to Faustus. "It was necessary when the king wrote to her asking to meet. You know you do. So go do it and see what he says."

"And if he says to tie her up in her bedchamber?"

Silvia stiffened.

"I doubt he will," Eirian said. "It may be that he will find no harm in it."

"Loarn could hold her hostage."

"Well then, she knows that, and so it would be her problem to solve, having been warned." She glanced at Silvia then. "It may boil down to what risk Silvia is willing to take."

Faustus considered the risks that Eirian herself had taken. Those had seemed to him to be her right even though the idea had terrified him. He hadn't thought Silvia had that kind of temperament. He still didn't, but Eirian was right about the legate.

—

Caecilius was eating his breakfast on his desk in the Principia over a pile of messages – an unrolled scroll in front of him, pinned down by his wine cup. He raised his eyebrows and considered Faustus's news while Faustus stood at attention. There was every possibility that the result was going to be immediate transfer to a desert outpost in Syria, which at least would solve the problem of Silvia and Loarn.

Instead, Caecilius said, "I'm not sure this is an entirely bad thing, Centurion, if we use the opportunity carefully."

"This is my sister, sir," Faustus protested.

"Of course. Of course. Her wishes must be taken into consideration, naturally." The legate paused, considering something, possibly Silvia's cooperation. "What do you think the king actually has in mind? If he were just trying to seduce her, I think he would be less obvious about that, don't you?"

"I have no idea," Faustus said frankly. "I don't understand the Silures as well as people think I do."

"Marriage to a high-ranking Roman woman might be just what would buy lasting peace, don't you think? These tribes often make alliances that way."

"Among themselves, sir." Aedden's predecessor had promised his niece to every chieftain in West Britain at one time or another during his war with Rome.

"Then why not with us? Hmm?"

"Our family is not high-ranking," Faustus said.

"True." The legate chewed a bite of bread and cheese. "However, Loarn doesn't know that."

"Do you imagine he actually wants to marry her?" That still seemed unlikely to Faustus. Particularly for a man who was almost certainly stockpiling grain and weapons in preparation for a revolt.

"He certainly seems to want her in some fashion, perhaps less official?"

"My sister is not a concubine, sir."

"Juno forbid, of course not, Centurion. No insult intended. He *is* being exceedingly public in his courtship, which argues an official approach. Does *she* want to marry *him* might be the question. If she doesn't, we should nip it in the bud to avoid further provocation. I suspect that rebellious kings are more dangerous when lovelorn. It affects their judgment."

"She wants to traipse about the countryside with him and see our mother's land," Faustus said. "Beyond that, I don't know. I don't think she does either."

"That seems harmless, and indicates she is considering the idea." The legate sounded hopeful.

"He won't let me send an escort with her, only her maid."

"Of course he won't. The man's not a fool. Tell her she may take the king up on his invitation, Centurion, if he hasn't changed his mind by spring. Or his own people talked him out of it."

"They may," Faustus said. He hoped so.

"Well, I trust not," Caecilius said. "This is really very useful. We all serve Rome."

"My sister is also not in the army," Faustus said but Caecilius had stopped listening, his attention returned to his messages. Faustus saluted and left.

—

Faustus spent the rest of the day in a foul mood, cursing the legate and Loarn alternately under his breath while his cohort worked on the new arena. The foundation was complete – tiers of seats beginning to rise above it – and the arena floor leveled, overseen by the enigmatic whiskered face and tufted ears of Cath Mawr. Nothing new had surfaced in the work and the legionaries on construction rota had taken to brushing their fingers across the plinth as they passed it, for luck.

Before the king's party drove out toward Porth Cerrig, a boy brought a small package wrapped in red wool to the fortress gate to be delivered to Silvia. The sentry brought it to the house himself, radiating interest.

"It's for the primus pilus's sister, from the Silure king," he announced as he handed it over.

"Thank you," Eirian said firmly, motioning to Paullus to show him back out again. As the door closed behind him, she said, "That will be all over the fort in an hour."

"Eirian, look." Silvia held out a gold brooch, an S-shape formed by two beast's heads. Blue enamel decorated their eyes and snouts and banded the midsection.

"It's beautiful," Eirian said, examining it.

"What do you think the legate told Faustus?"

"That he was to leave you be, I expect. Else he would have been back here by now to tell you that you're forbidden further contact."

Silvia laid her ears back. "He can try. Gwladus says British women have more rights than we had in Rome."

"He only worries for you," Eirian said. "The Silures are very different from the ways you are used to."

"Do you mean people in the villages? Loarn is the king. Loarn doesn't live in a village."

"He lives in a drafty great fort with no hypocaust," Eirian said. She had come to appreciate that function of Roman houses. "My father's house on the island was always cold. Or smoky. Or both."

"After Castra Borea I have some acquaintance with discomfort," Silvia told her.

"Well, you didn't like it there. And you *don't* know what it will be like to find yourself among people who do things differently, who have different gods, who have different customs, who *think* differently."

Silvia pinned the brooch to her mantle, wrapping the woolen folds around her shoulders. It was cold in the house even with the hypocaust burning. A gray autumn rain had settled in during the last hour. "What was that like for you?" she asked Eirian.

"I came to it gradually, you know," Eirian told her. "On the road with Cuno and Rotri, then at Castra Borea. To come here was… peculiar. I felt at home in the vicus, the people there are very like my own. Here in the fort… you know what it was like. The women in Loarn's house may not be kind to you."

"Well, I haven't said I will marry him. He hasn't asked me."

"He may have to ask the Druids first."

"I thought the Druids were all gone."

"I imagine that the Druids are only gone when Rome looks for them," Eirian said. "You have barely met this man."

"I had barely met Manlius," Silvia said. "That is almost always the way."

"Do you care for him?"

"I must, I suppose, or I wouldn't be angering Faustus over it. I want him," she admitted. "I never felt that way about Manlius, not really. Does that mean caring? Or just my body having its way?"

"I expect it can be both," Eirian said. "Maybe a better question is, do you trust him?"

Silvia shrugged her shoulders. An enameled eye on the brooch shifted its blue stare toward Eirian. "I trusted Manlius," she said.

VII. THE NONES OF NOVEMBER

Clio considered the lengths of cloth spread across the table in her work room at the back of the shop. Cadr stood to one side, arms folded, while she examined his goods. He was brown-haired, not so dark as the Silures or so fair as the Atrebates, with the mustache that most of the Britons wore, and hair cropped just below his ears. He might have been of any folk of the Gauls or Britons, or even a German. Even his accent was nondescript.

"You won't find better," he said. "Not for any price."

"I know that," Clio said. "I am thinking about what I can afford." She fingered a thin cherry-colored silk. "The aedile's wife at Calleva will buy this. It's finer than anything she can get there." The silk was entirely too light for the British climate, but the aedile's wife would not be troubled by that. Clio turned her attention to a pile of fine woolens, and a length of gauzy cotton.

"Egyptian, that is," Cadr said. "First quality. It cost me a bit to get it by the portoria office."

"Since when are you law-abiding enough to take your goods through customs?" Clio asked, rubbing the cotton between her fingers.

"Well, not through customs, you understand. Past them, so to speak. That costs a bit too, sometimes."

Clio surveyed the offerings again and slid beads up and down her abacus until she was satisfied. "I'll take all of it." She ran a hand lovingly across a fold of deep emerald, admiring its shimmer. "You have a good eye."

"We pay attention," Cadr said. "I told Ma we should bring more silk this trip, with Saturnalia coming up, and I was right."

"Your Ma is a wonder," Clio said. "You take her this belt from me for a present." She fetched a soft red leather girdle with a bronze buckle shaped like a stag. Cadr's Ma ran the family operation with an acumen that would have done credit to any businessman in Rome, and it paid to stay on her good side. Boats captained by her three sons and various other relations fetched back silk and fine wines, jewelry and Gaulish glass, and anything else of value that could be slipped past the harbor portoria offices on a dark night.

"She'll like that," Cadr said. He buckled it around his own waist above a serviceable belt from which hung his dagger, a money pouch, and a pewter spoon.

"Have a cup of wine with me before you go," Clio said. "I have a bit of that lovely Falernian left."

They settled up and she took him to the room behind the workspace that served as her private office. It held an olivewood desk, a bronze table with an onyx top, and cushioned wicker chairs.

"This is good," Cadr said, when Clio's maid had poured the wine and been sent off again. "I may have some more next trip if you want it. But what do you want now, my girl, because you want something."

Clio was unsurprised. Cadr's family were of no known tribe but their own and had been at their trade for generations. They conducted their business with care, and suspicion was their default approach. "I have a friend," she told him, "who will pay for something very specific."

"You know I won't run weapons," Cadr said. "Even if I would, Ma would skin me."

"It isn't weapons," Clio said. "Not exactly."

"Weapons aren't worth getting executed for."

"He only wants information. About who might be bringing weapons. I know it's not you. I've told him so."

"Who is he?" Cadr put his wine down. "This sounds to me like something you should keep your nose out of."

"It is," Clio said. "But he's an old friend."

Cadr snorted.

"Yes, that. But he was always nicest to me of any of the customers. And he brought me the money to start this shop. I owe him."

Cadr grinned. "You must have been good at your work."

"There actually are men who do more than follow around behind their cock!" Clio said. "The money came from Tuathal Techtmar, who is now High King in Hibernia. He sent it by my friend, because he promised me he would buy me a house when he was king. I never thought he meant it."

Cadr looked skeptical. "I'm believing you less the longer you talk. Who is this friend?"

"He's an officer with the legion at Isca Silurum."

"The last person I want dealings with then."

"He's not interested in your business. He wants to know who's bringing the Silures weapons and armor, and grain."

"It isn't us! And I don't know anything about it."

"Yes, you do. And I expect you know who it is, don't you? Or have a good idea."

Cadr's face was expressionless now. "How would I know that?"

"Because you aren't an idiot, and your Ma has more eyes that Argus," Clio said, exasperated, "and between you, you know what the competition is doing."

"Maybe," Cadr admitted. "I've no interest in starting trouble with the competition either. We have our territory and our clients; they have theirs. It doesn't pay to pry."

"It will pay to talk to my friend," Clio said. "If they don't find where it's coming from, the Sabrina Channel will be so thick with patrol craft you'll never be able to land there. Probably the southern coast, too. They want this stopped."

"Mmm." Cadr flicked a gnat out of his cup and drained it. "I expect Ma will see the reason in that, but she won't like it."

"I don't like it either. But better to see it stopped short. I don't want my supply of goods cut off any more than you do."

"That's what he threatened you with, was it?"

"Yes," she admitted. "But he wasn't wrong. That's what will happen. It won't be good for anyone's business."

"Who is this friend? I want a name. And no more tale-spinning about the king of Hibernia."

"Faustus Silvius Valerianus. Primus pilus of the Second Legion Augusta. Will that do?"

Cadr nodded. "Tell him it will cost him. He'll pay in silver same as if it was goods."

"I'm sure he expects to," Clio said. "Where would we be if people did something just because it was the intelligent thing, without having to be bribed."

"The poorer," Cadr said. "Ten denarii."

"I'll tell him."

"He can meet me at Cow's Inlet. Next full moon. And he's to tell nobody where, nor make no noise about it. He's to leave off the steel plate and not come bumbling along with his helmet shining like my Ma's new cookpot. If I can see him much before he gets to me, he won't see me."

"And you'll tell him what you know?"

"I'll decide that after I meet him."

—

Cow's Inlet – named for the horn-shaped headland that rose above it – lay where the Uxella flowed into the southern side of Sabrina Mouth. The land here was primarily reed swamp and salt works, little used for shipping as Abona farther upriver was the official port. Clio's message had instructed Faustus to meet Cadr at the shrine that sat on the far end of the horn, a limestone temple to Llyr atop the sea cliff. As instructed, Faustus came unarmored except for a mail hauberk under his tunic, because he wasn't an idiot. His scarlet tunic and cloak, that would have glowed like a beacon in the daylight, looked black under the moon. He approached from the landward side through the riverine smell of salt marsh and tidal mud flats and found the well-trodden footpath that ran up the headland to where the horn's tip jutted over the sea.

The full moon reflected off the dark water in the channel below and gave a milky glimmer to leaves still clinging to the scrub that grew atop the rocky promontory. The night was full of the chirring of insects, a last burst of life before the world froze around them. A crashing in the surrounding brush made him jump and he saw a horned head regarding him from above. After an unnerving moment it resolved into a wild goat that bounded off a stone outcropping, showering Faustus with loose pebbles.

The temple on the sea cliff was small, just four stone columns with low sections of wall between them on three sides, silvery in the moonlight. Inside was a plain stone altar with the face of the god looking out from a stele atop it. Faustus put a copper coin on the altar because it was always a good idea to honor the gods, any gods. Other visitors had left bits of coral and shells and fossilized sea creatures dug from the promontory's cliff sides. Faustus sat down on the low wall to wait.

"Are you alone, then?" a voice asked from the shadow of a column and Faustus could just see another shadow move beside it.

"Yes. Are you?"

A man emerged into the pale light. Faustus eyed him curiously: dark shirt and trousers, a patterned cloak that blended with the brush beyond the temple. He wore an amulet of some dark stone around his neck but no other jewelry. "Alone enough," he said.

Faustus decided that would have to do. "You are Cadr?"

Cadr held out his hand. "Ten denarii."

"When you have spoken to me. Clio has told you what I want to know."

"What if you don't like what I tell you?"

"I will pay anyway. You aren't responsible for whether I like it or not."

Cadr considered that. "You may not."

"I probably won't."

Cadr sat down on the stone wall beside him. "I can't give you names."

"Because you don't know them or because you won't?"

"Because I'm not certain."

Faustus raised his eyebrows. "High-minded of you."

"I'll not spoil a man's business over what I'm not certain of."

"A revolt will be bad for your business as well as everyone else's," Faustus said. "Except maybe the legitimate weapons dealers."

"I'm well aware of that."

"I need to know where it's being landed, and where it's coming from. We need to stop it. If I can stop it without names, it will serve as well. I'm not the portoria office."

Cadr laughed. "Clio assured me of that. If she's wrong, she won't get any more silk."

"Five denarii now," Faustus said. "Five when you've told me everything you know." He reached into the pouch at his belt.

Cadr held out his hand and examined the coins in the moonlight. "It *was* being landed off the Demetae's southern coast, southwest of Moridunum." He put the silver in his own pouch. "They'll have abandoned that one now."

"Two of our men have gone missing from Moridunum," Faustus said grimly. "Would that be why?"

"No doubt, but if someone has killed them, it won't be the boatmen. We contract to deliver goods, that's all."

"Even if you run into the portoria?"

"Killing portoria agents is bad for business. We'll put out to sea again and wait them out. We don't commit murder. Ask the Demetae where those two men are."

"Where are they landing the shipments now?"

"On the west coast," Cadr said. "We watch these things. Octapitarum or Dinas Head. Both. They'd like to bring it in by Dragon's Head but that's Ordovice territory and they haven't got the Ordovices to agree."

"Useful to know that they're trying," Faustus said.

"What did you expect?"

"Where is it coming from?"

"Some of it from Gaul, same as us. But buying weapons is more suspect than buying silk. Most of it is coming from Hibernia. That's the part I thought you mightn't like. That it's the Gaels selling it."

"Why would that be, then?" Faustus asked.

Cadr shrugged. "Clio told a long tale about the High King of Inis Fáil, and you and her and a bag of gold. It sounded better than the theater, but I don't know how much of it I believed. She claims you're friends with the king."

"Let's say I am acquainted with him," Faustus said. "And no, I don't like it very much, but the High King is a practical man, not unlike yourself. He will do what seems profitable for his kingdom. Are you reasonably certain it's coming from Hibernia?"

"That's the part I am sure of."

"And who's paying for it?"

"The Silure king," Cadr said as if that ought to be obvious to anyone.

It was, but Faustus wondered if Loarn had any direct dealings with Tuathal. It was not a long voyage to Hibernia from West Britain – for which reason the Silures and the Gaels raided each other constantly, almost recreationally. The buying of weapons would require some restrictions on that activity.

He reached into his pouch again and took out the rest of the silver. "Your information has been most useful," he said as he held it out. "I would ask one last thing," he added when Cadr had tucked the coins away.

"If I can," Cadr said.

"If you learn for certain who the boatmen bringing iron to Loarn are, will you tell me? Only if you are certain."

Cadr thought. "No," he said finally. "If you knew, Rome would find them and execute them. They are only doing business. It is not their affair that the business offends Rome."

Faustus didn't argue. The landing spot was what mattered. He could catch weapons runners without knowing their names.

"I'll see you off down the path now," Cadr said.

"You don't go that way yourself?"

"My way is my business."

Faustus heard a little rustle of loose stone from the cliff on the inlet side. There was a way down to the water, he decided, and someone was waiting at the top of it. He cocked his head toward the sound and Cadr looked annoyed.

"Goats, no doubt," Faustus said blandly. Of course Cadr hadn't come alone. Neither had he for that matter. Paullus was waiting at the base of the footpath, along the edge of the salt marsh.

"There's more abroad in the night than Rome knows," Cadr said. "Keep that in mind, Centurion."

If there was anything more than Cadr and his companion and the boat that no doubt waited for them in the inlet, Faustus didn't encounter it on his way back. Paullus heard him coming and led his horse up with obvious relief.

"Ten denarii well spent," Faustus said, mounting.

"The army's ten denarii, not the centurion's, I hope," Paullus said.

"Naturally. For which I shall have to file twenty forms, two per denarius." That was an exaggeration, but not by much. "And we'll have to go after them before the winter storms. Not even smugglers are mad enough to sail in that weather. They'll be trying to bring as much across as they can now."

Caecilius and the commander of the Fleet at Moridunum heard Faustus's report and agreed. Lupinus, the Fleet prefect, was in a touchy frame of mind over the missing men and illicit cargo run in under his nose and irritated to be summoned to Isca overnight. Solid information improved his mood somewhat even when Caecilius ordered Faustus and his men aboard Lupinus's patrol boats. There were marines stationed at Moridunum and the other harbors, but Caecilius was adamant about having his own officer in charge and he outranked Lupinus.

Faustus kissed his collective family and set off again with close to a third of his cohort, chosen from men who could swim or at least tread water until someone fished them out again. Most Roman legionaries couldn't, and Faustus thought longingly of his Batavian auxiliaries who swam like armored fish.

Lupinus inquired with a raised eyebrow as they boarded at the Isca docks how many men Faustus thought he needed to fight a handful of weapons runners.

"Enough that I don't have any casualties and I catch live ones," Faustus said.

Lupinus shrugged. That was the centurion's business although it seemed unnecessary to him.

—

Just past the Nones of November was on the edge of safe sailing weather, Lupinus said pointedly again as they stood on the deck of his flagship. The moon had waned to a sliver, barely visible even without the dank gray cloud cover that had formed over the western coast. Three liburnians, hulls and sails painted the gray-blue of water and sky, lurked off Octapitarum Head where it jutted into the Hibernian Sea. Three more sat off Dinas Head to the north with Septimus in command of their legionary crew.

Faustus peered through a gathering mist toward the likeliest sea road from Hibernia. That island's coast was studded with jagged cliffs fit only for roosting gulls; most traffic went in and out of Inber Domnann and the harbor at the trading port of Drumanagh. If the smugglers' venture had the Hibernian High King's blessing there would be no reason to sail from any other place.

The mist thickened into dense fog. Octapitarum Head behind them was an amorphous black shape, some dark monster rising from a place where water was indistinguishable from sky or land. Faustus wrapped his cloak around him more tightly and pulled the hood up over his helmet. Beside him, Lupinus was muffled in a heavy sea cloak of oily unbleached wool. Mist dripped off his nose. They both squinted from the *Pinnata*'s bow into the fog. If there was more than one boat, and Cadr had said there would be, they would carry lights to keep from being either separated or driven onto one another. Lupinus hadn't argued about the number of ships. *Fortuna* and *Draco* accompanied the *Pinnata*. The ability to triangulate their quarry increased the odds of catching them before they could land and douse their lights. The dark coast was studded with inlets and coves and the water off it with shoals on which the larger patrol craft risked running themselves aground.

Lupinus's ships waited with sails reefed and their own lanterns closed, all oars out to hold their place against the waves as they listened intently for the dip and splash of other oars approaching or the sight of a lantern or a sail through the fog. At full speed his crews couldn't keep at their oars for long, but they wouldn't need to. They would either catch them quickly or lose them and speed would be what mattered.

Faustus felt Lupinus's hand on his arm just as he heard it too – a murmur of voices carried by the wind and then the splash of approaching oars. It was hard to pick the oars' sound from the sea lapping at *Pinnata*'s hull, but the voices came clearly. Then an approaching light gleamed palely through the fog, another behind it. In another moment they could see their outlines through the mist. Small ships, of the sort that a ten-man crew could handle even if they had to row. They sat low in the water, heavy with cargo, the painted eyes on the prow barely above the waves. Faustus looked back and saw an answering gleam on the headland.

Lupinus snapped an order and *Pinnata*'s helmsman unshielded his lantern. In an instant, lights bloomed through the fog from *Fortuna* and *Draco*. They heard a muffled curse from the approaching boats and saw them begin to turn, putting back out to sea, out into the gray fog again.

The lean wolf-like shapes of the liburnians shot after them, all oars out, *Draco* pulling ahead, *Fortuna* and *Pinnata* hunting along each side. The light on the headland disappeared.

They were nearly on the larger of the two boats as the fog became a drizzling rain. A slingstone flew overhead through it. Faustus ducked as another thudded into the sternpost, and thanked Neptune for the waves that made their aim unsteady. An arrow shot into the reefed sail and flames began to spread along it despite the rain. A sailor scrambled up the rigging to douse it with a bucket.

The two boats were still trying to outdistance the hunters. Their defenses, meant to fight off pirates, were inadequate to argue with Roman patrol vessels. They were no match for the liburnians' speed but quicker than the liburnians to change course. They came about instead and ran in the other direction. The *Pinnata* swung about too, more slowly, but then the speed of her oars closed on the smaller craft before it could turn again.

"Prepare to board," Lupinus ordered. The deck crew raised the boarding ramp and held it in position. When dropped its weight would drive the corvus, the spiked iron beak at its end, through the quarry's deck.

"Hold her steady."

The helmsman and rowing crew were well trained. They brought the *Pinnata* alongside, shipped oars, and the corvus swung into position. It came down with a thunderous sound; the crow's beak punched through the smaller boat's deck and held it fast to the *Pinnata*'s side. *Draco* and *Fortuna* sheared off and pinned the second boat between them.

"Board!"

Faustus's men ran across the ramp as the boat's crew tried desperately to fend them off. A defender lunged at Faustus as he stepped onto the deck, sword in hand, while his legionaries pushed from behind.

"Put your weapons up!" Faustus shouted. He heard someone go into the water. He drove the boatman away from him with his shield, knocking him back into his crewmates.

"Give over! We are a Fleet patrol!"

"Sea Father drown you, then!"

Faustus struck the man again with his shield, counting on the weight of it to stun him. He wanted at least the boat's captain alive. This was probably him. The man staggered and two of Faustus's cohort took him by either arm.

"Tell your men to give over!"

The captive glared at him furiously and Faustus saw a blow from another sword coming in the instant before it could connect with his head. The deck was slick with rain, the shapes around him indistinct. Angry shouting carried across the water from the other boat. He swung his sword, blocking the blow and swung it down again, low into the man's calf. The man fell, blood pooling into the water on the deck.

"Call them off!" Faustus shouted again to the captain. The boat's crew was outnumbered by three to one and unarmored.

"Fuck yourself!"

The deck was swarming with Faustus's men now. The crew fought them doggedly; more, Faustus knew, in fear of being taken for slaves than for their cargo. That his men were heeding their orders to disarm rather than kill gave certainty to that fear.

The smugglers' captain shouted the order to stand down only when there was no choice. He spat at Faustus from his seat on the bloody deck, his hands bound behind him with his belt, rain washing the gash in his leg and the rag that someone had tied around it. Faustus surveyed the defeated crew, two dead, four bleeding dangerously, and four with their arms pinned behind them. Lupinus came across from the *Pinnata* while his crew pulled up anyone who had gone in the water. On the second boat the legionaries from the *Draco* had subdued the battered remains of its crew.

"Board any that are still alive onto the *Pinnata*, please," Faustus told Lupinus, a diplomatic effort to let the prefect give the order himself. In a fight, Faustus was in command of his men. In the aftermath Lupinus was in command of his ships. Just now the hierarchy was indistinct.

Faustus's cohort prodded the smugglers' captain and the bound men along the boarding ramp and carried the wounded, none too gently. A few of the legionaries had minor wounds, none deadly, but enough to give them a temper when dealing with the captives.

"Search the hold," Lupinus ordered.

The hold yielded three crates of sword blades and spear tips, and one of iron ingots. Faustus ran a fingertip down a long blade. The bare tang extended from it where a hilt and pommel would be affixed, and the naked blade looked dark and efficient. His crew carried the crates across the ramp to the *Pinnata*. When *Draco*'s boat had brought its captives and cargo and they too were hauled aboard, Lupinus's sailors freed the crow's beaks and hauled up the ramps to set the captured boats adrift.

"Out oars. Reverse to ram them!" Lupinus ordered. His crew began to back *Pinnata* away from the drifting craft, bringing her about again at some distance, head on to the nearest hull.

"Ramming speed!"

All oars dropped to the water, pulling fast. The ram, a dark shadow under the water line, hurtled toward the captured boat and the bronze-sheathed beak buried itself in the hull. Faustus braced himself at the impact and thought as the *Pinnata* backed away again at speed to keep from becoming tangled with the sinking craft that they could have accomplished the job with an ax. A ram was more theatrical though, and he supposed that was to the good in imparting the message he had to give. He heard a crash and saw the *Fortuna* ram the second boat. *Fortuna* backed away and the little boat spun in the current, listed with one painted eye to the rain, and went down.

Faustus lined his captives up on the *Pinnata*'s deck and stood silently before them a long while, time enough for them to think over all the numerous unpleasant things that might be going to happen to them. The fog was still thick enough that the lanterns on *Draco* and *Fortuna* were only faint splashes of misty light. He looked up at the dark bulk of the headland. Whoever had been guiding them in with a light there would be long gone, as soon as they saw the Roman patrol ships.

"There is a market for men used to rowing," he commented.

The smugglers' leader looked back at him steadily. He knew what the possibilities were and how little power he had to fight them. Merchant ships ran mainly under sail, but they kept crews to row when the wind died. If they were slaves, they got little care and less food since they were disposable. In the light of *Pinnata*'s lanterns, Faustus could see that the man was young, no more than five-and-twenty at the most. Smuggling was a young man's game.

"What is your name?"

"The man who betrayed us didn't give it to you?" His Latin was accented but clear. Latin was a necessity for his trade.

"No one betrayed you," Faustus told him. "You are not as clever as you think. Hibernia was the logical place to buy your cargo. You were running out of time for one last shipment before bad weather and Loarn was harrying you for it. All we had to do was wait. I asked your name."

"Madog," he said grudgingly.

"Well, Madog, you have thirteen men left to you, if they all live. Which four shall I send to the slave market?"

Madog's crew looked at each other and at him.

"I will go," Madog said.

"Not you," Faustus said.

"What will you do with the rest then?"

"I will tell you what *should* happen," Faustus said. "There should be a line of crosses along the road from Isca to Porth Cerrig."

"Ah. So you are saving me for that." He shrugged. "Harder than the slave market but sooner ended."

"Every decision has its consequences. The decision to smuggle arms to enemies of Rome, for instance. You should have stuck with untaxed wine."

"No doubt I will think on that in the time left to me."

Faustus decided to let him contemplate crucifixion a little longer. It was cruel, but it might cement certain things in his head, afterward. He turned to Lupinus. "The cargo has to go to Isca. It can't be shared out; we don't want it floating about the province."

"I suppose not," Lupinus said regretfully.

"Take two from among the prisoners," Faustus told him. "Whichever ones you want except Madog. And one each to the first men aboard the boats." He beckoned to the legionary who had followed across the ramp on his heels, and turned to the junior centurion in charge of *Draco*'s crew.

The centurion grinned at the man who had earned the second honor. "Your lucky day, lad."

"Only four?" Lupinus looked irritated. "It seems like a waste. I am prefect here, Centurion."

"You are," Faustus said. "But I have orders from the legate. I am to put a stop to the arms running. Removing these men won't do that, even if they are all sold, or executed to make an example."

"That is exactly what execution and the slave market are for," Lupinus said grimly. "Deterrence."

"Prefect, a man afraid of danger is not transporting smuggled goods. The trade has its territories, like wolves. They stay out of each other's business. But if you take one pack from its territory, another will move in."

"They will," Madog said.

"You were listening. Good."

The men entitled to a prisoner for prize were taking stock of Madog's men, bypassing the wounded. Besides Madog there were eight unharmed, sitting miserably on the deck in the rain, hair plastered to blood-smeared faces.

"They are waiting for you to choose," Faustus said to Lupinus.

Lupinus looked ready to argue further.

"We can of course take it to the legate," Faustus said, "but he may decide to keep them all himself. Best to sort it out first, I thought."

The legate almost certainly would and Lupinus knew it. "Very well." He inspected them. They looked afraid to be chosen and afraid not to, with Faustus's threat of crucifixion in their minds. "You. And you." Lupinus pointed at two of the youngest and motioned to his own slave who had come out from his cabin with a dry cloak and cup of hot wine. "Take them away and clean them up and feed them. I haven't any use for them at Moridunum but they'll fetch a decent price there. Oh, and bring the primus pilus some wine."

Faustus's junior officers looked wistful, but the invitation was not extended further.

The slave inspected the prisoners with distaste. He wore a good wool tunic and a silver armband of the prefect's household. "Come along then."

The two stood, looking desperately at Madog but he only shook his head. Faustus nodded at his men, and they made their own choices. He thought they would probably sell them too. A slave was more nuisance than not in barracks where men slept eight to a room. He could polish your armor for you, but he also needed to be fed and that out of your own pocket. It was highly unlikely any would go to the rowing decks. They were worth far more than that.

Faustus turned to Madog. "You have lost five men dead and four to the slave market. You have six wounded who may survive or not. Do those numbers incline you to think you have made a mistake?"

"Does it matter?" But Madog looked at his men and Faustus saw him wince.

"It matters to me. I want the arms traffic stopped. You are going to stop it. If you don't, then I will rethink things and come back and find you and you may believe that I can, and then there will be the crosses I spoke of. But I would rather leave you in place and keep some other fool from trying to fill the opening."

Madog looked suspicious. "What do you want of me then?"

"You control this territory, and the coast here offers the best landing for boats from Hibernia. You will keep others off it. You will not run arms for Loarn anymore, and you will see that no one else does."

Madog grunted. "I don't have that power."

"You do. Those of your trade are not at war with Rome. This was business. When they learn what a bad bargain it was, they will lose interest in Loarn's silver."

"It was ill business," Madog admitted.

Faustus nodded. Lupinus's slave brought him a cup of warmed wine and he stood sipping it while Madog thought. No matter who ruled in West Britain, whether Loarn or Rome, they would tax imported and exported goods. Madog's business, like Cadr's, did not depend on who ruled. The higher the taxes, in fact, the greater the profit.

Finally, Madog said, "I will say a word to the other families." Smuggling tended to be an inherited profession. "If I do, you will let the rest of my men go free?"

"So long as your word is kept," Faustus said. "That and one other thing."

"Of course, there is another thing," Madog said. He had known there would be. There always was. Still, he was surprised when the Roman spoke again.

"I have a message for the High King in Hibernia."

VIII. THREE-QUARTERS ROMAN

Tuathal Techtmar, High King of Inis Fáil, sat on his carved chair with his queen beside him. The dozen council lords assembled around him watched as the king considered the man who knelt in front of him and read again the scroll in his hand. It was filled with small, infuriated letters.

Outside the Great Hall at Tara a storm that had been brewing for days unleashed a howling rain and wind. The man kneeling before the High King was soaked with it. "Do you know what is in this?" the king asked him.

Madog coughed. The rain pelting the shutters and the roof thatch two stories above the open hall made the hearth fire smoke. "No, lord. I was bid to bring it to you, and I bought my life with it, so I didn't ask."

"Dangerous weather for sailing," Tuathal said, "this late in the year. You'll not likely get home again before spring."

"If there's aught left of it," Madog said. "I brought my wife's brother to her with a festering wound in his ribs that he may die of, and two cousins at the bottom of the sea and all the cargo confiscated. Four living men went to the slave market and the Roman who sent you that sold me back the rest for the price of the voyage. It was an ill business start to finish and I a fool to listen to kings."

"Lost cargo is your affair," one of the Inis Fáil lords said. "No one will be paying you for that."

"I did not ask!" Madog snapped. He had spent his own silver and only a little of Loarn's to buy it. Loarn was to have paid him when they landed. "I have two boats on the bottom as well and still I did not come here to ask for silver."

Tuathal nodded. "However, you are owed hospitality." He looked at the lord who had spoken, a man with a lined face over a dark mustache speckled with gray. "Fiachra, find this man lodging and see that he is fed and clothed until he can chance a voyage home. I would not have him lose another boat, or his life, since he took such risk to come to me."

"Come then," Fiachra said. Madog followed him.

"What news did he bring other than his own disaster?" another of the lords demanded. Cassan was younger, even more finely dressed than the king, with blond hair spilling over his shoulders, gold at his throat and wrists, his scarlet shirt belted with links of enameled silver.

Tuathal didn't answer until he had seen Fiachra escort Madog out. "That Rome is most unhappy," he said then.

Cassan grinned. "And if that message is from your tame Roman, he is unhappy too."

"He was my general and yours," Tuathal said. "You knew him well enough to understand that he does not make idle threats."

"So, it is a threat?" Dai asked. He was dark-haired, as plainly dressed as Cassan was gaudy. Sitting side by side they seemed reversed images of each other, reflected in sunlight and dark water. All of them had followed Faustus's command when Tuathal took the High King's throne.

"A statement of facts," Tuathal said, "and the facts are that he has bottled up the boatmen who have been buying weapons in Inis Fáil and so we will have no more trade there. He sympathizes with my lords who have been supplying them, for their loss of income."

The lesser kings of Laigin and Connacht, Eochu and Conrach mac Derg, stirred angrily and Eochu said, "You gave the trade your blessing, High King!"

"I did, nor do I retract it. Sell all you can, if you can, but that route is closed."

"When you refused the fianna their right to come home again from Britain," Conrach said, "there was nearly war between their fathers and you. The weapons trade was your concession."

"I do not withdraw it," Tuathal said again. "Make contact with Loarn of the Silures if you will. If you can." The tribes of West Britain and the lords of Hibernia had raided each other for centuries. There was little if any trust between them. Madog's family had been the go-betweens.

The queen spoke for the first time. "The fianna who made alliance with the tribes of Britain have taken up holdings in the highlands there now, among the Cornovii," Baine said. "Your sons have fared none so ill." The mainland Cornovii's war with Rome had left them defeated, with the predatory Gaels of the fianna in their lands. They would not be got rid of again. And Rome had no hand there now, if it ever had that far north. "They build a new kingdom there," Baine said. "Content you with that."

Eochu grumbled under his breath, but the queen's word held power. She was the old king's daughter — he whose throne Tuathal Techtmar had taken in battle — and a royal woman, and at certain times the earthly body of the Goddess.

"Are you forgetting," Tuathal asked, "why it was that I forbade the fianna to go to Britain, and why it was that I refused them return when they disobeyed me?"

"For fear of Rome," Eochu snorted. "Rome has not the power there now to even hold the north."

"Not now," Tuathal said. "But Faustus Valerianus and I marched with general Agricola and if our old general had not been recalled to Rome his next conquest would have brought him here. Rome fears a governor with too many legions under his command and so moves them about like men on a Wisdom board, patching up holes in their border that have been opened by the last withdrawal when some general got too great. That tide may well come in again after a few years. I would not give

Rome reason to look our way once more. And we have had this conversation, Eochu, and I will not have it again."

"Leave be, Eochu," Cassan said. "You were wrong then and you are wrong now."

"The arms trade was a fine income while it lasted," Dai said. "From what the boatman said, it is ended now. Take your profit and be content."

Cassan eyed Tuathal. "Is the High King going to read the message aloud?" A few of them spoke Latin; none could read it. Tuathal, who had spent his adolescence in Julius Agricola's charge, was a rarity among his people. That marks on papyrus could speak unsettled Cassan a little. It was too close to magic – something only Druids had the power to handle, and they disdained it.

Tuathal ran his eyes down the scroll for a third time. "I am not," he said.

–

The wind was still howling when the evening meal had been eaten and the council lords urged to the guest house to continue their drinking there, if they would. The fire in the queen's chamber smoked, throat-rasping gusts that blew sideways in the draft from the shutters. The sleeping quarters were on the second floor in a gallery over the Great Hall. The wind whistled in the wickerwork that formed the inner walls.

"*Bean-sidhe*," Baine's maid said, brushing out the queen's hair before her silver mirror. "It's a wicked night."

"Any hag that comes here will start with the fools in the guest house," Baine said.

They could hear the sounds of men growing steadily more drunken even over the voice of the wind. Tuathal had not summoned them; they had lingered at Tara after the autumn court, and now with the boatman's arrival clearly would not go away again until they had found out everything they could and quarreled and made poems about it. Baine heard Dai's voice, loud and argumentative, and a hoot of laughter from Cassan, and someone's voice declaiming muffled verse. Only Owain had had nothing to say on a matter to do with the greater island across the water. He had found his woman again but otherwise he had shut away his old life and the clans he had ruled in Britain in a closed chest somewhere in his mind. Anyone who bade him open it risked being bitten.

A torch just visible from her chamber doorway illuminated the High King's shield and a sword hung on the wall below it. Her father's skull, picked clean years ago by the crows, sat in a niche among other skulls, ancestors and enemies, some both at once, in the stone staircase that rose from the hall to the sleeping chambers. Baine had been married to the High King for six years now, had given him a daughter and a son and a pair of twins who had died borning. There was little that he thought that he did not tell her, and so she was not surprised when he came to the chamber door.

She took the hairbrush and sent Olwenna to bed. After a moment she laid it down and turned to him. "You did not come just to watch me brush my hair."

"I like to watch you do that," he said, leaning in the doorway. "But no. I am too restless for bed until you come with me."

A howl of laughter, an angry shout, and more laughter came on the wind from the guest house. Then the sound of a table being overturned.

"There will be blood feud over some chance insult if we aren't lucky," Tuathal said. His voice was irritable, a man far beyond his patience.

"You lived too long among Romans," Baine said placidly. She had told him that before. "Feuds keep the fianna employed. With no one to fight for, they are dangerous." The fianna – young and without land of their own – fought in service of lords to whom they swore for a season. Unoccupied, they were a liability.

"Very well, Most Wise," Tuathal said. "We will see who is standing in the morning."

"Owain will stop anything that goes too far. They respect him." She was dressed for bed, her night shift puddled around her feet like the snow that would come soon. She smiled up at him. "There were a great many letters on that message from your Roman to say merely that the boats are stopped. Did he really offer condolences for the lost coin?"

Tuathal took the scroll from his shirt. "I will read it to you." He sat in the chair opposite her and pulled the table with the flickering oil lamp closer to his side. He laid the scroll in his lap and put a hand on it to keep it open. The oil lamp sent fluttering shadows over the letters.

> *To Tuathal Techtmar, High King in Hibernia, from Faustus Silvius Valerianus, primus pilus of the Second Legion Augusta, greetings.*
>
> *I send this message by a man who has sworn to deliver it and has excellent reason to make good on that, to inform you that the arms smuggling from Hibernia to West Britain has been put a stop to and if I catch any of your countrymen aiding a new operation I will not hesitate to execute them in the most horrible manner possible and send you their heads.*

"Some would take that as a challenge," Baine observed.

"Precisely why I did not read it to them."

> *The new king of the Silures is intent on throwing off Rome's hand, taking advantage of the lack of a permanent governor. I am intent on stopping him. What you intend, I have no idea, but if it is to aid rebellion, you should reconsider. You marched with Julius Agricola, along with me, and you paid me to train your war band when you sought your father's throne. The highland conquest, I am sorry to say, has been undone for lack of manpower. I would not like to see your victory similarly*

> *overturned, but if you are counting on the same lack of numbers to prevent that, don't try your luck. Your countrymen were an undisciplined rabble except for the ones I trained personally. They fight each other like stoats in a barrel but they will not stand up to a properly disciplined force. Furthermore, the emperor never takes well to a revolt and legions which are now in Germany may be in Hibernia in a matter of weeks if the emperor gets a notion in his head.*

Baine looked over his shoulder at the small black marks flickering on the page. The words Tuathal read from them were as fiery and elaborate as a poet's recitation. It was like sending the poet to declaim your message. Tuathal went on reading.

> *While I regret not to have killed more of them because they cost me many good men, your Gaels now running loose among the Cornovii have rendered the Cornovii incapable of troubling us further since they now have troubles of their own, an unintended consequence that I appreciate. My scouts' information suggests that their new kingdom there has begun to encroach on the Epidii as well, unfortunately for the Epidii, who are kin to your people and thus gave them free passage. Their assumption that they would all pass through to settle elsewhere appears to have been erroneous.*

"You knew that would happen when you forbade them to come back," Baine said. "I told you and the Druids told you."

"I didn't need either of you to tell me. I had hoped to inconvenience Rome."

> *In sum, please keep your boats off West Britain and your fingers out of Rome's pies.*
>
> *You may convey my condolences to your lords over the sudden restriction of their income.*
>
> *Your friend, Faustus Silvius Valerianus*

"If they attempt to keep the trade moving directly," Tuathal said, "I won't be able to stop it. He actually knows that. It is a fine balance to keep."

"Between men like Eochu and Rome?"

"I am not an emperor. You told me yourself that I cannot rule here like a Roman. I have no wish to draw Rome's eye, but I also have no power to forbid them if they decide that Loarn won't play them false."

"They are as likely to play Loarn false and he knows it," Baine said. Trade between West Britain and Inis Fáil usually fell somewhere between an armed standoff and an outright raid. It was a sign of the importance of the arms and grain to Aedden and then Loarn that they had paid to use the boatmen as go-betweens.

"If he wants weapons badly, he will pay enough that no one plays false. That is what is in Eochu's head, I expect. Where they will land is a different matter, unless Loarn can convince Cadal of the Ordovices to ally with him."

"There is bad blood between the Silures and the Ordovices, isn't there?"

"There is bad blood between the Silures and nearly everyone," Tuathal said. He stood and stretched. "Come to bed. I do not care if Loarn throws off Rome, as long as the trouble he makes does not come to my shore."

Baine stood and gathered up the trailing hem of her night shift in one hand. She gave Tuathal the other. "Will you send a message back to your Roman?"

"It is late in the season to risk anyone's life on the water just to spite Faustus." Tuathal blew out the lamp. The fire in the hearth was banked and gave only a warm glow for light to see their way to bed. "In the spring," he said, laying her down on the furs that piled the wooden frame, "I may perhaps remind him that it was I who warned that his northern rebels were recruiting a war band in Inis Fáil. It is possible he has forgotten that."

"He hasn't," Baine said sleepily. "But he can't afford to let that rule him any more than you can."

—

The bare black trees were rimed with ice, and Llamrei's pony picked its way carefully over the frozen ground, but the sky was clear. A break in the weather that the Druids said would last had set her on the track to Bryn Epona.

A hare in its dark winter coat sat motionless as she passed, while a flock of crows watched her from the high branches, but nothing else moved. She kept a wary eye out, nonetheless, bypassing the Roman checkpoints on the main roads and the scattered outposts that supported them, following deer tracks and the little rivers that wound through the mountain valleys. Past the last outlying Silure village she was unsure of her welcome and slept in the woods, avoiding Roman and tribal settlements both. A burst of cawing made her spin her head around, but it was only a hawk circling overhead. The crows launched themselves at it in a series of furious dives, harrying it from their roosts.

Caer Gai was near the end of her journey: a Roman outpost on a low shoulder of land above a river, guarding the ford where a well-used chariot track swung north to Bryn Epona. She skirted through the woods around it, swam her horse through the icy water above the ford and, shivering, picked up the road once she was well past. She found a yew tree and tucked a green sprig through her belt, and more in her pony's bridle and saddle trappings. From here, Cadal's men would be well aware of her presence.

Cadal's mountain hold was set into a ragged slope encircled by seven concentric rings of mud-and-timber wall, now slighted in accordance with the peace treaty. A banked chariot track passed through each gate and six courtyards holding byres and dairy, ovens, granaries, woolshed, and smithy. A stream flowed down the mountain to pass through the mid-level of the hold on its journey and supplied water to the population within. It had taken Roman siege engines to force Cadal's surrender. Even with the walls broken to rubble in places it was still impressive, and the lower gates were manned by a spearman who barred her way.

"What business?" he demanded. "Silure," he added and spat.

"I am Llamrei, captain to Loarn," she said, evenly. He was still a boy, she saw, not more than a year from his spear-taking, with a boy's arrogance. "He sends me to Cadal with a greeting and a message."

"And what might that be?"

"That might be for Cadal's ears," Llamrei said.

He grinned, looking her up and down. Llamrei laid her hand on her belt knife.

"Prove it," he said.

Llamrei pulled off her glove and held her right hand out to show him a heavy gold ring, its red stone carved with the horned moon. "You may tell him I wear this," she said. Cadal would know it, even if this boy was too young to remember. Bendigeid had worn it, and after him Aedden and Loarn.

A wagon with a load of firewood came up the track. The spearman waved the driver through. "Tell Cadal there's a Silure whore to visit him."

Llamrei's face darkened but she didn't answer. The worst she was likely to get was insults, until Cadal had spoken to her. After that, matters were uncertain, but she doubted that Cadal would allow Loarn's captain to be ill-used. That would start the war that Cadal was trying to avoid.

The sentry jerked his thumb at the skulls set in Cadal's gateposts. "You can talk to them while you wait." He grinned at her.

The wagon driver, older and possibly wiser, took note of the wealth of gold and fine clothing worn by the Silure messenger, and of the silver trappings on her pony's saddle and the yew sprig in her belt, and sent a passing child running to take Cadal the message that a Silure envoy waited at the gate.

After a while, someone came down the track to fetch her and Llamrei followed him. At the top courtyard one of Cadal's hounds took the pony's reins, staring at her with curiosity. "I'll rub him down and give him a feed, lady," he told her. "And put him up where it's dry." A faint rain had begun to spit down.

"Thank you. He will appreciate that."

Another spearman halted her outside Cadal's hall and held out his hand for her belt knife. She gave it to him.

"Stand still." He ran his fingers down her boots and pulled out her other knife. He nodded at her. "Go in."

Cadal received Llamrei where he had once made council with Bendigeid against the Romans, and he nodded when she sat in the chair he offered and showed him the ring.

"I would not have doubted you," he said. "I remember you." She had been among those who accompanied the king to that council. "You serve Loarn now."

"I serve the king."

"Is it not the same thing?"

"No. Among your people maybe," Llamrei said. "Among ours, the kingship is a living thing. It absorbs the man who is king."

Cadal leaned back in his chair and touched a forefinger to his forehead, to the blue spiral of his own king mark. He was tall and battle-scarred, with tawny hair going gray. "That is the Old Ones' blood in you," he said. "We may give up the kingship if need be, in other ways than death."

"So you think," Llamrei said. "You may find differently when you try."

Cadal didn't answer until a slave had brought them cups of mead and a tray of bread and cheese. Then he said, "You have been a long way on the trail, Llamrei king's-messenger. Eat before you tell me why you are come." He waited until she had a mouthful of bread and cheese before he added, "If it is to war against the Romans again, Loarn knows my answer already and you have made a winter journey for naught."

Llamrei chewed and swallowed, unperturbed. "That is your prerogative, king, but not why I am here. By what reason would Loarn trust you in war again?"

"Nor should he," Cadal said, "when your people encroach on my hunting runs and thieve from my border villages, even under Rome's nose."

Llamrei shrugged. "A mutual occupation. The only border my offer has to do with is the one with the sea."

Cadal stroked his mustache and his hand hid a grin. "So Rome has stopped up your weapons trade?"

"We will pay for a landing place on your coast."

"Where?"

"Off Dragon's Head."

Cadal considered it. That might be safe enough with Rome undermanned; and the legions' presence galled him like a burr under his harness. If the Silures drove Rome back... then the Ordovices might finish the thing. And if the Silures were beaten back into their own burned villages... that too would not trouble Cadal.

"I will think on it," Cadal said. "And tell you in the morning."

"If I am to sleep in your guest house," Llamrei said, "I want my knife back."

"I will put a guard on the door," Cadal told her.

Llamrei cocked her head at him. "You would do so anyway, lest I go where I am not wanted."

Cadal nodded. "It will serve a dual purpose, then."

Llamrei's mouth tightened. There was no guarantee that one of Cadal's men, drunk and reckless, would not come looking for a right to boast to his fellows afterward. The laws of hospitality were stretched thinner than cobweb when it came to the bone-deep enmity between his people and hers. All the same, she said, "Very well."

She was escorted to the guest house and when she was left alone with a bowl of stew, another cup of mead, and a pot should she need it, she took out the knife that was strapped to the inside of her thigh and put it to hand under the furs on the bed.

—

Llamrei half feared that the weather would turn and strand her among Cadal's people, but the Druids in Bryn Epona consulted the stars and said it would hold, and it was doubtful they would lie. The Druids had stronger ties to their fellow Druids, even those of rival tribes, than to the affairs of kings. They wielded great power, including the ability to halt a war, but they rarely took sides, except against the Romans.

Cadal gave her his answer in the morning, and his price, to which she agreed in Loarn's stead. He gave her back her knives and did not remark on the one that already hung on her belt. Loarn would send ships of his own to Inber Domnann in the spring and they would bring their cargo to shore at Dragon's Head, the promontory west of Bryn Epona that jutted like a great beast's snout into the sea opposite Inis Fáil.

—

It was past the solstice when Llamrei rode into Dinas Tomen, where the king's court had settled for the winter as far from Roman reach as possible. Far enough, she hoped, to erode his interest in the Roman woman before spring came. She gave Loarn Cadal's answer and terms, and went to the captains' house across from the Great Hall to sleep until morning. She woke hungry, washed her face in the icy water barrel, and dressed in clean clothes.

It had snowed in the night – a storm that had followed on her tail for the last day – and the blanket of it covered the courtyard, crossed with footprints already filling in as the snow kept falling, shrouding the hillside below and the buildings in the lower courts. One more day, she thought, and she would have been caught. The scent of baking barley cake came from the hall, and she could sniff stew on the wind as well. Her stomach growled and she headed for the smell.

A sudden chill wind stirred the air, with icy flakes on its breath, and an insistent, unwelcome memory dogged her as she crossed the courtyard: of the starving winter when they had held out against the Romans in Dinas Tomen until they could hold no more, when everyone had been bone thin and Owen, who had been Llew's spear brother, had died from starvation as much as sickness.

As she pulled open the door to the Great Hall, angry voices inside told her what had brought back that memory. Llew stood stubbornly before the king, feet planted, fists curled, face dusky with fury.

"This is not your affair, Llew," Loarn said, his voice tight, with a measure of menace.

"They are a danger to you!" Llew said. "The boy is a danger. Why will you not see it?"

Llamrei stamped the snow from her boots and saw Rhodri and Pwyll finishing their breakfast, dipping barley cake into bowls of thick stew. They watched Llew cautiously, and Loarn even more so. Llew and the king radiated anger like a shimmer of light around them, an energy that made Llamrei think of the Dancers, a force so elemental it would burn you if you could actually touch it.

Loarn didn't move from his chair, but somehow he seemed to stand, towering over Llew. Llew held his ground.

"I will have the woman I want," Loarn said. "She is of our blood, and you have no right to gainsay me."

The others stepped in reluctantly. Llew looked ready to push the quarrel too far; his face twitched with fury.

"She was born to the Romans," Rhodri said. "She isn't worth it."

"There are other women, King," Pwyll suggested. He was the youngest of them, of an age with Loarn. "Women of your own people with whom you can also breed sons to come after you. Why not with them?"

"Because I do not want them," Loarn said between his teeth.

Llamrei spooned stew into a bowl. "Have you spoken to Teyrnon of this?" she asked quietly as she did.

"Yes," Loarn said. "He says it is possible. We are related only in the fourth degree."

Llamrei ground her teeth. The Druids would rarely order a king not to do as he wished. They would warn him of what might happen if he did, but not forbid it, not in this case if the woman was suitable by blood. It didn't matter if she was unsuitable in every other way. "What does Iorwen say?" she asked.

"Iorwen has gone to her husband's hold for the winter," Loarn said.

Llamrei noted that he had not answered the question. Iorwen no doubt had had a good deal to say – advice her brother was planning to ignore. For some reason the old god the Romans had unearthed came to her mind, and the idea that signs and upheavals came in threes. With the earthquakes and the old god, she had thought the Dancers made three, but perhaps it was this half-Roman woman instead. As if conjured by that thought, the floor beneath them rolled slightly and subsided. They waited but it didn't come again.

"That!" Llew said. "That is what you have brought on us, King!"

"You are a fool, Llew," Loarn said. "The tremors began before Aedden died."

Llew was shaking. "It doesn't matter."

Llamrei took Llew by the arm. "Sit and eat. Your head will be clearer when you have, and then you may form an argument that makes sense." When Llew glowered at her, she said softly, "I do not disagree with you."

"There is something in what Llew says," Pwyll added uncomfortably. "Take her to your bed if you will, if she will, but leave her with her people. If you marry her, the Romans will use her and the boy against you."

"Pwyll is right in that," Llamrei said and ignored the black look on Loarn's face. Of all of them, she had the best chance of forcing him to listen. "The woman might do no harm if she is safely wed to you, but the boy is three-quarters Roman. They will use him if you bring this woman into Dinas Tomen."

"She will bring the boy with her," Loarn said. "To raise him here among us."

"He is twelve," Llamrei said. "It is late for that."

Llew put down the bowl Llamrei had given him and stood stubbornly before Loarn's chair again. "He will be a threat to your kingship and to the succession of your own sons – or Iorwen's – as long as he is alive."

Loarn stood too, pushing the chair back hard so that it nearly toppled into the hearth. His face blazed with anger. "That is enough! I will wed where I will. Do any of you want the kingship? Did you when Aedden died? I will have the one thing that I desire out of all the others I did not wish for."

They were silent at that, even Llew. None of them were of the royal house, none could have been made king except in extraordinary circumstances if the royal line had died out entirely. And none of them would have wanted it if they could. None of them had lived with the possibility hanging over them, wishing for Aedden to get a son when he had not. Loarn knew it. "Leave me be," he said now, quietly, and they did.

IX. THE ROYAL HOUSE OF THE SILURES

Faustus was no more pleased with his sister than Loarn's captains were with him. At breakfast, he pointed to the blue-enameled brooch pinned conspicuously on her shoulder.

"You can't keep that."

"Of course I can. I have had it since Samhain, and you just now noticed it?"

"I have had other things on my mind. The arms being smuggled into West Britain by your suitor, for instance. Silvia, you are insane. You have to send that back to him."

"In this weather?" It was snowing outside, and frozen snow slicked the streets beneath the new fall. The hypocaust, privilege of a senior officer, warmed the floor but they had drawn two braziers near the table as well. Silvia smiled, a little smugly. "And besides, Caecilius approves. He told me so."

"He what?" Faustus reached for the basket of bread and knocked the little silver Lares over. He righted them with a murmured apology to the ancestors and glared at Silvia. "You talked to my commander about this?"

"He talked to her," Eirian said, before Faustus went further.

All three of them remembered Lucius and looked at him.

"I'm not stupid," Lucius said. "I know the king wants Mother. And the legate thinks that will make peace."

Faustus, diverted, bent an eye to his nephew. "And what do you think?"

"I think it might. And I think I will stay here," Lucius said. "And join the army when I'm old enough, just in case."

"You will not join the army!" Silvia snapped.

"Uncle is paterfamilias," Lucius said, dipping his bread in the bowl of honey.

"This is what comes of letting him go out with your patrol. He could have been killed," Silvia said, turning the talk from her own affairs.

"By Loarn's men?" Faustus asked, turning it back. "It was a local patrol, nowhere near any Silure village, they were armed to the teeth, and he was bored."

"I won't have it!"

"Then stop waving your tits at Loarn!"

Silvia stood, knocking the Lares over again. "Your *commander* stopped me in the village to tell me that he approves of my friendship with the king," she said between her teeth.

"How kind of him."

Eirian saw Gwladus hovering in the doorway, wondering if it was safe to clear the table. "We are finished," she said, whether they were or not. "Lucius, come with me to the storeroom. I want to see what we have on hand in case this snow doesn't stop. I would as soon not slop through it to the village if we don't have to."

Lucius followed her reluctantly. Faustus picked the Lares up again. He and Silvia glowered at each other across the crumbs on the table. He thought of going to Caecilius to tell him the many ways in which he was a fool, and restrained himself. Being booted down to junior centurion of the sixth cohort for insubordination would not improve matters. He went to the door and looked out. It might be clearing. If it was, he would take a sack of apples to Llanmelin. The Old Ones knew things, in ways that weren't entirely clear to him, and he remembered that there was old blood in the Silure kings. Curlew might know what he should do. At the very least it would remove him from the temptation to give Silvia a beating. He wouldn't – and if he tried she would probably stab him with the cursed brooch – but he wanted to.

The weather cleared to a blue sky and slush underfoot. Faustus announced his intention to buy a saddle from a saddler in Venta Silurum whose wares he liked. He would as soon the legate wasn't aware of his visit to Curlew until he had heard what Curlew had to say.

He told Eirian where else he was bound, just in case, but took no escort other than his own weapons. The road between Isca and Venta was well patrolled, and most bandits had sense enough not to be out in the dead of winter.

"I have been wondering if there is something the Old One hasn't told you," Eirian said. "And if she will tell you now."

He wasn't sure where that thought came from. Eirian's ways of knowing things were different from the Old One's, and mostly involved listening to the seals, but it might be that they crossed in some ways. Or the seals knew something. That was possible too. The seals had been in the waters off Britain longer than humankind. It wouldn't surprise him in the least if they talked to the little dark people.

He rode out through the Dextra gate to take stock of the arena's progress as a sop to his conscience. It was nearly complete. He eyed Old Cat on his plinth as he passed. *And how long have you been here?* he wondered. West Britain seemed to him lately to be the tip of some buried world, older than all but a few of the gods. He circled the fort to the north where the old hillfort rose above it. The Silures had lived there once, before the Romans had come, and before them an even older people, ancestors maybe of the little dark ones. And the flint men before them. On the other side, he picked up the Venta road. It was wet with melting snow, the eye of the sun bright overhead now, and the bridle path to the side slick with mud. Arion picked his way carefully along it, snorting at a hare that shot from the underbrush encroaching on the verge. That needed to be cleared again, Faustus noted.

He stopped at Venta to sleep at an inn and to buy the new saddle. He sold his old one – ragged from thirteen years of campaigning – to the saddler for the frame and hung his kit and the bag of apples from the horns of the new one. When he came to the grove at Llanmelin he found Salmon waiting there, sitting motionless beside the spring. He rose when he saw Faustus. How long he had been there, Faustus had no idea. The hill people could sit and wait unmoving for hours.

"You travel less noisily without your soldiers," Salmon said. "Even on horseback. They make noise standing still. They make my head ache."

"Too noisy still," Faustus said, "if you knew I was coming." The little dark people moved like smoke. Faustus would never match them, but he had thought he was getting more skillful.

"We always know. But, until now you have had others with you, so we wait until you come here to the spring, to be sure you want to see us. This time, the Old One said you were on the way alone. My brothers saw you as you left Venta. She said you would come to us."

"Did she say why?"

Salmon shrugged. "I did not ask. She would tell me if she wanted to."

Faustus thought there was a faint note of irritation in his voice. Curlew was Salmon's sister and somewhat the younger. His 'brothers' might be actual brothers, or just men of the same sidhe, but Curlew and Salmon were blood siblings. "I will tell you why I have come," Faustus offered. "My own sister is a trouble to me, and I think yours may give me advice."

He heard a small snort of laughter and then Salmon disappeared into the trees, leaving Faustus to follow. Faustus remembered what Salmon had told him the last time he had come to the sidhe of Llanmelin, when Faustus had said uneasily that he was learning the way: *You will have to decide what you will do with that knowledge.* The woods were mostly winter-bare, the scrub brush and bracken brown and sodden. He could have found his way without Salmon. He tethered Arion to a tree in the hawthorn thicket near the door and left his sword and knife tied to the new saddle. He had made sure that nothing else about him bore any iron.

Curlew was stirring soup over a peat fire in the round stone-walled room that was the only one Faustus had ever visited. Corridors led from it deeper into the hillside. Curlew's people often adopted the stone chambers that the flint people had once dug, enlarging to suit them, and with some exceptions at home with whatever old magic lingered there. He knew this hillside housed a multigenerational dwelling, but he had never been invited further into it.

Faustus knelt to Curlew and then sat up when she grinned at him and held out her hands for the bag of apples. She bit into one, juice running down her chin.

Faustus smiled. Apples seemed such a small thing to bring that much pleasure.

Curlew swallowed and called out something in her own language, and another woman came down the corridor and took the bag from her. Salmon looked indignant and Curlew handed him the uneaten half of hers. "We will have some now, and make the rest last," she said gently. "And Faustus will have soup with us while he tells me why he has come."

Faustus took the clay bowl from her reluctantly. The hill people lived always on the edge of hunger and could ill spare soup for well-fed Romans. But it was a matter of manners and friendship to offer it, and to eat it. The broth had shreds of meat in it, thickened with barley and heavily flavored with herbs and allium. Faustus sipped at the bowl. "Thank you, Grandmother," he told her. She was much younger than he, but the honorific belonged to her status as Old One.

"How have you fared since summer? Have you built Cath Mawr his altar?" she asked him.

"We have."

Curlew nodded. "That was wise of you. I would not have invited him to come, but since he did, he has his reasons, and it is always best to honor the ancient ones."

"My men have decided he is good luck."

"Luck may run in two directions." Salmon swallowed the last of the apple core. "Often at once."

Faustus considered the notion that luck was a tidal river: controlled by the distant moon on one hand and the weight of water flowing toward its natural place on the other; endlessly, stubbornly pushing against each other. It seemed likely. "I have a new dilemma, Old One," he said.

She nodded gravely. "We have heard. My people speak to one another, house to house. The Old One at Ty Isaf is disturbed."

"The new king of the Silures is courting my sister, and my legate is fool enough to think it will bring peace if he marries her." Faustus's voice was ragged with exasperation now.

Salmon's eyes widened. Among his people the women chose who they mated with, nor did they marry. Among the Sun People marriage was a serious matter.

"I don't even understand why he wants her," Faustus said. "Ordinarily, kings have not the luxury of following their desires."

Curlew looked solemn. "Remember that she is half Silure, like you."

"So are any number of children of the legions," Faustus said. "We settle where we serve, and often enough marry there. Why would a king seek a wife who's half Roman?"

"Lust," Salmon said. He sounded disgusted. "Sun People have no restraint and think only of their bodies."

Curlew seemed to be debating something and didn't answer.

"What happens when his lust burns itself out and he sends her back? He will too, although she won't believe that."

"He won't," Curlew said finally.

"How do you know?" Faustus demanded.

"Because, lust or no, Guennola your mother was a daughter of the Silure royal house. This is the thing my grandmother did not tell you, because she thought it would not be good for you to know. It probably still is not."

"Then we are kin to Loarn?"

"There is a link that is too far back to prevent marriage. But had your mother not been taken, she would have been the royal woman of her people, and the body of the Goddess on earth. Once he marries her, he cannot send her back."

Faustus was silent now. So she had not come from some wattle-and-daub hut. She had been a royal woman, a princess of her tribe. Another thing he had not known about her. He wondered if his father had known that, if she had bothered to tell him, if he would have thought it mattered.

"Your sister is a danger to both her people," Curlew said. "After I spoke to the Old One of Ty Isaf, I hoped you would come to me. I was even thinking how I might come to you."

"She doesn't know," Faustus said.

"That is worse. Loarn knows."

Faustus remembered their conversation at the legate's banquet. Certain things that had puzzled him about Llamrei's reaction and Iorwen's began to come clear. "The Silures are stockpiling iron and grain," he said. "We are certain of it. There will likely be a revolt in the spring. I would not have my sister in the middle of it."

"Nor do we wish your armies trampling over our houses," Curlew said. It was dim in the chamber, but he thought he saw anger spark in her eyes. "The Old One at Ty Isaf allowed them to hide iron in the barrow there for two days while your tribune was in Dinas Tomen for the king-making, because she hates your people even more than Loarn's."

"And you?" Faustus asked quietly.

"You are of our blood, and you have been kind. I am fond of you and Grandmother said you were important. But your people are no different to us from the Silures and every other of the Sun People who came and took our land and trampled us under their boots. It would not grieve me if they and all your Romans slaughtered each other."

Salmon had been silent, listening, lest she send him away. Now he said bitterly, "That will not happen. One side or the other will win, and our fields and gardens will go to ruin because an army on the march can find anything that grows."

"What should I do?" Faustus asked Curlew.

"I don't know." She looked in to the peat fire as if some answer might show itself and shook her head when none did. "I have asked the Mother, because this concerns her, but she has given me no answer. Sometimes that happens."

Faustus wondered uneasily if the Goddess would speak to Silvia if she wed Loarn, and if she did, what message would come. Juno, wife of Jupiter Best and Greatest, was a deity that Silvia understood. The Goddess as she resided in the Silure royal women might be different.

"You have until spring, I think," Curlew said. "He will want to wed at Beltane before Druids."

"Should I tell her?"

"I would have said no, but now it is best that she know it."

―

When Faustus untethered Arion from the hawthorn he was not surprised to see a faint mist beside him coalescing into the angry figure of his father. He ignored it and put his heels to Arion's flanks. Once they were away from the sidhe entrance the figure materialized again in his path as Faustus stopped to slide sword and knife back onto his belt.

"Sorcerers!" the old man said. "Witches. They will lull you to sleep in their caves and it will be a thousand years gone when you wake."

"They haven't yet," Faustus said. "Did you know about Mother?"

"What about her?" The shade looked evasive.

"That she belonged to the Goddess? Or would have if Claudius's army hadn't taken her?"

"She belonged to Juno like any good Roman woman." Silvius Valerianus stuck his translucent chin out, obdurate.

Faustus narrowed his eyes at him. His father's shade was paler than it usually was, as if something here in Guennola's country sapped his strength. Or maybe it was just that there was another fog coming down around them. Or both. "I suspect that the Goddess's aspect in Rome may be somewhat tamer than it is here," he said.

"She learned to cover the mark," Silvius Valerianus said. "That was all that mattered."

A farm dog barked somewhere in the distance and a memory slid into Faustus's head through the fog, of his mother bent over the coals in a brazier.

She had just come from the bath and not dressed yet. Faustus was young enough for that not to matter and he sat beside her playing with the clay dog he had been given for Saturnalia. She was singing.

It was not a tune he recognized, or even a form of music that was familiar. It sounded more like the wind in trees. If there were words, they were in her own language, which he was just beginning to understand. She knelt beside the brazier, the mark like a flower between her breasts lit by the embers' glow, and moved her hands above them while she sang.

Faustus grew silent. The clay dog ceased to bark at imaginary visitors. His mother's hands made a pattern above the brazier, back and forth, in and out, weaving something he could almost see. The air in the room was still. Her furniture – the bed dressed with woolen covers, the cushioned chairs, and dressing table with its perfume bottles and silver mirror – became ripply, like water in a pool when someone put their hand in.

When she was finished, she sat for a long time while the room grew solid around them, then sighed and stood.

What magic had she been trying to make, Faustus wondered now. As dusk fell, he recalled, a slave had come to say that the master had trodden on a loose stone and twisted his ankle, and his father had been abed for several days while it healed, and in a bad temper the while.

Could his mother have done that? Had she tried to do worse? Watching his father's shade ripple in the fog as the room had done in his memory, Faustus thought it might be possible. "I don't think you knew what mattered," he told the shade. "I don't think you do now."

"I know one thing!" the shade snapped. "Get the boy out of Britain!"

"To where, damn you?" Faustus asked, but he was gone.

—

Silvia was at the baths with Gwladus and Lucius when Faustus rode home in the evening, and he took the opportunity to tell his tale to Eirian. She listened with a look of growing unease while he hung up his wet cloak and pulled his boots off.

"You can't let Lucius go with her," she said. "A royal woman's son is too much of a threat to any other son."

"I'm certain Loarn doesn't want him, whatever Silvia thinks," Faustus said. "If I could get them into a succession squabble and thereby divert a revolt, I would do it. But not by using Lucius."

"Fortunately, Lucius doesn't want to go." Eirian tidied her distaff and spindle into a basket full of soft tufts of wool. "He says that when his mother comes to her senses, Galerius is going to be his father, and you and he will get him a commission in the Centuriate."

"I'm delighted someone has a plan. Loarn has far more reason to be serious about this than we knew."

"Are you going to tell her?"

"About our mother? I have to – and try to keep her from telling the legate. Mithras, what a mess. Maybe if she thinks that's the only reason Loarn wants her, she'll be insulted and change her mind."

"If she doesn't, I doubt you can stop her. You can order her not to do it, but if she marries him anyway with the legate's blessing, you won't be able to fetch her back even if she changes her mind."

"That's what worries me, and I'm willing to use Lucius for that," Faustus said. "I am paterfamilias. She can't take him with her without my leave. I have to hope she'll be unwilling to go without him."

"She won't forgive you for that."

"If she leaves my house to be queen of the Silures that's not likely to matter." And if she didn't? Would she feel about him the way their mother felt about their father, the man who had kept her from the people she belonged to? He couldn't believe that Silvia belonged with the Silures any more than he did, but what if he was wrong about that?

Eirian stood and put her arms around his shoulders. "You are wet."

"It rained most of the way." Outside they heard the sound of the Watch going past, splashing through the street.

"You need dry clothes and dinner then."

"I wanted to catch you before Silvia gets back. I can't tell her tonight or I'll make a mess of it and I won't be able to stop myself if she starts up on it. I ate at a stall in the vicus. Come to bed and save me from making matters worse than they are."

She followed him into their bed chamber and watched while he stripped off his wet clothes and found the dry undertunic that Paullus had laid out for him. She admired his naked body, lean and scarred here and there from spearpoint and sword blade. "You know what she wants, don't you?" she asked.

"Her own way," Faustus said shortly.

"She wants this. Someone to feel desire for. I don't think Manlius gave her that."

Faustus thought of Manlius: pompous, a little flabby – by Faustus's lights – his hair carefully curled across his forehead in the style favored in Rome. "No," he said.

"Well, then."

"Father picked Manlius out. Silvia thought it was a fine idea."

"She was young. She thought what she was told to."

"I wish she'd start doing it again." He put the wet clothes outside the door so Paullus wouldn't come in for them, and pulled her into bed with him.

"I'm finding it hard to blame her for what she wants," Eirian said as he began to run his hands down her thighs.

"She's my sister. I'm not going to think about it." He nuzzled his face into her breasts and put his hand between her legs, rubbing his thumb through the soft, pale brown hair. She wriggled under him contentedly and he forgot about Silvia and the Silures.

He was on top of her, breathing hard, her legs wrapped around his back, when furious shouting erupted beyond the door.

"Curse it!" He tried to ignore the row, but the momentum was gone and the shouting was growing louder. Two voices. Silvia and Lucius by the sound of it.

"Go and see what it is," Eirian said, pushing him off her.

"Typhon take it." Faustus rummaged on the floor for his undertunic and pulled it over his head. He stalked out into the corridor.

Silvia and Lucius were in the atrium, loud enough to be heard in Rome. Faustus hoped they hadn't been shouting at each other all the way back from the baths. Gwladus's expression said that they probably had.

"You are a woman! I don't have to answer to you!" Lucius's hands were balled into fists at his side.

Silvia's face was red with anger. "You are a child! You will do as I tell you!"

"Uncle is paterfamilias. You have to do what he says!"

"We are not in Narbo Martius!"

"Be *quiet*!" Faustus shouted at them both, louder than they were.

They quieted but Silvia gave a contemptuous look at his disheveled hair and bare feet. "Put some clothes on."

"I need to talk to you!"

"Not while you are half naked," Silvia said icily.

Faustus turned to his nephew. "Lucius, go find something else to do than talk back to your mother. That was disgraceful."

Lucius glared at Silvia, but he let his breath out. "Yes, Uncle."

Gwladus had disappeared in haste and Faustus saw Eirian beckoning Lucius to her. He looked at Silvia and said, "Sit." When she looked as if she would balk, he said, "Do it!"

Silvia sat. Her face was still scarlet with rage, but her expression was frosty.

Faustus sat opposite her and tried to get a grip on his temper. "You cannot take him with you if you marry Loarn."

"You said Loarn didn't intend to marry me," Silvia said stiffly.

"I have learned something since," Faustus said.

Silvia raised her eyebrows. "That I am not a whore?"

"From the Old One of the hill people."

"Why are you talking to them?"

"I told you. We have their blood. Mother did. If that makes you uncomfortable, you had best remember that all the Silures do, in some dilution. Particularly the royal house."

"Loarn said that," Silvia admitted. "Did this old woman tell you that Loarn is not toying with me?"

"She's younger than you are. Old One is an honorific. And she told me that our mother belonged to the royal house," Faustus said. "*That* is why Loarn wants you."

"It is not! Am I too ugly for someone to love?"

"Think, you fool. If he marries you, his sons will have a better claim than his sister's sons."

"He didn't tell me about Mother," Silvia admitted. "He does know, I suppose."

"Of course he does. And I expect he would prefer we didn't know. But you can't take Lucius with you."

"That's ridiculous."

"Silvia, listen to me, and stop thinking of yourself as the heroine of some drama. Guennola was a royal woman of the Silures. So are you, or you will be if you go to live with them."

"What does that mean?"

"It means that your son is a threat to any sons you have with Loarn, *and* to his sister's sons. The kingship often goes through the mother. You can't take Lucius."

"He's a child. Loarn wouldn't hurt him."

"Maybe not Loarn. There will be plenty of others with reason to. Lucius will be thirteen in the spring. Old enough to matter. Old enough for Caecilius to think him useful too. You cannot tell Caecilius this. I am only telling you because I see no way out of it."

"You insult me. And Loarn." Silvia stood and picked up the basket of bath oil and towels that Gwladus had abandoned. "I see no reason Caecilius shouldn't know."

"If you want to be a diplomatic piece on his latrunculi board, by all means tell him," Faustus said. "Then see whether you can do anything at all unless he wants you to. He might marry you to Loarn. He might try to overthrow Loarn and make Lucius a puppet king. How long do you think Lucius would survive then?"

That had got through to her, he thought. However rebellious she might be over Loarn, Lucius was the heart of her world. It drove her need to control him, to keep him out of the hated army, to make for him the life she felt he should have. The irony of her abandoning the life that her family had felt she should have was probably lost on her. Faustus thought he would save that for another argument.

"I am going back to bed," he told her. "I will let you think on this."

He thought she was going to snap at him. But she just said, "I will think."

The next morning's breakfast was uncomfortable. Silvia was distracted, and Lucius silent and tense, like a wound torsion spring. His spoon rattled in his bowl every time he dipped it in his porridge. Only Eirian looked placid, spooning honey onto fresh bread with Argos's head in her lap.

"That dog should be in the kitchen," Silvia said.

Faustus wasn't surprised when Lucius caught up to him at the door as he was buckling his helmet strap. "Come outside," Faustus told him.

Lucius followed him out. The rain had stopped and a chicken, escaped from the pullarius's pen behind the Principia, was prospecting for worms. "Uncle, I am not going with Mother. I don't care what she wants. Not about this anyway."

"Of course you aren't."

Lucius looked relieved.

"But you aren't to talk to her like that again."

"No, Uncle."

"I understand the temptation," Faustus added. "What is it that *you* want?"

"I've already told everybody what I want. I want a post in the army."

"Over your mother's objections?"

"You are paterfamilias."

"I wish people would stop telling me that and then objecting when I exert any authority," Faustus told him.

Lucius grinned. "That's natural, isn't it? We only like it when authority tells us to do the things we want to do already."

"That's cynical enough to be accurate," Faustus said. "Listen, Lucius, if you will try not to aggravate your mother any more than you have to by refusing to go with her if she marries this man – and you absolutely have to refuse – then I will write you a recommendation for the Centuriate when you are eighteen. In the meantime, study your Greek and make yourself fluent in British. I will find someone to teach you tactics and military history. Will that help?"

"Oh, yes!" Lucius watched a century of the Fifth Cohort pass them, marching in formation through the Sinistra gate, steel plate gleaming in the sun that had finally shown itself. "Mother says the army was all you ever wanted, too."

"It was." Faustus remembered the first time he had seen a column of the Tenth Gemina go by their farm and how he had yearned after the scarlet uniforms and the shining plate and the great gold Eagle of the legion.

The pullarius hurried past in the other direction in pursuit of the chicken, which squawked and pecked him in the eye as he scooped her up. He bore her off under one arm, cursing.

"The army is not entirely a glorious profession," Faustus observed. "Someone has to mind the sacred chickens."

"Well, that's an honor," Lucius said. The chickens were consulted before battle; their appetite for the grain offered them predicted the way events would unfold. "I wouldn't mind that. It would be better than having Mother hovering over me like a sheep dog with one sheep. Even when she's not there I feel like something is watching me. When can I go out with your cohort again?"

"When her temper cools down. And when there is a routine patrol making the rounds of very safe places. I am not going to put you in the way of any action, so don't think it."

"Of course not," Lucius said. He couldn't help hoping for unexpected action though.

Faustus knew that and couldn't blame him. But an almost-thirteen-year-old was not a soldier despite the sword and pilum practice that Faustus and Galerius had indulged him in, also over Silvia's objections. He should probably forbid Lucius telling his mother about the promise of a Centuriate recommendation, but Lucius's face beamed with that knowledge like a lighthouse. Silvia would know.

Faustus was right about Silvia's powers of deduction. She was lying in wait for him when he came home in the early dusk, looking for Paullus, towels, and a hot bath.

"Lucius is not going into the army! Lucius will come with me wherever I go! You will not decide for me where that is! I will go to Caecilius!" She advanced on him furiously and when he backed away, she threw herself at him and beat her fists on his lorica.

"Silvia, stop it!" He grabbed her wrists. She twisted in his grip. "Stop it!"

"You are trying to take my child from me! You went behind my back!"

"Silvia, he is absolutely suited for the army. He is *not* suited to be an accountant or lawyer or whatever civilian occupation you have picked for him with no regard to what he actually wants."

"You let him go out with your men! I want that stopped."

"And if you take him to live with the Silures he will end in Loarn's spear band," Faustus said. He let go of her wrists and pushed past her. "Paullus!"

"Of course he won't. I wouldn't permit that either."

"You are an idiot." He shucked off lorica and helmet. "Silure boys – and girls – start weapons training when they're eight or nine. What do you think will happen?"

Paullus appeared with towels and bath oil, and slid warily past Silvia to the door. Faustus followed him, leaving her shouting at his retreating back.

X. OWL

The weather that winter was as capricious as the earth, snowing one day, clearing the next, then freezing solid as a block of marble overnight. Lucius's restlessness increased along with his sense of being constantly watched, at which he kicked like a recalcitrant cart horse until the joyful silliness of Saturnalia offered a welcome respite.

Caecilius decreed a holiday for the legion and dispensed a generous ration of wine. Each household and century drew lots for Saturnalia Princeps and the winner issued orders to those above him for the rest of the day. Septimus failed in his attempt to give the army oath standing on his head, so his century threw him in the bath instead. Crispus, possessor of the first century's lucky bean, ordered Faustus to declaim a poem about beetles. When they had begun to settle, somewhat drunkenly, to their dinner, Faustus retreated to his house before Crispus thought of something else.

Master waited upon servant at Saturnalia. Silvia and Lucius poured wine for Gwladus and Paullus and Eirian brought them the best parts of the roast goose. A good deal of wine was going into Lucius too, Faustus noted, but let that slide. Gwladus looked happier than he had seen her since her man had died, and was head to head with Paullus, giggling. There were new clothes for both, and gifts between the family. Outside, his men had gathered about his door singing loudly and untunefully.

"If they keep that up, I'm going to give you back to them," Eirian said.

"I gave quite a good poem on the subject of soldier beetles," Faustus said. "Impressive, I thought, for an impromptu effort. I expect they were too drunk to appreciate it."

"Well sit over there and eat your dinner before it goes cold." She brought him a bowl and spoon and a small table to set them on. The guests of honor were occupying the dining couches.

Eirian approved of Saturnalia. It seemed to her a fine idea to trade places now and again to keep anyone's head from getting too big. Faustus had given her a pair of lapis eardrops set in gold, and she had made him a new cloak, deep heavy scarlet wool with a hood lined in fox fur. Faustus had bought Silvia ear drops too, and Lucius a latrunculi set with onyx counters. The only fly in their mutual wine cup was that Loarn had sent Silvia a present. It was his understanding, the note in Latin read, that her people gave gifts at this time. This one was a gold finger ring set with agate. Faustus had regarded it with horror and ordered her not to wear it, an order she had ignored. Now she was lecturing Lucius on the amount of wine in his cup and listening disapprovingly to the howling outside. It was growing louder.

"Go and see what they're doing," Faustus told Eirian. "If I go, they'll have me wearing your nightshift and a blond wig."

"I would pay to see that," Eirian said, but she went to the door. Paullus looked relieved not to have to.

The joyful howling stilled for a moment, and someone said something to Eirian.

"Thank you, no." She shut the door and bolted it.

The singing resumed. Now they had begun "The Commander's Horse", which had verses that grew increasingly scurrilous as it progressed.

"That's no good," someone said. "We've brought him a present. Sing something nice."

A mournful voice took up a new tune.

Livia said she'd wait for me

When I left two months ago,
Now she's drinking in Assisi
With a tribune from Brindisi
And I'm here digging ditches in the snow!

"They've brought you a present," Eirian said. "It's a pig."

"A pig?"

"A medium-sized pig. It has a ribbon on it."

"Where in Hades did they get a pig?"

Paullus got up from his couch and peered through the shutters at the gathering on the portico. "Stole it, I'd say."

Lucius came to look too. "From the village? It's not a wild one."

"Of course it's not. A wild one would take them apart."

They looked out the window again. Argos snuffled the air with increasing interest and came to stand beside them, paws on the sill.

"Why don't you want it?" Lucius asked.

Faustus didn't bother answering that. "Just leave the door bolted. If we're lucky they'll get bored and try to give it to Septimus."

"Well, I think it's a better present than a ring," Lucius said.

"More practical," Gwladus said. Faustus thought she had had a good deal of wine too.

"Loarn should have sent Mother a pig."

"Loarn shouldn't have sent Mother anything at all," Faustus said. But he had, and Caecilius had called the gesture "promising".

"You know, that might be the legate's pig," Paullus said thoughtfully. "His cook was in the vicus yesterday picking one out."

Faustus hoped it was.

In the morning the pig was gone – no one asked where – and Faustus's men all turned out for morning prayers with pounding heads. Lucius should have had a hangover as well, since he had been sick in the latrine and again in the garden the night before, but with the resilience of youth, he was sunnily cheerful at breakfast. Silvia lectured him on the evils of drunkenness and was ignored.

To her further annoyance, over the course of the next months, Lucius exhibited a growth spurt that made him taller than she was. The more she tried to control him, the more rebellious he became. He won a handful of silver throwing dice with the cavalry vet and spent it in the vicus on a military dagger which he wore sheathed at his belt, daring her to forbid it.

"Leave it alone," Faustus said. "It's much better than his old knife if he should need it."

"And why should he need it? Because you endanger him letting him follow your patrols?"

"I never send him on anything that's going to be dangerous," Faustus said. "We don't go far in this weather and he's always with Septimus. If he doesn't have some outlet, he'll do worse. He's not an infant."

SPRING, 845 ab urbe condita, from the founding of the City

The cold loosened its grip, and the land began to green, the verdant magical yellow green of spring on the trees and the road verges, and the pale uncurling new shoots of bracken and fern. Snowdrops and then the yellow stars of celandine pushed their way through the leaf litter in the forests. Eirian, Gwladus, and Silvia washed all the bed linens on the first warm day and hung them to dry like celebratory flags in the garden.

Caecilius marked the completion of the new arena with entertainments and an exhibition battle dedicated to Cath Mawr. His cohorts squared off against each other with wooden swords and the winning side received double pay for a month and bronze phalerae. The First Cohort acquitted itself well until Septimus, unscathed during the exhibition, attempted to imitate the troupe of professional acrobats who followed it and sprained his ankle. The cohort surgeon wrapped it and announced that he would need to stay off it for at least a month.

"You are an idiot," Faustus told him.

"I'll be all right by the time anything comes up," Septimus said optimistically.

Lucius visited him in his barracks quarters with a consolatory jug of Faustus's wine.

"Well, I made a fool of myself, didn't I?" Septimus said, grinning. His immobilized ankle was propped on a stool. "I can get about with a crutch but that's all."

"Naso can take them out, can't he?" Lucius asked. Naso was the century's optio; second in command to Septimus.

"They'll do well enough with him, but it's Typhon's own pain in the backside to me to be stuck like this. Now that the weather's turned, the legate and the primus pilus want us out there like ants on honey cake, just to give the Silures the idea we aren't asleep. Naso can handle the men, but your uncle won't want you following along with us anymore. It was all right in winter, but things are likely to liven up now. I wouldn't feel right about it."

Lucius considered that. Faustus hadn't actually told him he couldn't go anymore. No doubt he would if Lucius asked. "Well anyway I can cheer them along," he told Septimus. "When do they go out again?"

—

It was only a one-day patrol along the coast, and Faustus hadn't said he couldn't, Lucius reasoned. Not yet anyway.

"Are you sure?" Naso looked doubtful. "This is a bit further than you've gone with us before, isn't it?"

"Uncle thinks it will be all right," Lucius said. "It's a fine day and I always ride, so I can turn back if you tell me to." He smiled confidently and swung his horse into line beside the column. If you just did something, he had found, people usually decided that it was all right to do whatever you were already doing.

"Well, we're glad to have you if you have the commander's word. It's a fine day for sure."

The sky was bird's-egg blue, and a breeze carried the scent of growing things on it. They made their way along the banks of the Isca River to the Sabrina coast where the estuary gleamed under the sun. It was fine sailing weather too, and the legate and primus pilus wanted multiple eyes on the channel. The tide was nearly at full, the air washed with a salty, marshy, riverine smell. Sea birds made great clouds overhead. The coastline grew jagged with rocky cliffs outcropping above the water; the track wound sometimes into woods clinging to the coastwise slope and then along bare headlands where the land fell down to the sea.

Lucius dawdled, keeping the column in sight with one eye, but mostly watching the gulls wheeling over the cliffs, and the foam of the incoming tide. The cliff edge was crumbled in places, and he kept a cautious distance from it. He could feel a pricking like some insect on the back of his neck and he slapped at it but when there was nothing there, he shrugged. It was the same feeling of being watched he had had all winter while his mother fretted over him. By now she would have discovered him gone. He would pay for this adventure, he knew, but it would have been worth it. He lagged farther behind, stopping to look at the dark heads of seals near the shore, so like human faces at that distance. His aunt, Eirian, had told him about seals that changed to men and came ashore. What would it be like to slip out of the skin you wore every day and into some other flesh?

Dreaming of seals, he didn't see the ripple in the salt grass behind him, moving out of the cover of trees on the wooded headland, or that the column had wound out of sight. While he watched the seals, hands grasped him from behind by an arm and a leg and dragged him from the saddle. He reached for his dagger, struggling in their grip. They were pulling him toward the cliff, and he fought them furiously. One hit him across the face with a fist. He kicked at them, trying to free himself but they pulled his feet out from under him. He scratched one with his free hand, raking his nails down the scarred and tattooed cheek. He reached for the dagger again, but a hand grasped that wrist too and twisted it. There were two of them and they were stronger than he was. He could see the Sabrina far below, muddy with the tidal surge, as they wrestled him toward the edge.

Finally, they lifted him up and flung him out over the water. He had only a moment to try to twist himself in the empty air, catch at some stunted tree on the nearly vertical slope, break his fall somehow, before he landed with a force that turned his vision black and a hideous pain that he felt only for a moment, face in the foaming tide.

Above him, the horse struggled at the end of its reins while the men tried to drive it over the cliff after him, but it reared, lashed out with its hooves and broke free, going at a gallop down the track.

The men cursed and turned to the cliff edge instead. They kicked out a gap at the track's edge with their boots and then ran. A tumble of loose stone and clods of dirt rained down on the still figure in the water below.

—

The column had not noticed the boy lagging behind and their marching cadence drowned the hoofbeats until the horse was nearly on them, foam-flecked and panic-driven. Naso caught its reins and swore.

"About turn! On the run!"

They went back up the track, looking for the place where the hoof prints had changed to a gallop, and saw the torn-out cliff edge.

"Mithras! Something must have spooked the horse. It's a wonder it didn't go over too. Do you see him?"

Naso and the watch commander peered over the edge, keeping carefully away from where the stone and sand had crumbled away.

"No."

"Tide's turning," someone said. "It will have taken him with it maybe."

"We're going down there!" Naso said. They had to. He inspected the cliff. "There's a track that might be for goats along the way." He pointed to a faint precipitous path. "If we're careful we might get down that."

"Or go back to where the road follows the shore," the watch commander said.

"That will take longer." Naso shucked his lorica and helmet, and his boots. Bare feet would offer him a better grip.

—

Owl had been inspecting the shoreline to see what the tide would bring and if any of it would be something useful when the Roman patrol came by along the road above. She slid back into the shadow of the cliff while they went past. She had just crept out again when a man on horseback followed them, and she saw two more men hunting behind him. She was about to hide again, because the Sun People's business was none of hers — and if they saw her, they would hunt her too — when they caught the rider and hurled him off the cliff. She stared at them while they fought the horse. When it broke free and ran, they ran too.

Owl crept cautiously closer. There was no one left on the cliff now and curiosity got the better of her. When she reached the rider, he was floating face down. She turned him over and saw he wasn't a grown man at all, but a boy, just tall like all the Sun People. There was a bloody gash in his head that bled into the water.

Owl dragged the limp body above the tide line and knelt, inspecting it. He smelled like iron. She found the blade at his belt, took the bronze hilt gingerly between two fingers, and flung it into the water. The water could have the dagger in exchange for him. The sea would want something, and she had no use for iron.

Owl put her head against his chest. She couldn't decide whether he was dead or not. She put him over her lap, pounded his back, and some water came out. She put her face to the back of his neck and breathed in a startling, half familiar scent, there and then gone again into the heavier scent of salt water and sea wrack. She put her fingers in her mouth and whistled a long low note.

Then there were voices on the cliff top and she saw that the Romans had come back. They were staring down at the water. Owl dragged the body farther out of their line of sight into a shallow niche in the cliff wall. The tide was on its way out, but still high enough to wash away her footprints and the furrows his feet had dug in the sand. She whistled again, a different note, repeated impatiently.

One of the Romans began to climb down the cliff. He was cautious, clinging to the stony, nearly vertical slope, feet feeling for purchase. Owl's sisters came along the shore from the other direction, quietly as shadows.

"Help me carry him."

Plover looked at the body distrustfully. "What is it?"

"He's mine. Someone threw him over the cliff. The Romans are trying to find him, I think." She pointed at the man just below the cliff top, clinging precariously to the slope.

"He stinks of iron," Rail said.

"He had an iron knife. I threw it in the water. Help me carry him. We're going to take him to Grandmother."

Rail looked dubious. "She won't let you keep him."

"He's likely dead," Badger said.

"I want him," Owl said.

They peered out from the niche in the cliff face to see the Roman part way down the slope. Another had shucked off his boots and turtle shell of iron plate and begun to follow him down.

"I'm the oldest," Owl said stubbornly when her sisters still looked resistant.

Badger snorted. "We haven't found anything good this tide, and a dead Sun Man is likely not what Grandmother wants." Still, she put her hands under the boy's shoulders.

They took him two at the shoulders and two at the feet and bore him down the sand, through a fissure in the cliff face, and then up the steep path it almost concealed until they came out above the estuary.

—

The home house of Owl and her sisters lay to the north of Porth Cerrig in the shadow of the old barrow of Blaidd Llwyd from which it took its name. The entrance was concealed by forest and by the natural disinclination of the Silures or any other Sun People to go anywhere near it. They brought the boy through the narrow doorway and down the stone stairs it concealed and laid him on the hearth before the Old One. The room was warm and dim and smelled of peat. A bright thin shaft of light came from an opening somewhere above, crossing the boy's pale face and sea-soaked tunic.

Fox, Old One of Blaidd Llwyd, was in middle age, hair just beginning to go gray. She knelt beside the boy, pulled the wet pale hair away to look at the gash in his scalp, touched it lightly, then put two fingers to his throat and then to his wrist. She pressed her ear to his chest and listened.

"Alive. But barely." She looked consideringly at Owl. "Why have you brought a Sun Man's boy here?"

"Other Sun Men tried to kill him. Then Romans came looking for him. I think they wanted to kill him too."

"We should have let them," Badger said.

Owl ignored her.

"Maybe he's theirs," Rail said.

"I found him," Owl said stubbornly. "He's mine."

"He is not an orphaned hedgehog," the Old One told her. Owl had brought one of those home last summer. It had stayed to live in the woods by the old barrow. Fox looked at the boy for a long time. She put her face to his throat and breathed deeply. "Is that all?" she asked Owl when she sat up again.

Owl looked uncertain. "I thought... I thought he was ours."

"Yes," Fox said. "Very long ago, but yes. Take him and put him to bed and I will see if I can make him live."

"Ours?" Badger was scornful. "A great Sun Man's boy who is bigger than you are?"

"When you have learned to look closely at things, Badger, and can tell a rock from a turnip, you may question me," Fox said, and Badger closed her mouth.

"I will save him if I can," the Old One told Owl. "Then we will decide what to do with him."

—

The tide was well on its way out when Naso slithered and stumbled to the bottom of the cliff. The wet sand lay stark and empty before him, and he looked despairingly in every direction.

His watch commander came down behind him, half falling the last few feet.

"The tide..." the watch commander said.

"Yes." Naso looked for something, anything, floating on the retreating waves. He waded out and splashed up and down the shore, searching the water. Something caught his eye but it was only a piece of broken crate with shreds of cloth caught on it.

"Best we go back," the watch commander said.

It would take another hour to make their way up the shore to where they could climb to the road again. They wouldn't get back up the way they had come down. Naso shouted up at the column on the cliff to meet them and to wait for him. It had to be he that told the commander, he thought dismally.

—

Faustus saw the patrol coming through the fort gate leading Lucius's riderless horse and his blood went cold. When they had not found him that morning, a conversation with Septimus had convinced him that Lucius, probably through outright lying, had convinced Naso to take him along. Faustus had been angry but not overly worried. Lucius would regret it when he got home, but there was no sign of action yet from the Silures, and Loarn was still courting Silvia which argued that he would not start a war until he had her in Porth Cerrig. Silvia had been even angrier than Faustus, pacing furiously from house to the First Cohort barracks and back, waiting for them to come home.

Now, the moment that Faustus saw Naso's grim, frightened face, he knew. He walked to meet him.

"What happened?" He took the horse's reins from the century watch commander.

"We don't know exactly," Naso said miserably. "He lagged behind the column—"

"Which he should not have been with."

"He said he had your permission... Oh, Mithras, he didn't, did he?"

"No."

"We didn't see him getting behind and then the horse came after us without him. Something had spooked it and we turned back." Naso closed his eyes for a moment. "We backtracked. We saw a piece out of the cliff edge – we were along that bit where the road runs along the headland – where it looked as if the horse lost his footing. He must have thrown him. But we couldn't find him."

"Did he go over the cliff?" Faustus asked, his stomach churning.

"He must have but we couldn't see him," Naso said desperately. "I climbed down there, sir. Two of us did, but he was gone." He swallowed. "The tide was going out."

"Lucius!"

Faustus turned to see Silvia running toward them.

"Where is Lucius?"

Faustus caught her and took her in his arms. Paullus was behind her, and he handed him the horse's reins. "Come in the house." He looked back at Naso.

Naso met his eyes, face grim, waiting for whatever was going to happen to him.

"Take the century back and report to Septimus." He wanted to blame Naso, but Naso was no more responsible than any of them, than himself, and Silvia, even Septimus who should have realized what the boy was up to.

"Where is *Lucius*?" Silvia cried.

Faustus walked her to the house, murmuring softly, telling the horrible story in soft words, hugging her to him while he did.

Eirian met them at the door, her face white. He told it all over again while Silvia sobbed.

"We'll go out there," he told her. "We'll find him if we can." At least he could try to give her a body to bury.

Silvia pulled away from him. "You did this! Where is my son? You let him go out with your men! *You!*"

"He went without my permission this time. And do you think I don't blame myself? I should have known how restless he was and made sure my men knew not to listen to him."

"Restless?" Silvia flung the word at him. "You made him restless, with all your talk of the army!"

"*You* made him restless by trying to cage him!"

"Faustus, no." Eirian pulled at his arm.

"You took my boy from me, Faustus! I will hate you forever!"

Gwladus put her arm around Silvia. "Come, lady, and I will make you a warm drink."

"I don't want a drink!" Silvia sobbed. "I want my boy!" But she let Gwladus lead her away.

Eirian sank into a chair and put her face in her hands.

Faustus stood grim-faced, staring at the door that he would never see Lucius come through again. Guilt and anger and misery washed over him. They were all at fault. Everyone was at fault: Naso, Silvia, Manlius and his debts, but most at fault was himself, paterfamilias, the one who should have protected Lucius. The one who should have listened to his father's shade when he said to get the boy out of Britain, where even the landscape was a danger. *If* that was what had happened.

"That horse is as surefooted as a mule," he whispered to Eirian. "And Lucius knows not to go near the cliff edge, he knows the ground there is unstable. I should have thought of this when Loarn sent an ambush after me. They were trying to pick off officers, it was just their bad luck they got Blaesus instead of me."

Eirian looked up at him. "If you say that to Silvia, you will drive her to him, to prove you wrong," she said quietly. "But do your best to find him, to give her some comfort. Sometimes the sea gives them back."

—

The sea returned nothing but the knife. They found it half buried in the sand at low tide, proof that what they feared had been true. But of his body, nothing, not a scrap of cloth nor a sandal strap. Eirian stood on the shore and listened to the seals crying far out in the channel. They only said, *He is not with us.* In the face of Silvia's anguish Eirian wondered again how her own mother could have left her. No one had ever spoken of her to Eirian, only to each other, gossiping with the aunts who inspected her hands for suspicious signs of webbing and advised her father to keep her from the water. If she had a child herself, did she risk this pain? The seals had no answer to that either.

—

The legate ordered prayers for Lucius's shade, to Jupiter and Juno, Persephone and Hades, and to Mithras god of soldiers. "He would have been one of us," Caecilius said quietly to Faustus. "May the gods give him his command in the afterlife."

Silvia was silent and ashen faced, moving as mechanically as a child's clay puppet. Faustus ordered a memorial stone, and she approved it without really looking at it.

>Dis Manibus
>Lucius Manlius
>Beloved Son
>Aged thirteen years
>Silvia his mother set this up

A portrait of Lucius rested above the inscription.

Faustus had it installed beside his father's monument among the tombstones along the Venta road. Silvius Valerianus's ashes had been buried in Narbo Martius, but Faustus had once hoped that a suitable gravestone in Britain would make him lie quietly there as well. It hadn't. He half expected the old man to appear now, berating him, but all he heard was the unexpected sound of weeping hanging in the air.

—

Owl sat beside the boy's bed. The Old One had done what she could for the blow to his head and Owl could see him breathing faintly now that everything was still. They had undressed him and put him into a clean shirt belonging to Thorn, who was taller than most. Even so it was barely large enough for him. They did not disturb the charms around his neck, a gold locket and a winged silver phallus, thinking them lucky things that might help him live.

"Gold would buy meat in the Sun People's market," Thorn muttered.

"And luck turns when it is stolen," Fox said.

"He's mine," Owl said stubbornly. "You leave him alone."

Now that he was clean, she bent and breathed in his scent again. *You are ours*, she thought. *But long ago.* He stirred and she put her brown hand on his pale one. He had big hands like all the Sun People. Whatever old blood was in him was so far away it was no more than an echo.

"They won't let me keep you," she said sadly. Now he was not much taller than Thorn, but he would grow, in the way of all adolescents, shooting up like a tree in sun. What she wanted with him, she didn't know, but the fact that she had found him and saved him bound him to her. At least for now he was hers.

—

He opened his eyes slowly. The room was dim and peat-smelling. His head hurt. Even the dim light was too much at first and he shut them again. Slept again. Woke again. There was a child sitting beside him. She spoke to him, some language unintelligible, like birdsong. It was a pleasant sound. His head still hurt. He closed his eyes. When he opened them, the child was still there, although he saw now that she was not really a child, but a young woman, dark-skinned and blue-eyed. She fed him broth from a bowl.

"What are you?" he asked her, and she spoke again, the same musical bird notes. He shook his head.

She went away and he closed his eyes and when he opened them there were seven of them standing around the bed. They were small, no taller than nine-year-olds, with tribal marks like vines circling their arms and faces. A woman with blue beads knotted into her graying hair bent over him and touched his forehead. "Who are you?" she asked him.

This one spoke the Silures' language, which he understood somewhat. He thought about it. "I don't know." That seemed wrong. Surely he knew who he was. He thought some more. "Where am I?" he asked her.

"This is the sidhe of Blaidd Llwyd," she said. "I am the Old One of Blaidd Llwyd. My name is Fox. What is yours?"

He thought. That should have come easily. He knew his name, surely. There was only a gray, misty space where his name should have been. "What is the sidhe of Blaidd Llwyd?" he asked.

"It is our house. Are you Roman? Our daughter says she thinks you spoke to her in their tongue."

He tried the language that came easiest to him. Latin. Yes, he could speak Latin. He said so. His head began to throb, and he winced.

"You fell from a cliff," Fox said. "Do you remember that?"

Did he? A moment of falling, terror, something else – anger, maybe.

"Do you remember the horse?"

He shook his head. Had there been a horse? He thought there had.

"Sleep then. Sleep and likely it will come."

A babble of voices surrounded her in the bird note language he couldn't understand. She said something sharp, and they quieted. He closed his eyes again.

—

Badger glared at Owl when Fox had driven them all from the chamber. "What if he's a Roman? A Roman is worse even than the Silures."

"A lot of the Sun People speak the Romans' language," Owl said. "And so do some of ours."

"He is not one of ours!"

"A long time ago," Owl said. "The Old One said so."

Badger sniffed. "That one of his kind raped a woman of our kind does not make him ours."

"The amulets around his neck look Roman," Thorn said. "I have seen things like the silver one on dead ones. I will have to throw away that shirt."

"Owl is too fine for sidhe-men," Plover said primly. "She wants a man from the Sun People to keep for a pet."

"Shut your mouth." Owl balled her hands into fists.

"I think he's a Roman," Rail said.

"Someone was trying to kill him," Owl said. "They threw him off the cliff."

"Stop and think why that might be," Thorn said. "And whether they will come looking for him here."

"He's mine," Owl said. "They gave him away and I found him."

He opened his eyes carefully. The things he had forgotten were always just out of reach when he snatched at them. Maybe memory would come if he left it alone. He could feel it on the edge of his mind. When it didn't, he concentrated instead on looking about him at the chamber where they had taken him. The walls were stone and a faint draft told him that there was an air vent somewhere above them. It was chilly but not cold. He lay comfortably under a woolen blanket, and there was a wolfskin on the packed earth floor. The light in the room came from rushlights set into niches in the walls, only a few of them so the air had a twilight quality.

He got up shakily to use the pot they had brought for him and looked wistfully at the empty bowl by the bed. When he lay back down on it, the herbs in the thin mattress gave off a cloud of scent.

Fox, the Old One, came into the chamber and held out the clothes he had worn. "We have washed these for you, and done what we could with the boots. The sea water has spoiled them somewhat."

He sat up and stripped off what he was wearing. Thorn's shirt was tight in the shoulders and pinched him when he slept. He put his own tunic on gratefully. "You are kind." The British came more easily to his tongue now. Someone had told him to learn it. He tried to remember who, and the pain flared up. He winced.

"Let me see your head."

He bent his neck while she inspected his scalp. Her hands were light fingered, gentle, probing carefully. She smelled of peat smoke and the salve she rubbed into his hair.

"Do not think on it," she said quietly. "Rest and it will come. Rest. You are safe here with us."

Who was he safe from? He tried to remember that too and nothing came but a flashing memory of hands on his wrists and ankles. He thought someone had pulled him off a horse. "Are they looking for me?" he asked, suddenly frightened.

"We don't know," Fox said. "If they are, they will not find you here."

XI. BELTANE

Faces young and old looked out from gravestones lining the Venta road beyond the fort, cast in sharp relief by the morning sun; babies and young wives, centurions in crested helmets, cavalrymen on horseback. Silvia looked from one to the next as if they would tell her something. Her father's stone had no portrait, only an inscription much like Lucius's. His actual grave was in Gaul, and she supposed that by setting up a stone for him here Faustus had tried to do the filial thing at last. She also supposed it didn't matter anymore. Father and brother were as lost to her as Lucius, as lost as her old life.

Silvia unstoppered the little jug and poured the wine over Lucius's stone, letting the stain tell anyone who passed that someone had mourned him. Faustus had made an offering too. Silvia would have scrubbed that one off if she could.

She pulled the black mantle around her again, mourning clothing folded away since a year after Manlius had died, and returning took the path that ran around the north side of the fort past cropland that had been the Silures' corn fields and which now grew grain for the army, evading any place she thought she might meet Faustus. In the vicus she sold the Saturnalia ear drops for a ring that would fit a man's hand, gold with an onyx stone.

"Who goes often to Porth Cerrig?" she asked the jeweler. "Who could take a message?"

"It's time for the tinkers and such to be on the road," he said. "Look for a man with a birthmark on his chin and a piebald horse. Fychan. He'll likely be at the Capricorn if he's still in Isca."

Silvia bit her lip. The tavern was a favorite of the legion, which bore Capricorn as its badge. Still, early in the morning it would probably be empty of her brother's men.

She found the piebald horse tethered in the inn yard with a man adjusting the contents of the cart that stood beside it.

"Is this Fychan's wagon?" she asked him.

"It is." The man turned around. He was short, with a crop of dusty brown hair and a wine stain birthmark across the left side of his chin. "If you've pots to mend, I'm off on the road just now. You can leave them with me, and I'll bring them back mended if you want."

"No pots to mend," Silvia said. "I want you to take a message to Porth Cerrig if that's where you're bound."

"It is," he said again. She looked well-dressed enough to have come from the fort, with a gown and overgown, draped and pinned at the sleeves in Roman fashion. Officer's wife, he thought, although her command of British was good. Having a fling with a local? "What sort of a message?"

"This." Silvia held out a small leather bag with the ring inside. "You are to take it to Loarn at Porth Cerrig and tell him that it is my answer to his last message."

Fychan balked. "To the king?"

"Yes." Silvia laid a silver denarius on her outstretched palm, beside the bag.

"What's in the bag?"

"That is not your business, although you will look anyway. I do not owe you explanations. Do you want the silver or no?"

"How do you know I will not keep the silver, and what is in the bag, for myself?"

"I will know," she told him. "And Loarn will know, in time. It won't be pleasant for you. A king has a long arm."

Fychan scratched his mustache, thinking. He smoothed the ends. A king had as much right to an illicit fling as anyone, he supposed. She was good looking enough. Unless she was spying for him. That made Fychan uneasy. But silver was silver. And it was the woman who was most like to come to a bad ending for that.

"Very well." He held out his hand.

—

Loarn's answer came with April, not by the tinker but by a hound of Loarn's household who passed the message for Silvia to the sentry at the fort gates again. Fychan had written it out for Loarn, too afraid to go back to the fort with it himself and too afraid of the king to play him false, despite the fact that Llew had got Fychan drunk and tried to bribe him.

Silvia went to the legate before she went to Faustus.

"You are willing to do this?" Caecilius asked her. He thought of Faustus's protests. "Likely it can't be undone." Particularly given her mother's bloodline, a bit of information that Centurion Valerianus should have known he couldn't keep quiet permanently.

"I would not wish it undone," Silvia said. "There is nothing left for me in my brother's house. I will have my own life whether he wishes it or no."

"Women have braided warring nations together before now," Caecilius said. "You will serve Rome if you make this marriage." In Loarn's household she might or might not have as much of her own life as she thought, royal woman or no. He didn't say that.

"Then you will order my brother to let me go?"

Caecilius gave her an avuncular smile. "I cannot trample on the rights of the paterfamilias. But I can certainly convey that it is in his best interests to release you."

"I don't care what you do to him," Silvia said. "I will hate him for the rest of my life."

Caecilius winced. "Best you don't live with him then."

"Britain has cost me everything." Silvia's voice was icy. She sorted her possessions with her back to Faustus. "I cannot go back to Narbo Martius. I cannot stay here where my boy was lost to me."

Faustus listened miserably. Eirian had said it would make matters worse to argue and no doubt she was right. "But you hate Britain," he said anyway because matters were as bad as they could get.

"Perhaps I hate you more," Silvia said. "At least Loarn wants me, cares for me."

"Lucius's horse was surefooted," Faustus said grimly. He would suggest now what he had suspected, since she had made up her mind. "And your new husband has reason to want Lucius out of his way. Have you not once thought of that?"

Silvia spun around. She picked up her jewelry box as if she would heave it at his head. "You have no right! You have no right to blame Loarn for what you have done!"

"What I did was take my eye off him. What someone else may have done was throw him off that cliff. Who would want him gone, Silvia? Who would wish the son of a royal woman to be dead and out of competition with the king's own sons?"

"That is vile, Faustus! I will never believe it."

"Maybe not Loarn. Although I suspect he set an ambush on my patrol for the same reason. But his sister is a royal woman too, with a son of her own. And Loarn's council – they knew that Caecilius was bound to find out about our mother's rank, and has, because that began to spread as soon as he announced his intentions toward you. And then Caecilius would have seen Lucius, or even me, as a possible puppet king, someone he could install by force in Loarn's place."

"Caecilius would not do that."

Faustus snorted. "Caecilius would do what serves Rome, with either of us."

All the same, he made one more effort to change the legate's mind. Loarn would come for Silvia in the morning. Faustus went to the legate after evening prayers while the signifers were putting the standards away in their sanctuary.

Caecilius was not to be moved. "Men have often been known to put up their swords for a woman."

"Who was that, sir?"

"Kings in history," Caecilius said. He didn't elaborate.

Faustus's face said plainly that he couldn't think of any.

"And the smuggling has stopped."

"Off Demetae or Silure shores, yes, sir," Faustus said. "But the border wolves say that Loarn sent an envoy to Cadal of the Ordovices last fall."

"That would have been before your sister agreed to wed him. And what did they say Cadal's answer was?"

"They don't know."

"Precisely." Caecilius had heard the report of course. "We see no signs of Cadal readying for a war."

"No, sir. And no talk of what answer he gave Loarn or what Loarn asked of him. Would there not be talk if he had refused? They are old enemies. He would make his refusal known."

Caecilius sighed. "Centurion Valerianus, I understand your position regarding your sister. But she is capable of halting a rebellion against Rome, and that must supersede your own authority over her. Do I make myself clear?"

"Yes, sir."

"That is excellent. I will be proven right about this, you know. She will be a queen, and Loarn will give her more children, and both will ease her grief. Be joyful for her, Centurion. And for your late mother, for that matter, that her child is coming home."

Faustus said, "Yes, sir," again, saluted again, and that was that. Caecilius had always found his Silure blood a bit suspect. Faustus doubted that Caecilius cared in the least what their mother might have thought of it all. He was sitting on top of a rickety political position, with no governor to take the blame when things collapsed in revolt. If West Britain went up in flames, Caecilius's career would end with a command somewhere in Lower Tartarus. He would offer up Silvia or anything else to stop that.

Tribune Marcellinus was loitering – suspiciously, Faustus thought – in the corridor outside Caecilius's office. "I want you to know I tried," he murmured as Faustus passed him.

Faustus turned back.

"I'll walk with you," Marcellinus said, starting him toward the door again. "I think he's wrong, for what it's worth. I couldn't convince him, and I haven't the clout to go over his head to anyone as far away as Rome. The procurator here hasn't the will to go against him."

"I appreciate that you tried," Faustus told him.

"Well, I like your sister, apart from anything else, and I think she's making a disastrous mistake out of grief." He paused. "Fluency in British is useful, but it may not have been the best idea on someone's part to post you here."

"I suppose it seemed like a good idea at the time. Nobody knew anything about my mother's family. I doubt even my father did. Just that she was Silure."

"My housekeeper informs me that the Silures are all peculiar," Marcellinus said. "Based on testimony from the fishmonger in the vicus. *She* says that the royal women all have the Sight. I have to doubt that, given your sister's decision."

"If *I* had it, I would have arranged to be violently ill on the night of that cursed banquet."

Marcellinus clapped a hand on his shoulder. "I may write a book on the events that a good dose of scilla beforehand could have prevented."

Dinner on the last evening was strained, everyone tight-lipped with anxiety or anger. Silvia and Faustus did not speak to each other. Eirian served as intermediary between them – "Ask my brother for the bread" – until she tired of it and left the table.

Gwladus had decided, after a fierce argument with Paullus, to go with her mistress.

"You're just half in love with him yourself!" Paullus snapped at her in the kitchen. "You've been nattering about him for months – the king is so beautiful and strong, the king is just like a man out of legend. Oooh, the king."

Gwladus sniffed. "I'm a free woman that can make up my own mind, nor will I leave my mistress."

"Oh, throw that at me then!"

"You could buy yourself free any time you wanted to, the centurions said so. Talk to me when you're willing to do that and risk being on your own."

"Why should I? I'm not going to stick my head in that nest of adders."

"And no one asked you." She glanced at the skillet. "You're burning the fish."

—

A gawking crowd followed the king's procession as it neared the vicus. Loarn's chariot was pulled by a pair of sleek sorrel ponies, silver hub caps on its blue wheels, its side panels painted with a horned moon and golden sheaves of barley. Following behind Loarn rode a retinue of his captains, each in their own chariot, their drivers as finely bedecked as they in bright shirts and trousers, and gold at neck and wrist. The chariots were bright-painted red and blue and gleamed with silver and enamel mounts, the ponies with red ribbons braided in their manes.

They drew rein before the fortress gates, which swung open as they approached to reveal the legate with Silvia on his arm. She had taken off the dark mourning clothes and wore a rose-colored gown pinned at the sleeves with pearls and the enameled brooch and agate ring that Loarn had sent. Loarn leapt from his chariot and even Faustus, hanging reluctantly behind the legate, saw the king's face light up at the sight of his sister. Eirian, beside him, sighed quietly and whispered, "He does care for her. Mother of us all, that is worse."

Loarn bowed his head to Silvia and took both her hands in his. Caecilius beamed at them approvingly.

"Your marriage is a seal set upon the treaty of Aedden ap Culwych, king that was," Caecilius said. "May peace reign always between Rome and the Silure people, Loarn king."

Faustus noted that Loarn didn't answer that, but said, "I will honor always the woman you give into my care."

Silvia's face was pale, but her eyes shone. Loarn flicked a glance at Faustus; her brother's eyes were shadowed by his helmet.

Paullus loaded Silvia's trunks into a chariot less impressive than the others and inhabited only by the boy driving it, a hound of the king's household looking proud to be given the task of ferrying the new queen's belongings. Paullus reluctantly boosted Gwladus up beside the boy.

"She will send you back if you ask her to," he said quietly. "Remember that."

"I shan't ask."

"You may need to. She may need you to. Just remember."

Gwladus ignored him. She settled herself on a trunk.

Loarn led Silvia to his chariot. She saw his captains waiting, watching her as he brought her toward them. Their faces were impossible to read, expressionless as statues. Each bowed a dark head as she passed. The woman, Llamrei, was among them.

Loarn stepped up into his chariot and turned to help Silvia up beside him. A path opened for them through the crowd that had clogged the road to see the king and his bride. Men lifted children on their shoulders to see them go by and women called soft good wishes in their own languages, daughters of the Mother in all her guises. Loarn's driver shook out the reins and Loarn put his arm around her waist to steady her as the red ponies broke into a fast trot. The chariots were wood and wicker, lithe as snakes, and the floorboard swayed under her feet. She braced them against the jolting of the wheels.

Loarn's arm was steady around her. Silvia leaned her head against his shoulder, feeling the soft curtain of his hair brush her forehead. She didn't look back, but Faustus's face rode with her, with the face of her lost boy beside it. Faustus, she thought, would have preferred that the gods had transformed her into a laurel tree like Daphne rather than go with Loarn. She blinked both faces away, then looked ahead, toward Porth Cerrig. Loarn wore the ring she had sent and his closeness made her yearn for him with a force she had never felt for Manlius. She would be Loarn's, and Loarn's world would be hers — a change even more stark than her voyage to Britain had been. She would give herself to it because there was nothing in her old life left to her.

It was two days' ride to Porth Cerrig and they stopped at an inn near the Romans' auxiliary fort at Pen-y-lan. Loarn took her hand, kissed it, and then she found herself sharing a room, and its only bed, with Llamrei.

"He won't take you to his bed until you're wed to him," Llamrei said, pulling her boots off. "It's not like a roll in the meadow, not for a king and a wife taken before Druids."

Silvia sat down on the bed and let Gwladus unpin her gown and pull it over her head. She was glad for her presence but after Gwladus saw her mistress tucked into bed she went to sleep in the kitchen where the tavern wife had offered beer and a spot by the hearth in exchange for a gossip about it all.

Llamrei shucked her trousers off, put her gold torque and arm bands into her boots and blew the oil lamp out. She lay down on the other side of the bed, wrapped in her cloak. Silvia moved toward the wall to make room.

"It isn't too late," Llamrei said.

"Too late?"

"To change your mind. To tell Loarn to send you back to your brother at the fort."

Silvia sat up. A thin line of moonlight came through the shutters, casting black and silver bars across the other woman's face, across the blue lines on her cheekbones.

"Are you hoping I will change my mind?" she asked Llamrei.

"Yes," Llamrei said bluntly. "None of us wish to see him wed you. But he wants you, and therefore we obey."

"And why do you not wish him to marry me?"

Llamrei made an exasperated sound between her tongue and teeth. "Because it will bring trouble. To him. To you. To all of us." She rolled herself more tightly in her cloak and turned on her side, her back to Silvia.

Silvia lay back down, her face to the wall. She breathed in and out slowly, willing herself to sleep.

"We will do you no harm while you are among us," Llamrei said. "Nor give you reason to fear us. It is only that a king is not an ordinary man, not once he becomes king. Everything he does can sway the world. We are more afraid of you than anything else."

The next day they came to Porth Cerrig. The air was bright, and clouds of gulls swooped over the mud flats below the cliff. Silvia's legs ached with the jolting of the chariot floor. Loarn had made her a seat to rest on but that drilled the ruts in the track up and down her spine, and standing was easier. She could have asked for a wagon, but would not. She would not arrive like some pig bound for market. She was to be a queen. She would come to her new home like one.

Loarn's sister Iorwen met them just inside the landward gate. With her was an old priest with white hair and gown, a heavy gold sun disk about his neck. Loarn helped Silvia down from the chariot and steadied her on her feet. He bent his head to the old man and said, "Teyrnon Chief Druid, I bring home my bride."

"It is a ten-day wait until Beltane," the old man said. "She will bide with the Goddess on earth until then."

There had been no time to question that, no time to cling to Loarn. Iorwen had taken her arm, and with Gwladus hurrying after them, had led her to a chamber in the queen's quarters of Porth Cerrig, where there had been no queen in anyone's memory.

"You will bide here until morning," Iorwen had told her.

Now she sat in the queen's chamber alone except for Gwladus. What would come in the morning she didn't know. The chamber was luxurious by tribal standards, and even by the standards of the frontier fortresses where Faustus had served earlier. The bed had a wooden frame with carved and polished legs that ended in a beast's four-toed feet. It was piled with soft woolen blankets and furs, and a bronze oil lamp sat on an inlaid table beside it. There was a smaller bed for Gwladus, cushioned chairs against the woven wicker walls, and a small brazier to supplement the heat that rose through a central column from the ground floor hearth to sift through the roof thatch above them.

She yearned for Loarn with a ferocity that startled her but without him there, misery over Lucius clouded her head again. She had felt brave and in charge of her own fate when she made the decision to go with Loarn. Now she sat and waited to see what his people would do with her.

A slave brought her food and drink, a pot, and a bowl to wash in. Outside it was still light, the beginning of Britain's long summer twilight, but the interior of the hold was lit only by lamps and rushlights and the glow of the hearth. When Gwladus began to snore, Silvia was tired enough to sink into the furs and sleep. In the morning, Iorwen came back.

"Where is Loarn?"

"Loarn may not come to you. Teyrnon will come – or I will – to teach you what you need to know. Your woman may help in the kitchen when you do not need her."

"What is it I need to know that I do not already?" Silvia asked rebelliously.

"A great deal," Iorwen said.

Silvia looked at her suspiciously. "You don't want me here either," she said.

Iorwen made a noise somewhere between a sigh and a growl. "Llamrei is not known for tact. It is not that I do not want you, or that any of us do not, it is that we fear what will happen if my brother the king finds he has made a mistake."

"What if *I* have made a mistake?" Silvia snapped.

"That will make no difference now," Iorwen said.

Silvia was silent. She had not made a mistake, she told herself. She was certain of it.

"You may leave," Iorwen told Gwladus. "Do not go outside the walls."

"You have only to call for me," Gwladus said pointedly to Silvia.

"She is loyal," Iorwen said. "That is good. But you have lessons to learn and the more you speak with me the better. Your speech has the accent of your Dobunni maid, and that is not fitting for my brother's queen."

Silvia studied Iorwen. They were of an age, she thought, although the Silures had a way of looking young past their fifties. She had a fall of dark hair like her brother's and a gold fillet around her forehead. She did not look like a woman possessed by the Goddess so much as by a kind of authoritative exasperation.

"Your mother, Guennola, came from our line," Iorwen said abruptly. "That was never a secret that could be kept, when my brother decided he wanted you."

"Faustus told me," Silvia said. "He said the little dark people told him."

"They seem to have made a pet of your brother," Iorwen said. "They may regret that. Still, they know as much about our family as we do and have intermarried with us more than they like to admit. It was not always a case of rape. My grandmother was a sidhe women. Yours too, farther back."

"And Loarn?"

"Somewhere perhaps. The Druids know. But the king and I are only half siblings and my sidhe blood is on my father's side."

"Is this what I am to learn about? My mother's family?"

"Partly. Teyrnon will teach you that."

"What are you to teach me?" Silvia resented this stiff-necked woman's intention to teach her anything.

"To be Silure. To know the land. To recognize our gods." Iorwen's mouth twitched. "To doctor cattle, which is a thing even a queen must know."

Silvia looked suspicious.

"A man's wealth is his cattle," Iorwen told her. "I have had my arm up a cow's ass to make a calf come, and poured a draught down the other end too. Can you ride?"

"On a cow?"

"On a horse. Or drive a team?"

"Among my people, women do neither," Silvia said stiffly.

"You will learn, since they are not your people anymore."

"Now?" Silvia asked. Anything would be better than fidgeting in this room while even Gwladus had more freedom. And she might see Loarn.

"No," Iorwen said. "Now you will come with me to the bride's house and bide there until you are wed. I will come to you there, and Teyrnon. And your woman may come, but that is all. When you are wed you will return here with Loarn. Come."

Iorwen led her down the stairs again and out into the courtyard. The great court of Porth Cerrig held a whole village, houses as well as cow byres, dairy, pony shed, smithy, granary, shearing and weaving sheds. Water for the washhouse flowed from a small brook that bubbled past the walls and away to the sea, and several wells also fed the population. Most of them seemed to be milling about the courtyard now on one pretext or another. Silvia could feel interested eyes on her from every direction, but she didn't see Loarn.

"He has gone hunting," Iorwen said when she saw her looking for him.

The house Iorwen led her to was round, stone walled and thatched with a conical roof that came down to the top of the doorway. The inner walls were plastered white and painted with a pattern of red waves. Like the great hall, the only light came from the door. There were signs of hasty rearrangement, and it now contained a bed, another cushioned chair, a table, a stool, and a chest for her clothing. A fire was lit in the hearth against the morning chill. "Teyrnon will come when you have eaten," Iorwen said. A tray with bread and cheese and a jug of some drink sat on the table.

Silvia remembered the white-bearded old man with the sun disk. "He frightens me," she said.

"He frightens everyone," Iorwen said. "Do as you're told, and you'll come to no harm from him."

Iorwen left her there, and at mid-morning Teyrnon came. He carried a wicker chest under his arm and a staff with a gold wheel at the top. He leaned the staff against the inner wall and inspected Silvia when she rose to meet him. "You have a look of your mother," he said, not unkindly.

"Did you know her?" It was hard to tell how old he was. Ancient, by the white hair and beard.

"Somewhat. I was a young man then and in training when the Romans came."

"Why must I stay here?" she asked him. That he had once been young made him a little less frightening.

"You must stay here so that the gods may come to know you," he told her. "And so that you may be made clean of your father's people." He knelt to open the wicker chest. "And so the king may be certain of his mind," he muttered.

He seemed disinclined to curse her or cast a spell on her with his staff, as she had heard the Druids could do, so she said brazenly, "Do you also think that the king is making a mistake?"

"It does not matter what I think. We read the signs in the stars and in the earth's waters, and we see what may come. What a man does with that rests with him."

"What do the signs tell you?"

Teyrnon gave an irritated sigh and she thought she had gone too far. "What was stolen is returned to us again. And there is a price for that as there is a price for all things." He drew the chair into the rectangle of bright light from the doorway. "Sit there and pull your gown down to your waist."

"What?"

He brought up the stool and sat on it, a thin needle in one hand and a pot of blue paste in the other. "You are a royal woman. Had you not been born among Romans you would have been marked as such in your twelfth summer. I will do it now so that the king may wed you."

"The king said nothing to me about this." Silvia felt a flurry of panic. She saw Gwladus hovering outside the doorway.

"The king forgets how little you know," Teyrnon said. "He bears marks of his own. The marks of his household, the spear mark of a king's captain. The king mark that I put on his forehead only last winter."

Silvia hesitated, her fingers on the pins of her gown. Everyone outside could see her. That was probably the point, so that everyone would know it had been done. She remembered her mother and the faded mark like a five-petaled flower between her breasts. This was how it had been made. She sat and gritted her teeth.

The needle hurt, like tiny wasps, over and over again, tracing the same pattern her mother had borne. Halfway through, Teyrnon inspected the jug that had been brought with her breakfast. "Finish this," he told her.

Silvia looked rebellious. "I don't like beer."

He chuckled, surprising her. He told Gwladus, "Stop hovering like a hawkfly, and get your mistress a cup of mead from the storeroom."

He set the needle aside until Gwladus came back. *I can never go back to Narbo Martius now*, Silvia thought while the half-finished pattern on her breastbone throbbed. She nearly laughed at the absurdity of that impediment among so many greater ones, and when Gwladus brought the mead, she emptied the cup.

Teyrnon began to sing softly, startling her again. She followed only half the words, something about a magic child and the sea.

When he stopped, she said, "That is beautiful," because it was.

"I was a harper when I was young," he said. "It is the first level of our training, to learn the songs. Those who love music more deeply than anything else remain there. Those of us with a wish to see deeper into the worlds leave it behind except for pleasure." He sat back on his heels. "There. I am done. Take this salve and rub it into the skin twice a day starting tonight." He gave her another pot from his basket, stoppered with a piece of wax. "Tomorrow I will come back, and you will learn about your true people and how we came over-water to claim our land here. You will be Silure when you wed the king, since that is what he is determined on."

Silvia's head swam from the pain of the needle and from the mead. When he had gone Gwladus drew the door closed so that only a dim light filtered between the eaves and the walls. "No need for them gawping at you more," she said briskly. "And he's a fool if he thinks he can wipe all that away like mopping up milk. I went with my man to follow his legion, but I am Dobunni, and Rome didn't wash that off me. Druids have their heads in the clouds with the birds."

—

Llamrei, come from spear practice with the young hounds who would be made men in the summer, sat on the edge of the kitchen well to let the sea breeze cool her. She watched Teyrnon march across the courtyard from the bride's house, not occupied since Bendigeid's father had brought a wife home from the sidhe of Ty Isaf. Lately it had been a storehouse for the odd detritus that any household, even a king's, accumulated – broken chairs good enough to mend, a child's chariot that had once been Aedden's, dented pots awaiting the tinker's next visit, although Fychan might not be back any time soon. Llamrei thought that he had been more than uneasy over his part in the courtship of the king.

She took a deep breath of spring air, feeling the world as it turned from winter to summer stopped here on the balmy midpoint. The sky above her was full of birds returning to their summer nesting places. She heard the bubbling call of a cuckoo hen and thought again of the half-Roman woman and what they were going to do about her. Loarn had come in from his hunt as she was finishing with the boys, Llew beside him. "You should be grateful to me," she had heard Llew say to Loarn as they rode past.

"I am not," Loarn had said, but he hadn't asked why. Llew would go to his grave angry that he had lived and Owen had not. Spear brothers' bond was often greater than lovers'. Llamrei knew she should find a way to make Llew be still and cease the veiled talk of something everyone knew but Loarn's bride.

Rhodri sat down beside her then with a napkinful of honey cake charmed from the kitchen. The spring air whispered in her ear again, green with yearning. She and Rhodri were both: spear companions always, lovers when the mood took them.

He grinned at her and gave her a piece of honey cake. "The air tells me that I am not so old as I felt yesterday," he said. "Or may feel tomorrow. What does it tell you?"

"That I ought to make Llew hold his tongue, but that I would rather go to the woods with you," she told him, grinning back. The day was seductive, urging abandonment of *should* for *could*. Her hounds had been erratic as young goats and set her to laughing so hard at them that she hadn't the heart to punish anyone. They would carry their spears with the men soon enough.

Rhodri said, "I will go with you to speak to Llew, because you are right about that. And we will go to the woods first to steel ourselves for the task."

Llamrei bit into the cake. In a few more days it would be Beltane and the king would wed the half-Roman woman, and they had best silence Llew before that. But in the meantime, it was spring and there were few pleasures as sweet as this one. It had taken her a long while to grow into this easy way with Rhodri and she treasured it, particularly now with war coming. She stood, scattering crumbs from her lap, and took his hand.

—

Beltane fires dotted the countryside but the greatest of them blazed outside Porth Cerrig, twin bonfires under an onyx sky washed with stars. Loarn's people crowded around them to see him meet his new queen. She was gowned in blue-and-yellow checkered wool, girdled at the waist with painted leather, a gold collar at her throat and gold bands on her wrists. Her dark hair hung loose down her back, crowned with a gold fillet.

You would not know her for the woman who had come a ten-day ago from the Roman fort, Llamrei thought. In the firelight and under that wild fall of dark hair she looked wholly one of their own. Iorwen had seen to it that she learned the rituals of the Goddess, the proper propitiation of Lleu Sunlord, Epona and Llyr, all the spirits who watched over her reclaimed people. Teyrnon had lectured her on the history of their kind from the beginning of the earth when men had been giants and walked across the water. Llamrei had helped Iorwen and Gwladus dress her in the bride's house and make up the bed in the queen's quarters to which Loarn would take her. Perhaps most importantly, she and Rhodri had gone to Llew and threatened him if he did not keep his tongue still.

Loarn had reached Silvia now and he held out both hands to take hers. She gave them to him, and he turned her to face their people, and then to walk beside him between the fires. The sound of pipes accompanied them, not the solemn tune that had marked his king-making, but jubilant notes above a soft patter of drums like a frisking pony's hooves. The Beltane Walk was a joyous entreaty to the gods to give fertility to the king and queen, to their people and their beasts, and the crops that sprang up new in the fields.

Beyond the fires Teyrnon waited, the flames repeated in his white beard and gown and shining from the sun disk on his chest and the wheel atop his staff. Behind him two younger Druids stood holding the halter of a red cow, her horns crowned with twigs and green buds of elder.

"Say before the gods that you are willing to make this marriage," Teyrnon told Silvia.

Silvia took a deep breath. She would be someone new now, newer even than she had grown in the ten-day in the bride's house, learning how her mother's kind had conquered, mated, and fought their century-long battles across the green hills beyond Porth Cerrig. She could feel her heartbeat flutter and then steady under the pattern that Teyrnon had pricked into her skin. "I am willing."

"And you, king."

"I am willing." Loarn's voice was loud enough to reach the outer edges of the crowd. "I take this woman to live beside me and be queen over my people."

"Then it is done," Teyrnon said. He turned to the watching crowd. "That which was stolen comes home to us."

A shout of acclamation came from the crowd around the fires – for the new queen who was the first thing taken back from the Romans.

Teyrnon nodded to the two younger priests and one of them led the cow forward. The fire glinted on the bronze blade in the other's hands, and she fell without a struggle: a good omen. Another shout rose from the tribe.

Loarn and Silvia walked back again between the fires while the pipes and the drumming cheered them on. A silver-mounted chariot with blue wheels waited for them, the one Loarn had driven to fetch her from Isca. The red ponies' bridles and the chariot itself were twined with rowan and alder and the early-blossoming flowers of wood anemone. Loarn boosted her into it and took up the reins. The ponies snorted, edgy from the fires and the crowd and the drums. They shot down the track away from the sea hold.

"Where are we going?" Silvia clung to him. She had thought they would go back to Porth Cerrig and the bed that Iorwen and Gwladus had so carefully made up for them. Ahead, instead, was the black night and a road she could barely see.

Loarn laughed. "Where we will not have an audience listening outside our chamber door. There is a cloak here for you. Put it on if you are cold. We are not going far."

Silvia found it folded on the floor of the chariot and put it around her shoulders. There was just enough moon to see by now that her eyes were away from the fires. It hung in the sky like a cupped hand, and she saw that he wore the onyx ring she had sent him. They left the track, the ponies surefooted in the darkness. They wound across open pasture and then into young woods that encroached on it. They were nearly upon a hut in the trees before she saw it. A glow from the doorway spoke of a fire inside and there was a pail of water and another of grain for the ponies. She watched, curious but asking no questions while he unhitched them, put them in halters, and tied them to a post beside the water and grain. He turned to her smiling and held out his hand again.

"What is this place?"

"My childhood refuge, made somewhat more comfortable for us. It was a shepherd's hut when this used to be sheep graze. Before the Romans came, when there were more of us. Before the last king fell and my line and Iorwen's was the only one left, except for Aedden."

"Oh." She wasn't sure how to answer that.

"And now we take it back, you and I. I sent Gwydion and Pwyll to chase the foxes out and improve it for us. Come inside."

She followed him and found a banked fire in a stone hearth and a bed heaped with layers of blankets, pillows, and furs.

Loarn pointed upward where the thin drift of smoke from the fire sifted through the thatch. "See, they have patched the roof. And here is a fire for us which I need only stir up and feed."

He set to doing that while she watched, bemused. He began to whistle between his teeth, some variation on the Beltane Walk. When he was satisfied with it, he stood and pulled back the covers on the bed and raised an eyebrow at her. Then he sat down and pulled his boots off.

That made her laugh. She had been married before, she was no shrinking maiden, and she suspected he knew how badly she wanted him. *You are not Manlius*, she thought while he stripped his shirt over his head and the fire glow flickered across the spiraling spear mark on his chest. She thought of a wild thing come tame to her hand.

"Your turn," he said, eyeing her. She dropped the cloak. He stood again and came to her, to lift each foot and pull its shoe off, unfasten the painted belt and the gold collar, the gold fillet and the arm bands, and finally to lift her gown over her head. He put a gentle fingertip to the five-petaled flower on her breast. Then he unbuckled his belt, pulled his breeches off, and laid her down on the bed with him under a blanket that smelled of wild mint.

"I used to come here as child." He turned her in his arms so that her head was nestled in his shoulder. "Whenever I ran away from my nurse, or some chore, or a beating I thought I was likely to get. It was falling down, even then, and there were things growing in the thatch, but it seemed like a private kingdom to me. Nurse didn't know where to look for me because I never told anyone else, not even Iorwen."

"Would she have told on you?"

"No, but it was something I wanted to be mine to me." He slid one hand down her belly and felt her quiver. "As I wanted you." He stroked her between her thighs while he kissed her and felt them open to welcome him.

Afterward while they lay entwined, he said, "I will make you glad you came to me, I swear."

XII. CADAL

To Centurion Galerius, primus pilus, XX Valeria Victrix
From Faustus Silvius Valerianus, primus pilus, II Augusta
In the name of Aulus Caecilius, legate, XX Augusta at Isca Silurum

My dear friend,
Aulus Caecilius wishes me to inform you that our scouts – and yours, I have no doubt – are now reporting signs of boats unloading on the Ordovice coast. As your legate is still in Eburacum, he wishes to know what you are doing about that. I can only assume that he thinks you are sitting about eating jam tarts and playing rota with the pullarius for eggs.

Galerius grinned. Faustus's letters were always most informative when he was in a temper.

Caecilius ought to know better but he's the sort who feels that no one but he can do things properly, or at all. I have not bothered to call his attention to the fact that he was certain that my sister's marriage would put a stop to any ideas of war, since it would be pointless.

Galerius winced. He noted the legion's senior tribune eyeing the scroll, and walked away to the window, ostensibly in search of better light.

> *It doesn't look as if Cadal is actively arming his own people, as all the cargo seems to be going south. Knowing you of old, I am certain you are doing everything you can to lay hands on the boatmen or their clients. Please send a report to that effect with all possible detail. If we even have an idea of the route they are taking south, that would help.*
>
> *I am sorry about Silvia.*

Faustus's handwriting was never good. Here it began to crawl down a ragged slope.

> *She blames me for Lucius's death, and I am horribly afraid that her new people were behind it. Bloodline matters more to the Silures than to most of the tribes, who may just choose a man suited to the role, or fight for it. But then kings among those people are not like the Silure kings.*

Galerius could feel Tribune Terentius's interest. He ignored it. The next few lines leveled somewhat but remained an unhappy, ungainly scrawl.

> *Despite what Silvia thinks, Caecilius absolutely would have tried to install Lucius as a Roman client-king if he thought he could manage it. And it has crossed my mind that he may think of using me if matters go sideways. I am desperately afraid they are going to. Silvia was too besotted to see that marrying her was never going to keep Loarn in line. He just wanted her because he wanted her. His council certainly didn't want her; she was right about Lucius's death being my fault. I didn't think of all the ramifications soon enough to protect him. No doubt I will deserve whatever the gods send me in retribution for that.*
>
> *Faustus*

Galerius rolled the scroll back up and tucked it into the leather case it had come in.

"Is that a report from the south?" Terentius asked him. "May I see it, please?"

"It's a personal letter from a friend," Galerius said. "But a report of its kind. The legate at Isca wants to know what we know about the Ordovices letting boats land in their territory."

"That's a report then. I should read it." Terentius Priscus was convinced that all matters were his business in the absence of the legate.

"I've told you what's in it." Galerius put the case in the pouch at his belt. "Optio!"

The headquarters optio, who had been filing supply lists and pretending not to listen, stuck his head up cautiously. The primus pilus and the senior tribune were prone to give him conflicting orders.

"Go find me Aurelius Rotri," Galerius told him.

Terentius said, "This is no longer a matter for the scouts. If you already have evidence of the Ordovices allowing contraband to be landed on their coast, then it's a matter for discipline. Sanctions must be imposed. Why was I not informed of this before?"

"Tribune, I have been in West Britain a long time." *Longer than you have* was implied. "We have handled Cadal very carefully and it has paid off in peace. If he is letting the Silures land smuggled goods on his coast, we can't confront him with the accusation without solid evidence."

"Of course we can."

"He will deny it," Galerius said with elaborate patience, "and then we will still have to figure out how to stop it, which is where we are right now, except that he will know we are trying to."

"We impose consequences until the smuggling stops," Terentius said. "That ought to be obvious, Centurion."

Galerius gritted his teeth. "Only on the surface, Tribune." *Yes, I am aware that you outrank me.* A primus pilus was second to the legate in legionary hierarchy and in experience. A broad-stripe tribune was a political appointee but also nominally second in command.

"On the surface?" Terentius snapped.

"When Cadal surrendered to Agricola – I was there," Galerius added pointedly "–the terms given were practical ones, such that Cadal was given no reason to fight longer, and we could leave stable country behind us while we campaigned in the north. It was a delicate negotiation that has paid off in peace with the Ordovices since. Draconian response to smuggling that we have no concrete proof of will overset that at a time when we are undermanned and cannot afford it."

Terentius looked dismissive. "And what do *you* suggest, Centurion?" His tone said that he didn't particularly care.

"I suggest that we get solid information that will give us the ability to stop it without involving Cadal. That's what I want with Aurelius Rotri. He served with the border wolves in the north. If anyone can get in among the Ordovices and see how best to put a hole in their boat, it's him."

"That would be wasting a fine opportunity, Centurion. If the Ordovices are involved with smuggling for the Silures, then they can be made a channel for intelligence."

"They won't betray the Silures to us," Galerius said, "if that's what you're suggesting. They will deny everything, and we will be back where we are now except that they will be aware of how much we know."

"Why should they not? The Silures are old enemies."

"The Silures are paying them. And we are a new enemy and the greater one."

"Exactly. That is our strength. I shall speak directly to Cadal and make it clear to him that this is a diplomatic request from the highest quarters. He cannot refuse what Rome asks."

Galerius stared at him. "You are proposing to go to Bryn Epona and order Cadal to inform on the Silures?"

Terentius looked pleased. "As I said, it is a fine opportunity. He can't refuse, not and keep his treaty with Rome. I shall require that he become more involved in their enterprise and then report directly to me."

Galerius tried again. "We should consult the legate before we take further action."

"It would take far too long to get a message to Eburacum and back. The legate is concerned with weightier matters and may even be in the field."

Galerius's optio reappeared. "Aurelius Rotri is here, sir."

The three narrow-stripe tribunes attached to Deva appeared behind him, having got wind of what was afoot.

"I wish to say, sir, that perhaps—" one of them began and Terentius cut him off.

"Send Rotri away again. I am in charge of this matter. He won't be needed. I shall take an escort," he told Galerius. "But you needn't accompany me." He eyed the narrow-stripe tribunes and dismissed them as well. "I shall handle the matter."

—

Terentius rode out with a full century marching behind him under their silver standard and the legion's boar's head banner. Galerius and the three narrow-stripe tribunes watched silently, but when the last man was through the gates, one of the tribunes said pessimistically, "Now we're for it."

"Can't anyone stop him?" another asked.

"If the primus pilus can't, we can't."

A broad-stripe tribune *laticlavius* was of senatorial family and would advance to command of a legion himself, or a governorship. Tribunes *angusticlavii*, for the narrow stripe on their tunics, were career army men with substantial experience, and in the way of armies, outranked by the broad-stripe man.

"Cadal may send him back across his horse," the first one said.

"That wouldn't break my heart."

"It would push us into war."

"Pity no one's put an adder in his bed yet."

Galerius decided he had best take notice. "This is not a subject for public discussion," he said, and they nodded. But he sympathized with their anger. He considered the wisdom of reporting on this development to Aulus Caecilius in Isca. He would wait, he supposed. There wasn't any way to stop Terentius and he might as well see what came of it.

—

The tribune's route took him past the garrison at Caer Gai where they halted for the second night and then by the same way that Llamrei had come through the now greening hills to the lower gates of Bryn Epona. The sentry there gave them much the same look he had given Llamrei.

"Move aside," Terentius told him. "I have come to speak with your king."

The sentry was used to the presence of Roman patrols circulating through the Ordovices' hills, inspecting road maintenance, collecting taxes, requisitioning grain and meat for the forts, for which they never paid full price. They were as ubiquitous and welcome as fleas and as impossible to get rid of. This one was grander than most. His silvered cuirass was embossed with figures of the gods and tied with a scarlet sash, and a fine display of scarlet feathers topped his helmet. The sentry shrugged his shoulders, indicating lack of comprehension.

Terentius beckoned for one of his escort to translate. It had not seemed worth it to him to learn British for a one-year posting. Cadal would speak Latin.

"We were not told to expect you," the sentry told the translator when he repeated Terentius's request. "It may be that Cadal is not here." He paused thoughtfully. "Someone said he went hunting."

"We will wait for him in his hall," Terentius told the sentry.

"Likely he might be gone for a day or so," the sentry suggested.

Terentius knew that he and his escort had been tracked since they left Caer Gai and that someone had gone running to the upper courts as soon as they saw the Romans were coming to Bryn Epona itself. He let his eyes run over the damage to the gates and outer walls. Rome had ordered that and it had been done. Rome would not now be kept waiting. "Stand aside," Terentius said. "The king is not so foolish as not to be here to greet us. Send someone to inform him that we have arrived and to order food and drink for my men."

The sentry pondered this and beckoned to another man. "Tell him there is a mannerless Roman come to see him." He stepped aside and they proceeded up the track through the six courts to Cadal's hall. Cadal's people watched them on their way, curious and unfriendly, and spat at their backs as they passed.

A graying man who said in Latin that he was chief councilor to the king met them outside the great hall. "Your men may wait for you here," he said. He glanced at the sky, which was darkening ominously. An elm that overhung a stream-fed tank in the courtyard rustled its leaves. "Likely it won't rain for a while yet."

Terentius looked as if he might argue, but the centurion of the escort said, "It's all right, sir. Best they be where they can keep an eye out." He had a healthy distrust of being under any British roof.

"Very well," Terentius told him. "But you come with me." He dismounted and handed the reins to the slave who trudged along behind him. "Take us to your king," he told the councilor and they followed him, picking their way carefully across the courtyard. Someone had recently spilled a load of manure.

Cadal of the Ordovices sat at the far end of the hall in the great chair from which he met with his council and heard petitions from his people. Its arms were carved with beasts' heads, open-jawed and snarling; the seat was piled with hides dyed red and green. There was another, smaller chair beside it. The king wore a finely embroidered shirt and checkered trousers. There was a heavy gold torque at his throat, four armbands on each arm, and a gold crown on his graying fair hair. He was somewhat more splendid even than the tribune, and his expression was haughty. "It is considered good manners," he said to Terentius in Latin, "to send a messenger ahead of a visit. To make sure we are prepared to offer you suitable hospitality. As it happens, we are not, since we begin sheep-shearing today. Still, you may sit." He gestured at the smaller chair. "I can spare a few minutes."

Terentius bristled but he took the chair. The centurion stood at attention by the door.

"Why are you here, Tribune?" Cadal inquired.

"It has come to our notice that you have allowed the Silures to land contraband cargo on your shores." Terentius leaned forward toward Cadal, who leaned back.

"I have no idea what you are speaking of," Cadal said blandly. "We do not even have diplomatic relations with the Silures. They are an unpleasant people. I have as little to do with them as possible."

The graying councilor nodded solemnly at Terentius as if to confirm that.

"You are lying to me," Terentius said flatly.

Cadal stiffened and so did the councilor.

"Do you question my word?" Cadal asked.

"I do," Terentius said. "We have evidence. This will stop and you will cooperate with me in the matter or there will be consequences."

The councilor's eyes widened while Cadal's narrowed. The centurion watched them uneasily.

"What exactly are you asking for, Tribune?"

"We wish you to continue your relations with the Silures and to report to us on their plans. It's perfectly simple, and you will be allowed to keep whatever they are paying you for the arrangement."

There was a small, dangerous silence.

"Let me understand this clearly," Cadal said softly. "You wish me to play spy for Rome, and to betray Loarn of the Silures to you at your bidding?"

"Precisely." Terentius nodded his satisfaction at the king's understanding.

"And you will *permit* us to keep what they are paying?"

"We will. We could confiscate it, of course, but I am inclined to be generous in exchange for your cooperation."

"And if not, you threaten consequences." Cadal gave him a long stare. "Explain what you hint at, Tribune."

"The consequences need not concern you if you do as we ask," Terentius told him.

"I see," Cadal said quietly. "And if I do not?"

"Then there may be another king on your throne," Terentius said. "Rome is not to be defied."

The gray-haired councilor put his hand on his dagger and the centurion on his, but Cadal shook his head. He stood. "You will have a message from me soon then, Tribune. When I have information for you."

—

The rain began to come down as the tribune left the hall, washing the manure into little runnels across his path. He ignored it, his aim achieved. He remounted his horse and signaled to the century to follow him. They squelched unhappily through the water in formation, shields and the poles that carried their packs slung behind them, pila at the ready. It would take three days to get back to Deva. Terentius considered waiting out the rain at the village that lay just past Caer Gai. There was a tavern inn there with more comfortable beds than the garrison had offered, and the men could be housed in the civilians' huts. That would probably be good reinforcement of Rome's authority. When the rain began to pelt down like water from a bucket as they passed Caer Gai he decided on it. It would likely clear by morning and in the meantime, he remembered the wine at the inn as passable.

The gray curtain of the rain blanketed everything, the road ahead barely visible. The uncleared land beyond the Roman road disappeared behind the wall of water and if anything moved through it, it was unseen.

The tavern keeper welcomed the tribune and his men, although he was fairly sure that the village headman would not. Nevertheless, they would make room for them.

The centurion of the escort declined the offer of a bed in the tavern, preferring to sleep with the most unreliable of his men, and administer a stern warning to the rest about the local women, remembering that it was a rape that had begun the worst rebellion in Britain that Rome had seen.

"Good man," Terentius said. "Excellent idea. Wouldn't want to stir the pot just now." And Centurion Galerius would see that he had been right. Galerius was too easy on the natives, in Terentius's opinion. There was no need to let the men run savage among them, but they needed a firmer hand than Centurion Galerius's. He had been too long in Britain. Officers were usually transferred into other provinces from their first posting as they were promoted, but the lack of strength in Britain since Agricola's day had made legionary legates inclined to hold onto their best officers. That was what Vitruvius Arvina, the legate of the Twentieth had told Terentius, but in Terentius's opinion, if a man stayed too long in one spot, he went native and nothing good came of it.

He settled into a chair before the fire and drank hot wine while the rain hissed on the thatch. The tavern wife went past with a bowl of stew for a sodden traveler, and Terentius held out his cup for more wine.

A small knot of men came to the tavern not long after the Roman patrol. They were muddied and clothed in nondescript shirts and trousers like shepherds come from the pasture, or crew from the road repairs beyond Caer Gai. They found the tavern keeper in the stable feeding the tribune's horse and spoke quietly to him.

The tavern wife brought Terentius another cup of wine, a gift on the house, she said. He drank it sleepily, lulled by the rain and the fire and the wine which was warm and spiced and nearly unwatered. He set the cup down, yawned, and threaded his way through the other drinkers to the room that had been made up for him. The mattress was fairly free of lumps when he prodded it. He stood while his slave unbuckled his cuirass and greaves and helped him out of his tunic. A fresh one for the night went over his head and he lay down and closed his eyes, composing the report that would put Centurion Galerius firmly in his place.

The tavern wife met Terentius's slave as he lay down to sleep outside his master's door. "My husband sent you this." She put a cup of wine into his hands. "Noticing that the tribune didn't bother."

"He doesn't," the slave said. He smiled at her, drank gratefully and slept.

He was still sleeping when two men stepped carefully over him and eased the chamber door open. He didn't wake when they came out again carrying the tribune, nor when they picked him up too. The tribune stirred when they tied a gag around his mouth but by then it was too late. The slave woke with the jolting of the wagon, found his hands tied behind his back, and kept silent.

—

The escort centurion stuck his head past the chamber door in the morning to wake the tribune and saw it empty. He found no one behind the counter in the tavern either, although the door had been unbarred. A furious thumping came from the back of the house, past the kitchen. The centurion pushed the door open to find the tavern keeper, his wife, and the girl who had waited on customers the night before, all tied with their hands behind them, their ankles together, rags stuffed into their mouths. The tavern dog was shut in with them.

The landlord swore when the centurion pulled the rag free. "The Morrigan fly off with the motherless bastard sons of whores. Likely they've taken every bit of silver in the house and the good pots too."

"Where is the tribune?"

"Asleep most likely. He was drunk as a bargeman last night. Ask his boy."

"He's gone too. *Where is the tribune?*"

"He's not here? Untie me, curse you."

The centurion cut the thongs around the man's wrists and ankles with his dagger and freed the wife and girl.

"What happened?"

"How in Lleu's name should I know? Someone grabbed me from behind, hit me with a brick." The tavern keeper rubbed his head. "Woke up like this."

"And you?" The centurion glared at the women.

"Don't know," the girl said sullenly. "It was dark, then."

"Dark and no one about to help us," the tavern wife said. "My husband being hit with a brick. I was just finishing the washing," she added helpfully.

The centurion pointed at the door. "Go and see what's missing."

They took stock of the tavern's main room, and the kitchen. "The small porridge pot, I'm thinking," the girl said.

"What about the till?"

The tavern keeper inspected it. "Still here. Box is locked, you see. I expect they couldn't carry it."

"And the tribune?"

The tavern keeper looked uncomfortable. "I'm thinking, since they didn't take much else, they took him."

The centurion ground his teeth. That much had been obvious but he couldn't decide whether the old man had been in on it. There was a raised raw spot on his balding head that argued that the brick had been real. The sky had cleared outside, and the air was full of carefree birdsong, indicating that any invaders were gone long ago. They wouldn't be hunted down by a single century when they had the whole countryside to hide in. There was nothing for it but to go back to Deva and report to the primus pilus.

—

A horrible cold feeling crawled all the way up Galerius's spine when the centurion galloped through the Deva gates on the tribune's horse. A considerable number of people who should have been elsewhere had begun to gather. Galerius shouted at the nearest man to take the horse and the rest of them get back to what they should have been doing, and took the centurion into the Principia.

"Mithras," he said quietly when the centurion had told his tale. "I told the fool to go carefully with Cadal."

"It was Cadal, I suppose?"

"Without a doubt. The arrogant ass insulted him. You don't insult an Ordovice king unless you want serious consequences yourself."

"What do you think they'll do with him? Leave his body somewhere? My patrol is on their way in. I can take them out again if you have any idea where we should look." He fidgeted unhappily with his helmet strap. "We'll have to find it."

"They'd have left his body in the bed if that was all they wanted," Galerius said. "They'll keep him alive to bargain with. And not with us, I suspect."

"The Silures?"

Galerius thought it through. "Loarn has been pressuring Cadal to ally with him. Cadal doesn't want to be pulled into a war. Letting them land goods on his coast was a sop to that. My best bet is that he'll sell the tribune to Loarn and get a pact to leave the Ordovices neutral."

"Mithras." The centurion's face paled. "His father's a senator, isn't he?"

"And an *amicus* of the emperor. I don't fancy being the one who let Cadal grab him."

"That was me then, wasn't it?" The centurion looked miserably afraid, and trying hard to cover it.

"It was himself," Galerius said. "He's as stupid as an ox. I *told* him not to go, but I doubt Cadal would have gone this far if Terentius hadn't threatened him like that. You don't do that to a stiff-necked native king if you have half a brain. But it's us they'll blame so we've got to get him back." The fact that the tribune had made his own trouble was irrelevant.

"What do you think Loarn will do with him?" the centurion asked uneasily.

"I don't like to think. We need to find him *before* they give him to Loarn." Galerius picked up a pen and a handful of tablets. "Get me two riders. I want dispatches to the legate in Eburacum or wherever in Pluto's name he is, and to the command at Isca. They'll be heading south once Cadal exchanges messages with Loarn."

—

Mostly they called him the Sun People's boy, but Owl had named him: Sedge, because of his hair, pale and bristly like the windblown tufts that grew along the dunes.

She took him with her to gather the berries that were just coming ripe and to catch eels in the stream. They had a bucket of them now, yellowy brown creatures bumping their noses against the sides. An otter on the opposite bank was eating an eel of its own, working its way from the head on down. It watched them with bright eyes but didn't seem afraid. None of the wild creatures seemed to fear Owl. The boy stared. He had a fleeting memory of someone taking him to see otters in a river and then it was gone. He shook his head, trying to bring it back, but it wouldn't come.

Owl dipped her hand in another bucket and brought out a fistful of berries.

"There won't be any left to take back," the boy said as she ate them, her face smeared with juice.

"There are more," she said happily. "Here." She handed him another fistful. "We'll fill the bucket again on the way back."

A sound in the forest behind them made both snap their heads around. It stilled all the other sounds, the birds and the rustle of small things in the leaf litter. "Something's coming!" he whispered, and they melted into the trees to watch, motionless. Hoofbeats on the track to Porth Cerrig.

They crouched to watch the rider go by. "Ordovice," Owl said. "From the north. What is he doing here?"

"Whyever he's here, he's in a hurry," Sedge said. He had begun to think of himself that way because it was dreadful to have no name.

"He has a green branch tied to his spear," Owl said. "He must have some message from the Ordovice king to Loarn."

That name moved something inside his mind and then it vanished again. It was like trying to catch a trailing rope that the wind kept snatching away.

Owl watched the thought move across his face and fade. He still didn't remember falling from the cliff. Owl had told him about that. They had seen Romans looking for him along the beach, but there was no way to know whether he was their lost one or they were hunting him like the others. Fox said that memory would come, and until it did, they would keep him in Blaidd Llwyd. Maybe he wouldn't get his memory back, Owl thought, and then she could keep him.

The rider disappeared down the track and they went cautiously back to the streambank. The otter had gone, slipping into the water at the first sound of the intruder. Owl picked up her buckets. "We should tell Fox about him," she said.

The boy looked back along the track where the rider had gone. He had no feeling that the errand was to do with him but still there was the sense that Loarn of the Silures had crossed his path somehow. *I don't like him*, he thought, and didn't know why. He followed Owl down the hill people's track, one he could barely see, through woods that a month ago had been white with the frothing bloom of hawthorn and now grew dark and mysterious as the canopy leafed out to a thick dark sky above them. He knew his way through it now, as he must have known his way home once. There was the oak with the bees' nest that he and Owl had raided for honeycomb. The place, overhung with willows, that was the best place to catch the slick, spotted trout; Owl could do it with her hands. The rocky spot in the shallows where cress grew along the bank. The hidden garden in a clearing where the people of Blaidd Llwyd grew peas and barley. He watched Owl's slight figure with affection as it darted through the trees ahead of him. He didn't think he had ever had a friend who was a girl before. Since his head had healed, she had become his minder in an unfamiliar world, until her sisters and Thorn laughed and said he was Owl's pet. Plover and Rail had warmed to him since, and Thorn had taught him to shoot one of their small bows. When he consistently hit his target with the little bronze-tipped arrows, Thorn and his brothers had warmed to him, too. Only Badger remained grumpy about his presence. He was too big, she said, and growing bigger and if he didn't leave, he would plug their doorway like a pig stuck in a fence.

The Old One was washing clothes with Badger and Rail at a pot over a fire when they came out of the trees. They put their buckets down and Owl said breathlessly, "There was a rider from the north with a green branch on his spear, going to Porth Cerrig!"

"Indeed?" Fox said. The Old One dropped the shirt she had been wringing out back into the pot. "There is always some trouble between the Sun People. They are like rutting deer in the spring. I will send Thorn to see what he can see."

"Why?" Rail asked.

"Because it is better to know what they are doing than not."

Badger's eyes slid toward Sedge. "Maybe it is to do with him. He should not be staying here and drawing their eyes to us."

"You shut your mouth!" Owl said. "It is not to do with him! Why are you such a pig?"

"I am not a pig!" Badger said.

Owl oinked at her.

"It's not to do with me. I don't think so anyway," the boy said. "The Silures and the Ordovices don't like each other but the Silures want the Ordovices to fight the Romans for them."

Badger stared at him. "How do you know that?" she demanded.

He stood gaping at her, frozen by a sudden isolated piece of certain knowledge. "I don't know," he whispered.

XIII. "HE IS OURS"

Lucius's stone was dark with the wine that Faustus offered every morning before prayers at the standards. Faustus brushed his hand across its legend in the almost-dawn, the surface cool under his fingertips, and one word, *paterfamilias*, hammered in his head. He had lost everything he had been entrusted with – Silvia, Lucius, the men who had died under his command in the north while the army had given him a grass crown for it. Including, it seemed, his father. Even in the presence of the other weathering stone, dedicated to Marcus Silvius Valerianus, he felt no sign of the shade that had dogged him for so many years. The old man had not appeared since Lucius was lost. He had told Faustus to get Lucius out of Britain and Faustus had not listened. Maybe that was all he had wanted, Faustus thought: to be right about something.

As he had left the house in the pre-dawn darkness, he had caught Eirian already up, crying and washing out bloody rags in a bucket yet again. He couldn't even give her a child, as if the Fates had no intention of trusting him with more lives.

The sun made a pale glimmering line above the hills now amid the morning bird chorus. Faustus turned to go before he was late to prayers. He was primus pilus. He stood before the golden Eagle of the legion with the legate and Marcellinus to give the gods their due on behalf of the whole Second Augusta. It would be an ill omen for them all if he was late, and mark him as suspect in his duty. The legate had been kind but increasingly irritable at his distraction.

He nearly was late. The aquilifer had already brought the Eagle out of the Chapel of the Standards and his cohort was paraded before it with Septimus at their head. Septimus stepped back when he saw Faustus, relief plain in his face. The Eagle's wings caught the growing light. The silver spearpoints of the cohort standards were ranged around it, and in the massed legion the standard of each century marked its place.

Caecilius and Marcellinus led the invocation to Jupiter Best and Greatest, Juno and Minerva, and to Mars Ultor, god of war and armies. Faustus had always found the prayers almost joyful, a sign that he had found his home and his calling. They raised the hair on his arms, and he felt a glow in his chest. That reaction had grown less and less since Lucius died, and now he could not feel it at all, only a leaden weight like a sling bullet where his heart should have been. He had failed his family and now the shattering fear came to him that he would fail his legion. He saw Caecilius looking at him oddly and straightened his back, made his face a blank.

Morning prayer was the time for announcements, for important messages from Rome to be read, for the day's duties to be laid out if there were special orders. Caecilius tightened the scarlet sash around the waist of his silvered cuirass, adjusted the folds of the blood-red military cloak at his shoulders, and surveyed his legion from beneath a gilded helmet rim.

"Men of the Second Augusta." He paused, surveying them. "You have done well in troubled times. The Britons have so far held the peace, rather than swelling in rebellion. This has been due to your vigilance. We have every confidence that this will continue if we continue vigilant, but the rising of Cath Mawr, taken in combination with the late rising of the ground beneath our feet, has been a sign, according to your haruspex."

The haruspex, at his elbow, looked portentous.

"To that end, I have consulted with the Tribune Laticlavius," Caecilius said. He nodded toward Marcellinus.

And not with his primus pilus, Faustus thought. And why would he, when the primus pilus could not be trusted? Had the haruspex told him that too?

"We have devised a form of drill," Caecilius announced, "that will increase our understanding of the natives' way of warfare."

That produced an inquisitive murmur suppressed by swift glares from centurions among the ranks. It bubbled up again when Caecilius gave his orders. The cohorts were to be split in half, one side to become Britons carrying round shields and spears, the favored weapon of the tribes. The spears would be blunted, and the other side would wield wooden practice weapons as well, and regulation shields, and when they had fought each other to a standstill, or one side had won, there would be turnabout.

"Not a bad idea from the old boy," Septimus said under his breath to Faustus. "It helps to have experience with the enemy without having actual experience, so to speak."

"We'll end with some in hospital anyway," Faustus predicted, diverted for now from his black thoughts. Wooden practice weapons could break bone. "We'll have to lay down some rules about when a man considers himself dead or the fools will hop back in it like Prometheus's liver until they get serious damage."

Septimus looked relieved that his commander seemed to warm to the plan and come out a way from his gloom. In Septimus's opinion there was nothing like a good fight to lift the spirits.

The men of the First Cohort felt the same and the 'Britons' derived a good deal of amusement from drawing rude symbols on their faces in blue paint and slogans like 'Bite my cock, Roman soldier' on their shields. The 'Roman' side responded with a chant regarding the hairiness of British genitals.

Faustus saw no reason to intervene in that. He set out rules for when a combatant was to be considered dead. "A heavy blow to anywhere on the torso or head and you're out, and your centurion will be watching. A hamstring blow puts you down on one knee. A blow to an arm means you can't use it." He marched them down to the new arena in two columns, Briton and Roman, and noted how many of the men touched the head of Cath Mawr as they passed.

"No chariots?" a Briton asked plaintively when they were arrayed across from the enemy, one of several battles to be fought along the arena's length.

"There is a limit to the verisimilitude we can scrape up on short notice," Faustus told him.

"Chariots are for show anyway," his mate said scornfully. "They never stay in the line long. Kill yourself right off trying to drive one anyway. You can be a horse's ass retreating, if you like."

"Quiet!" Faustus snapped. "Shields up and at them!"

He moved into place at the end of their line, hefting the unfamiliar round shield and spear to test their handling. The shield felt small to a man used to the rectangular curved shield of the legions, and the spear was a weapon he used only for hunting, although like every man in the army he had been trained with a throw spear. The quartermaster's shop that provided the wooden weapons had padded and blunted the spearpoints, but a good deal of damage could be done with one anyway. Faustus had ordered his men to pull their blows and strike just hard enough to convince an opponent to drop out.

A flight of wooden pila rained down from the Roman side and the Britons ducked under their round shields. When the supply of pila was exhausted, they threw themselves into a screaming imitation of the native tribes, and Faustus found himself caught up in it, glad to be given something to fight.

Despite the war cries and blue paint, they fought more like Romans than Britons, holding the line steady, watching their centurion, keeping the Roman opponents at bay with a bristling line of spears until the Romans formed a pig's head wedge and drove it into the Britons' line.

One of Faustus's men came at him with a wooden short sword, aiming to drive it up under his commander's guard. Faustus blocked the blow and then used the rounded metal boss in the center of his shield to push the legionary backward. The Roman's helmet flew off and Faustus pulled his blow before he broke the man's skull. The legionary went at him again.

"You're dead!" Faustus bellowed at him.

"Aw, sir, you barely touched me!"

"I have no intention on putting my own men in hospital. You're dead! Get off the field or I'll touch you again when I have my vine staff. I may do it anyway for not having your helmet properly fastened."

"Yes, sir!" The legionary saluted and fell dramatically. His fellows began to scramble over him, and he cursed them and rolled out of the way.

Faustus devoted himself to trying to put a hole in the Roman line, thrusting his spear at any opening. All the same, the Romans carried the day, no doubt as the legate intended, since the Britons weren't used to their weapons or shields. It had started to drizzle when the last of the Roman units overwhelmed their opponents and the legate called a halt.

"A fine showing," he told the victors. "Tomorrow we will reverse the sides. Tonight, both sides can be proud of themselves, for the superiority of Roman discipline and equipment but also for the ability to fight with unfamiliar weapons. That has saved a legionary's life before now."

"He's wilier than you might expect," Marcellinus said, stopping at Faustus's side while Faustus inspected his men for actual damage.

"West Britain is an excellent tutor," Faustus said. "Usually."

Marcellinus nodded. "Water under that bridge, though, isn't it? I'd like to try a bout against British weapons myself." He eyed Faustus. "Are you game?" He didn't seem to mind that rain was pooling on the arena floor around them.

"It's a bit muddy now," Faustus suggested. The rain was soaking the tribune's helmet crest and the feathers drooped like wet chickens.

"All the better. War doesn't wait for sunshine."

And you want to see if I'm still functional. "All right." Faustus caught a man hurrying by with a wooden sword and Roman shield. "Here, you, give the tribune your equipment."

The man looked startled, but Marcellinus held out his hands and the legionary put the shield and short sword in them.

"That's a good man. I'll see you get your shield back."

The legionary looked as if he thought he might get it back with the tribune on it, but he didn't argue.

Faustus didn't either, just squared up on the sopping arena floor, his now battered shield and blunted spear against Marcellinus behind legionary shield and wooden sword.

They circled, feeling each other out, and Faustus saw from the corner of his eye that they had attracted an audience. He raised his shield arm and leveled his spear, angling for a way past the curved shield that covered the tribune from neck to knee. Marcellinus in his turn was looking for a way past the spear, where the short legionary sword would be at an advantage. Faustus lunged and the spear slid past Marcellinus's guard but there was no need to pull the blow. Marcellinus sidestepped as he swung his sword against the spearshaft and drove it downward. He pulled back out of reach, and they circled each other again.

Marcellinus grinned at Faustus. "They're making bets on us."

Probably on who would end in hospital, Faustus thought. The blunted spear was capable of taking out an eye and the wooden sword of breaking bone. He aimed the spear again, at Marcellinus's head, feinted, and came from the side to the ribcage instead. Marcellinus stepped back and then rushed him, knocking the spearshaft away with his shield edge, feinted to drive the sword under Faustus's guard and then brought it up to swing at his neck. The arena floor was growing slicker and Marcellinus skidded just enough with the blow to miss his stroke. Faustus backed up, lowered the spear and thrust it between the tribune's legs.

Marcellinus sat down heavily in the wet sand, swung his short sword desperately and caught Faustus across the back of his calves, a blow that would have cut hamstrings with a sharpened blade. Faustus drove the wooden spearpoint into Marcellinus's ribs as he fell.

They lay on their backs for a while in the rain, drawing air into their lungs. Then Faustus sat up.

"Are you all right?"

Marcellinus laughed. "I'll have a bruise as black as Styx water tomorrow. Are you?"

"I think so."

Marcellinus got to his feet and stood bent over, hands on knees for a moment. When he straightened, he held out his hand for Faustus. "Thank you. I enjoyed that."

The rain had begun to sheet down, and the spectators retreated. Faustus shook away the water that was dripping from his helmet rim. "What possessed you?"

Marcellinus put a hand on Faustus's shoulder as they squelched across the sand, now cut through with rivulets running with mud. "I'm to command a legion someday if I do things right. I never pass up an opportunity to know things."

"What did you learn then, just now?"

"I'm not sure yet. Sometimes knowledge takes a while to manifest itself." Whatever it was, he sounded content with it.

It was only midday, but the rain now cast a curtain like dusk over the arena and the rolling hills to the north. The way back to the fort was clogged with sopping Briton and Roman teams, cheerfully insulting each other on their performances, and bound for the baths and a hot meal. Faustus and Marcellinus followed them. They had come nearly to the Principia and the row of senior officers' houses when they were waylaid by the rider thundering from the Decumana gate, waves of gray mud and water flying up from his horse's hooves. He passed them at full gallop.

Something important. Something wrong. Good news did not travel on a galloping horse through a storm. Faustus and Marcellinus reached the Principia as the sentry there was ushering the rider in. They followed, handing off sopping cloaks to a clerk in the forecourt, and hurried after the courier as he stopped to salute the standards and the statue of Jupiter Optimus Maximus in a halt so brief it was clear that his message was urgent.

Caecilius was at his desk and looked up startled at the three of them. The courier handed him a leather dispatch case and all three stood dripping on the floor tile while Caecilius pulled the scroll out and read, face reddening into fury. He looked up at the courier again. "Do you know what is in this?"

"Yes, sir."

"Very well. Wait for a reply. Optio!" A headquarters optio appeared. "Get this man dry clothes and food. You two." He motioned to Marcellinus and Faustus. "Sit down. Terentius was always a damn fool. I told the procurator I wouldn't have him, so they foisted him on the Twentieth instead. And their legate's in Eburacum, so he's running loose like a maniac. Or he was." Caecilius crumpled the dispatch in his fist.

"May I inquire what has happened, sir?" Marcellinus's voice was soothing and official, a voice that could sort out a conversation and get it to the point.

Caecilius spread out the scroll again and stabbed a forefinger at it. "According to Centurion Galerius, the primus pilus at Deva, Tribune Terentius's response to our request for any information on what the Ordovices might be allowing the Silures to land on their coast was to go to Cadal and demand that he play spy for Roman interests and report on the Silures under the threat of being replaced with a king who would cooperate."

"Mithras," Marcellinus said. "Are we at war with the Ordovices yet?"

"Not yet," Caecilius said. "But they've got him and now they have a reason to ally with the Silures over the insult or else use him as a bargaining piece." He cast a wary eye at Faustus. "Pray your sister has as much influence on Loarn as we hoped."

"Got him, sir?" Marcellinus asked quickly before Faustus could say anything unwise.

"As in hauled him out of an inn in the middle of the night, under his men's noses," Caecilius said. "And if that wasn't Cadal's doing I'll retire and raise pigs."

"What does Centurion Galerius think?" Faustus asked.

"He thinks they're going to sell the idiot to Loarn for what they can get, and an agreement to keep the Ordovices neutral in a war, if there is one. Now there probably will be. If they kill him, we'll have to start one. His father's a senator and *amicus* of the emperor. The garrison at Deva is looking for him in their territory of course, but Centurion Galerius thinks they'll send him south to Loarn once they've negotiated something."

"Might they just demand a ransom?" Marcellinus asked.

"Not if they don't actually want a war. As it is, we don't have any real evidence it was them."

"Trading him to Loarn is risky, isn't it? They're old enemies."

"Neutrality is risky, but Cadal seems determined on it. What he'd most like would be to mop up what's left of the Silures after we're through with them, I expect."

"I agree," Marcellinus said abruptly. "And we need to intercept him before they can deliver him, given that he knows that half of the Twentieth is in the east." That was a fact that both legions had been at pains to hide.

"Would he talk?" Faustus asked. That piece of knowledge was dangerous. They were all fairly certain that it was only the threat of two full legions in West Britain that had kept the Silures peaceful until now.

"Centurion Galerius is of the opinion that he will," Caecilius said. "Anyone will eventually if it comes to that."

"We haven't a lot of time," Faustus said. He sifted out the possibilities in his head.

"As long as Loarn is in Porth Cerrig, it's a seven-day ride from Deva, even moving fast," Marcellinus said, calculating. "Their rider to Loarn will be on the heels of Galerius's man. Then they'll wait for an answer. But the chances are good that Cadal has sent someone with the authority to negotiate on the spot."

"And also that Loarn will go north to Dinas Tomen once he has him," Faustus said. "Where he will dig in." *And take my sister with him.*

"We'll find them if they move him south – Jupiter granting before they can reach Loarn," Caecilius said. "Two centuries ought to do it, but then it's war, no matter who has him." He smacked his fist on the desk hard enough to topple the ink pot. He righted it. "Typhon take him."

Faustus started to speak again and hesitated. How much reason was there for him to interfere in the legate's plan, which was a perfectly sound one even if it was likely to bring back a dead tribune rather than a live one? How much reason to try to save a foolish man from his own stupidity when he couldn't save his sister or his nephew? More than enough maybe. The gods rarely let you choose. He said, "If we go after him, there's a good chance they'll kill him as soon as we approach."

"Unfortunately, yes," Marcellinus agreed. "All the same, we have to get him back one way or the other, and fast."

"I am sorely tempted to allow Terentius to take his chances in that respect," Caecilius said grimly. "But naturally I cannot if a solution can be found before they get any information out of him. The tribune is one of ours however little we desire him. Do you have something else to suggest?" he asked Faustus.

"Try to pry him loose before there's an outright battle," Faustus said. "I might be able to. I can pass for Silure as long as the Silures don't see me, if we can get to the Ordovice riders bringing him south before Loarn's people can. I've seen Loarn's signet ring. He wore it at your banquet. I can get something similar made in the vicus. Loarn won't go himself, he'll send an envoy."

"You've lost your mind," Caecilius said flatly. "Valerianus, I have been worried about you."

"I'm perfectly sane," Faustus said.

"You are also perfectly clean-shaven, with a military haircut," Marcellinus pointed out.

Faustus gave that some thought while they watched him uneasily. Not as sane as he claimed, maybe, since he hadn't thought of that. "I have taken a vow," he said after a moment's consideration. "Disgraced myself in some fashion. It is penance. The border wolves all have long hair and mustaches. I'll go with them."

"And why not leave it to them?" Caecilius asked.

"They aren't troops of the line. They'll find him, but it may still come to a fight after I get him loose, particularly if Loarn's actual men are hard on our heels. I need regular troops under my command. And I need the authority to use them."

"Someone has to be in command, legate," Marcellinus pointed out. "It may be that Centurion Valerianus is the best man for it."

"No one else has a better chance of tricking them into handing him over," Faustus insisted. "I look like a Silure, I speak like one, and I've hunted all over these mountains, and campaigned over them too when we first took West Britain. I know the country and where they're likely to lair as well as the border wolves do."

"And what exactly do you do when you have got the tribune in your talons?" Caecilius asked. "And are who knows how far from a fort?"

"Head for the nearest one," Faustus said. "I don't think anything after that is predictable."

"He will have regular troops at his back that can be brought up after there is no longer any need for subterfuge," Marcellinus said. "The Ordovice contingent won't be large, they won't risk us noticing a large armed band traveling south. Nor will the Silures."

"They are equally likely to notice our men if the detachment is large enough." Caecilius ground his teeth. "I don't like this. I don't like anything about it."

"We can send the scouts out and have them put an arrow through him as soon as he's spotted," Marcellinus said.

"I would like to," Caecilius snapped. "But no. He is ours. We will go after him. Centurion Valerianus, if you pull this off, I will be grateful. If you don't, I will see that your widow is cared for."

—

Silvia could hear their voices in the hall below: Loarn and the tall fair-haired stranger who had ridden in with a green branch that morning. Llamrei and Rhodri and Pwyll. If she knelt at the withy screen that circled the gap in the upper floor where smoke rose from the central hearth to Porth Cerrig's roof, half their words came up on the smoke.

"What does Cadal ask for him?" That was Loarn.

She froze. She had heard enough before Loarn had sent her upstairs to learn that the Ordovices to the north had stolen a Roman tribune from the fort at Deva and wanted to sell him to Loarn. That would start a war with the Romans, the war that Loarn had told her their marriage would forestall. She had thought he would send the man away again. Her nose itched from the smoke, and she put a hand over it, pinching it closed before she could sneeze.

Below, Loarn gave a bark of laughter. "Tell Cadal he grows soft."

"Which is more useful?" she heard Llamrei ask. "The thing we can readily use, or the thing we would have to force? Cadal has made it clear he is not easily forced."

"Clear to the Romans at Deva," Pwyll said with a laugh.

"What are you thinking to do with him?" That was Rhodri. Loarn valued his advice and took it more than any of the others'.

"Tribunes are high in the Romans' command," Loarn said. "They know what there is to be known."

"So your wife says." A new voice: Llew, Silvia was certain. He was polite in her presence, but of all her husband's councilors, Llew was the one who actually hated her. "She has come home to us," she heard Pwyll say to him once, "leave her be," and Llew said only, "She has been too long with the Romans." Silvia had prayed to the Goddess to give her the power of a royal woman and a way to show Llew to his sorrow how wrong he was, but it never came. That role had gone to Iorwen and lived in only one woman at a time.

Silvia pressed her face against the withy screen, close enough that the smoke that drifted through made her eyes burn.

"The queen knows what she speaks of, Llew," Rhodri said. "She has lived among them, as you are fond of telling us until we are tired of it. Tribunes like this one are high officers, second to the commander of a legion."

Llamrei asked, "What will you do with him when you have emptied this jug of its knowledge?"

The flurry of half-heard suggestions made Silvia's stomach turn over.

Then Loarn was speaking to the Ordovice man again and she strained to hear but his voice was too soft. His voice was always softest when he most meant something, for good or ill. When he caressed her and whispered to her in their bed, for instance, and nothing else mattered. Loarn had given her a body she hadn't known she possessed, and until now she had barred her door to any doubts over what she had done. Gwladus had said to her worriedly that a little experience with the world often taught a soul that there was no need to be stone or water, there were a good few places in between, and Silvia had drawn back her hand at that to slap her, threatened to send her back to Isca, and then been ashamed of herself.

The voices rose again in the hall below.

"The agreement on coastwise trade," the envoy said now. "The silver for that must double."

"That is separate. And if there is interference, we will know that Cadal has broken his word."

"The tribune is worth more than one handful of silver and a promise of neutrality," the envoy said. "The Romans have their spies, but it would be dangerous, you understand, to insult Cadal with the idea that he might be one of them."

Loarn laughed. That was what the tribune had done.

And would pay for that foolishness, Silvia thought queasily, in any number of horrible ways. The Silures and the Ordovices warred constantly with each other, and any alliance between them was subject to abrupt betrayal when it suited one or the other, but not in a matter like this.

"The Roman tribune and his armor and weapons for a fourth-part increase in the silver and my word to leave Ordovice lands untouched, asking no levy of men or horses."

"A third."

A chorus of voices talking over each other debated it.

"Tell Cadal it is done," Loarn said when they quieted.

"We will give him to you on the border between our lands and these," the envoy said. "At the stinking spring below the ruins at Lleu's Well, that neither may play false."

"You have my word," Loarn said angrily.

"And you have Cadal's," the envoy said. "And still."

Silvia crept back from the withy screen. Loarn would not be happy to find her listening although surely a war with her people – her other people – would be her business. Loarn would not see it that way and most certainly his council would not, not even Gwydion who liked her and sat for hours while she told him stories of the gods and their doings, new tales for his harp song. She was queen of the Silures until she crossed Loarn in some way and then she was his pet, scolded then petted and made love to. Mostly that was enough, a solace against the early morning moment that came every day on waking when she remembered with a lurch in her heart that her son was dead. If she had lost Lucius, then she would have the only other thing she had ever wanted with the same ferocity.

Now... Now for the first time she considered how little power she had here at Porth Cerrig. And how often she was alone except for Gwladus. When she slipped back to her chamber, she found Gwladus there sorting an armful of linens.

"He has bought a Roman tribune that the Ordovices took in the north," Silvia told her. Everyone would know soon, there was no reason that Gwladus shouldn't.

"For what price?" Gwladus folded the linens into a chest and closed the lid.

"Asking no levy of men or horses from the Ordovices." Silvia said. "And silver. I didn't understand entirely."

"What he wants of the tribune is more likely what you'd best know," Gwladus said.

Silvia shivered. "Whatever the tribune knows. Information."

Gwladus nodded. "Well then. That will be war."

"No!"

Gwladus stood and put her arm around Silvia's shoulders. "You should have known this was coming. You did know, lady, you just would not look."

"I did not. And you can't know that now." Silvia balled her hands into fists, stubborn, as if she could turn events by force.

Gwladus sighed. She didn't answer.

"Then why did you come with me?" Silvia demanded.

"I am Dobunni," Gwladus said. "This is my country. Not these hills, but near enough to here. If Rome left it would not grieve me. Not now that my man is gone."

"That was my brother's fault," Silvia said. "Your man's death."

"It was not. He served Rome just like your brother his commander and he did what he had to. That was no one's fault. When you are older you will maybe not be so quick to look for a fault instead of a reason."

"I am the same age that you are. And what about Paullus?"

Gwladus snorted. "Paullus may court me when he has the courage to buy himself free."

"Paullus was born a slave," Silvia said. "It's all he knows, and Faustus is kind. I will give him that," she added, tight-lipped.

"Paullus is afraid to leave that comfort. There's many a slave would buy himself out, or run if he could, that have masters worse than the centurion. Paullus is too comfortable. He'll have to give that over if he wants me." She shrugged, stone-faced now and maybe not as uncaring as she seemed. "In any case it won't matter now."

"What will they do to the tribune?" Silvia whispered.

"We'll not talk about that, and you stay away, or it will mark the child you're carrying."

Silvia put a hand to her belly.

"Have you told him?" Gwladus asked.

"I'm waiting to be sure."

"Wait a while more," Gwladus said.

XIV. BIRDS OF PREY

The rain had let up, but the forest was still mist-shrouded, full of the smell of wet earth and last year's leaves. A war spear and a round shield were lashed to the little horse's saddle along with a bag of silver. The blanket beneath was a native weave, and Faustus's trousers, loose about the leg in the British fashion, were boldly checked in blue and red. A sword with tribal mountings hung at his belt and the gold torque at his throat and gold armbands befitted a Silure lord, even a disgraced one with a ragged stubble on his upper lip. The tribal pattern on his cheeks was paint but authentic enough in shadow. He would have to hope for shadow. It was likely, as the Ordovice men were keeping to deer trails and hidden tracks far into the trees. Faustus had ridden over the Silure Hills before while hunting and always felt the presence of something else at his elbow, something belonging to the woods and the wet places. The deep green of the forest was studded with patches of bog, bright green moss, and boulders that might have been tumbled from a god's hand. It was a place that would not surprise him to find the Oldest Ones living.

The handful of border wolves with him included Aurelius Rotri; back in the job he loved and grinning. They were dark men, mounted on native ponies, their luxuriant hair and mustaches and gold ornament proclaiming them lords as well. Yesterday they had sighted the Ordovice party on the trail, with the tribune in their midst, hands tied behind him and bumping unhappily in the saddle. Today they had shed the nondescript clothing that blended with the trees for the bright adornment of the high-born and set a course to intercept them from the south.

The scouts had spotted the envoy from Cadal as he left Porth Cerrig ten days ago and they had let him through to set the thing in motion. All concerned considered it unlikely that the Ordovices would take the tribune clear into Silure country; there would be a handoff somewhere on the border. The Silure party would by now be probably a day's ride behind, with Septimus and a century of the First Cohort on their tail. If they were lucky, Faustus thought, he and his border wolves would be there first and gone again before the Silures caught up. If not… two more centuries of Faustus's men trailed them carefully in the distance on the Roman roads, near enough, with luck, to hear a trumpet call.

Faustus thought that Caecilius held little hope of their success, but Faustus would save someone if he could, even if only the tribune, who had a father and wife and small child in Rome, who belonged to someone who would mourn him if he didn't come home. The rescue party would also kill him if they had to, and Caecilius was aware of that too. If Loarn learned that the West Britain legions were even more undermanned than he had thought, if Cadal learned that, then everything might turn over on that knowledge, even Cadal.

And Silvia. He would not be able to get her out when she changed her mind. If she did. How deeply she hated him and now hated Rome in the incarnation of the legions, he was not certain. It didn't matter, not to his responsibilities. His job was to look to his legion, but if there was open rebellion, civilians in its path would be caught up in it too. He felt as if they all perched on his head and shoulders, clung to his shirt like starlings fighting for a place in a hawthorn's branches – the ones he hadn't saved, the ones he couldn't save, the ones he might yet save.

Septimus halted his men and squinted through the trees. He could just see the glint of steel, spearpoints catching the afternoon sun. Not many, thirty maybe: the Silures or he was a daffodil.

"We could take them easy, Centurion," Naso said. They were two to one at least.

Septimus shook his head. "Not unless we have to. We want to give the commander a chance to pull him loose without a fight, nor their knowing it was us."

"Why that then? Keep the tribune alive, I can see, but why not know it was us, and give the Silure bastards notice we'll not be having that?"

"Because likely they and Cadal's men will quarrel with each other over who's got him, you see? And that's to our advantage. Our job is to track these and if they get too close to the border with Ordovice lands – that's where they'll make the hand-off for the tribune – *then* we take them out, but not if we don't have to." Not if the primus pilus got to the Ordovices first, brought off his impersonation, and didn't get himself or the tribune killed in the process. Septimus was pessimistic about that outcome, but he had his orders.

A scout materialized between the trees and saluted Septimus. "They're making camp, sir. I counted thirty-two, a couple that might be council lords and thirty spearmen. All mounted."

"Is there a spot to halt where they won't sight our fires?" If they got ahead of the Silures they stood the chance of losing them.

"A ridge north of here and east from them. If we camp on the far side and put a watch up top we'll be able to see when they break camp – they'll have to go past us. They've been staying to the trees, best luck for us. Horses won't outpace us through trees."

Septimus considered the possibilities. They had two days, he thought, before he'd have to take his optio's advice. They would trail Loarn's men out of sight, and then they would either get word from the primus pilus that he had the tribune and they were to back away, or they would have to waylay them.

That was confirmed in the night when the scout crept out of camp, lay in the bracken outside the Silure camp with his ears pricked, and came back again to wake Septimus.

"They're making for Lleu's Well," he said.

"What's that?"

"North two day's march. Near – under – a hill fortress that's from before our day. The place has been abandoned for years, centuries maybe, but the hill sticks up on the skyline like a great tit. I've been there. There's a stinking spring that comes out of the rock a few miles away."

"Stinking springs are holy," Septimus said. "One way or the other. That will be the spot."

"I think so. It's just on the border between the Silures, the Demetae, and the Ordovices and if it's holy it will help bind any bargain they've made."

Septimus rolled over and tried to sleep, but it didn't come, and neither did a dispatch rider from Faustus. Two days later in the gray pre-dawn he rose and stood listening to the birdsong that told him that still no rider came. Nor was the Silure camp half a mile away stirring yet. He shook his watch commander awake as a late-homing bat flitted past them.

"Now. We won't wait any longer. Move them out. Battle order and leave the tents. We'll catch them in camp and be done with it."

—

The Silures had halted in the lee of a stony bluff, studded with wind-bent scrub. The Romans poured from the trees on the other three sides, down bracken-covered slopes and the rocky scree where a shallow stream fed one of the silver rivers that laced the Silure Hills like a fish net. Before they had closed on the camp it was in furious motion. A gray-mustached man in an iron helmet shouted orders, cursing, and a whirr of slingstones flew into the oncoming legionaries as Silure spearmen snatched up weapons and bridled their ponies. Mounted in haste, they bunched together, pushing at the weakest point in the Roman line, trying to shove through before they were trapped. They were outnumbered, but on horseback and spear-armed they held the Romans off at first until the legionaries closed ranks, pushing them back against the bluff. Two went down before slingstones hurled by retreating horsemen trying to scramble up the hillside, and another under the hooves of a rider forcing his pony through the advancing shield wall of the attackers. The pony and its rider were cut down and the shield wall stepped over them.

The Romans went for the horses, smaller than Roman troop horses, and for the riders' legs, hacking with the sharp, short legionary sword that could either stab or slash. They used their heavy shields to block downward driving spears, duck under, shove at the spearmen, push them off their saddles. The loose horses panicked and scattered, trampling unhorsed Britons. The Romans opened ranks to let them go and closed again.

The gray-mustached man and a second helmeted warrior rallied the spearmen around them, lordly figures in ring mail and gold at the battle's center, armed with long swords; weapons that like the war spears had been treaty-banned. The Romans pushed harder, trying to close the circle completely, bunch them up until they could no longer fight. The Roman shield ring in places was still only one man deep.

The gray-haired lord swung his sword at Septimus. Septimus pushed his shield into the blow, staggering from the force of it. His watch commander, in the line beside him, took the Briton through the throat with a slash of his short sword that cut through the helmet strap and sent it spinning away. The man fell in a gout of blood that soaked the ground and slicked the rock under their feet until Septimus lost his footing again.

With a bellow of fury, the other lord spun his mount around, put his heels to its flanks, and rode it hard at the shield ring where it was weakest. The pony leapt, higher than Septimus would have thought it could, clearing the heads of legionaries who swung their swords up in haste and tried to gut it as it passed. Then horse and rider were down the other side and gone at a gallop into the trees.

—

The Ordovices halted at Lleu's Well, tied the tribune to the ill-gaited pony he had ridden from Bryn Epona, and the pony to a tree while the rest dismounted, stretched, and shared a loaf of bread and skin of mead.

Neither Cadal nor Loarn would come to the exchange that would deliver him to the Silures. Both were too wary and too wily, nor did either expect the other to appear. The matter would be done by proxy between council lords, each bearing their king's ring in proof of authority.

The tribune's stomach rumbled. They had not fed him since morning and plainly did not plan to. His escort had amused themselves on the four-day ride by prodding him with their spearpoints when he slumped in the saddle, and decking themselves in his silvered cuirass and greaves, posing and declaring themselves Caesar come to rule West Britain. His threats of crucifixion when he was restored to his office were met with hoots of laughter by those who understood some Latin and translated for the rest, and who held his own sword to his throat and grinned. It was only this morning that he had realized he was not being ransomed back to Rome but was to be given to the Silures. An evil smell rose from the spring that bubbled out of the rocks where they had halted and hung in the air like an emanation from the Underworld. He shivered. The land was hilly, high wild country under a leaden sky and inhabited only by wild things. The night had been shattered by the scream of something in an owl's talons.

The scent of brimstone in the air suggested to Faustus's party that they had most likely come to the meeting place. Lleu's Well was an ancient treaty site. Faustus settled himself in his pony's saddle, sitting loosely to shed the telltale posture drilled into every soldier since his first march, by centurions with vine staves. Aurelius Rotri drew rein beside him. Rotri had taught Faustus that particular talent in the north. It was an ability that all the border wolves possessed and Rotri inspected them as they readied themselves, checking everything, the false tribal patterns on their faces, the way they held their reins, sat their mounts. The only Roman thing among them was a cavalry horn, its length cut short and hidden in the pack of a border wolf from the auxiliaries at Moridunum.

"Go," Rotri said, and melted into the trees to wait. If the Ordovices wouldn't know him, the tribune would, or should, and was too likely to give that away, in Rotri's estimation.

Faustus and his men made no secret of their presence now, moving through the green tree shadow with a show of grumbling conversation of saddle-weariness and thirst. Faustus snapped at them to be less querulous: "This is a holy place."

An Ordovice sentry met them before they reached the spring. He stared at Faustus. "What do you want here?"

"I am Rhys," Faustus said. "Captain to Loarn."

"You are bare-faced and shorn," the sentry said.

"Yes. It was punishment. I have no need to speak to you of it. The king has entrusted me with this." He held out his right hand, a heavy gold ring on the forefinger, red stone carved with a horned moon.

The sentry hesitated. "It may be you bring ill luck."

"Are you Cadal's envoy?" Faustus snapped. "If not, that is not for you to decide."

"Ill luck for the Roman, anyway," the sentry said. He seemed to decide. "Follow me and remember there are more watching."

The spring came from a cleft in a tree-covered hillside, thick-shaded by spreading oak, ash, and hazel, the stones moss-covered, the damp ground green with leaves of the little woodland flowers that had bloomed and faded again with summer. Cadal's envoy, marked by his wealth of gold and lordly air, sat on a fallen log some distance from the spring. Faustus saw the tribune tied to a pony nearby, bruised but apparently otherwise unharmed, and he let out a breath of relief. He halted his horse beside the spring and dismounted while Cadal's man watched him silently. Faustus took a silver piece from the bag at his belt, touched his forehead in respect, and laid it in the spring water. Only then did he speak to the envoy.

"I am Rhys, king's captain to Loarn." He extended his hand to let the Ordovice see the ring.

"I am Ula." Cadal's man kept one hand on his belt knife. "Why are you shorn?"

"It is punishment," Faustus said.

"For what?"

"For matters that are private to me and to my king and to the Druids." Faustus glared at him.

"The Druids decreed this?" Ula raised his eyebrows. The Druids rarely meddled in personal matters, unless it was one of sacrilege. Still, they had left him alive. "And these men still follow you?" A man that much disgraced was lucky to live much less to command loyalty from others of his tribe.

"Rhys's fate is not yours to question," one of the border wolves snapped.

Ula's men stiffened. They glared at Faustus's men and the border wolves glared back, lordly-wise themselves, the flowing mustaches and dark hair tied at their necks in stark contrast to their leader's shorn face and head.

They were a dozen strong, even numbers with the Ordovices. Ula might consider that Loarn's man would need more than that to get the tribune back through his own lands, if the Romans got wind of it, but that was not his affair. Ula would have no illusions that the Romans were ignorant of who was behind the tribune's abduction – they had been hunting him since he was taken. They just had no proof and a tenuous treaty they did not want to overset. Loarn would overset it soon enough and the Ordovices would enlarge their borders afterward. Still, Faustus thought Ula might be eager to get the man off his hands.

"How long has it been since you let him off his horse?" Faustus asked when Ula sat unspeaking as his men and Faustus's eyed each other.

"Since morning," Ula said.

"He probably needs to piss," Faustus said. "Take him down now. And his armor and weapons." He could see a pair of silvered greaves tied behind a saddle.

"Those were not part of the bargain," Ula told him. He seemed unconcerned about the tribune's bladder.

"They were," Faustus said, guessing. "I am not a fool."

Ula shrugged. "Do you speak for Loarn? Do you have authority to bind him to a treaty?"

"The armor," Faustus said. He held his hand out again to show the ring. "And take him off the horse."

"I don't trust a man with shorn hair."

"Did Cadal tell you to decide whether you liked Loarn's envoy? Or did he tell you to give the Roman to us? And where is Cadal's token that I may know you have not stolen the man from Cadal yourself?"

The day was growing warm. The paint that the border wolves used would stick, Rotri had said, but don't wipe your face. Faustus resisted the urge to. His neck itched. A cuckoo somewhere in the forest was wooing a wife with its maddening *cuck-koo cuck-koo cuck-koo*.

Ula seemed to come to a decision. He held out his hand to display a ring set with squares of carnelian and green chalcedony that covered nearly all of his thumb. "Take him down," he told his men. "And bring his belongings." To Faustus he said, "The horse is not his."

Faustus knew that to be true since Terentius's centurion had ridden back to Deva on it, and this was a native pony. Terentius had had a slave with him, but there was no way to admit knowing that. "Agreed," he said. He motioned to one of his men who brought up a horse with an empty saddle.

Ula's men began to untie the tribune. The man was white-faced under the bruises and clothed only in what looked like his undertunic.

"Put his armor on him," Faustus said with a grin. "Let him wear it one last time. I've no mind to encumber my own gear with it."

Ula's men brought it out then, laughing, and made the tribune lift his undertunic and piss in front of them if he wanted to – he had to – amid jokes about the size of his balls. Then they pulled his silver-mounted harness tunic over his head, none too gently, and his silvered cuirass over that. Faustus took the tribune's belt with his dagger and sword and buckled it around his own waist. He pointed at the tribune's bare feet.

"Did he have boots, then?"

One of Ula's men scratched his head and laughed. "Must have been lost. We were in a rush, you see."

Terentius, driven to fury shouted in Latin, "I had boots! They were new. Red boots. He has them." He pointed to one of Ula's men, who mimicked looking around him for boots.

"Be quiet and maybe you'll get to Porth Cerrig with both your ears," Faustus told Terentius. The threat was clear from his tone and the tribune fell silent. "Tie his hands in front and get him in the saddle," Faustus told his men. They heaved the tribune onto the pony and tied his wrists again, this time to the saddle horns. One of the wolves took his reins.

"I will agree that boots were not in the bargain," Faustus told Ula, mounting. The back of his neck itched with the urge to be gone.

The shrill alarm call of a sparrowhawk made him jerk his head up. The cuckoo fell silent. A cloud of rooks flew up from the tree canopy to the south and a magpie's rattle joined the alarm. Something was coming fast through the trees.

Faustus took the bag of silver off the saddle horns and tossed it at Ula. They had no way to know what Loarn had offered but the amount in the bag was generous. By the time Ula had counted it they had better be gone.

"Ride!" Faustus shouted while Ula and his men were still staring into the forest.

They rode at full gallop through the trees, leading the tribune's mount and risking the ponies' legs, not waiting to see what was coming. It would not be anything to favor them. Rotri fell in with them as they went and the cavalry wolf from Moridunum pulled out his horn and put it to his lips. The high-pitched scream of the horn rang in their ears. He blew it as they rode, then blew it again. The Ordovices would hear the horn too, but there was little point in trying to disguise their purpose now.

—

Ula was in a rage, bellowing orders at his own men, at the Silure rider who had come crashing through the trees, at Faustus's fleeing riders to halt.

"Romans!" the Silure rider gasped. "Waylaid! Where is the hostage?"

"With your men!" Ula said. "And if not, then they are false or you are." His men surrounded the rider and pulled him from his horse. Ula took him by the throat. "Now tell me which!"

"Romans!" the rider said again, furious now. He was mud-covered and bloodied, his horse lathered and heaving, head low. "I am Pwyll, envoy of Loarn. Romans waylaid us and I was the only one escaped them. And you have let him go with someone else?"

Now they heard the horn.

"He had Loarn's ring!" Ula shouted in his face. "What have you?"

Pwyll shook his fist back in Ula's face, a fist with a red stone carved with a horned moon.

"Ride!" Ula snapped. He looked at Pwyll and snorted. "If you can." The horn sounded again, and his face grew scarlet with fury.

—

Faustus's wolves thundered through the trees, dodging low-hanging branches that threatened to sweep the tribune from his seat. There was no time to stop and cut him loose, to let him have the reins. Terentius was clutching the horns of his saddle, bent over and trying to untie the knots with his teeth.

Faustus shouted, "We are Roman!" at him but the tribune looked uncomprehending. Faustus cursed him, hoping the ties would hold. He and his wolves would likely have to stop and fight, risking that the column was close enough to back them, and Terentius would be a liability.

Faustus listened for the Ordovices behind them now. Whatever had been coming through the trees had most likely eluded Septimus and if so, Ula knew he had been fooled. A slingstone went past his ear to confirm that and he wished desperately for his helmet and lorica. He ducked low over the pony's neck. The Roman road was two miles east by his estimate, the column somewhere along it and it would have to march cross-country to intercept them. They had not known until today where the meeting place was to be, had had to guess, to let the column trail them far enough away not to be seen by Cadal's men, close enough to march if need be, a desperate geometry of chance and supposition.

The trees thinned and there was open ground, a small valley, and another of the hundreds of streams that wound through the Silure Hills. Beyond was bog land; he could see the water shining here and there, mirroring the pewter sky. A lot of it would be dangerous. The Ordovices might know the safe paths, but he didn't. The road would be on the other side. They could follow the river to it maybe.

Faustus swung them down the streambank, keeping to the clear ground where he could, thrusting their way through trees again where they encroached on the water, watching for patches of 'soft' masked as shallows. The ponies' hooves splashed up mud and made squelching noises at each step. The Ordovices were hard behind them. Rotri had taken the tribune's reins and was shouting at him in Latin. Terentius nodded now, recognizing him and seeming to comprehend, and Rotri gave him his reins, slowing enough to fling the offside rein across the pony's neck. The tribune clutched them in his bound hands and Rotri pulled his spear and shield free of their bindings.

The cavalry horn sounded again, and Faustus heard an echo returning from the direction of the road.

"Again!" he shouted.

Again the horn wailed, and after it came the reply: two separate tones this time, not an echo but the column taking their direction.

"Keep sounding!"

Another slingstone whirred overhead and thudded into the bare leg of one of the border wolves. He howled but stayed on his horse. His companions began to fire their own stones at the oncoming Ordovices. One pulled an arrow from the quiver on his back and nocked it, turning backward in his saddle. He loosed it at three Ordovice riders grouped together, horses flank to flank, and hit the right hand man in the shoulder.

The stream flowed into a broader one, running in an old channel cut over centuries through rock. It was brown and frothing with runoff from the rain, but the ground along it was drier, tufted with grass, and the ponies' hoofbeats were solid on it. Faustus wrapped his reins around his saddle horns long enough to unbuckle the tribune's sword belt. He hung it across the saddle in front of him and shouted to Rotri, "Untie him when you can!"

They would have to turn and fight soon. The ground here was better but likely not to stay that way. The Silure Hills and all of West Britain were woven with bogs, springs, rivers that erupted from the rock and vanished again, marsh, and flood meadow that dried and refilled seasonally. He wouldn't risk the Ordovices driving them into bog. Whether Ula would risk losing the tribune by doing that would depend on how angry Ula was, and Faustus's guess was that he was very angry. The Ordovices were stiff-necked and did not take well to insult, as Cadal had proved. And they were very close, their howling war cries coming clear over the drumming hooves. He heard the trumpet from the column again and made up his mind.

"Form up to meet them!" They would have to hold the Ordovices off long enough for the column to catch up, but it was near. The column's centurion would have had scouts in and out of the land beyond the road; they would know the ground with more accuracy than Faustus could guess at.

They halted on solid ground beyond the stream and made a ring around the tribune. Rotri cut the bindings with his dagger and Faustus handed Terentius his sword belt.

Terentius took it and buckled the belt about his cuirass. His mouth was a tight angry line. Faustus wasn't sure who he was angry at. Everyone probably.

"Stay behind us and don't try to fight them unless you have to," he told Terentius, "and if you have to, it will have gone to Hades so you might as well."

"Who are you?" Terentius snapped. "I doubt you are senior to my rank!"

"I doubt it too," Faustus said, "but you will take my orders until we have you clear, or I'll give you back to the Ordovices."

There was no more time to argue with him. The Ordovice band fell on Faustus's men, spears out, shields up, angry at being made fools of. Ula went straight for Faustus and Faustus brought his shield up to drive Ula's spear sideways and down, thrust with his own at Ula's face and missed. Rotri was beside him, heaving a broken spear into the Ordovice ranks and drawing his sword.

The Ordovice men were warrior-trained; spear brothers since childhood and veterans of the ceaseless border raids that pitted small bands of similarly armed men against each other. They fanned out around Faustus's men, angling to come at their rear. The border wolves too were brothers under the skin, even those who had been strangers until now, and more importantly they were Roman soldiers beneath their long hair and insubordinate outlook. They locked their ponies into a defensive line, spears out, a bristling barricade around the tribune. Spear and shield clashed against spear and shield. Two of the border wolves fell, one dead, the other rolling from under his pony's hooves as he bled from a spear thrust to his collar. Among the Ordovices, three went down, and the loose ponies fled through the battle, breaking lines open, some of them bleeding from wounds, some merely panicked.

Like Faustus's wolves, the Ordovices wore no armor except for Ula, whose shirt was covered by a coat of ring mail. A slingstone hit Ula in the chest as he shifted his shield arm to strike at Faustus again and he slumped back in the saddle. Ula righted himself, but the force of the stone would have driven mail through his shirt into flesh and he would likely begin to bleed internally. Faustus pressed his advantage while Ula tried to lift his shield. The sentry who had mistrusted his shorn head thrust his spear under Faustus's shield into his thigh. Faustus slammed the shield edge down on the spearshaft as the man pulled it back. He pressed past the spearpoint to bring the shield up again against the man's face, dropped his own spear and drew his sword, driving it under the sentry's guard. The sentry fell and his mount trampled him in panic. Faustus felt blood streaming down his leg. It pooled on the ground, and he swayed in the saddle. Rotri was beside him then, reaching to knot a cloth around his thigh, drawing it tight, grunting with the effort. The blood slowed somewhat. Faustus's head swam. The trumpet from the column blared.

"Get off before you fall off!" Rotri pulled at his arm. The sun shimmered in his eyes, brighter than it should have been through cloud, limning the steel of the column, the silver standards of two centuries, the sanguine splotches of tunic and helmet crest, redder than the blood.

Rotri caught him as he slid from the saddle. He laid Faustus on the ground and added his belt to the bloody rag around his thigh, pulling it tighter. Faustus tried frantically to see what was happening. The roar of the battle came as if through a layer of wool. He tried to sit up.

"Lie down!" someone snapped – the medic from his own century, easing his trouser leg up past the wound, tightening another tie-off about his thigh, carefully unknotting the first ones. "Be still!" the medic said again. "We've got them, but they nearly got you and I need to stop this bleeding. This just missed the big artery and it's torn a nasty hole coming out. Sir," he added as an afterthought.

"The tribune," Faustus said, gritting his teeth.

"He's here and trying to order our men about but Septimus isn't having it, so you can relax."

"Septimus?"

"They caught up to us this morning." The medic pressed a thick pad to the wound and eased the tie-off from around the leg. Blood soaked the pad, but it was slowing.

The sound of battle faded to angry shouts and the scream of an injured horse. Rotri disappeared and then came back again to report that after one last furious onslaught the Ordovices had fled at the advent of a column nearly three centuries strong. Four were dead and Ula rode slumped in his saddle.

"He'll not live to tell Cadal the tale," Rotri said.

"And ours?" Faustus asked him.

"One lost – Natta. Merula took a slingstone to his leg, and it's probably broken. Nasica got a spear in the shoulder. He'll be all right if it doesn't heal twisted."

"Centurion!" Tribune Terentius stood over Faustus. The feathers cresting his helmet were sodden and he was splattered with mud but uninjured.

"Tribune." Faustus looked up at him and nodded.

"I must be in Deva as soon as possible. On a decent mount."

"We are closer to Isca," Faustus said, trying to fix his focus on him. "I am to report to my legate there and would be ill advised to split my detachment here to send you north." He paused. "The Ordovices will not be above hunting you north if anyone is foolish enough to give them the chance."

"And thank you, Centurion, for saving my ass," Rotri muttered.

Terentius snapped his head around at Rotri.

"Regrettably, you must ride with us until we reach Magnis," Faustus said. "There will probably be a troop horse available there, and an escort to Deva."

"You have threatened me and been insubordinate, Centurion." Terentius's fingers tried to adjust his sash of office and found it missing.

"Verisimilitude," Faustus said faintly. The sky kept spinning overhead. The medic was picking threads of cloth from the wound with tweezers.

"You encouraged them to make sport of me."

Faustus pulled his wits together. "Tribune, you would otherwise be dead, once Loarn had extracted all the information he desired from you. The extraction would have been painful. We have forestalled that. And you are not dead."

"Information?"

"The fact that half of your legion and its legate are in Eburacum was not something we could allow to be told to Loarn," Faustus said flatly. "So mull over the ways we could have prevented it."

Terentius started to bristle, then was silent. His face had gone white again. "You would have killed me?"

"I would."

"It would have been easy," Rotri said. "An arrow from the trees and we're gone. But you're one of ours, Tribune, so we came after you."

"I see," Terentius said. "It would have been simpler to kill me, wouldn't it?"

"Well, your father wouldn't have liked it," Faustus said.

"He wouldn't. All the same, I'd still be dead. Very well, Centurion, I understand."

Faustus thought of asking him if he understood that he had now pushed them all into war. Instead, he said, "You had a slave with you." He wondered if the boy had fought for his master and paid with his life for that.

"The wretched beast asked safe haven of Cadal and he took him into his household," Terentius said, angry again now.

Faustus grinned, then changed it to a grimace before Terentius saw it.

"I need boots," Terentius said, remembering that injustice as well.

"Magnis," Faustus said. He lay back, signaling an end to what he would discuss. Terentius could go and gnaw his helmet feathers.

The medic inspected Faustus's leg and pressed another wad of wound dressing to it. "You'll do, sir, if I bandage this tightly. I'd rather you were on a litter though."

"Carried by these?" Faustus looked at his men, loricas shining, barely bloodied, and jaunty at their rout of the Ordovices. Being carried by them was a last resort. "Even that hill pony has a better gait." The little horse, placidly cropping grass nearby, snorted at him.

"Very well, sir. As long as we camp here tonight, and you don't move until morning."

"I have no intention of it," Faustus said. He still felt light-headed, as if he was floating on the trampled, bloody grass. The air felt like a warm hand on his skin. He watched a flock of crows settle on the spreading branches of an elm, their bright eyes cocked at the bodies on the ground. "The Ordovices will come back for their dead when we're gone. But move them away from our camp."

"Crows will start in first," Rotri said.

"Crows feed snakes, snakes feed the boar, the boar feeds us, we feed crows," Faustus said. "But put Natta over a saddle before he stiffens, and get a tent over him."

Faustus looked up at the sky, brightening from the morning's pewter to blue strung with cobweb wisps of cloud. Two soaring shapes rode the currents of the air. Buzzards, he thought at first, by the fanned feathers of their wingtips and the blunt wedges of their tails, but they were too large. Eagles. Messenger birds of Jupiter, emblem and personification of the legions. A hunting pair. A red kite sat on the edge of a spinney, watching a patch of grass but when the eagles dropped down into the cover of the trees, it flapped away from them. The larger of the eagles shot from the spinney, rose with nothing but flew on, fast over the grass, driving something. The second circled, dove, came up with the hare in her talons.

We are all birds of prey, Faustus thought foggily. *The Britons are like the red kite and hunt what they can, but we are the Empire's eagles that take what we want.*

XV. MEMORY AND FORGETTING

Thorn trotted through the garden rows toward his sisters, picking beans with the boy and the Old One, Fox. "The Sun People are buzzing like hornets that someone has heaved a rock at," he said. Thorn had heard them, crouched in the shadows of the landward ditch. The men that Loarn had sent north hadn't come back, except for one. Then another Ordovice rider had come south, and there had been shouting when he spoke with Loarn.

"That is nothing to do with us," Badger said. She looked at Sedge. "Except for this one, maybe."

The boy shook his head. "Those are not my people."

"Who are not?" Fox asked quickly.

"The... the Silures," he said without thinking. "Not really. Or the Ordovices." He paused. A memory came suddenly, sharp as crystal: a wooden horse. His mother, and a man in Roman uniform. *Come and meet your Uncle Faustus. He is going to be your father now.*

Fox pressed him, fishing for whatever image had risen. "What is your name?"

"Lucius," he told her, not knowing quite where it had come from. But it fit. It was his. It settled on him like a cloak.

Fox smiled, approving. "Does your head hurt?"

"No," he said, realizing that it didn't.

"And where do you come from?"

"I..." He almost knew that too, but the name went away. Four great columns, a river. A house with a lion painted on the wall beside his bed. He shook his head, but nothing more came. Except… no, it was gone.

"You are beginning to come back to yourself," Fox said, "but you cannot rush it."

"Lucius is a Roman name," Plover said helpfully.

"We know that, stupid," Owl told her. She looked unhappy. "Mind your own business."

Plover threw a clod of dirt at her, and Owl threw it back.

Roman, Sedge-who-was-Lucius thought. *I am Roman.* That felt right too. He turned the thought into Latin, and it sat neatly in his mind. He had been thinking in British among Owl's people because it was what they understood, but Latin felt like his own tongue. He plucked at the image of the wooden horse and the man in armor to see if any more threads would come loose. They had been speaking Latin.

"The Old One at Ty Isaf says that there was a battle at Lleu's Well," Fox said thoughtfully now. "Between Ordovice men and Silures — maybe — those didn't look right to her. And then Romans. And another fight south of there between Romans and Loarn's men. That will be why they did not come back but one."

He didn't ask Fox how the Old One at Ty Isaf knew, or how she spoke to her. The people of the hills had a language of drums and whistles and bird calls that could take a message for miles under the noses of the Sun People.

The tilled earth of the bean rows was warm under his bare feet, holding the last of the afternoon sun. There was a garden where he had come from too, more orderly than this one, laid out in straight lines with herbs and flowers all along the edges, and a sundial in the middle. Why had he been on a horse along the cliff road, to be pulled from it and thrown over, a thing he still didn't remember? A feeling of shame came to him when he thought about it. He thought he should not have been there.

The Old One had gone back to the beans but he saw her watching him, bright eye cocked toward him like a wren, waiting to see if he remembered more. He felt enormous next to her. He had grown just in the three months he had been in Blaidd Llwyd. He was a cuckoo in her nest, and maybe Badger was right – a danger if there was going to be a war between the Silures and the Romans or the Silures and the Ordovices, or all three.

He said so worriedly to Owl as they were spreading the bean pods to dry on a wicker frame. Would they send him away? To where?

"Loarn's men and Cadal's fight each other for amusement," Owl said disgustedly. She thought a moment, "But I will tell you another thing. The Old One at Ty Isaf told our Old One that Cadal took a Roman officer out of his bed at night and tried to sell him to Loarn. That is what will bring your people, if they are yours, in."

"I think they are mine," he said.

Owl nodded. "We think so. But you are ours too, many mothers back." She frowned. "The Old One promised not to send you to them unless you remember whether it is safe."

"I'm trying," he said. "Someone else told me that we had your blood, I think, someone of my own people. I wish I could think who. Maybe it was my uncle." He knew somehow that it would not have been his mother.

"Your uncle?" Plover asked, arranging beans on the drying rack, making a pattern with them.

"Faustus," he said. "He's my mother's brother. We had to come live with him." He shook his head hoping more knowledge would slide out.

Plover and Rail cocked their heads at him as Fox had, listening to see if it did. Badger was silent, her small fingers separating beans on the rack, but he could feel her eyes on him too. Only Owl didn't seem to wish to know.

"Do you know your mother's name?" Plover asked.

"Silvia," he said. It floated to the surface of his memory, another small certainty.

He heard a quick intake of breath from someone. "Roman names all sound alike," Owl said. "And mean less." She tapped him on the shoulder. "Go and tell Grandmother we need a cover for these. It's going to rain again tonight." Dusk was falling. The shrill voices of crickets and the rattling call of a nightjar filled the twilight.

—

"That is where the boy's old blood came from," Badger said furiously to Fox. "I told you he was dangerous."

"It is possible," the Old One said. She was stirring yarrow and bearberry in a bronze pot, boiling it down for salve. She kept her eyes on the surface, skimming off the scum as it formed.

"He is!" Badger insisted. She squatted beside Fox on the hearth, glaring at her.

Owl stamped through the doorway, "He isn't your business, Badger!"

"Just because you think you can keep him for a pet," Badger said.

"He is not a pet!"

"You'd as well bring home an adder. He'll have Sun Men breaking open our houses, trampling our gardens. The Romans and Loarn's men will both be looking for him!"

"Likely," Fox admitted. "If that is who he is, then it was Loarn's men who threw him over the cliff."

The people of Blaidd Llwyd made it their business to know what went on in Porth Cerrig. The new king's determination to wed the Roman woman had been talked over from all sides and opinions. The consensus had been that it was no business of the people of the hills; the sidhe blood in the Silure royal house was diluted over many generations. But if this boy was the son of the new queen, then Loarn had every reason to wish him dead. All in all, it explained a great deal.

Fox sighed. "I will talk with him. You are not to." She looked at them to be sure they were listening, particularly Owl and Badger. "None of you."

Lucius was turning the beans over on the drying rack and watching the sky the next afternoon when the Old One came and sat down on the grass beside him under the leather roof that was stretched between four poles.

"There is a storm coming," he told her. "Not just rain. These need to be moved maybe. If this wind strengthens, they'll be wet."

Fox cocked her head to the trees. The leaves of a tall poplar were turning their pale undersides to the air. "Likely," she agreed. "We'll take them in before it starts, you and I. They can finish drying by the fire, don't you think?"

"Gwladus dries peas in the kitchen," Lucius said. He looked at Fox, startled. Who was Gwladus? He could see her at the stove with Paullus, arguing over seasoning a fish.

Fox smiled. "It's coming, isn't it? It will come best when we sneak up on it, as we just did. Who were your mother's people?"

"We had a house in Narbo Martius," Lucius said, trying just to answer and not think first. "Until Father died." That scrap came unbidden. "Her mother was Silure but they are *not* my people." That too, with a furious emphasis. He put his fingers to his temples. "My head hurts now."

"That is enough for this evening," Fox said. "You can help me get these beans in."

Beans were solid things, Lucius thought, piling them in a basket. Homey, comfortable, something you could put away for the winter. He wouldn't be here by winter, he knew that now. Even as he worked, he felt memories sliding into his conscious mind, like fish slipping free from a bucket back to the water. As they swam past, he saw his mother, Uncle Faustus, the primus pilus's house in Isca Fortress – he knew its name, and the name of the gray dog asleep by the brazier in the atrium beneath the household gods and the painted octopus swimming in green water.

Did they think he was dead, he wondered, those people in the Roman fort? Did they know who had pulled him from his horse? He still did not – could not – remember that. After the evening meal of eel broth with barley and wild greens, when as always he tried not to eat too much of what these small people grew, he crept out of the dwelling in the hillside to sit under the black sky and wait for the storm. He didn't know what it would tell him, but the air felt alive, full of portent. The wind blew his hair, longer now, around his face and a moth caught in its stream tumbled by. Everything was being carried on that wind to somewhere else.

Owl appeared, as if the wind had brought her too. "I'm not supposed to be here," she said, sitting down beside him.

He turned to her, glad of her company. "Why not?"

"The Old One said so, while she thinks about who you are, but I don't care." She smacked her small fist on her knee.

"Maybe she has reasons," Lucius said.

"It's because of the new queen," Owl said. "Loarn's new queen. And I still don't see why you can't stay with us. With me," she added.

"I don't understand."

Owl sighed. "I don't either."

"I don't think I can stay," Lucius said helplessly. Somewhere in the still walled-off part of his mind was the reason his presence threatened these small and vulnerable ones.

"You belong to me," Owl said stubbornly.

He touched her cheek with his fingertips. "But I can't stay. I am danger. I don't know quite why, but I know that much."

She laid her head against his shoulder. Her dark hair was braided with two blue beads like eyes that reflected the faint light from the storm sky. The rest of her was a warm dark shadow against him. "You'll forget about me," she said.

"I will not." He put his arm around her small waist.

"You will need to," she said practically. "If you are Roman, you will need to forget we are here."

—

The snatches of memory were still jumbled when it began to rain and they fled into the hillside, but two mornings later he woke with them all in place. The Old One was standing by his bed, watchful.

"You have come back to yourself," she said as he sat up and pushed the blanket away.

He had to lift his head only a little to meet her gaze. In another month they would have been at eye level; he sitting and she standing. He would not be here another month.

"I come from the Roman fort at Isca Silurum, on the river," he said because he might as well get it over with. "My uncle is the primus pilus of the legion there."

The Old One nodded. "We thought so. The Old One at Llanmelin says they have raised a gravestone for you."

Lucius's stomach lurched. His family thought he was dead, and they were not conjecture anymore but intimate to him, and now heartsick. "My mother…"

"Your mother has wed the king of the Silures," Fox said flatly. "Does that tell you anything about who pulled you from your horse?"

His stomach turned over again. He remembered, shamefully, wheedling his way into accompanying the patrol, but still nothing past that, not until he woke in Blaidd Llwyd.

"I still can't remember it."

"It doesn't matter. You may not get that part back ever. Sometimes that happens."

"When did she marry him? My uncle will be furious. I told her if she did, that I wouldn't go with her."

"That was prudent of you," Fox said.

"When did she marry him?"

"When Loarn thought you were dead no doubt," Fox said. "Think, child. Who would want a son of Loarn's new queen by another man, out of their way?"

"Why? I wasn't going to go with her." The certainty of that came clearly, and the battles they had waged over it.

"Perhaps not just then. But you cannot tell me that certain things did not occur to the Roman commander. You have the same lineage as your mother. You would make a king who could be set over the Silures and impose Rome's will. The Romans are far thinking."

"The legate would not—" He stopped. Caecilius would. Caecilius had wanted Mother to marry the Silure king. He thought it would forestall war. Or he thought... thought exactly what the Old One was suggesting. Lucius put his head in his hands. "Mother couldn't have known," he said miserably.

"No. They think you fell when your horse balked."

"Uncle Faustus doesn't think that," Lucius said with certainty. Uncle Faustus had taught him to ride. He looked up at her. "What do I do now?"

"You must go back to your people. To Isca fort, not to your mother."

"Yes. Of course." He felt stupid, his head thick with too much new knowledge.

"And you must go now," Fox said softly.

Lucius looked around the small stone walled chamber. The bow that Thorn had taught him to use stood against the wall with his mended boots. Besides that, he had only his belt with its empty scabbard and the tunic he was fast outgrowing.

Fox saw his eyes light on the bow. "You must leave that. It is not good that you remember your time among us."

"I won't forget," he said indignantly. "You or Owl or—"

"You will," she said. "And Owl must. You and Owl – that is not a good idea. Put your boots on, Lucius."

They gave him only time to go into the bushes and piss, and then Fox and Thorn were leading him away. It was barely light. The dawn birdsong filled the trees. Owl tried to come, but Fox sent her back again, sobbing.

"That one should not know where you are," Fox said. She reached into the sack at her waist and handed him a barley cake. "Eat this. It is a very long walk to Isca."

"I don't know how to get there," Lucius said, terrified now that they would send him alone into the forest.

"We will stay by you until you are in sight of the fort," Fox said. "Did you think we would not guide you?"

"I didn't know," Lucius said, shamefaced. "You have been kind to me, but…"

"But now we are making you leave us? It is the way of things, child."

"I am not a child."

"You are," Thorn said. "You are a great large child, even though you are taller than we are. You are somewhat quieter on the trail than you were when you came to us—"

"Owl taught me," Lucius muttered.

"But you are still like a boar trying to come into a badger sett and you will draw the Romans to us, *and* the Silures."

Lucius was silent at that. He followed Fox and Thorn along ways that stretched beyond where he had roamed with Owl, paths he could not see at all even looking as she had showed him for the small signs of trodden stem or snapped twig. It was high summer, and the world was deep green, the forest laced with the black contorted limbs of oak, with rushing brooks that fed streams and then rivers, with limestone outcrops, deep pools with otter slides, and mossy shallows where dipper birds hunted mayfly larvae and fish eggs. The people of the hills moved silently, and Lucius had indeed learned from them. The wild ones watched them go by and were not alarmed until Thorn took up his bow and shot a hare. The otter dived into his pool and the noise of wren and woodpecker stilled. They cooked the hare in a damp glade, hastily because it was beginning to rain again, and before they had eaten it the forest noise began to murmur around them once more, blending with the curtain of the rain.

Twice where there was no ford they swam. Fox and Thorn cut through the water like otters and Lucius followed, climbing up shivering on the far bank while Thorn and the Old One shook themselves off and beckoned him onward. It was well into the long summer twilight and his legs ached when they came within sight of the Isca River estuary. They followed the riverbank north in the dimming light until Lucius saw the lanterns on Isca Bridge glowing ahead of them.

Fox put her hand on his shoulder. "We will leave you here." She smiled at him, not unkindly. "You are home now. We will fade from your mind in a day or so. Let us go."

Lucius looked from her face and Thorn's to the lanterns on the bridge. "It is night already, Grandmother. Where will you sleep?"

Thorn turned away. "Go home now, Sun Man's boy. What does it matter to you where we sleep?"

"I don't know," Lucius said. He felt bewildered. They had been kind to him, even Thorn, and now they would drive him from them.

"This is how it must be." The Old One put a hand up to his face. "Go back to your own world. You cannot live in two places, nor take anything of us with you."

"Owl," he said unhappily. "Tell her—"

"No." Fox turned away too and then both of them were gone.

Lucius walked toward the bridge. The lanterns cast his image in multiple shadows across it. In the vicus the hot food stalls were lit with torches and hanging lamps. Shouts of laughter came from a tavern and a quarrel from the apartment above a fishmonger's shuttered stall. He trudged past them, battered by so many sounds and smells, dodging a cart full of bricks left in the street, until he came to the fortress gates.

—

"Your uncle's here." The senior surgeon of the Second Augusta prodded him in the shoulder and Lucius looked up, uncertain of where he was. He had slept the day around and it was twilight again. The small ward in the Isca hospital was whitewashed and cool, its window shuttered. There was no one else in the other bed. Faustus, his face drained of color, stood over him, dressed for some reason in ragged blue and red checked trousers.

"Uncle?" Lucius stared at him to be certain.

Faustus dropped to his knees beside the cot. "They told me you were here as soon as I got in, oh thank the gods, where have you been?" The words spilled out one on top of the other.

Lucius tried to think. The Old One had been right. His memory of Blaidd Llwyd was dimming. He struggled to call it back. "Owl," he said, the British word.

"What owl?"

"Her. She found me. She lives in the hillside."

"With the little dark people?" Faustus pressed him. "Where?" Not at Llanmelin, or they would have told him.

Lucius opened his mouth but the name of Blaidd Llwyd wouldn't come.

"You've been gone three months," Faustus said.

"Have I? They sent me back... When I remembered."

"Remembered?"

"You. Isca. Everything. I didn't before."

"He's had a blow to his head," the surgeon said. "See here." He lifted Lucius's hair to show the healing scar. "When memory returns very often the period when the patient couldn't remember fades away instead. We don't seem to be able to keep two selves in our heads at once."

Lucius closed his eyes again.

"He'll need to rest. Leave him here until tomorrow and then take him home and have someone keep an eye on him. Your wife has been to see him. She'll know what to do. The mind is fragile after an injury."

"Thank you for your care of him."

Lucius heard them murmuring together as they left the ward. He sank into a dream of wet green woods and a brown girl like an otter.

"There is blood on those disgusting trousers and you're limping," the surgeon said to Faustus in the corridor. "Let's have a look at it."

Faustus sat obediently where the surgeon directed him and stripped off the red and blue checked trousers.

"Hmmph." He peered beneath the bandages and then unwrapped them. "Not a bad job by your medic. And you were lucky. Mithras, an inch over and you'd have come back over your horse."

"So he said."

"I'm going to clean this and redress it. Let me look at it again on the overmorrow. I think it will heal cleanly, but it's going to scar."

"I am not renowned for the beauty of my legs." Faustus gritted his teeth while the surgeon cleaned the wound with vinegar and rebandaged it. It ached but it didn't feel hot. He thought that was probably a good sign.

By the time he stood outside the hospital and took a deep breath to still the shaking in his rebandaged leg, the evening sky was beginning to darken and show the stars above the trees beyond the vicus. The surgeon had given him a stick to lean on until he retrieved his vine staff, and had told him to use both and why hadn't he come to get that leg looked at first thing?

Faustus had sent a fast rider south to Caecilius while he arranged to get the tribune back where he belonged, and tonight when he reported the legate had been at his dinner and told him to come back in the morning but thank you very much, Centurion, we are pleased with your results. Then Caecilius had told him his boy was back and he hadn't thought of anything else, not even to see Eirian.

As he stood gathering his wits in the hospital portico Eirian appeared out of the dusk and flung her arms around him. "Paullus saw you ride in!"

"I was coming to you next," he said, staggering a little. "I promise you."

She looked up at him, eyes shining. "And Lucius too, you see? Did he tell you where he has been?"

"He doesn't remember well."

She stepped back and linked her arm through his, guiding him toward their house. "You're limping."

"I'll be all right. It was a spear in the thigh. It was just cleaned and dressed again. What did Lucius tell you?"

"Well, it was garbled and mixed with other things. He says in the hillside. I think it must have been some sidhe of the Old Ones but he's forgetting them as he remembers us. The surgeon says that happens."

"I don't care. Only that he's here." There was still probably going to be a war, but Faustus felt a weight sliding from his shoulders like mail slipping off. "I'm filthy and I need a bath and the only clean part of me is under the bandage, but can I come to bed with you first?" He wanted her desperately now, bodily proof that they were all still alive.

Eirian had seen him dirtier than this, she said when he was undressed in their bed chamber, with the moon coming through the shutters, and a little oil lamp splashing its light across his body, but she gasped when she saw the wound dressing that ran down most of his thigh.

"Just be careful of it," Faustus said, reaching for her hungrily. "The rest of me is fine, just filthy."

She lay down next to him, letting him find a way to keep his injured leg clear. It was not easy and managed with a good deal of laughter punctuated by yelps of pain, but he was determined he would have this homecoming, something to wash away the last of the despair that had been enveloping him.

Afterward he stretched and said, "The surgeon says not to get this wet yet, so I suppose you'll have to bathe me."

She lay with her chin propped on her hand and traced the lines of his face. "You came home in bloody trousers, but you stopped to get a shave somewhere," she said, amused.

"Magnis," he said. "I couldn't come on a uniform tunic to steal but I couldn't stand my face. It felt like I had a fungus."

Eirian chuckled. "My brothers were very proud of their mustaches. The Druids have beards. Some down to their chests. I wonder how you'd look in one."

"Horrid." He pulled her to him again, carefully, and ran his fingertip along the clan marks on her breast, blue-gray against white skin, like dappled leaf shadow in the oil lamp's shimmer. "Rotri was with me."

"Is he—?"

"He came out of the adventure with a whole hide and says to give you his regards."

Eirian smiled. "He probably enjoyed himself. I am glad they've let him go back to the service where his heart is."

"He told me something," Faustus said. "That when you were on the run together and it didn't look good for getting out, he asked if he should kill you if you were going to be taken, and you told him you would cut off his balls if he tried."

Eirian snuggled her head into his bare shoulder, smiling. "It was kindly meant, but men who think death is preferable to rape are men who have been told a woman has no value afterward."

"I think you changed a number of Rotri's assumptions about women."

Eirian propped herself back up on one elbow. "If men want to understand women, they should ask women, not other men."

Faustus was silent at that. How hard had he tried to understand his mother? Or Silvia? Had he asked Silvia what she wanted or just told her what she shouldn't want? Had she tried to tell him? If so, he hadn't listened, although he thought that Eirian had. "What are we going to do about Silvia?" he asked her.

Eirian sighed. "There's going to be a war, isn't there?"

"Very likely. Cadal may actually change his mind now and ally the Ordovices with Loarn if he's angry enough over the tribune. Or he and Loarn may be at war with each other over whose fault it all was, and who betrayed whom."

"Or both," Eirian said.

"My bet is both, based on their history, but it doesn't help."

"Is there any diplomatic way to get her back, before a war can start?"

"Not if she doesn't want to come," Faustus said gloomily. "Loarn isn't likely to let her go in any case."

"Lucius was with the Old Ones. I'm practically certain. They sent him back to us when they could have given him to Loarn," Eirian said.

"The people of the hills don't like the Silures any more than they like us. We're all Sun People." Faustus thought for a while, stroking her bare thigh. "I don't know where he was, but it can't have been Llanmelin. Still, I could go to the Old One there. They all talk between sidhes. And she likes me, at least somewhat. She might help me get Silvia out."

"No," Curlew said. "These are not matters for us to meddle in."

Faustus sat cross-legged by her fire in the smoky dimness of the hillside. The senior surgeon had obligingly put him on the Hospital List despite knowing he intended to use the excused-from-duty time to ride to Llanmelin with a bag of apples and another of grain tied. The food was appreciated, but it had done no good otherwise.

"She is my sister," he persisted. "Also of your blood as I am, which is why I have come to you." What he didn't say was that he had had no guide this time, but had ridden straight there, making the point, if she wished to take it, that he knew the way. He fingered the small blue bead he wore around his neck. "Your grandmother the Old One gave me this," he said, "to remind me that a part of the people of the hills lives in me."

"That is true," Curlew said. "But when one of ours leaves to live among the Sun People, neither they nor their children may come back again later."

"We would only take her back into our own keeping," Faustus said.

"It was an Old One of ours who sent the boy home to you when she learned who he was. But your sister, no. Not from Loarn's house."

"There is going to be war," Faustus said, letting her decide what that would mean.

"Then we will wait while it passes over us, as we have before."

"If it does."

Curlew's eyes reflected the glow from the peat fire, small red embers in the blue iris. "If you lead your men here to dig us out, we will be gone before you get here."

"I will not do that." It was one thing to let her know he could, another to make good on the threat, turning these small ones out like foxes dug from a den, and for what? It would not bring Silvia to him. "I will swear that on whatever you like," he added, ashamed of himself.

Curlew considered him. "Sun People's gods matter little to us."

Faustus said, "By the Mother, then. And by Cath Mawr. May she and the land both devour me if I forswear."

Curlew smiled at him then. "The land wants to devour something, but I don't know that it is you. We will see what it eats this summer. Faustus, I wish I could help you, but this is not a thing for us to meddle in. Unlike you, Loarn of the Silures would track us to earth. The king before Aedden did that to the people of Ty Isaf for helping the Romans once before. It is not something I will risk."

"I understand."

"Does she know the boy is alive?"

"I have been afraid to send her word. It was Loarn's men who tried to kill him."

Curlew's mouth tightened again. "Loarn overset the balance when he did that. The boy was wholly Roman despite his blood, and to be taken to a sidhe has broken the pattern and pulls him into three worlds at once. That is never good. Those who sent him back to you may tell her, but that is all they will do."

"How do you know this?"

"We have survived by knowing the pattern. That is what we fear, Faustus — what chews holes in the fabric of the world, and goes from one place to another where it should not be." She nodded at him, a formal dismissal, but then she said gently, "Thank you for the apples, Faustus, and the grain. We are grateful."

It was his kind, he thought unhappily, riding back to Isca with the wound in his leg throbbing, that gnawed at her world. How long until it vanished for good, sinking into the earth beside the even older people who had built the barrows and set the stone dancers in their rings? He saw his people and Loarn's as rats now, gold torques around their rapacious throats, loricas buckled about their torsos, long teeth chewing ever deeper, eating and spoiling and burrowing, making their nests where hers had been.

XVI. THE MORRIGAN

"I thank you, Centurion. Rome is in your debt. But no." Caecilius shook his head again. "Your sister may return to Isca if she so wishes. But you may not go to Porth Cerrig and force her, and start a war."

Faustus tried to think of another argument to offer. There wasn't one. "Likely he has taken her to Dinas Tomen. Or he will." Dinas Tomen would be even harder to get into.

"That is irrelevant." Caecilius gave him a long look. "I mean it, Valerianus. You are not to go after your sister. Not to Porth Cerrig. Not to Dinas Tomen. Not anywhere. Not unless she comes voluntarily. And I was wrong," he added. "I will give you that. The marriage will not mend the treaty. I fear that ink is dissolving while we watch it."

"Yes, sir." Faustus was surprised that the legate would admit that much. Caecilius looked weary to him, and suddenly older. He kept shifting in his chair as if his back hurt. "And when there is war anyway, sir?"

"Then you may retrieve her afterward. I need you. I was willing to risk you over the tribune. I am not willing to do so over a civilian woman, not even this one."

"Yes, sir," he said again. *Yes, sir. Of course, sir. I realize she is unimportant, sir.* And she was, that was the problem.

"Be pleased that you have the boy back." Caecilius turned his attention to an optio hovering in the doorway with a sheaf of reports. "You are dismissed, Valerianus."

Faustus saluted. "Yes, sir." On his way out he made his respects to the statue of Jupiter. The chief of the gods looked impassive. One civilian woman wouldn't matter to him either. To his wife maybe. Silvia had been a faithful devotee of Juno. Faustus hadn't really expected to convince the legate, but he had promised Lucius he would try. There would be war anyway, Caecilius knew it now and didn't want it begun before he was ready, nor over a grievance that could cost him his primus pilus if things went badly.

Outside the Principia he skirted a cart full of drainpipe and a pile of stone half blocking the street; the fortress of Isca Silurum was constantly building, replacing old peat-clay and timber walls with stone, adding new barracks, new warehouses, repurposing others. His own cohort was on construction detail this morning, forming roof tiles from wet clay and spreading them in the field outside the walls to dry under the promise of a fair day.

They had cheered his return to command, the dressing on his thigh visible under his harness tunic but smaller and no longer leaking blood. He suspected that in his absence at Llanmelin, Septimus had entertained them with accounts of the extraction of the tribune and the finer points of their commander's native disguise. Septimus eyed him warily now on his return from the Principia and Faustus shook his head.

"I'm sorry to hear that, sir," Septimus said sympathetically. "It would have been another grand adventure, wouldn't it?"

"The legate has his reasons," Faustus said. It was never a good idea to complain downward. Or upward for that matter. Only between equals was it safe, and that not always. He missed Galerius and his cheerful agreement with any insubordinate remark.

"I'd rather have fetched lady Silvia out than the tribune," Septimus said. "If the Ordovices handed him off to Loarn like they meant to it was to take the place of an alliance, wasn't it?"

"It may still, if they're fighting each other over whose fault it was," Faustus said. "But Rome can't lose a tribune. Tribunes are essential personnel."

Septimus snorted.

"There's one now," Faustus said. "Buckle it, Centurion."

"Indeed," Tribune Marcellinus said, showing no sign of offense. "If they had handed him over, we'd just have to get him loose from the Silures instead."

I might have got Silvia out at the same time, Faustus thought, followed by, *While I was murdering Terentius before he could talk.*

"That might not have gone well," Marcellinus added, possibly with the same thought. "As it is, I have sent a message to his father and the senator is very grateful." He nodded at Faustus and Septimus both. "There may be some reward for the men who brought it off."

Septimus brightened at that.

Marcellinus laid a hand on Faustus's shoulder. "Walk with me a bit, Centurion."

They strolled past the tile field. A small child and a puppy dashed across it, leaving a trail of footprints.

"Out!" the centurion in charge bellowed at them.

"No child can resist wet clay," Marcellinus said. "I remember putting my handprints in a tile field on my grandfather's estate. It was very satisfactory until the steward caught me. Your boy came to see me," he added.

"What about?" Faustus asked warily.

"For one thing he wanted to know why his mother has gone to the Silures. He says you won't tell him."

"I told him she was determined," Faustus said.

"Not that his mother thought he was dead and in her grief, she went to Loarn to spite you?"

"No," Faustus admitted. "I didn't want him to carry that."

"You didn't think it would occur to him? When he knows he went out with a patrol when he shouldn't have?"

"I suppose so," Faustus said.

"He told me he is old enough to own his own foolishness," Marcellinus said. "He wants his mother back, but he knows it has to wait. He had a request though."

"For something else?"

"A letter of recommendation to the Centuriate."

"I've known he wants the army. I promised him a letter myself, when he's older."

Marcellinus smiled. "I told him he was somewhat premature, and he said he wanted everything lined up. I suspect he meant before she can come back and make him feel enough guilt to change his mind."

"That's complicated self-knowledge for thirteen," Faustus said dubiously.

"I don't think so. Think back to when you were thirteen."

Thirteen. Three years after Marcus died. Marcus, the brother who should have inherited the farm. The brother who had wanted it; whose death had hung it around Faustus's neck like an anvil. At thirteen, Faustus had wanted to army too. Desperately. "What did you want when you were thirteen?" he asked Marcellinus.

"I wanted my grandfather to die," Marcellinus said promptly.

"Did he?" Faustus asked, startled at the bluntness of that.

"Yes. He was an evil old beast who made my mother and my father's lives a misery to them. He caught a fever, and I really began to believe in the gods."

"He hasn't, uh, come back, has he?" Faustus asked.

"No, I expect he's safely in a pit in Tartarus. I hope so. But my point is that people know what they want at thirteen and are capable of some complication about it."

"And did you promise him a recommendation?"

"I did. He is excellent material. Important to make him thoroughly Roman too, don't you think?" Marcellinus clapped him on the shoulder again and went on his way.

Thoroughly Roman. Too Roman for there to be a chance of installing him as a client king of the Silures.

"Marcellinus tells me he offered you a letter for the Centuriate," Faustus told him at dinner.

Lucius nodded. "Don't think I don't know things," he said, dousing his fish with garum.

"What things?"

Lucius ignored that, chewing. He had been ravenous ever since he had come home. He was half a foot taller than before and Gwaldus and Eirian had let down the hems on all his clothes as far as they would go. He swallowed. "Garum is one of the things I missed. At least it seems like it." He paused, staring at his plate.

"It's all right if you don't remember," Eirian said. "The surgeon says that's normal."

Lucius shook his head. "I wish I could remember them better. They were kind to me."

"It's enough to remember that you owe them a debt if you meet the little dark ones again."

Lucius grinned. "The people in the vicus think the fae took me. The fishwife made me show her how many fingers I have."

"Did she decide you aren't a changeling?" Faustus asked.

"I don't think she's sure."

Paullus put a loaf of bread on the table between them. "Argos knows you." Argos had laid his gray head hopefully across Lucius's thigh.

"He wants fish." Lucius slipped Argos a bite from his plate. "Mother hated it when I did that," he said. "Marcellinus says there's war coming, and we can't get her back until it's over."

"I tried," Faustus said. "But I can't disobey a direct order. In the meantime, your tutor is glad to hear you are still alive and he will see you tomorrow. He's very interested in your adventures so please be careful."

"He's writing a natural history of West Britain," Lucius said. "He believes anything anyone tells him. I could tell him a bonasus carried me off and he'd swallow it."

"And what is a bonasus?" Eirian asked.

"Sort of a cow thing with useless ingrown horns," Faustus said. "It shoots a stream of caustic shit at its enemies."

"Three hundred feet," Lucius said. "It can burn your skin off." The bonasus was his favorite animal, and that description had induced him to read Aristotle without complaint.

Eirian snorted. "It sounds like something my brothers would think up after a barrel of beer."

"Plinius said it lives in Paeonia," Lucius said.

"Then don't tell your tutor there's one loose in Britain," Faustus said. "Seriously, Lucius, don't embroider your story. Rumors have a habit of metamorphosis. I'm not worried about a bonasus, but I don't want stories about fae abductions circulating."

"I wouldn't," Lucius said. "I told the fishwife that a shepherd's woman found me and nursed me back to health, like Romulus and Remus. Will that do? I didn't want to talk about them, and I don't really remember anyway."

"That is best," Eirian said. "People will hunt what they fear, just out of spite."

—

Porth Cerrig was a bustle of activity, some overt, some secretive. In two days, they would go to Dinas Tomen for Lughnasa, taking more supplies than Silvia knew they would need for the announced ten-day stay, nearly everything from Porth Cerrig's cellars. She knew they were not coming back.

Did that matter to her? She wasn't sure. When Loarn came to her bed at night, then she was sure it did not. When she saw the stockpiled weapons set aside to be carried by mule back along a different route because there were inspection posts on the wagon road, then she wavered. But there was nothing to go back for. She had cast her lot with Loarn.

Silvia went with the rest of Porth Cerrig's women to gather the first of the ripening summer crops, every young turnip and stalk of grain and small sour apple. It was hot. The air shimmered with it, a welcome relief in its way after a week of rain. A few parsnips overlooked last fall sprouted among the young ones, woody and beginning to set seed. They pulled those too, mindful of the sap that would burn on a day like this. Silvia's hands were wrapped with oiled linen.

Larks cavorted in the clear sky, their bubbling song like liquid sunlight. Silvia set her basket down and shielded her eyes carefully with one hand to watch them from the shade of a hedgerow. Such small things to make so much cheerful noise.

"Lady." It was a small voice, as soft and musical as the larks and she didn't hear it at first.

"Lady."

Silvia looked for the voice. A little shadow in the depths of the hazel and blackthorn.

"I have a thing to tell you, lady."

"Who are you?" Silvia whispered. She looked to see if anyone was watching. Gwladus was pulling parsnips, tucking them into her basket. Iorwen was across the field. Beyond them four or five other women bent to rows of ripening grain, sickles in hand, cutting the first crop.

The small figure came closer, pushing through a thicket of bramble heavy with berries. She was brown-skinned and tiny, with red and blue beads braided into her black hair, and a ragged-hemmed gown of checked brown wool.

Silvia stared at her. "What do you want with me?"

"The Old One sends me to tell you a thing."

"What thing then?" Silvia peered through the leaves trying to get a better look.

"The boy is alive, and I am to tell you that and also that it was your lord's men who tried to kill him."

The light was suddenly blinding. Silvia closed her eyes. "He can't be."

"We tell you only because you are a royal woman and thus belong to the Mother as we do. Your man unbalanced our world when he did that, and your boy more so when my sister found him and brought him to us."

"Where is he?" Silvia whispered.

"We have sent him back to the Romans' fort at Isca. We want no more to do with him, or with your people."

The blinding light faded to gray and darkness and then back to the sunlit sky where the larks were still wheeling. Silvia's stomach felt as if it held a fistful of cold lead. "How did you find him?"

"My sister, who maybe should have minded her business but did not, saw them throw him from the cliff."

"He has been with you all this time? Where?"

"There are more of us than you know, in more places," the small woman said. "We were here before your people rose and we will be here when you fall. Now I have told you what the Old One sent me to." Before Silvia could ask anything else she vanished into the thorny shadows of the hedgerow.

Silvia stared after her. Lucius...

She had never seen one of the little dark people before and had only half believed in them, despite Faustus's assurance that they were both real and kin by some long ago mating. Why would one come to her to tell her Lucius was alive if it was not true? And that meant Loarn... Oh, surely he could not have. Faustus had warned her though. She stood frozen, staring into the hedgerow.

—

At dusk she found Loarn with Pwyll in the lower courts, ordering the sorting of goods to go to Dinas Tomen, marking them on a handful of tally sticks. He glanced at her and went on speaking to Pwyll, shaking his head at some question. There would be no talking to him until he came to her bed.

She waited, grimly patient, while Loarn ate dinner with his household at the table in the great hall. Silvia had not eaten, her stomach churning with fury, the appetite that pregnancy had given her turned to lead. Loarn hadn't noticed, his head bent now to Pwyll, now Llamrei or Rhodri or Iorwen, leaning past her, the scarlet-embroidered sleeve of his shirt nearly in her plate, to speak of weather and grain supply and the dispatch of an envoy to Cadal with a demand for men and horses in lieu of the tribune.

"Do we consider that likely?" Rhodri asked. "They are blaming us instead."

"Cadal will agree, or regret his bad faith," Loarn said.

He didn't notice when Silvia tucked her feet under her to slip off the bench. In the queen's chamber she settled herself with her spinning because she must do something or go and take him by the throat in the great hall before all his people and scream at him. Gwladus bustled about the chamber, packing the last of the queen's clothing into trunks, sprinkling fleabane between the folds, until Silvia snapped at her, "Leave it! I will send for you when I need you."

It was late when Loarn came to the chamber, and raised his dark brows in surprise that she was not in their bed.

"I am going back to my people."

He halted halfway to her. "You cannot."

She pulled the agate ring from her finger.

"There is nothing for you among them," Loarn protested. "You belong here with your mother's kind. Are you afraid because there will be fighting? I will see you are safe in Dinas Tomen."

She threw the ring at him, and then the spindle.

"What is the matter with you?"

She looked for something else to throw. Her hand closed around a silver cup, a bride gift from his council. "You sent men to kill my son!"

He eyed her warily now. "I did not."

"Do not lie to me, Loarn."

"How do you know this?" he asked carefully.

She didn't answer that. Nor would she tell him that Lucius was alive. "You murdered my boy. How can you think I could stay with you, knowing that?"

"Look you," Loarn said helplessly, "I did not order it. I knew afterward, yes, but I did not order it and the man who did has died fighting the Romans."

"Llew," she said, positive of that. "And when you knew, you did not avenge my boy."

"Llew is dead. Is that not enough?"

"He did you a service," Silvia spat at him. "Whether you admit ordering it or no."

"Who told you this?"

"What does it matter? You can't tell me that they didn't all know. Everyone but me. The foreign queen. I am going back to my people."

"You cannot," Loarn said again. "Not now." She knew how many spearmen he had, how many horses, how much iron for spearpoints and sword blades. Whether Cadal would come to his standard or not. All the things he could not let her loose to tell the Romans. "You cast your lot with your mother's people."

"I cast my lot with *you*, because you said you loved me," Silvia said. That still stung. "But you didn't want me, you wanted to convince the Romans you didn't intend rebellion. Until you were ready."

"War, not rebellion. They are not our masters. I wanted you as much as I have wanted any woman. More. I fought my council to wed you."

Silvia turned the silver cup in her hands. She still wanted to throw it. To scream and throw herself at him, pull her belt knife and drive it into his chest, hunting for the heart. "I tried," she said grimly, "to be the woman that you wanted."

"Is that not the way of marriage?" Loarn asked.

"You have tried little enough to be the man that I want," Silvia said. "Except in bed."

"What other way to please a wife? Besides gold, which I gave you."

"You may keep the things you have given me. I tried to be the woman that my father wanted, and that my first husband wanted, and the woman that my brother wanted. To be what some man required. I thought that marrying you was different, because no one else wanted me to, and the difference was that I loved you." She stared at him, thinking. "Or that I lusted for you. They may not be the same. They don't feel the same now. I am going home."

"This is your home."

"It is not. Not now that I know how my boy died."

Loarn came to her and tried to take her hands in his. She let him, sitting stiffly. She would not look at him now. Not while he was this close to her, his familiar scent of horse and saddle leather and the nettle with which he washed his hair.

"Silvia, you cannot leave here now." He bent his head to hers and she turned her face away. "I will stay out of your bed if you wish, but you cannot leave Porth Cerrig until you go to Dinas Tomen with me."

"And then I cannot leave Dinas Tomen."

"No."

—

It did not take long for the word to go out, quietly, that the queen was not allowed outside Porth Cerrig's walls. If she came to the outer gates there was always a sentry kindly, gently, insistently pushing her away. "No, lady. It isn't safe out now," he would say. Silvia did not argue. There was no privacy in Porth Cerrig. Everyone knew the king's business and that Loarn had stopped going to her bed, as he had promised.

Preparations for the journey continued. They would sweep Porth Cerrig bare, something the Romans were not to know until it was too late. The king's household, his captains, servants, hounds, and hunting dogs, would go by the paved road, the road Loarn had taken to his king-making. The rest, the gathered spearmen, the laden mules, everything that should escape the Romans' notice, would go by the forested mountain tracks with Gwydion to lead them, along the same ancient paths that Teyrnon had taken to seal Loarn's kingship.

Llamrei unearthed a crate of rushlights to be sent north and found that mice had eaten half the tallow. She swore and set about sorting out the good ones. The new queen had been something to give Loarn heart, she had thought. A compensation for the role he must play, like it or no. She had heard Loarn forbid what Llew had done, had known Llew was going to do it anyway, and not stopped him. *The Mother forgive that*, she thought. Llamrei had never borne a child, could only guess at Silvia's mourning, but it had been necessary. A king was not like other men. If he had been before his king-making, he was not afterward.

She carried the crate of tallow dips to the courtyard and found Pwyll fussing because a barrel of mead had cracked and leaked. He and two small hounds were trying to drain it into another cask. While they struggled with it, a gull swooped down and stole the piece of bread he had set down.

"Nothing goes right today!" Pwyll growled. He threw a rock at the gull.

"That's ill luck," Llamrei said. "Undo it."

"Llyr, accept my gift to your bird," Pwyll said. "Of a surety, all goes as it should."

Llamrei stalked past him, trying to shed the feeling that he was somehow right, that mice and cracked barrels and gulls were signs of something greater, some force at work to push against them. The door to the wash house stood open to light the tubs where bedding was soaking. A dark woman in a black cloak was washing something in one of them – a white shirt with scarlet embroidery down the sleeves. She turned as Llamrei neared and Llamrei's breath caught in her chest. There was no face under the raven hair, only a dark bright eye and a great beak. The long thin hands dipped the shirt in the water again and then woman and shirt both vanished.

Llamrei stood blinking. "No, Mother," she whispered but there was no answer.

"The king is looking for you." Rhodri tapped her shoulder. She jumped at his touch, and he stared at her. "What is it?"

I saw the Morrigan washing Loarn's shirt. No, she couldn't say that, not even if she had. The Morrigan came to wash the clothes of those who were going to die. That was a vision not to be spoken, a vision to convince herself she had not seen after all. Some new woman among the slaves, and a trick of the light.

"I thought the ground had tipped up again," she said, "but I think I only stumbled. Did you feel it?"

"No, and Teyrnon says it has settled now. Loarn wants a last council before tomorrow."

Llamrei saw Silvia's Dobunni woman carrying her own bundle to the wash house. The Dobunni woman was solid and earthly, but Llamrei shivered. "What does he plan to do about the queen?" *Let her not be his death.*

"Send her by the other road, with Gwydion and Iorwen," Rhodri said. "He'll not let her get near the Romans now."

"So he will drag her to Dinas Tomen and bar her door there," Llamrei said.

"Until the war is over. He will let her go, then, I'm thinking. Who would keep a hornet in a bottle longer than he had to?"

"He won't be able to marry again unless she dies. And to where, when we have driven the Romans out?"

"Where she will. She was an ill-omened thing to begin with."

"He wanted her," Llamrei said. "I came to think that he should have something that he wanted."

"Because he didn't want the kingship?"

"Would you have?"

Rhodri didn't answer.

"Tell me," Llamrei said, "do we make this war because we must? Or because we cannot let go of the idea of being free of Rome?"

"If we are not free of Rome, then what are we?" Rhodri asked. "How many years have we fought to be free of them?"

His face in the bright sunlight showed the years in lines around his eyes and the gray in his mustache.

"How many kings?" Llamrei asked in turn. "How many kings and spear brothers and hounds not a year into their manhood? How many widows?"

"As many as the gods ask for," Rhodri said. "What are we if we are not free? And what has come over you?"

"We can field more men than they just now," Llamrei said, thinking it through, unsure herself what had come over her. "But they are like tide, ebbing and coming back again. And never driven out."

"This time we will."

"Has Cadal agreed?"

Rhodri shrugged. "Best not to trust that one anyway."

She thought of Rome, driving its roads straight as a spearshaft through forest, fields, whatever stood in its path. She had seen them break up an outcrop of rock the size of a cow byre rather than turn the road around it. Was that what the gods required? For them to fight until they too were paved over with stone? She thought again of the dark figure in the wash house. But she had negotiated the first peace they had made with the Romans, and it had sat like a burr under her shirt ever since. Until the gods said otherwise, they would fight.

XVII. THE RIVER

Silvia stared furiously at the red and white pony. "I will not."

"There is no path for wheeled traffic on the track," Iorwen said. "You must ride or walk. I told you that."

It seemed the last insult, the final indignity. She had never ridden on a horse. Gwladus put her arm around her, firm and sympathetic. "You will get the way of it. I'll stay by you."

The saddle was heavy with enameled bronze trappings, the bridle adorned with a silver faceplate as befitted a queen's mount. The pony looked at her curiously and snuffled at her sleeve. Silvia gritted her teeth, shaking with anger while two of Loarn's spearmen lifted her into the saddle. Iorwen nodded to them, and they backed away respectfully, clearly with no wish to have further doings with a queen at odds with the king. The King and the balance of his household had left in the early morning to make a great show of travel on the Roman roads – the yearly trek to celebrate Lughnasa from the heights of Dinas Tomen.

The pony snaked its neck around again to look at Silvia. Iorwen smacked it lightly on the nose. "He only wonders what you're doing," Iorwen said. "Here, hold the reins like this. You're confusing him."

Silvia adjusted her grip and the pony snorted, apparently satisfied.

Gwladus swung into the saddle of a black pony with little trouble and Iorwen told her, "Stay beside your lady when you can, or just before. Follow Gwydion. I will ride behind with Teyrnon."

There was a pretense that she was not a prisoner, but it was only a pretense. They had put her at the center of the column among the laden baggage mules with spearmen ahead and behind. The pony started abruptly when Gwydion's mount moved off. Silvia grabbed the saddle horns and the pony snorted and flung its head up. She loosened the reins, keeping her grip on the horns.

It was a four-day journey to Dinas Tomen, at a minimum. Longer allowing for bad weather or lame mules or unexpected Roman patrols. Silvia watched everything as they passed, trying to fix the trail in her memory. The glint of a river in the distance showed through the trees from time to time, although she was never sure whether it was the same river or many. The Silure Hills were laced with rivers carrying the rainfall that fell on the mountains. This was her mother's country that Loarn had promised to show her, she thought sourly. Indeed.

When they stopped to eat a noon meal, Iorwen tethered her pony and came to sit beside Silvia and Gwladus. "You'll be saddle sore by evening," she told Silvia. "I will bring you some salve, but if you stretch your muscles it will help."

Silvia didn't answer. She bit into the boiled egg that Iorwen had brought her.

"I am sorry that it has come to this," Iorwen offered.

"He is keeping me for spite," Silvia said.

"No, he does not want you to go home to your people and tell them how many men we have in the war band, and what he plans to do. Do you not understand that?"

"I have no idea how many men he has!" Silvia snapped. "Did he ever talk to me of these things? Marrying me was supposed to *stop* a war."

"He told you that?"

"No," Silvia admitted. "The legate at Isca did."

"Who is a bigger fool than my brother," Iorwen said. "Men will believe what they want to before they will see what is under their noses." She stood. "Gwydion will want us on the move again."

They climbed higher into the afternoon and then descended again on the other side of some nameless ridge. Silvia itched with impatience. The farther they got from Porth Cerrig, the farther they were from Isca. She eyed Gwladus and Gwladus shook her head. *Not now.* Gwladus rode easily, her feet swinging along the pony's flanks, her reins loose in her hand. Gwydion's men stopped their patrols along the track to chat with her. Gwladus was still pretty, her pale hair with no more than a few silver threads, and she had a way of making a man feel he was interesting, and no doubt cut from heroes' cloth. So far as Silvia knew she never went further than that, but she was an expert at flirtation.

At nightfall they came to a clearing beside a stream and camped there. Gwydion's men pitched a tent for Silvia and Gwladus, and a second for Iorwen and Teyrnon. The old priest climbed from his horse with some difficulty and Iorwen set about making him comfortable. She brought him a cup of beer and a bowl from the pot of barley and thick broth set over the fire. She put a blanket across a downed tree trunk for him to sit on and another across his knees.

Gwydion had brought his harp out of its bag and began to sing, and when Teyrnon joined his voice to Gwydion's Silvia remembered that he too had been a harper.

Gwladus shook her head. "It seems a pity to make him travel this road. His bones are too old to be jolted in a saddle."

"That is my brother's doing," Silvia said. "And the legate. Rome's anyway." There seemed to be no end to the people she was angry with. The music ran up her skin like cold water, the tale of some ancient battle against ancient foes, told and retold with bloody satisfaction.

When his song was finished, Gwydion made the rounds of the camp, speaking softly to each sentry, and pausing, watchful, at Silvia's side. "Best to sleep, lady."

Iorwen helped Teyrnon into his tent and the rest rolled themselves in their cloaks. In the morning Gwydion roused them even before the birds began. Silvia looked for Gwladus and found her just coming into the tent.

"Did you sleep at all?" Silvia whispered.

"Enough. And the youngling with sentry duty tonight thinks I am faint with longing for him."

Silvia's eyes slid to the little traveling chest that held her clothes for the journey, a luxury she had furiously demanded until everyone gave in just to quiet her. "Are you sure you know how much?"

"I would not kill a man just for wanting his hand up my skirts. I know how much."

"You have had this since we left Isca? And never told me?"

"If I told you I had begged poppy tears from a medic who also wanted up my skirts, now would you have let me bring it?"

"I don't know. And you had best keep your skirts down or I won't be the only one to worry over."

"No sign yet?"

"My belly is cramping. But so is everything else."

"The stiffness will ease once you've been in the saddle again. For the rest — it doesn't always work."

Silvia knew she had been late in changing her mind. She had wanted a child with Loarn to ease her heart. Now she did not. It would only be another one for Loarn's people to hunt down and kill or take from her.

"Now is not the best time anyway," Gwladus said. "I told you that."

Silvia began to say *sooner better than not* and quieted instead because Gwydion's men were taking the tent down around them, impatient to be on the trail. They were not the only band making their way through the mountains north to Dinas Tomen. Other scattered levies, Silure and Demetae alike, would all be moving north, slowly past the Romans' noses, gone to Dinas Tomen before the garrisons realized their villages stood empty.

Gwladus helped Silvia into the saddle. The sun was barely up somewhere behind a lowering bank of cloud, and the air felt oppressive. "Rain would help," she said quietly, adjusting Silvia's skirts around her knees.

"Only if it holds off," Silvia said, worried now. Rain later would wash their tracks out. Rain now would make mud to show them.

"Ask your lady," Gwladus said. "Doesn't her husband bring the weather?"

Silvia looked at the sky again. Juno was wife to Jupiter Optimus who commanded the wind and rain with a thunderbolt in his hand. Juno had had Silvia's devotion from the time she was a child; she had promised her a heifer if Lucius was found alive. That had been before she went to wed Loarn. Would the goddess forgive her for that desertion? For her lack of faith? Silvia prayed for forgiveness as they rode, a lengthy prayer with vows of the heifer and the gold bangle that had been her own before Loarn. The sky stayed leaden, but no rain fell.

At dusk they camped near another stream, bubbling between moss-covered boulders under thick tree canopy. It flowed, Gwladus's spearman told her, into the river they had seen yesterday.

"And that one goes to the Isca, I'm almost sure. South anyway," Gwladus said.

"We can't wait longer."

"No." Gwladus set a bowl and cup down before Silvia. "Eat, and drink half of this and I will save half of mine."

Gwydion had pushed them until he had to rest the laden mules and even now in late July it was almost full dark by the time all his men had eaten and drunk. He did not take out his harp this night but set the sentries and ordered the rest to sleep. The moon was close to full but under the tree canopy and the cloud it gave little light to show Gwladus slipping past the banked fires with a cup in her hand.

She found her sentry on the streambank and sat on a rock beside him. Something scrabbled in the ferns and Gwladus shivered. "So many things abroad in the trees on a night like this."

An owl hooted and he laughed. "Just hunters of the little things. Nothing big enough to catch you. Besides, you have me."

"I brought you something."

He took the cup. "Keep your voice down. Gwydion has ears like that owl." He sat on the rock next to her and drained the cup. He put his arm around her waist. "And what Gwydion doesn't hear will do him no harm."

When he sagged against Gwladus, Silvia stepped from the tree shadow and together they laid him down beside the empty cup. Gwladus picked up his spear and Silvia his belt knife. It began to rain.

Iorwen stood over the sentry. He was alive but Gwydion was going to make him wish he wasn't. She sniffed the cup and weighed what to do.

Gwydion was cursing the fact that all the dogs had gone in Loarn's train. Teyrnon stood huddled in his cloak, rain beading his white beard. One of Gwydion's men poured river water over the sentry, and he spluttered and stirred. Gwydion kicked him.

"They won't have got far on foot," Iorwen said. "Not in this weather. And we've more important matters than my brother's whore. The king may be well rid of her."

"That is for the king," Gwydion said.

"She doesn't know what Loarn thinks she does. She doesn't know the way back either."

Teyrnon stared into the rain. "What was stolen from us was returned only to be driven away again, and that is on the king."

"It wasn't just Loarn," Iorwen said.

Teyrnon looked at her. "No." Iorwen had feared what the queen's son might bring to them. They all had.

"She'll not forgive him that," Iorwen said. "No matter how many times we bring her back to him. No woman would."

At least she hadn't been party to it. Had feared what the boy might mean for her own son, even what a child of the queen and Loarn would mean, but murder? No.

"That is for the king," Gwydion said again. He stood thinking. "Ten men." He kicked the sentry again. "And this one. Shave half his face. He can remember not to listen to his cock while it grows out again."

—

Loarn's household did not stop at Isca on its passage north. The legate sent a delegation to pay his respects and was told that the king appreciated the courtesy, but they were late on the road and it was important to reach Dinas Tomen by Lughnasa. If not, such tardiness angered the gods, and naturally the legate would understand that. And the queen was sleeping in her carriage and wished not to be disturbed.

"She's had her chance," Marcellinus told Faustus. "That's all we can do. We're not ready." The legate of the Ninth was theoretically prepared to send the vexillations from the Twentieth back to Deva, but they were still in Eburacum while the two legates weighed which was more unstable – the Brigantes or West Britain. That hinged on what Cadal decided.

In the meantime, the garrisons in West Britain prepared for war. Counts were taken of each outpost, and couriers went between Isca and Deva daily, the news always at least four days old. The legion abandoned roof tiles and digging new drains and drilled endlessly, on the parade ground and on patrols in every direction. That the Silure villages were almost abandoned became obvious.

When he wasn't drilling his cohort, Faustus was at his desk, poring over a map of the terrain between Isca and Dinas Tomen. Much of the map even now was speculation, estimates by scouts and surveyors supplemented by practical notes marking marsh and fords. Faustus was cursing Loarn, and Silvia and Tribune

Terentius equally when his father materialized in the chair opposite the desk. Faustus growled at him.

"I thought you had gone back across the Styx."

"What about Silvia?" the shade said.

"When have you ever given a copper as about Silvia?" Faustus nearly shouted at him.

"You let her go to the natives."

"I didn't *let* her."

"You are paterfamilias."

Faustus's fingers gripped the edge of the desk, knuckles white. "If you tell me that one more time, I will call a priest. There's got to be something that will get rid of you. *You* were paterfamilias."

"Not now. Now you know what it's like." The shade sounded sulky. "None of you were ever satisfied."

"Well, no one is satisfied with me either."

"Not even Silvia," the shade said smugly. He rearranged the folds of his ghostly toga.

"Why are you wearing that?" Togas were for important occasions, weddings and funerals, unless you were a senator in Rome.

"Your mother's funeral is this morning. The mourners will be here now. Why aren't you dressed?" He glared at Faustus's sweat-stained harness tunic and untied scarf.

Now Faustus saw that the toga was gray. The old man had leaned over Guennola's body, weeping, while Faustus and Silvia stood in the doorway, with the funeral workers behind them. It was the only time he had seen his father weep, not even when his brother Marcus died, or when their mother was dying. Then he had only commanded her angrily to live. When she had not, he seemed bereft. He had died himself two months later, and his parting words had been her name. Gaia, not Guennola. The name he had given her that still could not tether her to him, despite its inscription on her tomb.

Faustus sometimes thought that the old man had come to Britain in pursuit of her, not himself; Faustus was just the one he could find. "Best you look for her in Annwn," he said now; the underworld of her own people.

"Nothing here will let me in," the shade said fretfully.

"Then give up!" Faustus said, exasperated. "I have work to do."

"What about your sister?"

Faustus gritted his teeth. Silvia might be as lost to him as his mother's ghost was to the old man. It was also possible that nothing here would let her all the way in either, leaving her like Faustus alone in the doorway, able to see two worlds and inhabit neither completely. And there were the little dark people – an old current running through all of them, surfacing inconveniently. Curlew had said about inhabiting all three worlds that that chewed holes in the fabric that wove them together side by side, pulled them through each other, and unbalanced all. Maybe two worlds was possible though, if you picked one and gave the other collateral respect. And if the other wasn't making war on the one you had chosen.

When those thoughts had exhausted themselves, he said, "I don't know about Silvia," and found that he was alone again. His father's shade had vanished.

The rain came steadily, the cloud-covered sky giving only enough moonlight to see their own feet, and that barely. The sound of the stream kept them oriented to its bank while they clawed their way through underbrush along the jagged shoreline. Gwladus slipped and fell face down in slick mud and Silvia tugged her up again and they kept running. Always along the streambank, always downstream. When they came to a fordable spot, they crossed to the other side. At dawn, as the sentry had said, it joined with a larger river, and they followed that.

By morning they were well downriver, filthy and wet and starving. Bread, dried meat, and berries filched from the kitchen at Porth Cerrig had been in the bottom of Silvia's chest with the poppy tears and they shared it sparingly. Then they moved on through a tangle of nettle and blackthorn that reached to snag cloaks and sleeves, always following the river, afraid to stray out of earshot of its waters. At midday they came unexpectedly to falls. The water tumbled down a nearly vertical cliff to a pool below in a necklace of fern and moss-covered stone. As far as they could see on either side the bluff dropped away as if it had been sliced with a knife.

Silvia stood above the fall's lip, balancing carefully on wet stone. "We've got to get down there some way. They'll be hunting us by now."

Gwladus looked back the way they had come. "And following the water because they know we will, even if they've no dogs."

Silvia said a swift prayer of thanks for the absence of dogs. Her belly was still cramping. If she started to bleed, she would give thanks for it, but she would also leave a sharper scented trail.

"Stay there," Gwladus said. "Let me look." She lay on the bank and peered over. On this side the drop was sheer and offered no foothold. Across the falls tufts of sedge and a stunted rowan clung to the slope, offering what might give handholds.

Gwladus stood again. "We'll have to cross."

"That means going back." Silvia could feel Gwydion's men on their trail.

"We've a six hour start on them."

"And we need to keep it. They have horses."

"The way is rough enough for two on foot. Men on horses will have hard going. And we still have to cross. There was a place we might do, not so far back."

Silvia looked upriver. It felt like turning into the jaws of the beast that pursued them. It was still raining. The bank wouldn't hold footprints, but the river was the only logical way for them to have gone, to find their way south again. It still was.

Wherever it went it would flow to the Sabrina somewhere. "All right."

They went back upstream. Silvia's boots were wet, and her feet hurt. She had worn the heaviest of her clothes against the rain but now every stitch was sodden, weighted with water. The rain began to slacken by the time they reached the place where Gwladus thought they might cross, and Silvia didn't know whether to bless or curse it.

It wasn't really a ford, only a wide spot where the water spread out and lost some depth. Flowering rushes grew along the margins where the current slowed, a cloud of pink blooms in the drizzle, and the shallows were choked with pondweed. Farther in it would be up to their thighs. They tied the bags with food high up on their chests. Gwladus still had the sentry's spear and she used it to prod the bottom and to steady them both, her other hand in Silvia's. The surface water was frothed brown with the rain, the bottom soft with silt and stones slicked with small mosses.

Silvia followed Gwladus cautiously, feeling for solid footing with the toe of her boot. They would have to find a way to dry wet boots, or their feet would be blistered raw in another day, but she couldn't stop to think about that now, not with Gwydion's men behind her.

The current wrapped around her legs and tugged her downriver. Her foot slid on something slick, pulling her legs from under her; she sank into the current and swallowed a mouthful of water. Gwladus kept her grip on her hand as Silvia floundered to her feet again, gagging, water streaming from her hair and the sack of food. The river roiled on either side of them, deeper than it had looked from the bank.

"May Orcus swallow up that dog's prick for his lies to me!" Silvia spat out water and mud with her curse.

"We're almost across," Gwladus said, cajoling her on. "You'll be swearing like a cavalryman before we get back, just think how Lucius will laugh." She tugged Silvia on, and they took two more steps, and then three and then they were in the rushes, pondweed trailing about their ankles as they climbed the bank. Gwladus let her breath out.

Silvia stood shivering on the bank, "My older brother drowned," she said. "I have always been afraid of water."

"I know," Gwladus said. "It's wonderful what rage can get you past."

"You didn't have to come with me, you know," Silvia said. "Either time."

"And that's my doing." Gwladus wrung the water from her skirts. "I used to see the Silures come into the market towns when I was a girl. They always seemed like something wild, out of a nursery tale, that black hair and so lordlywise even driving pigs to market. It seemed an adventure to go with them."

Silvia didn't believe her, but she was grateful for the comfort the excuse offered as they started back downriver. The sky had cleared of rain by the time they halted at the falls to peer over the edge again. The downward slope appeared to be mostly stone, the striated product of some old upheaval with pockets of dirt that held clumps of rough grass. Below the lip a rock ledge jutted out, offering perhaps enough room for two feet, and below it the branches of the rowan reached up. Below the rowan there looked to be more outcrops and the tufts of sedge they had seen from the other side, but the rowan's leaves made it hard to be certain. The drop was steep but not vertical. It was also the only way down.

"It's this or wait for Gwydion," Silvia said grimly. She lay face down on the edge and slid her feet over, hands wrapped in the tough stems of the grass at the top.

"Here, take my hands," Gwladus said.

"And pull you over on top of me? And who'll hold yours? If I fall you might as well just sit there and wait for Gwydion." She slithered backwards, feet dangling, shifting her grip through the wet grass on the lip of the drop. When she was as far down as she could get, face pressed to the muddy slope, she felt with her toes for the ledge. Nothing. It might be two feet below her at least. If she loosened her grip she would slide quickly, but the grass also grew in smaller tufts down the slope wherever there was a pocket of earth. There was no going back up now, so she unwound her fingers from her anchor. She snatched at a clump as she slid, and it halted her just enough to brace her toes on the stone when they touched it. She stood there panting, splayed against the cliffside.

When she looked up Gwladus had stretched herself along the edge. Silvia nodded to her. Then she prayed and stepped off the stone into the air, catching at anything her fingers could grasp to slow her as she fell into the branches of the rowan.

Above her through the rowan's fringed leaves she saw Gwladus brace herself and begin to edge over the lip after her. Gwladus was taller than Silvia; she might find a foothold more easily. But then she would have to follow down to the tree where Silvia clung. Silvia was caught on the rowan's mid branches, the hem of her gown snagged above her, and everything else twisted into a knot of wet cloth. She tugged at the hem, and it tore away but she felt the branches shift under her. She stilled, looking below her for handholds among the leaves and clusters of green berries. The falling water misted her face; the river where it pooled below her looked very far away.

Silvia had climbed trees as a child, chasing her brothers through their limbs. She had been beaten for it too, once she reached the age when girls became women and did not do such things if they wanted a husband. So her father said, wielding a strap. She didn't know how that child had come back to her now to remind her that before Marcus died, she had swum like a fish and climbed trees like the monkey that Manlius's mother kept for a pet. But somehow the child was there in the tree, pulling the cumbersome bag from around her neck and dropping it, unwinding her cloak and sending it falling too. Silvia began working her way down the tree until she could see below its branches. It clung to the wall of the falls like a gnarled hand, roots sunk deep in fissures in the stone. Below it the sedge had found homes too in the pockets of earth that were more numerous on the lower slope where the drop grew less steep.

She looked up to see Gwladus with her feet on the stone ledge. "Wait till I tell you," Silvia called, "and then let the tree catch you."

She began to make her way cautiously down through the lower branches and finally to the base of the trunk, where she halted, clutching it, to scout the slope below. There were enough stands of sedge to work her way carefully from one to the next. She put one arm around the rowan's trunk and let herself down, on her backside this time, to slide into the sedge below her and grasp it to halt her before the next descent.

"All right!" she called to Gwladus and Gwladus stepped off the ledge.

Silvia heard the rustle of the rowan's leaves as she slid farther down the muddy slope, and then a sharp cry. As she looked up, Gwladus tumbled past the rowan's trunk, her skirts caught in a broken branch. Silvia put one arm out to catch her and Gwladus's weight tore her from her grip on the sedge. They fell together down the rest of the slope to the rock-studded pool under the falls.

Gwladus went into the water; face up, thank Juno, but unmoving, with her hair floating like the pondweed around her. Silvia struggled to her feet, every battered bone screaming, and waded into the pool. It was deep enough that she had to swim. The current had pulled Gwladus under the falls and now it tried to pull her from Silvia's grip. Silvia fought the water, holding Gwladus by the shoulder of her gown. There was a flat ledge behind the falls, narrow but nearer than where they had gone in. Silvia pulled Gwladus up over it, heaving her onto the rock. Gwladus didn't move and Silvia turned her on her face and pounded her back. Water ran from her mouth and Gwladus brought more up with a great gasping cough. Silvia crouched on hands and knees, spitting up water too.

When she could breathe again, she looked around her. The falling water made a curtain between them and the outside world. And behind them the rock face opened in an arm's-length gap. Silvia turned Gwladus on her side and crawled toward it to peer in. The narrow gap opened into a cave, its back wall receding into darkness.

Silvia dove into the water again and fought the current to pull out Gwladus's cloak and her bag of sodden food, found the spear, and went back for her own bag and cloak caught in the moss-covered rocks along the pool's edge. Her legs and arms were shaking uncontrollably by the time she climbed out of the water again. She dragged Gwladus into the cave, pulled their salvaged belongings in after them, and collapsed beside her.

—

When Silvia opened her eyes again, the sun had come out finally and was turning the water gold with its setting. The light filtered like candle glow through the falling water and the narrow door of the cave. She saw with relief that Gwladus was still breathing steadily. Silvia looked in her bag for her fire starter among the soaked mush of their bread, and wondered where in all this sodden world she would find dry tinder.

Gwladus stirred when Silvia spread the soaked bread out on the wet bag. "Did you pull me out?" she asked her. "I think I went in the water."

"You did, and yes." Silvia's head was swimming. "We need to make a fire. And eat something."

Gwladus sat up, coughing. She pushed her wet hair from her face. "The meat will be all right if we still have it."

Silvia prodded the mush of the bread. "This may dry. If it doesn't, I suppose we can still eat it."

She crawled past Gwladus to inspect the interior of their lair. It went no more than ten feet farther back. Something that might once have been a small creature's nest of dried grasses was scattered along the far wall. There was no sign of any other habitation. Anything larger than a mouse would have had to come from the water.

Silvia gathered the strands of grass into a pile. "If they decide we were fool enough to go down that cliff they will look for us downriver. Best we stay here and let them go by." She began to braid the grass together.

"We're likely only another day from Isca, if we can find it," Gwladus said.

Silvia added more grass to her braid, single-minded in her task. It was something she could do, besides sit in shivering terror and wait for Gwydion's men.

Gwladus rose cautiously. "Best I get something in now to dry before we chance being seen, or you'll have nothing to light with that." She shed her wet clothes and Silvia gasped at the bruises that ran up and down her body. Gwladus took her knife from its sheath on her belt and limped to the cave mouth.

Silvia set the braided grasses aside to spread Gwladus's gown and cloak on the floor of the cave. She stripped her own off to dry as much as they might.

Gwladus edged along the pool's lip and cut an armful of the nearest reeds, clinging to the stones along the rim to keep from being taken again by the current. Silvia watched uneasily but Gwladus hoisted herself safely back onto the ledge, shook herself off, and laid the rushes out. She squinted at the sunset. "If it warms and stays dry these might do tomorrow night. At any rate, we won't get wetter. Best to start flexing those boots though, or they'll dry like stone."

They ate handfuls of the mushy bread and most of the rest of the dried meat and then settled at the back of the cave as far from the mist of the falls on naked skin as possible. They took up their boots. Gwladus was right. They wouldn't be able to walk in them else.

Silvia ached from head to toe, everywhere her own bruises had formed. The air on bare skin was only slightly less clammy than her soaked clothes. She said, "Gwladus, I am heartsore that I pulled you into this."

Gwladus looked up from her work on her boots. "Lady, I have been free all my life with no one to blame but myself for whatever I've decided."

Something about the comical intimacy of sitting naked together in a cave, as if they were at the baths, prompted Silvia to ask, "How did you come to marry a man of the auxiliaries?" Gwladus's man had been in Faustus's cohort when Gwladus had come into their household.

"Ah, he was an adventure too," Gwladus said. "Look you, I was a farm girl with no prospects but some farm boy to marry and never seeing anything of the world but the nearest village on market day."

"Could he have taken you with him?" As a rule, no one under the rank of centurion was allowed a wife.

"No, but I didn't know that then, being too eager to ask. When your brother wanted a woman to tend to you it was pure fortune."

"I remember your seeming happy about it," Silvia said ruefully. "And my not understanding at all. The last thing I wanted was to follow Faustus about in the north."

Gwladus considered. "You weren't married to him," she offered. "Likely you might feel different if it was your own man."

"No," Silvia said flatly. The army would come first, just as Loarn's lot as king to war with Rome had come first. She should have known that. "I don't know what I want now. Not a man at all at this moment."

Gwladus worked her hand into the toe of her boot. "That's best, I should think."

"Considering my choices until now," Silvia said grimly. "Yes."

"Your first man," Gwladus said. "Young Lucius's father… servants can't help hearing things, you know."

"I wasn't quiet about it, was I? He spent all his money and mine on racing ponies, got into debt, caught a fever and died."

Silvia flexed the top of her right boot with fingers that looked rather as if they gripped a throat.

"What would you really want?" Gwladus asked, setting her boot aside and picking up its mate.

"I thought I wanted to go back to Narbo Martius, but I don't think I do anymore. Not even if I had money and all my friends would speak to me again. Anyway, I would just be a scandal now."

"Paullus says that things are easier in the provinces," Gwladus said. "Not so comfortable maybe, but easier."

"Paullus says." Silvia snorted. "You don't know what you want either."

"Then best we both stay single," Gwladus said.

And trail about after Faustus. Whatever Gwladus said, there wasn't anything a woman alone could do, other than keep a shop or sell herself, and Silvia didn't want to keep a shop. It was romantic to think of being like Atalanta or Diana and never marrying, living alone in the forest, but Atalanta was nursed by a bear and Diana was a goddess. They weren't real women and Silvia had no desire to live in the forest. The forest that grew beyond the waterfall and their hidden cave was darkening now, becoming a mass of shadow as the sun fell behind it. The night sounds had begun, insects and the screech of an owl. The rattle of a nightjar came from somewhere beyond the riverbank. Silvia eyed the darkness uneasily.

"Those always sound like the voice of the Underworld to me," she said. "The Boatman's oars. Particularly near water."

"If he's making noise, then there's no one else about," Gwladus said. "Be glad we can hear him."

Silvia's stomach clenched. She bent double, dropping the boot. Something warm was between her legs.

"Lady..." Gwladus put a hand on her shoulder.

"It's coming," Silvia grunted. "Juno, that hurts."

Gwladus put her arms around her, pulled her to her to rub the small of her back. "Best to come now. Your lady is looking after you, to take it now and not on the trail."

Silvia buried her face in Gwladus's shoulder. She heard the nightjar again.

"Hush. It's only a bird," Gwladus said.

Whatever was dying here had never really lived, wouldn't be distinguishable from the clots of blood that came now, but Silvia knew that she had wanted it dead and now she wept for it. Gwladus held her as the last of her marriage to Loarn left her.

—

Gwydion's men came in the morning. Silvia and Gwladus heard them above the falls, arguing, words half distinguishable through the noise of the water.

"—not fool enough—"

"—turned back—"

"They'll have gone around—"

"We'd have found them—"

Then there was silence. No one came sliding or falling down the bluff and there was no further sound.

"They'll have gone around," Gwladus said. "They'll know the way."

"I'm so cold," Silvia said. "I can't think."

Gwladus felt their clothing. "Dry enough to be warmer than we are now," she said. They had slept huddled next to each other for the little warmth each body gave off.

Silvia stood, shivering. Gwladus brought her undergown, and she put it on. The heavy folds of the overgown were still damp, the gold thread woven into sleeves and hem snagged into knots, the rest ragged and mud-stained. The blood on the cave floor was dark and sticky and Gwladus put a handful of rushes down to cover it.

"We'll give them two days," Gwladus said. "To give up."

"We'll starve."

"There are fish in that river," Gwladus said. Salmon. She had seen them, leaping at the falls where a tumble of rocks jutted out above their cave. "And I have a spear. Those rushes will be dry enough to light by nightfall. You'll feel more optimistic by a fire."

Silvia stared out through the cave mouth at the water, bright as glass, that curtained their world. She shrugged and gave over to Gwladus, as if all decisiveness had left her with the unformed child.

Gwladus set about spearing a fish. The sentry's war spear was unwieldy, and it took most of the day, but she struck one finally, almost at dusk; the heavy blade cut it nearly in half. The oiled leather case and tin box that held Silvia's flint and steel both had leaked and the fire sticks, splinters dipped in brimstone, had crumbled to a useless mess, but the braid of grasses caught the spark. The rushes smoked and burned fitfully and Gwladus cooked the fish in a basket of wet reeds before they could burn out. Silvia watched her despondently, but she ate when Gwladus handed her a piece of the fish.

The sun had stayed out and on a last expedition before full dark, Gwladus gathered up small branches that would burn for longer than the rushes. At the back of the cave, apart from the other fire, she lit the rushes that she had laid over the blood and let them burn to the stone.

Silvia rose at that and stood over the blackened stone. "I'm sorry," Silvia told the ashes. "It wasn't your fault."

Then she sat back down again, motionless and silent. Gwladus observed her uneasily through another day, but at the second dawn, Silvia sat up and put her boots on. She took a few experimental steps. They were stiff but not badly so. Then she pulled them off and put them in her bag with her clothes. The cloak wouldn't fit but she tied it into a ball with threads pulled from her raveling sleeves. Gwladus watched her with a surge of relief.

As they perched on the ledge behind the falls Silvia said, "Your arms are longer."

Gwladus nodded and slipped into the water, clinging to the ledge with one hand. With the other she took Silvia's bag, held it overhead, and heaved it as far as she could. It fell among the moss-covered rocks at the edge of the pool. Her own bag and Silvia's cloak followed but Gwladus's bundled cloak went into the water. She swore and dived after it, climbing dripping to the shore.

Silvia slid into the cold water after Gwladus. It was like an ice bath but the air when she emerged and clambered shivering across the rocks, was warm. She shook herself like a dog and opened her bag, pulling out gown and undergown and boots. When she had dressed, she pulled a bit of the gold thread from her torn hem and rolled it into a knot. She stood on the mossy rocks above the pool, in the mist of the falls, and threw the little offering out into the water; something small for a soul so tiny. Water was sacred, the abode of gods, the gate to the Underworld. All rivers and wells ran eventually to that river that was all rivers.

They set out again downstream, following the bank where they could, diverting into the forest when the bank grew impassable, keeping the sound of the water always in earshot. At midday, Gwladus stopped and pointed. "Look!"

A wooden tower rose over the tree canopy, just visible in the distance. A watchtower. It would be on the riverbank, and probably at a ford. They made their way back to the bank and saw that the water's flow was slackening, and mud flats had appeared on either side, newly exposed.

Silvia could smell the sulphurous stink of brackish water and hear the gulls that wheeled overhead looking for leavings in the mud. If the water was tidal here, they had to be nearing the lower reaches of the Isca, which swelled with the tides of the Sabrina Channel.

Gwladus studied the current. "Still going out. We'll make best time in the riverbed."

They stepped off the bank onto the soft exposed mud, leaving prints plain behind them. Silvia eyed them uneasily, but the tower was so close and there had been no sign of

Gwydion's men. As the river bent south, they could see the base of the tower ahead, a solid bulwark belonging to Rome in the wilderness. Silvia ached with every bone in her body and the sight of that distant refuge drew her like a tether. Gwladus stumbled beside her. They both knew they could not go on much longer.

And then there were voices from the forest on the bank behind them and Gwydion's men came out of the trees. Silvia and Gwladus ran, fleeing toward the tower and the watchers at its top.

"We are Roman!" Silvia called to the tower and whoever might hear her across the mud flats. "Go back, Gwydion!" she shouted at the pursuing men, "if you don't want your head on that rampart ahead!" Then she saved her breath for running.

The voices behind them were triumphant now, the baying of hounds that have sighted their prey. Silvia and Gwladus dropped all their bundles except for the spear but the pursuers were gaining ground. The watchtower was still a quarter mile away when Gwydion's men caught up to them. Gwladus faced them down with her spear and Silvia drew her belt knife. They moved in on Silvia warily and she saw that they were trying not to hurt her. But they would kill Gwladus to get to her.

"Run!" she told Gwladus. She held out her hand for the spear. Gwladus hesitated and Silvia shouted, "Go!"

Gwladus obeyed; Silvia gripped the spear with both hands. She had no experience with a spear, but her advantage was that they were afraid to kill her, and not only for fear of Loarn's anger. She was still a royal woman and belonged to the Mother, and the repercussions from that would be deadly.

"It will cost you," she said to them through gritted teeth. That she didn't see Gwydion among them said that he had thought her easy prey, sent a handful after her and taken the rest to Dinas Tomen.

Gwladus's sentry came at her with his spear ready to block hers and let the others grab her. Half his mustache was shaved away. Silvia drove the spear at him and backed up steadily, trying to keep them from coming behind her. He blocked her thrust with his own spear expertly, knocking the shaft aside and nearly out of her hands. She felt another set of hands grip her shoulders and she twisted in their grasp, thrusting her blade at anything in its way. There was a shout of anger, and a hand smacked her across the face while others pulled the spearshaft from her. She drew her belt knife and slashed with it at the arms that held her and then at the face that loomed over hers. The sentry's throat spurted blood from under his chin. He fell away from her but there were more, all in a ring around her, hands clawing at her.

-

The centurion of Batavian auxiliaries at the watchtower peered at the commotion upriver. He put his helmet on. Best to see what it was in these touchy times. He shouted at his men and the gates opened.

The jumble of men in the riverbed were Silures, he saw now, and with no business here – ten of them, trying to catch someone in skirts. And a figure running for the tower, a woman too. He wasn't having that, he decided, whoever they were, being a man with sisters.

"At the run!"

The garrison poured through the gates after him.

-

Silvia thrashed in the hunters' grip while they tried to pry her knife from her fingers. She bent her head and bit one of them, sinking teeth into muscle and tendon. He howled and three of them shook her back and forth like dogs with a kill, getting in each other's way, slipping in the mud. Then the hands abruptly loosened their grip. She heard bellowed orders and the sound of running feet.

"Pull back!" someone shouted.

One of Gwydion's men made a last try to drag her with him as he ran, and she laid his arm open with her knife. He let go and she fell in the mud.

"Leave her!" the same voice shouted. "Look to your own!" She saw them pick up the sentry from the riverbed where he lay. She couldn't tell whether he was dead or not.

And then someone picked her up, someone in the familiar ring mail hauberk of the auxiliaries, with a weathered, friendly face under his helmet.

XVIII. THE SHADOW ON THE SKY

The Second Legion was readying for war and the return of the primus pilus's sister was of interest only to those most involved, but those included the legate, who sent amphorae of wine and olive oil and a basket of summer fruit from his personal garden. Faustus left Silvia alone for the first day and she spent it in her chamber with Lucius – weeping and hugging him until Lucius insisted she stop doing both and eat.

Gwladus told Eirian what had happened in the cave, because someone ought to know, and it wasn't her place to discuss female matters with the primus pilus. Eirian told Faustus as they were going to bed, and he breathed a sigh of relief.

"It would have been a complication," Eirian admitted, brushing out her hair.

Silvia was fed and asleep in her bed, Lucius was asleep in his, and Gwladus was coming to whatever arrangement with Paullus they were going to, if any.

"That's an understatement," Faustus said. "Caecilius would have been thrilled and the whole idea makes me shudder."

"She'll be grieving it, you understand," Eirian said.

"She hasn't said a word to me," Faustus said. "About anything."

"She will. Just let her sift it all out on her own. The legate is going to want to talk to her. Let her get through that."

"She won't know anything Caecilius wants," Faustus said. "She didn't come back out of a sudden loyalty to Rome. She came back because she found out about Lucius. I had that much from Gwladus."

"Maybe," Eirian said.

As it turned out, Silvia did know things. When Caecilius summoned her, she asked him for a sheet of papyrus and drew the route they had taken north as far as she had gone with them, as well as the way she and Gwladus had taken to flee south. Then she listed the stores, including weapons, sent by that route, and her best guess at the number of men in the spear band, and in the Demetae ranks. Gronwy's loyalty was uncertain, but she thought him too afraid of Loarn to refuse.

"What about Cadal?" Caecilius asked.

"Loarn sent an envoy to demand men and horses, since they lost your tribune," Silvia said, embellishing her map. "He had no answer by the time we started north." She drew little trees to indicate the forest and a fish in the pool where they had climbed down the waterfall.

"That's very pretty," Caecilius said, diverted.

"I used to paint."

"Are you sure about these numbers?"

"As sure as I can be. I started paying attention when I found out what Loarn had done, and that he lied to me about a war."

Caecilius looked chagrined, if only mildly. "I fear we were all deceived."

Faustus wasn't Silvia thought. *Neither was Lucius.* "I appreciated the wine and oil," she said. "That was kind of you, Legate. I will go now if you haven't any more questions."

"Of course. You have been invaluable. If you think of anything else, please come to me with it."

"Naturally." Silvia hesitated.

Caecilius noted it. He waited.

"Afterward," Silvia said. "When you are making peace. Give the kingship to Iorwen's child, with Llamrei as regent if she survives."

"And why Llamrei?" Caecilius had found Llamrei unnerving.

Because I think she is tired. Tired of war, tired of the way the Silure kingship ate its kings. Caecilius wouldn't understand that, so Silvia just said, "She negotiated the last peace. She is practical and will know what needs to be done."

Silvia took Lucius to the row of tombstones that lined the Venta road, and together they uprooted his stone and pulled it in a cart to the stonecutter who had carved it.

"Take out the inscription," Silvia said, "and write that Silvia has fulfilled her vow to Juno for the return of her son."

"Well now, that is good news," the stonecutter said. "It's not every man gets to see his own tombstone while he's still alive." He nodded at Lucius. "What do you think of it?"

"It's very nice," Lucius said politely.

"And for the new inscription? The usual formula? 'Gladly, willingly, and deservedly fulfilled, etc?'"

"Yes, please."

"It may take me a while. I've a backlog of orders from the fort." The stonecutter made notes on a tablet. "If you make a vow and the god grants what you ask for, it's a good idea to record the fulfillment before you go to war and maybe lose the chance."

"I will pay for it now," Silvia said, "but you may put me at the end of your list." So many men going off to be killed. It wasn't right they should die without paying their god his due, and maybe suffer for it after. The goddess would understand. Silvia had promised her gold bangle and a heifer as well, and that could be accomplished now.

They bought the heifer at the cattle market and took her to the priest at the shrine of Juno, Jupiter, and Minerva, along with the gold bangle. Silvia led the heifer herself. She couldn't help feeling sorry for it and it would have been easier to have the cattle market's drove boy deliver it instead, but it felt like a thing she should do, penitence for having forsaken her goddess.

A cart full of grain sacks lumbered by the temple as they were leaving, and then a line of cattle from the market where Silvia had bought the heifer. The legion was stockpiling supplies in the same way that Loarn had done, and the vicus was exceptionally busy while also exceptionally empty of Silures come to trade from the surrounding farms and villages. The streets were clogged, even in the afternoon, with men from the fort buying new boots and sturdy cloaks and using up the leave they had coming in taverns and houses like Abudia's. Lucius looked with interest at the girls who leaned from the balcony above Abudia's purple door. A bronze phallus served as the knocker. Silvia gripped his arm.

"Do *not* give me something else to worry about."

"If I ever go to a whorehouse, I will make sure you don't know about it," Lucius said. He grinned at her, and she actually grinned back, somewhat to his surprise. He put his arm around her. "When are you going to make peace with Uncle Faustus?"

"It's on my list," Silvia said.

Lucius laughed. "Item one: spill your husband's tactics to the legate. Item two: revise my tombstone. Item three: buy a cow. Item four—"

"It's not that easy," Silvia said. "I have to tell him he was right. Nobody likes that."

"No. But was he?"

"Yes and no. That's why it's not easy."

—

Silvia said as much to Faustus when she found him alone in his office, staring at maps again. He had circles under his eyes. "I've been a trouble to you, haven't I?"

He put his hand out to her.

"It wasn't your fault that Lucius snuck off with that patrol," she said. "It was your fault for not watching him better, but his that he needed watching. That's the best I've been able to come to. That and that it's my fault for listening to Loarn."

Faustus kept his hand out. She put hers in it.

"I'm sorry about Loarn," he told her. "I do think he cared for you."

"Not enough."

"No, sometimes it's not enough." He squeezed her hand and let it go. The edges of Teyrnon's tattoo just showed at the neck of her gown, the mark of a royal woman that she would carry the rest of her life, a tether to their mother's people whether she would or no. "There are things you can't weigh against love because love will lose."

"You sound like Father."

"Father." Faustus ran both hands through his hair. She could see that it was beginning to go gray just over his ears.

She sat down in the chair across from him. "You and Father were like an explosion every time you crossed paths."

"I see him sometimes," Faustus said abruptly. "He talks to me."

"In your mind, you mean."

"No. In the flesh or whatever it is."

Silvia blinked at him. "You asked me once if I ever saw him. I thought you were joking."

"Well, I wasn't. He mostly shows up to tell me what I'm doing wrong."

"You must be imagining that," Silvia said firmly. "Although I can understand why. He was always hard on you just because you weren't Marcus."

"Eirian senses him sometimes. And Gwladus thinks he's a cobweb and keeps trying to sweep him. Paullus has seen him although he won't actually admit it."

"Then why don't I ever see him?"

"Maybe you're too strong-minded."

"I'm not though. I've never been."

Faustus snorted. "You got home through land you didn't even know."

"I had paid attention. Is that your map? Here, I'll show you what I showed Caecilius."

He gave her a pen and watched her shift a river here, a hill there, and mark Gwydion's path north. "If you're right about this, Caecilius owes you a reward and I'll see that he pays it."

Silvia handed him back the pen. "Why didn't you ever tell me about Father?"

"I thought you would think I was mad."

"I do. But I thought you were mad when you joined the army." She stood and kissed his cheek. "Just come back alive."

—

A legion preparing for war settled to a different task from that of occupation. Grain was baked into army biscuit that could be eaten on the march. Cattle were slaughtered and the meat dried. Stores of oil and wine rations were assembled, cooking gear inspected by each eight-man tent for leaks and missing implements. Wagons were loaded, ready to re-supply the column. Reconnaissance patrols went farther and farther out with stakes to mark safe routes through bog land.

The surgeons checked their stores and instruments, and the field medics emptied the hospital warehouse of bandages and wound dressing. Couriers went back and forth between Isca and the outlying auxiliary garrisons, whose commanders rode into Isca to confer with Caecilius and his senior officers and rode out again with copies of Silvia's map. Legionaries wrote letters to wives and parents and brought them to Faustus, who as primus pilus had charge of the pay chest, to be stored with their pay until they came back, or didn't.

The noise from the armorer's shops was endless, beating out new pilum points, mending loose fittings in lorica and helmet that came suddenly to their owners' attention. An ample supply of lead sling bullets was cast, the legionaries of the workshop competing to produce the mold with the rudest messages: Up your wife's twat; Eat a turd; Love from Caesar.

The catapults were set up for calibration and practice on the drill field outside the fort and in the grain fields behind it, shorn of their summer harvest: an onager, the monstrous stone-thrower built for sieges, and two bolt-throwing scorpions. This war would not end with a battle on open ground. Loarn's people might retreat to Dinas Tomen if the tide turned, to regroup and harry the Roman forces from there. Caecilius intended to take Dinas Tomen.

Marcellinus directed the arrangement of targets and put up a prize for the team with the best aim. Calibrating a catapult was complicated, a fidgety business of adjusting the torsion springs and noting the range and force of each trajectory. The springs were animal sinew of varying elasticity and unequal tension between the left and right torsion would throw the aim to the side; Marcellinus cleared the field around them in all directions. Once calibrated, they would have to be taken apart again and loaded on the artillery wagons, but today's work would turn up any missing pieces and provide detailed notes for the crews manning them in the field.

Faustus took his household out to watch. None of them had ever seen these monstrosities in action and Lucius was enthralled.

"Keep your hands away from the works," Faustus said. "Plenty of catapult men retire with one less finger than they started with."

Eirian stared at the onager as its crew loaded a stone into the bucket and wound the arm down further, four men on each side.

"Stand back!"

The centurion in command hit the trigger pin with a mallet and the stone soared into the air. The onager's frame bucked with the recoil and dug itself an inch into the dirt. The stone, with no enemy's wall to halt it, soared down again from the apex of its flight and they felt the impact as it hit the far end of the field only a little short of the X chalked in the grain stubble.

Eirian put her hand to her mouth. "Death from the sky," she murmured.

"Well, yes," Faustus said. "That's what it's for."

The onager's crew adjusted the tension while the centurion made notes on a tablet. "Two more turns," he said.

One of the scorpion crews overshot their own target and recalibrated. Septimus was taking odds on the competition.

Silvia noted that as Lucius edged away from her. She put a hand on his shoulder.

"Let him," Faustus said. "He hasn't got but two sesterces with him. I made sure."

"You knew they'd be betting?"

"They'll bet on anything, especially before a battle. It's a way to unwind your own springs."

Silvia rolled her eyes. "Galerius says you won half a denarius off him once, racing snails."

"Are you writing to Galerius?" Faustus looked hopeful.

"No. This was some time ago. I don't know why I said that."

"I like Galerius," Lucius said.

"Go bet your two sesterces," Silvia said, "and mind your own business. If you lose, I'm not making it good."

Lucius came back grinning. "I bet on the left-hand scorpion. When I join the Centuriate, could I be in command of a catapult?"

"Probably," Faustus said. "No one else wants the job, as a rule."

"I don't see why." Lucius looked at the catapults longingly. "They're wonderful."

The second scorpion let fly its bolt and a cheer went up when it landed squarely on the target. It was beginning to rain and Marcellinus called a halt to the practice and awarded the amphora of wine to the scorpion's crew. Lucius collected his winnings with delight.

As they made their way back through the gates, a ripple of voices and hurrying feet met them, flowing outward from the Principia where a riderless horse was tethered. The Demetae had been seen gathering at Dinas Tomen under Gronwy's banner. Of Cadal, there was still no word.

—

Cloud banks wreathed the lower slopes of Dinas Tomen. Gronwy's men came up out of them like an army from a gray sea as Loarn watched grimly. Gwydion had ridden in the night before, shame-faced, with word of the fugitive queen and while Loarn's temper had cooled somewhat since then, he was angry still; no one accompanied him on the topmost wall of Dinas Tomen lest it flare into flame again and singe someone.

"Leave him be," Llamrei had said, and Teyrnon had agreed.

"Let him speak to the god," the old priest had said. It was Lughnasa and the king must be the first to greet the Sun Lord. "The matter of the queen falls on his shoulders; he is king." No matter who had had a hand in it, it came home to the king. That was the way of kingship. Still, the new hangings and soft cushions that the Dinas Tomen people had put in the queen's chamber had been taken away again before he could see them.

Above the cloud banks the sky was clear; a red kite sailed in it, giving its shrill call. The sun beat on Loarn's back now. He had not wanted it done, but he had known that Llew would do it, known that no one would stop him, not even himself. Nothing was stoppable now. He turned from the kite to watch Gronwy's men and saw instead the sign that Teyrnon had said he would find if he asked for it: A great shadow rose on the air, taller than Dinas Tomen, encircled in bands of light.

Loarn stared. The shadow was that of a giant – a man whose arms and legs went down, down, into the valley below. The circle of light around it glowed blue, faded outward to gold and then to blood red as the farthest ring sank into darkness where spectral feet stood on some unearthly plane.

A god come to aid in the coming battle? Or to sweep the war band into Annwn with one stroke of its hand? Loarn lifted his arm and saw the shadow ripple on the sky. He stepped to one side; the shadow and the circle of light vanished. He stepped back and it formed again, paler this time, the light a mist about its head.

Not a god. Himself.

The shadow vanished. The kite swept back across the sky, calling. Loarn climbed down the steps from the high wall.

Teyrnon met him at the foot.

"We will win," Loarn said. "My hand will reach across the mountains."

"What did you see?"

"Myself. A shadow on the air greater than the mountain that Dinas Tomen sits on. With a circle of light about me."

Teyrnon looked across the mountains. The last of Gronwy's men were coming through the lower gates, with their women and children behind them. A wind had sprung up and the clouds moved before it, taking with them whatever Loarn had seen.

"There will be some other thing coming now," Teyrnon told him. "So great a sign will bring more on its heels." Other men had seen their shadow on the sky before and followed it, thinking it some separate being, never to catch it. That the king had known it for his own fetch meant that he was marked by the gods.

By midday everyone knew what Loarn had seen; the lord of the Silures was touched by some great force. Whispers had run through Dinas Tomen like water, and through the Demetae before they were even past the last gate. Gronwy had bent his head to Loarn, and even the red cow sacrificed to Lugh had dipped her head to the knife.

The next thing was not long in coming. At the last light, a rider with a green branch came from the north to say that Cadal of the Ordovices would send to the war band the men that Loarn asked for, and would lead them himself.

"How came Cadal to change his mind?" Loarn asked suspiciously, but only after the man had been feasted as befit an envoy and the mead jug was going down the table.

Ula sat back on the bench and stretched. He took a long swallow of mead, and nodded his approval. "This is good brewing."

"My sister is keeper of the hives," Loarn said, "and you have not answered my question."

"The insult given to our king by the Roman tribune is not reason enough?"

"For which you stole him out of his bed," Gwydion said. Still smarting from the king's temper, he was on his fourth cup of mead. "And would have sold him to us, if you could tell a Roman from a Silure."

Ula reddened and Llamrei snapped, "That quarrel has been mended. Gwydion, you are in an ill position to make mock."

Ula said, "The same tribune came from their fort and annexed two Ordovice villages by force when the Romans got him back."

Loarn nodded at that. He had heard rumors and, apparently, they were true. The Romans were as vengeful as Cadal. He asked Ula, "Do you bring assurance of alliance between your king and myself?"

Ula showed him the ring set with carnelian and chalcedony. "Cadal's token. There are only matters of command and spoils to settle."

"Cadal's men will follow his standard," Loarn said. "Cadal will follow mine."

Ula shook his head. "I am not given authority to put Ordovice men under your banner. Nor would I if I had it."

"Then there is no alliance," Loarn said. "And no share of spoil."

Llamrei signaled to the slave with the mead jug, and it went down the table again, although she shook her head when it came to Gwydion. Negotiation of command, and hence of rights to spoil, was never simple. And Loarn could not grant better terms to Cadal than he had to Gronwy when Gronwy was kin and Cadal an old enemy. Nor did anyone trust Cadal to command more than his own spearmen and chariots. The foolishness of the Roman tribune had driven Cadal to alliance with Loarn, but he had been cautious in his dealings with the Romans until then. Still, Cadal was as stiff-necked as any king, and maybe more so. She thought he wouldn't change his mind.

It took a great deal of mead, and a great deal of care to fill Ula's cup twice as often as Loarn's, before matters were settled. Loarn would be in nominal command but would give no orders to Cadal's men. Cadal's lords and his spear band would have a quarter share of the spoil, and Gronwy's a quarter, and of the remaining half, Cadal and Gronwy would each take a twentieth for themselves and Loarn and his men the balance. It was not unreasonable. They would likely be fighting on Loarn's land.

When they stood finally, and slaves began to clear the wreckage of empty cups and spilled mead while the Dinas Tomen dogs and Loarn's quarreled under the table over the leavings, Ula slapped Gwydion on the back. "Anyone might lose someone," he told him, grinning, and it was plain he had heard that tale and waited for the chance to amuse himself with it once the bargain was struck.

Rhodri stepped between them. "Come with me, Cadal's envoy, to a bed in the guest house. Best to stay there the night," he added pointedly.

Llamrei prodded Gwydion in the opposite direction. "Go to bed, Gwydion, or I'll take you there by the ear."

She left him with his harp in his lap in the captains' quarters, singing to the rest of them of yet another bloody ancient battle and the great king who had won it, and stood looking out over the lower courts and the small fires of the sentries at the gates.

The thing that Loarn had seen was a great portent, but signs had a way of holding meanings that were only clear when you had been mistaken about them. Cadal had come to Loarn's banner, yes, an alliance that no Silure king had ever brought to fruition before. Was it enough? *I grow old*, she thought. Two years ago, there had been no question in her mind.

A shape moved beside the well and she froze as she saw the dark figure with a length of something in its clawed hands, outlined by the lantern that hung over it. It dipped the thing in the well, pulled it up again and wrung it out, scrubbing at it on the stone. She wondered if it was hers this time.

—

If Cadal had had any thoughts of playing Loarn false, they had vanished with the annexation of his villages. The evicted families trailed into Bryn Epona in a ragged stream, some with injuries incurred in trying to fight off the Roman occupiers with sickles and kitchen knives. Cadal gathered the rest of his scattered clans, spearmen and farmers alike, and herded them and their animals through his gates. The damaged walls were mended. Old blades were unearthed from hiding places in byres and rafters, and the final cargo of weapons landed on Cadal's coast was diverted to his own use.

—

Galerius's furious message to the Twentieth Legion's legate in Eburacum was followed by one to Caecilius in Isca, accompanied by a private note to Faustus.

> *Terentius has brought the Ordovices into the war to soothe his wounded feelings. Two villages! The ones nearest us. I told him it would drive Cadal to ally with Loarn but as he likes to point out, he outranks me, and he confiscated their stores and annexed the land and fields*

> *to the fort. This should bring the rest of our legion back, but I hope to Hades that it's in time, and meanwhile that Terentius is carried off by basilisks. Give my affectionate regards to Silvia and tell her that I am glad she has returned to us.*

Faustus did so after he had cursed Terentius, and Silvia said that she hoped that Galerius was well, and would Faustus please see to sufficient fuel for the hypocaust before they marched, since Paullus would be going with him.

"Her concern is touching," Faustus told Eirian.

"She's terrified," Eirian said. "About you, I mean."

"Are you? I'll be all right."

"When you got that tribune away from Cadal, the gods were looking after you," Eirian said. "So I'm counting on that. I just wish I could go with you. It's worse sitting here not knowing what's happening." No one's household would follow the legion on this campaign. Caecilius wanted the column capable of forced march.

"I suspect it will be quick," Faustus said. "Unless we have to lay siege to Dinas Tomen. And then it will be very boring for a long time, and I can send for you."

"If you know enough to think it will be quick, Loarn must, too. Why is he doing this?"

"Because he has to, I suppose."

To Eirian's mind, the army of Rome and the war band of the Silures might have been two great stags, driven unthinking to bellow and gore each other for the same territory. But she had known Faustus's profession before she had married him, had run with the border wolves herself in service to Rome. He would serve out his time with the army and she would serve it with him. She had known that was the cost to have the man she wanted. He had paid to have her too, she knew, in terms of his career and a wife who brought neither money nor connections.

And tomorrow he would be gone with the column. Already the auxiliaries were moving out, and Galerius's cohorts marching west from Deva to try to halt the Ordovices before they could join Loarn. Vitruvius Arvina, the Twentieth's legate, had sent word that he was on the march too finally, to everyone's relief. Eirian put her arms around Faustus, holding him here just for the while. She tugged him toward their bed chamber.

After dawn prayers, sacrifices and auguries by the haruspex and the sacred chickens, the legate's signifer raised his personal banner. The aquilifer lifted up the golden Eagle of the legion and the trumpets sounded the third call. Shields in their leather covers, packs on backs, every century and cohort slotted into its place: five cohorts in the vanguard, the artillery wagons, the baggage wagons and the hospital carts, the legionary cavalry, Caecilius and Marcellinus with the narrow-stripe tribunes, Faustus with the First Cohort and then the last four cohorts. More than one man put out a hand as they passed Cath Mawr to touch his plinth. From the outlying garrisons came the cavalry and auxiliary troops, including Faustus's old milliary cohort of Batavians behind their emerald shields, fox fur caps atop their helmets. The sun was rising in a brilliant sky, and it made the marching line of polished steel fling back its light until anyone watching it was dazzled.

Eirian waited until the last rider, the last wagon, the last rearguard scout, had disappeared. Then she took two eels from the eel tub in the kitchen, put them in a bucket, and made her way toward the riverbank.

The docks south of the empty fort were still a cacophonous jumble of barges ferrying iron and tin from upriver, lighters unloading larger ships, and smaller craft dodging between them like water striders. The scent of pitch and the gulls squawking over garbage filled the air. The eels moved in endless circles in the bucket and a gull flew down to snatch at them. Eirian swatted it away.

Past the docks and the vicus there were fewer houses, and the trees grew thick along the water's edge. The day was already warm, with midges swarming beneath the osiers on the bank. In mid-river three seals raised their heads at her approach. They were hauled out on a rocky shingle exposed by the retreating tide that frothed and bubbled around it, singing their eldritch song.

Eirian had heard them crying early that morning when she had risen to say goodbye to Faustus. Seals didn't often come upriver out of the Sabrina Channel, but she had been calling to them, and these had come. And so, she would ask them the thing that was on her mind even if she feared the answer.

Eirian took one of the eels from her bucket, a slippery yellowy-brown creature like a thick rope. She threw it into the water and the seals exploded off the shingle. They tore it between them in a thrashing frenzy and looked at her expectantly, heads bobbing in the current.

Eirian showed them the bucket with the other eel.

What am I?

She had never known how true the stories about her mother might be but after three years there was still no child. She had asked the Goddess again and again for one, an anchor to bring Faustus home safely each time he went to war. But none had come. Iorwen had spoken at the legate's banquet as if there would be children, and she was Goddess on earth, but might they instead have been babes unknowingly conceived, mismatched creatures carried only a few days? What if like a mule she couldn't breed?

The seals cocked their sleek heads to her voice, broad spotted backs like floating islands in the river. *We come ashore to mate, we have pups, it is simple*, they said.

It is not simple for me. Eirian pulled the other eel from the bucket. It thrashed in her hands. *Am I kin to you?*

They watched the eel. *Maybe. But you must choose.*

Choose? She threw the eel and they fell on it.

Sea or land. One or the other.

Choose. She had talked to the seals since she had been able to talk at all, a gift that had made her feared by her village and beaten by her aunts. The seals had been her refuge, had let her swim with their pups, and drowse with them, head on a warm flank, where they came to bask on the rocky coast of her island. There was no question about her answer, but she looked wistfully at them. There was always a price. Then, "Land," she said.

Whiskered faces nodded solemnly. They were still singing but now there were no words to be untangled from their voices. There wouldn't be again. They bobbed a little longer in the river and when no more eels appeared they set their noses to the current that was hurrying southward, only their great heads visible before they dove under.

XIX. FORTUNA

Galerius suppressed a blazing fury at Terentius while they gathered the cohorts garrisoned at Deva and began to move them southwest as Cadal's forces flowed southeast. They took half the auxiliary garrisons of the northern forts as well, leaving the rest as assurance against any unexpected attack, although the scouts reported that Cadal had left behind only enough to man the gates at Bryn Epona, and those mostly women and old men.

"We can take Cadal's hold easily now," Terentius said at that news.

"By killing all their defenseless ones?" Galerius asked him.

"Surely they would surrender."

"They would not. And we would give their war band the best possible reason to fight to the death." He felt his temper slipping. "Tribune, if you want to live out your year on the frontier, I advise you to rethink. You have already taken actions that will cost Roman lives."

Terentius stiffened. "Are you threatening me, *Centurion*?"

Galerius spoke through gritted teeth. "Certainly not."

"Then what do you mean by that?"

"Only that it's easy for an inexperienced man to have an accident. I have known several commanders who fell in bogs." Galerius turned on his heel and stalked to his tent.

Terentius watched him thoughtfully until he had ducked under the tent flap. A primus pilus's tent, but not so grand as the senior tribune's tent. Terentius had made sure of that; his own tent had a fine rug as well as a wooden floor. Things like that mattered. In the morning, he issued his own orders, to Galerius and the *angusticlavius* tribunes.

"We will take Bryn Epona and thus force Cadal to turn back to fight for it," he announced. "That is the most promising tactic."

"It isn't," Galerius said.

Terentius ignored him. "Cadal will have to turn back from the Silure band. We will split them in two." He looked pleased at his plan.

"He won't turn back, and without us the Britons will have the advantage," Galerius said, desperate now.

"March!" Terentius snapped. "I am in command, Centurion."

The tribunes murmured to each other, although they made no protest. There wasn't any point. The cohorts swung hard west toward Bryn Epona.

—

By nightfall the Twentieth Legion should have reached the old fort built by Julius Frontinus on a tributary of the River Deva. Instead, they were camped in a valley to the west on the road to Caer Gai. They would be at Bryn Epona the next evening and proceed to swarm over its slight defenses, losing at least some of their own in the process, and then to slaughter women and old men. Galerius felt sick. And then Cadal would fight to the death, taking more needless lives with him, Roman and Briton. There would be no surrender, after Bryn Epona.

Terentius had seen little need for digging in extensively and ditching the perimeter when they halted, since Cadal's forces were known not to be near. Galerius had ordered it done anyway and they had fought over it. Galerius didn't see the tribune anywhere now and assumed him to be in his tent, attended by his new slave, bought to replace the man who had stayed with Cadal. The narrow-stripe tribunes were nowhere to be seen either. They had made a habit of joining the primus pilus for a cup of hot wine in the evenings, but perhaps they would as soon not be associated with him just now. They too had looked sick at the orders, but defying a senior tribune was impossible.

The lower ranks of the Twentieth, with the resignation of the professional soldier to misguided commands, were drinking their own wine and singing beside the lingering warmth of their camp ovens. When they began trading rude verses of a song about a tribune and his horse, Galerius considered shutting them up but decided he didn't care. He had been drawing a map in the dirt, over and over, calculating the chance of taking Bryn Epona and still being in time to get between Cadal and the Silures. There was none. Not even if they ran the whole way and Bryn Epona opened its gates at the sight of them.

It had just gone full dark when rain started to spatter the camp. The legion quieted, rose from its fires, and moved under the shelter of tents. Galerius stayed, getting morosely soaked, until the rain washed out his map.

"Centurion!" The voice came out of the darkness near the ditch. "Primus pilus!"

Galerius stood and peered through the rain.

Quinctilius Rufus, one of the narrow-stripe tribunes, materialized out of the watery night. "There has been an accident," he said.

"An accident?" The other two were carrying something.

"Tribune Terentius, sir."

Galerius took a lantern off the hook by his tent and squelched through the mud to meet them beyond the ring of campfires. "What happened?"

"He took a fall." The body they carried looked inert.

"Into the ditch."

Galerius held up the lantern. "How bad is it?"

"We're fairly sure he hasn't survived it."

"A fall in the ditch?"

"There was a rock in it."

They laid him down in the trampled grass. Terentius's face was white and wet with the rain and the right side of his forehead was a hideous cavity. The rain had washed the blood away and no more flowed from it.

"Mithras," Galerius whispered.

"He didn't have his helmet on, you see," one of them said.

"The ditch is steep. Regulation depth," another said. "Per orders."

Galerius looked from one to the other. He began to feel colder than the rain.

"He wasn't going to rethink," Rufus said abruptly. "And we didn't think it ought to be you."

"Mithras," Galerius said again. What he had said to Terentius about a bog came back to him. He looked at Terentius's body. "That's the end of this subject, permanently. I'll write to his wife and father and assure them he died nobly. Find an escort tomorrow to take him back to Deva."

"And the column?"

"We'll try to catch Cadal if it's not too late." He looked from one to the other. They were nearly as white-faced as Terentius. Murder of a bad commander was not unknown, but the punishment was draconian. He had no doubt that it had occurred to them that they each would hold the others' fate in their hands for the rest of their lives. As well as his own.

—

The Ordovice territory was mountainous, a forested land of rocky uplands and looming cliffs, webbed with the rivers that flowed throughout West Britain, running full spate in summer, swollen with the runoff of rain and snowmelt from the high peaks. It was not possible to simply turn the column south. The scouts, more nimble and more familiar with the terrain, knew best the ways to intercept Cadal, and Galerius followed their lead, moving at as close to forced march as the landscape allowed. The supply wagons fell farther and farther behind, a decision made out of desperation. Each man had enough rations for three days. They would catch Cadal by then, or he would have slipped past and it wouldn't matter.

Every track and river valley that narrowed to slow the column, every ford that necessitated careful crossing, gnawed at him. The narrow-stripe tribunes were grim-faced and businesslike. Murder had been done in the name of Rome, but Rome would make no distinction for motive if the truth came to light. And Mars Ultor, father of Rome and god of armies, would expect that it not be wasted. Like every other man of the legion, the tribune had belonged to him.

Dispatch riders came and went, trading horses at each outpost, riding sleepless, to monitor the positions of the Second Augusta, the Silures, the Ordovices, and the balance of the Twentieth Legion, on the march from the east with their legate. Galerius and his staff drew and re-drew their maps, tracing the spiderweb of possible paths, marking projected meeting points, calculating miles and supplies and the remaining stamina of their men.

Just as Galerius was certain that Cadal had already slipped past them while they were detouring toward Bryn Epona, a scout came in at dusk to report that the Ordovice war band was camped half a day away. At forced march, they could cut them off. It could still be done, barely.

Galerius didn't need to think about it. "This is our best chance. How many men?"

"Near six thousand at a guess," the scout said. "Some look like farmers to me."

"That many?" Rufus said. "Cadal is angry, then." To call farmers and shepherds into his war band, Cadal was very angry indeed. Those owed enlistment to that service only in dire circumstances.

Galerius considered the possibilities. He had five cohorts and the Twentieth Legion cavalry, plus two auxiliary cavalry cohorts and one of infantry, all undermanned. Three thousand

and some. They would need to surprise them, and to choose their ground. If they could.

"Where is the balance of the legion?"

"One day away now by the last courier's calculation."

"What are the chances of holding Cadal until they get here?"

"Maybe," the scout said. "But I got close enough to hear talk. They know we've only half the legion. Whatever we bring against them, they'll know that's all we have."

Rufus looked at Galerius. "Talked anyway, didn't he? Before your border wolves got him back."

"He said they hadn't mishandled him," Galerius said. "It was Loarn who wanted him to talk."

"He was always a fool with a loose tongue. Threatening vengeance, no doubt, and listing all the forces he could call up. Something like that."

Galerius let his breath out, trying to still his fury at a man who was dead anyway. "All right. The best we can do is try to slow them down." He turned back to the scout. "Give me a route that won't leave us open to ambush. And send a rider to Arvina. We'll try to drive them toward him."

—

The upland moor where Cadal's war band was camped was thick with mist. Galerius, on the ridge above them, could see nothing, but they were down there. The scout had said so and the border wolves were rarely mistaken. Cadal wouldn't see Galerius's cohorts either until the mist cleared.

"Slingstones," he told Rufus. "We'll give them a surprise."

A cohort of Asturian auxiliaries came forward quietly on Rufus's order, slings in hand, lining the edge of the ridge. They measured the distance and loosed the first barrage, with another and another behind it. Their lead bullets, cast with a hole through the center to shriek as they flew, sliced through the silence of the fog.

Cadal's camp erupted in panic, stumbling through the mist. A slingstone smacked into a tent pole and snapped it. Another chanced to hit a spearman and broke his arm. Another drove its weight into a second man's chest, caving in the breastbone. Many fell harmlessly but they caused chaos in the camp, dropping unseen from the sky and screaming as they fell.

Galerius could hear the shouted orders as Cadal pulled back. Cadal was camped on the near side of a ford, the scout had said. The ford offered an easy passage, but it would be dangerous to cross blindly. They were apparently doing so anyway to retreat beyond the slingstones' range.

Galerius ordered his men off the ridge then, out of sight of the war band below when the mist burned off. It was starting to thin as the sun rose higher. They descended by the route that the scout had marked, through bracken and gorse, as quietly as possible and clearing only as much as they needed for passage. The cavalry dismounted, led their horses down the slope. At the base of the ridge, around a jutting embankment from Cadal's band, they halted and formed up. A silver loop of the river shone through the clearing fog, a thin veil that was dissipating rapidly. Galerius nodded at the First Cohort standard bearer. He lifted the standard, a silver spear pointed at the sky, and the cornicen blew his horn.

As they came around the embankment, they saw Cadal's band on the far side. The Ordovices had fought their way blindly across the ford and as the mist cleared had begun to sort themselves out to meet whatever had attacked them. At the sight of the Romans, a rank of spearmen formed a front line with horsemen on either flank. The lords of the Ordovices mounted their chariots spears-in-hand while their drivers shook out the reins. Galerius could see Cadal at the forefront, in a hauberk of bronze scale, his tawny head bare and his face painted with blue lines to either side of the spiraling king mark on his brow. His driver drew his ponies to a halt on the riverbank.

"You are making a mistake, king!" Galerius shouted across the water.

"The mistake is Rome's!" Cadal called back. He held a spear in one hand and three more in the other with his shield.

"Rome wishes only peace with you."

"Rome annexed my land!" A roar of anger rose from the men behind him.

"Let us discuss that," Galerius suggested. "It is possible that can be undone."

"And done again at Rome's whim," Cadal said. "No."

Galerius nodded his head. "I cannot deny that." He leaned forward on his saddle horns. "But after today we will take every hectare of your land and parade you in chains in the streets of Rome." He waited to see if that angered Cadal enough to launch an attack. It didn't. Cadal had no more intention of coming back across the ford than he had of surrendering.

Galerius eyed the river. They would have to cross to attack, or else let them go. The ford was wide from bank to bank and the current swift but shallow; a chariot wheel broken off in the blind crossing showed half out of the water. Both upstream and down the water was swift and studded with moss-grown stones and the length of bank that bordered the ford was narrow. Across the river lay a flat valley. On the near side rose the ridge they had come down, and a series of further ridges, falling to the south into the far side of the same valley. All along the river the Ordovices waited, and Galerius thought the scout had been right about their numbers.

He put the Asturians shield to shield to make the first crossing with the heavy legionary cavalry behind them to break through Cadal's lines on either edge of the ford, clearing the way for the main body of his army. There was no other way than this to stop Cadal's war band or even to slow it, and no waiting for the rest of the Twentieth. He signaled to his cornicen and the trumpet sounded once more.

Cadal's chariots raced along the riverbank, hurling spear after spear into the ranks crossing the river. The Asturian front line held their shields before them and the rear ranks over their heads, but some of the Ordovice spears went home nonetheless, and the advancing line stumbled over the bodies in the water. When the Britons had exhausted their throw spears and the Asturians were clambering over the bank, returning fire with a volley of pilum points, the Ordovice lords leapt down, sending their chariots to the rear, swords in hand, hacking their way into the front ranks of the Romans. On either flank the Roman cavalry drove into Cadal's spearmen while Cadal's cavalry skirmished with them to push them back into the river, over the bank beyond the ford into rougher water.

Galerius, still mid-river, estimated that more than half of Cadal's band was armed with axes or pitchforks, but they were numerous and likely more deadly with the axes they used daily than with a war spear. The advantage that the Romans had was their formation, the ingrained discipline, the memory of each maneuver locked into the muscles of the body, that kept them moving forward, shields opening up to pull in a man from the rear as one in front fell, locking shields again, moving on another step, stab with the wicked, efficient short sword, take another step. But they were badly outnumbered. There was no keeping the legionary cohorts in reserve. Galerius signaled to the cornicen; the cohorts of the Twentieth Legion followed the Asturians.

He came ashore at the head of the First Cohort and by then his army had pushed the Britons back from the riverbank and made room for themselves to hammer at Cadal's front lines. Farther from the bank however there was more room for Cadal's army to envelop Galerius's on either flank. As they pushed farther into the valley they turned outward on either end of the line, forming a rectangle, holding off the Britons that hammered at either flank. The cavalry skirmishing with Cadal's horsemen had better going. Roman troop horses, even those of the light cavalry, outweighed the Britons' ponies, and were taller.

But now Galerius could see men and horses both slowing. Three days of forced march had taken its toll. He felt it himself when he barely got his shield up in time to block an axe blow from a fox-haired farmer in a scarred leather shirt and ragged trousers.

The bodies of a hundred men lay in the waters of the ford, their armor preventing the current from taking them downriver. On the shore, more had fallen, Roman and Briton both. As they pushed at Cadal's war band, they climbed over the bodies of their dead and his. Cadal's superior numbers were beginning to break Galerius's line. And there were no reserves.

Rufus reined his horse in next to Galerius's. He had a bloody gash down one thigh. "It's getting bad," he said.

"I know." Galerius looked at the sun, beginning to slide down the other side of the sky. They had cost Cadal a day. That might be enough. "Fall back," he said. They still might tempt Cadal to chase them, toward Arvina and the other half of the legion.

Rufus signaled the cornicen; the trumpet sounded *Pull Back*.

The Twentieth and its auxiliaries fell back in formation, the cavalry on their flanks, still deadly but tempting pursuit. There was none. Cadal halted his war band at the riverbank. A few hundred, unheeding, began to cross after the Romans anyway. Cadal ordered them back while the Romans turned and taunted them to follow. Roman cavalry encircled the ones who disobeyed, and they went down into the water under the troop horses' hooves and the heavy cavalry long swords, and the ford ran red again. A commotion on the far bank said that Cadal's lords were arguing with him, but he shouted them down and no more crossed.

Galerius made camp on the ridge to wait for the hospital and supply wagons to catch up to them, and watched as Cadal's war band moved away down the valley while the pyre for the Roman dead burned.

"At the least, we cost him," Rufus said. "It's a shame though, the bastard wouldn't chase us."

Cadal was too wily to waste more lives here, Galerius thought, when very likely his own scouts had informed him that the other half of the legion was on the march. "We did what we could," he said ruefully. "If we hadn't been delayed, we could have picked better ground. Now we wait for the legate."

"The legate…" Rufus began.

Galerius said, "Legate Arvina has been informed of the unfortunate accident suffered by Tribune Terentius." He paused while Rufus waited uneasily. "He completely understands that ill luck sometimes comes to a man unexpectedly." Galerius hoped that would reassure Rufus and his fellow tribunes. What Vitruvius Arvina had said in a private message to Galerius was *Whatever Fortuna has raised on high, she lifts but to bring low, according to Seneca, and I don't doubt it. I hope you have thanked her properly.* Galerius thought it best not to share that.

Vitruvius Arvina stayed only long enough to take Galerius's report and hand him command, with orders to follow at speed, before he rode south to meet Aulus Caecilius.

The two legates conferred by lamplight in Caecilius's scarlet tent, accompanied by Marcellinus, Caecilius's junior tribunes, and Faustus. The marching camp of the Second Augusta and its attendant auxiliaries sprawled over a high moor protected on one side by bog and on the north by an elevation that commanded a view across the valley floor and anything that moved on it. They bent their heads over a map and discussed command in careful phrases. With no military governor, overall command of the legions stationed in Britain was vague. Faustus was unacquainted with Vitruvius Arvina, who had been at Eburacum since Faustus's posting to the Augusta. The legate of the Twentieth was a tall, spare man with a beaked nose and a brush of graying dark hair, senior by a few years to Caecilius. Faustus expected him to assume command, or try to.

"Has the situation in the east stabilized?" Caecilius asked Arvina when they had exchanged greetings and reports. "Or is West Britain merely the greater emergency?"

"Both and neither," Arvina said. "The Ninth is solid enough to trust, if the Brigantes are not. The Ordovices…" He hesitated.

"Yes," Caecilius said. "It's surprising how much damage one ill-chosen man can do."

"I am told that you refused to have him," Arvina said.

"I did," Caecilius admitted. "I had a bit of inside information, having known him at school." He paused. "I am sorry to have foisted him on you," he offered.

"I serve Rome, as do we all." Arvina also paused and then shrugged his bony shoulders. "I do not care to be another ill-chosen man. Someone must command in this war and I have not only been absent from West Britain for over a year, but it was a man under my command – who I should have taken to Eburacum with me – who provoked Cadal. Your officers know that, as do mine. I intend to defer to you."

"That is generous of you," Caecilius said carefully. Faustus thought he was startled.

"Nothing of the sort," Arvina said. "I assure you I have never been called generous. Only practical."

"Very well then." Caecilius abandoned polite argument. "Here is my thinking: Loarn will wait in Dinas Tomen for Cadal. I have no wish to lay siege to Dinas Tomen if I can help it. I want them in the open."

"The Twentieth will be on Cadal's heels," Arvina said. "And on their rear when they venture out."

"Precisely. And then they will move south where we will be waiting, somewhat before they wish for us." Caecilius spread the map on his camp desk. "He will be trying to take the most advantageous ground. Here." He tapped finger on the map. "We need to stop him here…" Another tap "… before he can reach it."

Arvina inspected the map. "This is very detailed. How accurate is it?"

"It is a compilation of everything the surveyors and scouts have recorded, and some new information from my primus pilus's sister who has an adventurous soul. Valerianus recruited her help in combining them all. We feel that it is fairly accurate."

Arvina noted Faustus's stone-faced demeanor and asked no questions about the adventurous sister. "Where is the advantage to us in this particular place?" He poked a finger at the spot south of Dinas Tomen where Caecilius had inked a small circle.

"They will have to come through this valley if they take the path we believe they will follow. This place…" Caecilius tapped the circle on the map "… offers an uphill slope with forest on either side to force them together, and cover to wait for them unseen."

"How many days' march from here?"

"Another day. Two days for them from Dinas Tomen. The trick of course is being sure they are actually coming that way, and not being spotted ourselves before they are where we want them. Right now they have no doubt where we are camped. When to move is the question. And how."

"How many alternate routes are there?"

"For Loarn? Not many." Caecilius turned to Faustus. "Valerianus?"

"Only two," Faustus said, "that won't spread his army into multiple columns threading their way through the high mountains and down different glens. Or taking all by one narrow way and having the rearguard days behind the van."

"And they are?"

"West of Gobannium toward Pen-y-Darren, and then south to the coast to come up along the settlements there. Or maybe east to Ariconium and down to Sabrina Mouth. Either way, they could do great damage before we could turn around to stop them. If we guess wrong."

"Either of those routes takes them through British towns and mixed settlements," Tribune Marcellinus said, leaning over the map. "If Loarn wants to rule as king after this war, he won't want to despoil his own people."

"Nor will he," Caecilius said. "How long until Cadal comes to Dinas Tomen?"

"Four days at a guess."

Discussion went back and forth across the map while Caecilius sent his slave for hot wine.

"How if we laid siege to Dinas Tomen first?"

"It would take more than four days to crack that egg and then we'd have Cadal at our backs, cutting supply lines."

"If it was only Loarn's men, we could do it."

"If it was only Loarn's men we'd have met them by now. Loarn wants to make war, not hide."

"It will have to be done in the open," Caecilius said flatly. Rome's strength depended on pitched battle where the discipline of long drilling gave whole cohorts the ability to change formation and move on a trumpet call to outmaneuver greater numbers. "And where we have the advantage of surprise. The question is how to achieve that when they know where we are now."

In the king's hall at Dinas Tomen, Loarn and Cadal faced each other at one end of a table laden with the remains of a meal of beer and mutton. Dark head and graying fair one, a raven and a kite forced to some unorthodox alliance. They had been quarrelling all afternoon.

Loarn pointed a finger at the Ordovice king. "Look you, Cadal, this doing must be done completely. The Romans swept from our land clear past the iron mines in the east and the cities and forts on their main road north, clear of all the Westlands. So that even if their slaves in the east let them bide there still, they will not come back to us again. And for that, I will command."

"No man but me commands my own." Cadal held up his hand with the carnelian and chalcedony ring. "In any case they would not follow you."

"They will follow you. And you will follow me. That was the bargain made for your share of the spoil."

"I could have stayed in the north and driven the Romans only from our land," Cadal snapped. "And taken spoil there would be no need to share."

"To have them come back again. If indeed you did drive them out."

"My spear band follows Loarn," Gronwy interrupted and Iodoc nodded. They sat at the end of the table between the quarreling kings, with Cadal's lords down one side and Loarn's the other. "He speaks truth in this," Gronwy insisted. "We must be united against them or fail again." Since Lughnasa, Gronwy had been Loarn's man, not for love but for awe of the thing that Loarn had seen.

"I am not a Silure lapdog," Cadal said. "Not for any share of spoil."

He opened his mouth to say more and Llamrei asked abruptly, to forestall them both, "What does Teyrnon Chief Druid say? Or you?" She looked at the younger, red-haired Ordovice man who sat beside Teyrnon, sharing a place on the bench a little away from both sets of council lords.

Before Teyrnon could answer, if he would, the younger man said, "Druids do not belong to kings, nor to a tribe except that they are born of it. We serve the gods. I am not the priest of Cadal but of my own order. As is Teyrnon."

Teyrnon stood and leaned on his staff. "As he says. We have spoken to the rivers. We have studied their currents and the fish that swim there. We have looked to the sky and its birds, and the patterns in their flight. Thus the Sun Lord speaks, as does the Goddess in all her aspects light and dark, and Ocelus of Battles. Thus they speak and have spoken to us."

"And what have they said?" Llamrei asked impatiently although she knew that she could sooner hurry a snail.

Teyrnon looked up and down the table. "In every pattern, in every cloud and ripple and blade of grass, we have seen the same: the vision that came to Loarn king on Lughnasa. He will lead because it is his fate to do so."

"Is this as he says?" Cadal demanded of the younger Druid.

The red-haired man touched a fingertip to the heavy gold sun disk that hung across his chest. "It is, Lord."

Llamrei let out a quiet breath of relief. Cadal would listen to the Druids, no matter how much it went against his pride. The alliance would stand. She hadn't been sure. Cadal was prideful and volatile, and he hated Loarn. And the younger priest, for all his high-flown words, might have been inclined to back him if it were not for Loarn's vision. She wondered if anyone had asked the Druids if they would win.

"That would be pointless," Rhodri said when she muttered as much to him later in the captains' house. "Druids never give a direct answer because they don't think that way and the way they do think confuses ordinary people. Their idea of victory might be that the Romans actually leave a hundred years from now. No point in asking more than they've said. They put great store in Loarn's vision. I'm satisfied with that."

"That vision frightens me. Teyrnon says it was himself he saw."

Rhodri fished in the pouch at his belt. "I have something for you."

He put four rings of enameled bronze in her hand. Not jewelry, but a set of terrets for a pony harness, finely enameled in red and white.

"Where did you come by these?" she asked, admiring them.

"They were given me by Loarn at the marriage."

Llamrei winced. Loarn had given bride gifts liberally to his captains, and lesser gifts to lord and villager alike. He had given Llamrei a gold arm band.

Rhodri said, "Bride gifts are lucky, no matter the bride. They will match your ponies' headstall fittings. I thought of that as soon as I saw them."

If Loarn and Cadal didn't kill each other, the war band would ride out tomorrow. A new piece of gear brought luck in battle. Llamrei stood and took Rhodri's hand. "Come let's put them on my harness," she said. "Then they will give us both luck."

Pwyll and Gwydion watched them go and smiled and shrugged. There would be many courting luck that night. Gwydion took out his harp and Pwyll laid his head on Gwydion's thigh.

—

In the house allotted to the king of the Ordovices, both to honor him and to keep him under watch, Cadal lay wakeful while his slaves and his dogs snored on the floor beside his bed, and two of his spearmen stood outside. Three bars of moonlight came through the shutters across the one window that pierced the wall, and their pattern was a message. Three was the number of his grievance against the Romans: for the insult by the tribune, for the theft of the tribune, for the annexation of his villages. Three was the vengeful number, three the number of power. Three times he would make the Romans sorry. The peace that had seemed propitious to him since the last war was no more. Peace was only the answer until someone else betrayed it. It was clear to him now what he should have known before: Rome was not to be trusted. Whether or not Loarn could be trusted was not settled. Any man might claim a vision, and no one but Loarn had seen his. Cadal would follow his own vision if Loarn's did not lead where he wished.

XX. BLOOD AND BONE

The figures scrambling across the destruction of the camp's walls might have been so many great beetles, plates catching just the faintest sheen from the waning moon. They moved in a silent wave through the forest and after a while another wave came after them. The ditch had been mostly filled in with the turf from the walls on striking the camp, as Romans always did, lest their fortifications be used by their enemies.

Faustus counted each century as it left, counted in his head the time to delay the next, tapped its centurion on the shoulder at the next owl hoot from the trees. One more cohort out. A quick silent prayer to Mithras that they should be right. There was no guarantee that Loarn would move as they thought, nor any guarantee of finding him if he didn't, in this wild country that Loarn knew like the courtyard of his hall.

The First Cohort would be the last, with the legate and his staff following with Caecilius's personal escort. Marcellinus was in the vanguard, to sort everyone into position before dawn. An owl hooted again up ahead, and Faustus nodded to the legate and moved the last of his men out, over the broken wall and the soft earth of the newly filled ditch. They crossed the cleared ground around the broken camp and vanished in the darkness of the trees. Only the silence of the wild things in the forest betrayed their passage.

Small figures watched them go. The people of the hills were often about at night, and it paid to investigate anything out of the ordinary. The great machines that threw bolts and rocks had gone away earlier, with the gold bird that was the legion's token, accompanied by wagonloads of enough supplies to feed the people of Blaidd Llwyd for weeks. It was no matter to them why the Romans were leaving in the night, but Sun People didn't see well in the dark and likely that meant there would be things spilled or left behind.

When the last humped shapes, even more beetle like for the packs on their backs, had gone, they waited a bit more, listening to see if anyone or anything stayed behind. When they were sure that none did, they swarmed over the ditch and wall and spread out through the abandoned camp, putting into their bags a dropped copper coin, an onion, a broken saddle girth. Then they melted into the darkness. Wars between the Sun People were no business of theirs, except to follow like the crows and glean whatever spoil the winners left behind. There was always something.

—

The cohorts of the Twentieth Legion, reunited, marched south toward Dinas Tomen along the main road that ran from Deva through Viroconium to Magnis. As they passed, Arvina and Galerius pulled detachments from their auxiliaries and left them at both settlements. The civilians at Viroconium had moved within the walls of the decommissioned fort there and greeted the detachments with relief. They had been at peace with Rome for decades but always uneasy with their Ordovice neighbors. The spear band marching south was not to their liking. Nor was it to the Dobunni town of Magnis which looked to Rome for protection from the Silures.

Arvina made no attempt to hide his progress, and indeed made as much noise of it as he could, with regular trumpet calls, and a column that clogged the road for miles, accompanied by auxiliary and legionary cavalry, mounted archers, and baggage wagons carrying supplies and the hospital tents and equipment. The Second Legion's camp had been struck and appeared to have joined the Twentieth; their Eagle and the legate's personal standard were seen among the moving column. The heavy artillery wagons and disassembled catapults had lumbered along the same road to join it. The whole Roman army seemed to be converging on Dinas Tomen from the north to lay siege there.

–

Liking neither the ground he would fight on nor the prospect of a siege, Loarn led the combined war band out of Dinas Tomen toward Isca before the Romans could reach him. Favorable ground to meet Rome lay three days south. There they would halt where they could force the Roman commanders to come at them at a disadvantage.

–

Vitruvius Arvina looked up and down the wide valley; his column flooded it from side to side, a mass of steel and scarlet, the green and blue of the auxiliaries, the gold and silver of the standards. He had been chasing Loarn's war band south as it tried to outmaneuver him, lose itself in the wild hills and forests. But there was only one logical way for it to go, and it was a great mass of men to hide easily. And he doubted Loarn would risk waiting much more – the conscripted farmers and townsmen, particularly Cadal's, would drift off to their homes again if he delayed too long. Arvina bent his head to the scout's report again and nodded, conferred again with Galerius, and went off to say a private prayer to Mithras.

–

Faustus lay with his nose an unlovely inch away from stinking mud that released small bubbles of gas every so often, brewed by eons of decaying forest floor. Midges swarmed around his face. Thick tree cover surrounded them, and the heavily overgrown slopes below concealed further cohorts and the men of Faustus's old First Batavians. Unfortunately, most of the overgrowth was gorse.

The valley below them sloped slightly upward to the north and then again just past the ridges and slopes where his men lay concealed, with a flat plain between. On the southern upward slope, the ridges on either side bore inward, narrowing the way. Caecilius's orders were for absolute stillness. "I don't care if you've an adder up your skirt, nobody moves," Faustus said. They had been there since dawn, with midges up the nose and gorse spines in the nethers, and the tension of waiting hung over the valley like heat shimmer. Faustus thought it would be a wonder if the Britons couldn't actually see it. Assuming that they came this way, and there was always the gut-wrenching possibility that they wouldn't.

When the war band did come, they felt it before they heard it, a vibration in the ground of chariot wheels and hoofbeats, and marching feet. No war horns sounded, to Faustus's relief. Loarn was on the march, not readying for battle, no doubt trying to keep far enough ahead of Arvina's Twentieth Legion to reach their chosen ground before they turned to fight. Would they assume the Second Legion to be with it? Caecilius had done everything he could to assure that: sent the catapults north with the Augusta's standards, even its Eagle, an almost unheard of action; moved the Augusta's actual men and auxiliaries out of the camp at night in small groups, silent in the darkness, horses' hooves wrapped with cloth, bridle bits and buckles muffled.

"Get ready." Faustus spoke softly to Septimus and to the First Cohort's standard bearer lying beside him. With the Augusta's Eagle in Arvina's custody, the standard of the First Cohort, hung with a vexillum bearing the legion's Capricorn badge, would serve temporarily in its place. The legion's aquilifer had gone with his Eagle, flatly refusing to hand it to anyone else or trust anyone else to bring it through a battle to its legate and its legion as soon as the conflict was joined.

Now Faustus could see them in the distance, the front ranks of spearmen followed by chariots moving at a walk. Behind the chariots came mounted spearmen and rank after rank on foot. Trailing those would be the levies of the villages, farmers and sheepherders, many newly equipped with the smuggled weapons that Loarn had bought. They were untrained and their ranks would be more easily broken than the spear band. But they filled the valley. Faustus thought he could see the rear ranks, but he wasn't sure. More than ten thousand, nearer fifteen.

Even with a recent rain, they raised a dust cloud that filled the air, casting a yellow-brown haze across the valley. Loarn's sun wheel standard marked the king's place in the front line. Cadal was among his own chariots; his standard, the silver figure of a running horse, lifted above his head with his standard bearer's every stride.

Now the front line began to narrow as the valley narrowed between the gorse-covered slopes that led to woods on east and west. The watchers in the trees tensed. Almost. Almost. Wait for them to reach the dead tree that marked the point two thirds of the way down the valley on the southern upslope, too far to turn back. Wait for the signal from Caecilius, sitting his horse on the highest ridge, a vantage point from which he watched the approach; watched, Faustus hoped, as Arvina's cohorts appeared.

The trumpet call, sharp, repeated, cut through the air. They rose to their feet from the gorse and the trees while the trumpet sounded again and again and was answered by a sister in the distance. Faustus let out a long breath of relief at that.

The spear band halted a moment in confusion and then Loarn's war horn bellowed its answer, an undulating wail that made the hair rise on Faustus's arms. Loarn's voice could be heard shouting between the bellowing of the horns. The Roman auxiliaries were first in the attack, loosed to batter at the center of the war band and hold the slopes on either side to bunch them together. Faustus's old cohort of Batavians lumbered through the gorse, keeping formation, and their green shields locked into place as the Britons' chariots galloped at them. The drivers urged their ponies as near to the shield line as they would go, but they didn't like what appeared to be a solid wall and balked. As the chariots swung around, riders ran along the poles to hurl their spears deep into the Batavians' line. Some went down but the Batavians held until the chariots drew off, driven by the auxiliaries' spears and flights of arrows and slingstones from the slopes above. The horsemen and foot fighters behind them took their place and it was then that the sheer numbers of the war band began to tell. The trumpet sounded again, and six legionary cohorts moved up to reinforce the line.

The noise of the battle was deafening. Faustus listened for the trumpet that had sounded far up the valley but the sound of steel on steel, of wounded men, of shrieking wounded horses beat at his ears. The heavy legionary cavalry were at a disadvantage on the slopes to either side; a calculation that Caecilius and Arvina had weighed against the chance to bottle up Loarn between them. The Batavians and other auxiliaries, less likely to break a leg on a slope where the gorse might hide outcrops of rock or a badger's sett, pulled to the sides to encircle Loarn's flanks. The First Cohort pushed forward now, on the right flank where the ground gave the Britons the best advantage. They moved with the precision of pieces on a game board, the most experienced soldiers of the legion who had earned the right of their assignment to the First. The cohort standard with its Capricorn banner waved over them. Faustus had whistled Arion out of the trees at the first trumpet and now from his back, he could see a gleam of something in the distance – the Twentieth on the march. Their horns sounded again, and he could just hear them over the din.

A blue-painted warrior, a Silure by his dark hair, with a spear in one hand and three more gripped in the hand that went through his shield strap, aimed an already bloody blade at Faustus, clearly intent on taking the commander out. Faustus swung his long sword down into the blow as Arion pivoted with the expertise of an experienced troop horse. Beside Faustus his front ranks hurled their pila into the Britons' line. A pilum point sank deep into the Silure shield, dragging it downward. Its owner yanked angrily at the shaft with his spear hand, losing the spear in the process, but the softer iron shank of the pilum had bent on impact and could not be dislodged. Faustus swung his sword again as the man abandoned his shield and faced him, a spear in each hand; they were too close now for the spear to have the advantage and Faustus's sword sliced deep into the shoulder muscle. The Silure fighter tried to stay on his feet, but his spear arm was useless and pouring blood. He lost the spear he thrust at Faustus with his other hand and then staggered backward through the Silure line, but another man took his place, and another and another; the Roman line wavered.

—

Caecilius, on his ridgetop, watched the advancing Twentieth Legion as it poured down the valley to strike the Britons' rear. He nodded at one of his junior tribunes. "Those are conscripts at the rear, not fighting men. Tell Arvina to use the scorpions and to hold them until they grow desperate. Then let them through and see if they run. It will cost us fewer lives to hunt fleeing farmers down than to fight those with nothing to lose."

"Is he to take prisoners, sir?"

"Not among the lords. This will be the last rebellion."

The tribune saluted and rode at a gallop.

—

The men at the rear of the war band were not desperate. They were angry – at their king who had called them to leave their farms to fight over a slight to himself, at the Romans who now stood between them and the way home, at the Silures, subject of an ancient hatred who had led them into a trap. They hefted the axes with which they split firewood and lifted their scythes above their heads to swing at the Romans' throats. They were helmetless, armorless, and mostly with a small ancient shield or none, but they fought doggedly and gave no ground until Loarn ordered warriors from Cadal's spear band back through the battle to reinforce them. Cadal quarreled with Loarn over that for pride's sake, but the men at the rear were mainly his, and so he pulled the spearmen belonging to his lesser lords and sent them to hold the line.

The British war band outnumbered the combined legions by nearly five thousand men and the auxiliaries struggled to contain their efforts to come around the Roman flanks and encircle the army that had encircled them. Caecilius and Arvina had both underestimated the ferocity of a sheepherder removed from his sheep and facing a Roman cohort between him and his home farm. While the high lords and their household spear bands fought the legions, the conscripted farmers spread out across the slopes and battered at the auxiliaries trying to pen them in.

Faustus could see the Roman flanks collapsing as they struggled across the sloping hillsides. A trumpet call told him that Caecilius had ordered the auxiliary cavalry to their defense. He narrowed his eyes at a figure in a lionskin hood who dodged among them and swung a pole topped with the gilded iron Eagle of a legion at anyone who got in his way: The Augusta's aquilifer, bringing its Eagle home. Faustus pointed and the First Cohort signifer waved the silver standard with its Capricorn banner above the chaos of the battle, guiding him in.

When the aquilifer halted, bleeding, gasping, but still upright, the sight of the Eagle drew a roar from the cohorts of the legion. The line stiffened, held, began to push back.

"For Rome!"

"For your Eagle!"

As the chariot line drew off, Llamrei sent her ponies, with their fine new terrets, to the rear. Years of war had taught her people that chariots never served against the Romans. A thundering pair of ponies and a spear-armed rider balancing on the pole could unsettle the enemy before them enough to break their formation. But then, after that, the war was fought on foot, spear to spear. Now she drove her spear into a Roman's throat, pulled it back and went for another. His short sword slid across her scale hauberk, catching in the links and she twisted back and thrust her spear between his legs and then into his neck as he fell. The Romans had made a wedge of their front line, trying to split Loarn's men from Cadal's and their lines were intermixed with the Britons now, struggling to hold and each to break the other.

The smuggled iron and blades had been worth the silver: the Silures were nearly as well armed as the Romans, even their villagers, and it was making a difference. Some old-fashioned lords still went naked into battle but most, like Llamrei, were helmeted and armored in scale or ring mail. She caught a glimpse of Rhodri fighting with a Roman officer on horseback and then lost sight of both. She put Rhodri from her mind. To lose concentration was to die. She had seen Gronwy go down when a Roman took Iodoc who was Gronwy's spear brother and something more. An instant's mourning had killed him. She called Gronwy's lords to her and because Gronwy had bent his head to Loarn at Dinas Tomen, they followed.

The battle raged down the whole valley, but the heart of it was Loarn on a black horse, swinging a long sword with a hilt of twisted gold and crowned not just with gold and the king mark but with the vision that had come to him at Lughnasa. Loarn's captains clustered around him, but they gave him room to fight. A king did not lead a war band from a hilltop like the Roman commanders. A king won or died.

As the opposing sides struggled and the Romans pushed farther in – and their danger there was that the Britons would come around their rear – she caught a glimpse of the tribune who had been at the legate's banquet, and then of the centurion who was brother to Silvia, and the thought flicked through her head that the old legends thick with tales of blood feud quarrels born at feasts no doubt had some truth in them.

Loarn's sun wheel standard waved over him, catching the alternate light and shadow of cloud moving overhead. The sky was darkening in the west. Rain would churn the ground to a swamp, and she tried to think, in the instant between one enemy and the next, who that would give advantage to.

–

Faustus also looked at the sky and calculated the chances of rain. Rain would turn the trodden dirt to slippery muck. If they could drive the Britons back down the slopes, they wouldn't get up them again. Penned in the lowest part of the valley they would be trapped. He wasn't surprised when a junior tribune rode hard toward him carrying that order.

"Legate says to pull back a bit and bunch them up," the tribune said and put his heels to his horse, riding to the next commander.

"Pull back! In formation! On me!" Faustus bellowed into the din and the First Cohort coalesced around him, a moving wedge flattening to a rectangular line across the valley, the other cohorts to either side, the Eagle over their heads.

"Hold them now!"

It wasn't long before a drop spattered on Faustus's foot, and he heard others hit his helmet. The auxiliaries on the flanks were beginning to close ranks, pushing hard while the Britons fought to climb the slope. The reserves of the legion came out of the trees to reinforce them, and the Britons began to fall back. It was a calculated risk. To try to fight your way through a packed enemy was dangerous and there was no guarantee they would surrender, even surrounded. If the legions had to wade in and simply kill people until they were all dead, they would lose men themselves.

Marcellinus rode down the front line under the legate's banner. The increasing rain washed the dust from his silvered cuirass; it gleamed in the wet air. He halted opposite Loarn as the battle raged around them. Loarn was mounted on a black pony, helmetless, the red-gold crown that had been Aedden's and Bendigeid's before him bright on his dark hair.

"Surrender now!" Marcellinus shouted. "You are surrounded. Surrender and the terms will be merciful."

Faustus doubted that, but then there were many ways to be merciful: an easy death as opposed a parade through the streets of Rome with an execution in the Tullianum afterward.

Loarn put his hands on the saddle horns and leapt up to stand in the saddle. He raised his sword in one hand and his bright-painted shield in the other. A gilded sun wheel circled its bronze boss, blazing through the rain. "There will be no surrender but only war until Rome has left the Westlands!"

Not Britain, Faustus noted. Loarn was giving the legate an out: *Pull back from West Britain, and there will be peace.* What Loarn did not understand, or simply refused to, was that there would not be peace even if Rome lost today's battle, and they might. There would only be vengeance. More legions, a military governor finally, a siege of Dinas Tomen.

A flung spear skidded across Marcellinus's cuirass. A volley of pila returned the gesture and Loarn's captains pulled him down into the saddle again.

Caecilius watched from his ridge and swore. He sent a tribune to Arvina far up the valley.

"The general says to let them through now and see if they'll run," the tribune said, rain dripping off his helmet. "Cut off the lords and the spear-trained, but let the farmers out. That may be the last that Cadal sees of them."

"Very likely," Arvina said, and gave the order.

The scorpion bolts that had rained down on the rear of the war band ceased. The whistle of sling bullets overhead ceased.

A gap opened up in the Twentieth Legion's ranks. Men began to drain from the valley like coins through a torn purse.

"You betray us!" Loarn shouted angrily at Cadal when the word came from the rear.

"I promised men to the war band, and you promised we would meet the Romans a day from here. I owe a fool nought." Now Cadal shouted angrily for the driver who held the reins of his chariot ponies, trapped like the rest in the seething mass that filled the valley. The driver brought the ponies up and Cadal mounted his chariot. "I will see to my own folk!"

The Ordovices followed his horn and the galloping silver horse as Cadal fought his way through the roiling mass on the valley floor. The Ordovice lords battled furiously, with the Romans and with their own villagers, trying to stem the tide. Cadal, atop his chariot, shouted louder than the wail of his war horns but the shepherds fled home to their sheep and the Romans sifted out the high lords of the Ordovices, surrounding each whose gold and fine clothing betrayed his rank; and each died fighting. None were offered surrender. Cadal laid about him with his sword, the silver horse standard long lost in the chaos, and when the Roman officer who blocked Cadal's blade and struck his own fatal blow saw who he had killed, he spat in the mud and cursed.

"May the Furies tear him limb from limb," Galerius said, and every man of his cohort knew he meant the dead Tribune Terentius. "For the waste of a good man."

"That'll get you an award though," Quinctilius Rufus said.

"I don't want it!" Galerius snapped. But he would take it. Tainted or not, battle spoil and honors made a vital part of an officer's income. He turned his back on the dead king. "Close up that line! We aren't picking flowers!"

The Twentieth and its auxiliaries pushed the rear of Loarn's army farther up the valley as Cadal's went under. From his vantage point Caecilius saw the tide flowing south and took his helmet off to scratch his head, thinking. Rain poured off his hair, but it wasn't possible to get wetter than he was.

"He's not going to surrender, sir," Marcellinus said.

"Nor will his conscripts. They aren't like Cadal's people."

"The Silures regard their king as something close to divine," Marcellinus said. "Touched by the gods at any rate."

"So is the emperor of Rome," Caecilius snapped.

Marcellinus coughed.

"Yes, I know," Caecilius said. "The difference is the Silures believe it."

"Is there a way to cut the Demetae loose from them? Offer them terms? I saw their chief go down."

"Unlikely. Our scouts say Loarn saw some sort of vision at Lughnasa and now they think he's fated."

"I don't like that word," Marcellinus said. "*Fated*. It makes me itch."

"Let us say it's ambiguous at best," Caecilius said. "We will have to do this the hard way. Put the auxiliaries in the front again as long as they can hold out. I won't destroy two legions if I can help it."

—

The change in the front lines was short-lived. The auxiliaries had already spent most of their strength and their lines were ragged. Caecilius swore and the legions came up again in the pouring rain, pushing the Britons from both sides, leaving the auxiliaries to defend the muddy slopes from anyone who tried to climb them again.

Faustus could see Loarn at the center of it all, astride his horse, urging his men on to... to what? Faustus knew the Silure king was doomed now, and Loarn must know it too, but he wore that doom like some kind of glittering cloak, to be free of Rome in whatever way he came to it. And what did Faustus fight for now, in this mud-choked valley? For Rome of course. But also in some bone-deep way for Britain? For what Rome could give Britain whether it wanted it or not? Because hundreds of years from now it might matter, that the men who served Rome here on the frontier might have left something that would be needed? Where had that thought come from? A screaming Briton threw himself at Faustus, shieldless, a spear in one hand and a sword in the other and he abandoned all thought, as Llamrei had. Fight and don't think. Go by instinct, go by training, watch their eyes, don't think, focus.

The mud was mixed with blood now and the horrible smells of death: blood and opened bowels that even the rain could not wash away. He fought with the blue-painted Briton, slashed at his scale cuirass, sliced it open enough to go back for another blow, sword point through the scale this time, blood gushing. A wounded horse screamed and thrashed on the ground before him. A broken chariot lay like a barricade. The dying Briton fell backward across it and another leapt atop it to swing an axe at Faustus. Faustus kneed Arion out of the way and Arion screamed as the axe cut a gash across his haunch. Faustus swung his sword into the Briton's ribs with a force increased by fury. When the man fell, he dismounted while men of the First Cohort closed shields around him.

Faustus sheathed his long sword and drew the short blade. He passed Arion's reins to his optio. "Take him to the rear. Paullus has my spare horse."

He slotted his shield into line with the first century. It wasn't going to matter whether he could see over the battle or not. It had wound down to a rain-drenched slog and a contest of numbers, weapons, and wills. Man after man of his cohort went down taking three or four Britons apiece. The valley reeked like a slaughterhouse. Loarn was still mounted. Faustus could see him, head and torso above the milling chaos, the red-gold crown shining on his wet black hair even in the rain.

Slowly the Roman army tightened the noose around the war band. It cost them dear. Faustus forced himself not to think about that, not now when thinking about things got soldiers killed. He stabbed with his short sword, shield up, blinking away the rain that sheeted from his helmet rim into his eyes and down his nose. He hooked the next man's shield away with the edge of his own, drove his sword in under the man's guard, into a bare, blue-painted chest – one of the old lords who followed the old ways, when a man went to battle naked to show his courage and ferocity. The spear pattern tattooed on his breast was old too, faded nearly to gray. On the ridge, the crows hunched on wet branches, waiting.

Loarn died when the First Cohort hacked its way through his captains and pulled him from his horse. By then the battle was a straggling mass of fleeing Britons and vengeful Romans angry at their losses. Septimus and two more of Faustus's men pinned Loarn to the ground and he writhed in their grip.

"Give over!" Septimus grunted, but Faustus could see there would be no surrender. Septimus began to pull the king's arms behind to bind him.

A Briton in ring mail and a heavy gold torque, bleeding from a gashed thigh, knocked Septimus away with a spear thrust that opened up his arm. Loarn shook the others off in a fury and reached for his fallen sword. Septimus shifted his to his left hand and Faustus pushed past him, stumbling over a broken chariot wheel.

Loarn rose, sword in both hands, and Faustus's blade slid across the king's throat as Loarn aimed for his head. There had been no time to speak, to say anything at all. And what would he have said to acknowledge their left-hand kinship? Loarn lay still amid the chaos now, that dark, glittering force extinguished. The blood that flowed from his throat was already beginning to stop. The crown rested in the muddy grass.

"I'd of done that," Septimus gasped to Faustus. "Shouldn't have been you."

"It wouldn't have mattered," Faustus said. Silvia would thank him or hate him. Maybe both, no matter whose sword it had been. And best let Caecilius be angry with him instead of Septimus, for losing his prize.

All around them the battle had devolved to hand-to-hand fighting, the British numbers dwindling. The rain was still falling steadily, washing mud and blood into a quagmire. The death of the king turned the tide of the battle at last and Loarn's subjects began to surrender. Caecilius kept his word: no prisoners were taken among the high lords of the Silures but one, who had been Loarn's last defender. A blow with the edge of a shield had knocked her helmet off and they had balked at killing a woman for just long enough that Faustus, recognizing her, ordered her taken to the legate instead.

"He said kill 'em all," a centurion objected.

Faustus eyed Llamrei, standing stone-faced. "Tie up her leg. He will need someone to negotiate terms with, and this one will serve." Silvia had said so, and he thought she knew. Someone would have to be in charge, or the villagers and plain folk would starve this winter. There would be levies taken for the slave market, but the rest must be fed and their strongest would be the ones taken.

They camped on the ridge where they had hidden in ambush, felling trees now for space for a marching camp. The Roman dead were brought to biers outside the camp walls to be burned, their names and ranks noted first by weary commanders, and the British dead looted before being left to the birds. There were too many Roman dead. Faustus sat dispiritedly by his campfire while Paullus fed both him and the spare horse that had never caught up with him in the battle. Arion, Paullus reported, was with the cavalry in Arvina's camp and would heal, so said the cavalry vet. It was the one encouraging piece of news, a live horse among so many dead men.

In the morning the rain stopped and Caecilius ordered the siege engines retrieved from the Twentieth's train and on the next day he took the legion to Dinas Tomen with them.

Llamrei accompanied the legate under guard, on a captured pony. Her wounded thigh had been cleaned and stitched by the legion's surgeon and Caecilius had given her a clean tunic and army breeches from someone's stores to replace her filthy shirt and trousers. She had no idea what he was going to do with her.

"Watch," he said to her now, as the great machines were ratcheted back, buckets loaded with stones that took two men to lift. There was no one within the walls. Everyone inside Dinas Tomen had fled at news of the defeat and the approach of the column. This was a matter of vengeance. For costing him so many Roman lives, the legate had said explicitly.

There would be no more rebellions in West Britain. It would be two generations at least before the Silures or the Demetae could do much more than fend off vengeful neighbors who saw a chance to encroach on abandoned lands. Rhodri was dead. Iorwen and the boy would be in hiding, with Teyrnon and the younger Druids and anyone else that Rome's eye might light on. Even the birds had fled Dinas Tomen, lifting off in a great cloud as the catapults were brought up. The onagers' crews were fighting with the mules that had pulled the carriages up the mountain. For reasons known only to mules, they didn't like the place and they didn't like something in the air, or maybe just something in their long-eared imaginings, but they were restless and stubborn and bit the centurion in charge. When they were unhitched, they kicked loose from their tethers and thundered back down the track while their cursing drivers chased them. Above, the first stone slammed into the walls of Dinas Tomen, and a great cloud of dust rose as a piece of wall crumbled. Then another and another. When they ran out of stones, Caecilius sent men forward to roll the ones already used down the hillside to load up and throw again. Wall by wall, terrace by terrace, she watched Dinas Tomen come down. It was empty and the Romans could have dismantled it from the inside, but as Caecilius said, this was vengeance. Vengeance and a display of how Rome could crack any hold open like an egg if it so wished.

The rumble of the great machines and the thunder of the falling walls made an almost constant vibration in the earth so that, at first, she didn't feel the swaying of the rocky ground under her feet. Then one of the great stones went awry, flying past the walls to slam nearly into the camp of the legion at the foot of the mountain. The frame of the onager tipped sideways, and its crew fled as it rolled over. The mountain shook.

Shifting muscles deep beneath its skin, the earth remade itself. It spread its great paws from mountain to ridgetop like a cat stretching its back, turned and resettled and finally slept again amid the rubble.

XXI. CATH MAWR

The birds had gone still nearly an hour before Eirian walked down to the vicus. She had put the quiet down to the unusual heat of the day, but as she passed a dozen cattle being driven through the street, they balked and milled in the road while the herd dogs barked frantically, and the herd boy swore at them all. Then the sign that hung from the oak tree beside the Capricorn swayed violently and a fishmonger's stall collapsed in a flood of herring. Eirian turned around. She stumbled over paving stones heaved up from the street. The vicus was full of milling people now, shouting and praying as second floor balconies came down and the contents of shop counters were flung into the road. An overturned crate of turnips bounced across her path and a falling chair flew past her head. Eirian ran for the fort gates as the ground heaved under her. The plinth that held Cath Mawr buckled as she passed it; the statue fell and cracked in two. She stood staring at it, hand to her mouth, while a crow screamed from the trees along the riverbank and a dog on the bridge barked furiously at it. Then no more movement came; the ground stilled. Old Cat's enigmatic eyes watched her from two directions now.

Inside the fort one of the columns that adorned the Praetorium had shifted, leaning drunkenly into the portico, and Eirian waded through the flow from a cracked water pipe that two workers had already begun to dig for. Their own house looked mostly undamaged, and she found Silvia restoring the family gods to their niche in the atrium. Argos padded at Silvia's heels as if to see that she wasn't stolen by whatever force had shaken the ground.

"I thought we were done with this beastly land shifting about," Silvia said by way of greeting. She looked ready to cry, clutching the silver Lares to her chest and brushing the crumbs of dislodged plaster from their shelf with the other hand. "And thank Juno it didn't set the kitchen on fire. We'd just started to heat water for the wash. It's all over the floor but at least it put the fire out."

Eirian took the end of her mantle and brushed the gods' niche clean. "You washed yesterday – everything that could be washed except the dog," she pointed out gently.

Since a rider from the legion had brought the news, Silvia had been constantly and grimly busy about everything but any kind of mourning. Faustus had sent them each a private message – to get that over with, he had told Eirian – to say that the king was dead, and by Faustus's hand, and he would be home when Dinas Tomen was rubble. Silvia had put her letter in the fire.

"Everyone brings mud in. I was going to wash the cushion covers."

Eirian righted an overturned chair. Its cushion was perfectly clean. She could hear Gwladus and Paullus putting the kitchen to rights. "This is the worst one we've had. Where is Lucius?"

Silvia sat down wearily. "He went to see after his tutor. That apartment he lives in looks as if it would blow over in a high wind, and probably has."

"The quake toppled Cath Mawr's altar," Eirian said. "It split in two. That will mean something." Everything meant something. If it had come before the battle, it might have meant the death of kings. It still might. Signs moved backward in time as often as not.

"What will they do with him?" Silvia asked abruptly now, as if the quake that had broken Old Cat's altar had finally shaken that loose too.

"I don't know," Eirian said. "Faustus said they took him from the field, so maybe…"

"Maybe they won't mutilate his body and send his head to Rome?" Silvia closed her eyes, her face unreadable.

"I don't know," Eirian said. "Maybe." Depending on how politically useful, or dangerous, it would be, to be the general who had taken such a prize. She had learned that much in her years with Rome.

The greater question now, which Faustus had not addressed, was what the legate intended to do about the kingship of the Silures. He was reasonably sure that was what was on Caecilius's mind when the legate summoned him to his tent in the dusk, with the ruins of Dinas Tomen looming above them. There had been no more quakes but the one that morning had completed the wreckage that the onagers had begun. As soon as the legion left, the wild would begin to retake it, the green creepers and the small trees whose roots seized a purchase in any unmended crack.

Faustus saluted Caecilius and waited, vine staff under his arm. Neither Marcellinus nor any of the junior tribunes was in attendance. A brazier warmed the tent in the evening chill. Caecilius's cuirass and helmet sat on their stand, newly polished. Caecilius offered him a cup of warm wine and a chair. Faustus took both suspiciously.

"That woman, Llamrei," the legate said. "*She* is not of the Royal House?"

"No," Faustus said, increasingly suspicious at the emphasis.

"And you suggest her as regent. For Loarn's nephew?"

"Yes," Faustus said, avoiding the legate's suggestion that there might be a different candidate. "Silvia thought her the one we should go to, when it was all done with. I actually trust my sister's judgment in this instance. She lived with them."

"Yes," Caecilius conceded. "She told me the same."

"Iorwen's husband is dead," Faustus said before the legate could say anything else. "This will eliminate the possibility of a new husband attempting to rule."

"Iorwen's boy is very young. Might not an older candidate be preferable?"

"No," Faustus said. "I will resign first and take him with me."

Caecilius did not ask what he meant. He nodded thoughtfully. "Or yourself?"

"No. And no."

"It would be ideal, however."

"Only if you are staging a tragedy," Faustus said. "The kind that ends with everyone dead. I am not interested in playing that role. Nor will I allow my nephew to."

"Centurion, that is almost insubordinate."

"I know. That should demonstrate my absolute sincerity."

Caecilius nodded. "You are dismissed, Centurion, while I think on that." Outside in the falling dark a fox called and its mate answered from the valley floor. "They'll den in the king's bed by winter," Caecilius said as Faustus saluted.

"The human footprint is fleeting here." Faustus gripped his vine staff. "I could plant this and it would sprout."

Llamrei sat opposite Caecilius in the morning, her hands unbound, with only a guard at the tent flap while she considered his proposal. He had put on the silvered cuirass and scarlet sash of office and the helmet that made his face hard to read.

"Legate, I am tired," she told him when he had spoken. "Perhaps too tired for your purpose."

"Drink your wine," Caecilius said. "It will revive you."

She took the cup in her hands but didn't drink. "I negotiated the last peace. Why do you wish for me in that role?"

"Given that it fell apart? That would depend on whether you wish to raise Loarn's sister's son to fight against Rome again. Do you?"

No. As many times no as there were dead spear brothers lying under a bare sky for the crows. *No* for Rhodri, for Pwyll and for Gwydion. "If I say no, how will you be sure I speak the truth?" she asked him.

"Would it be better if I installed my primus pilus's nephew? The one your people tried to kill once already? We could make sure he lives this time."

"You could not," Llamrei said flatly.

"No? You tried to kill his father too, and we burned out a village for that."

"Do you threaten me with that?"

"I want peace," Caecilius said. "I want West Britain firmly allied with Rome. With Cadal dead, the Ordovices will choose a new king subject to our approval. By their laws he need not even be of Cadal's blood. Your people are different." Primitive, he thought, almost primeval, not far developed from the little dark people who lived in the hillsides. He understood the Ordovices. Llamrei's people made his head ache, but they would be best ruled by their own laws. He asked her, "Do you wish an internal war among you for the kingship? Or do you wish to raise Iorwen's boy to be a client of Rome? Those are your choices."

Llamrei put the wine cup down untouched. The kingship consumed the king. She had watched as it consumed Bendigeid. Then Aedden. Then Loarn. She would not have that for Iorwen's boy. "Leave me to think, legate. I wish to speak with someone whose wisdom I value. You may send soldiers to watch me, but they must stay well back. I have nowhere to run."

—

Llamrei rested beside the curbstone at the southern door into Ty Isaf. There was very little if any of the dark people's blood in Llamrei but all the same they would know she was there. The Lower House seemed unaffected by the quake, the thorn scrub and rowan that shielded it undamaged. The sun was out, and bees were humming among the red and white clover in the long grass. She drowsed as she waited, while her escort threw dice a hundred paces away.

"Something will come upon you if you sleep in Ty Isaf's door overnight, Sun Woman."

Llamrei opened her eyes as the old woman in the chair motioned to those who carried it to set her down. She looked tiny among the piled skins that cushioned the seat. Llamrei scrubbed her fist across her face. She had not meant to go to sleep.

Heron, Old One of Ty Isaf, gave her a long look, noting the Roman tunic and breeches and the bandaged thigh. She sniffed the air and Llamrei called to the escort at their dice game, "Go farther away, you have too much iron about you."

The escort moved but they put up the dice and watched the Old One and her sons suspiciously. The sons were there and then not there, and then there again. The escort's centurion rubbed his own eyes. The Old One wore a brown wool gown and a cat fur cloak. A bronze band sat on a cloud of thin gray hair. She looked at the escort and said, "You presume, Llamrei, that you bring Romans to Ty Isaf."

"And yet you have come to me anyway, Old Mother," Llamrei said. "Nor could I come without them."

"I came to you because I knew you would sit here with them until I did," Heron snapped. "What do you want of us? Sun People's business is not our concern, not even your kind's."

"Dinas Tomen is ruins," Llamrei said. "What the Romans did not do, the quake brought down. Are the people of Ty Isaf unharmed?"

"We are not your concern. The mountain spoke to us beforehand and so we were prepared."

"That is fortunate," Llamrei said. "I am glad of it. May there be no more."

"There will not. That is not why you came here. What do you want?"

"The Roman commander wishes me to make his peace with our people and the Demetae. And raise Iorwen's boy to be a Roman vassal. Old Mother, tell me what to do."

"You do not know?" Heron looked exasperated. "I will answer only because Iorwen belongs to the Mother, and a little to us: Learn to live with them as we have learned to live with you."

Llamrei grimaced. She had suspected that would be the answer and it came hard, but worse would be another king raised to feed the Morrigan's crows. "Will they ever leave?" she asked Heron.

"You have not."

"We are different."

"No, not different. Ask the land. Ask Cath Mawr."

Heron's sons picked up her chair and then there was nothing where they had been but grass and one trampled clover blossom.

Llamrei signaled her guard. "Take me back to your legate."

—

Caecilius next considered the question of Loarn's body. His branch of the Caecilii had negotiated the poisonous waters of Roman politics by the expedient of not calling attention to themselves since before the days of the deified Augustus. The less glory an emperor's general claimed for himself, the longer he was likely to remain in office. Even the present of a defeated king's head reminded any emperor that it was the general who had taken it and not himself. Therefore, the legion marched back to Isca Silurum leaving Tribune Marcellinus to escort Llamrei and the body of the king to Porth Cerrig. There Marcellinus would oversee the installation of Iorwen's son as nominal king and Loarn would be buried. Part of Caecilius's demands had been that he not lie at Dinas Tomen, not lie where his body would give that place power again.

"I will take you there if you wish to go," Faustus told Silvia. "To see him laid down."

"Caecilius agreed to that?"

"He did. He will even give us an escort."

"He would have to," Silvia said. "But I don't think I could bear it."

"I'm sorry it was me," Faustus said.

"It isn't that." Silvia shook her head, trying to make him understand. "How could he love me and do that?"

Loarn had lied to her about the war. Worse, he had allowed Llew to murder her son or try to, known and not stopped him. "They were separate," Faustus said helplessly. He knew that wasn't a satisfactory answer. "He took what he was given."

"So did I," Silvia said bitterly. "Every time, like a fool."

"The gods don't always make that easy," was all he could think to say. It was all that anyone knew in the end, that the gods were not always benevolent.

Silvia laid a hand on his arm. "I am glad it was you. I hated him for it but…"

"But you would not wish him in chains in Rome? No, nor would I. Nor would I wish for myself what the Fates asked of him."

Silvia shuddered. "Better Lucius go into the Centuriate than that." She put a hand to the neck of her gown, tugging it up again to hide the mark that wouldn't leave her.

Still, the gods seemed to have decided to stop prying the earth from its bed and construction on Isca Fortress began again. The legate had ordered Cath Mawr mended and reinstalled on his plinth and since then the ground had stayed still. For inscrutable reasons the legion credited Cath Mawr with that and increasing offerings were left on his altar. His whiskered likeness began to appear on the clay antefixes adorning the new barracks roofs.

"See those?" Paullus said to Gwladus. "The new adopts the old. It always does."

"Maybe," Gwladus said. "But it's getting it to go the other way round that gives the trouble."

"I went to the centurion this morning," Paullus said. "I bought myself out, except I don't want to leave the army."

"Then don't," Gwladus said. "It's being able to that matters."

"Matters to you, you mean."

She nodded. "Matters to me."

Fall slid past Samhain into winter, hung with green branches and holly berries and warmed with the solstice fires that everyone, Roman and Silure alike, brought home to kindle some life into the starkness of ice and snow. The primus pilus's house smelled of pine boughs and the baking that Gwladus and Paullus had begun for Saturnalia.

Faustus was adding up the household accounts the last time his father visited him. Silvius Valerianus appeared to be dressed for the baths, in a linen tunic and sandals, a towel around his shoulders. "What are you going to do about your sister?" he demanded.

Faustus stoppered the ink bottle and put his pen down. "I am going to let her do whatever it is about herself. She is twice widowed, and I suspect that neither marriage inclines her to look for a third. She can live with me as long as she likes."

Silvius Valerianus looked around. "I've lost my bath oil," he muttered. He peered at Faustus's desk.

"That's ink," Faustus said.

"The man I married your sister to was a spendthrift," the shade said morosely. "I failed her."

That was a startling admission. "No doubt you did the best you knew how," Faustus said, although not entirely kindly.

The shade stared at him – a wispy figure caught in the circle of light from the desk lamp. "Do you see now that I did my best?" he asked hopefully. "Do you really see that?"

"I do," Faustus admitted. His best had been awful, but maybe it was all he had. He felt a little sympathy for the old man now.

Faustus had done the best that he knew too, since he had come to Britain, and so often it had been the wrong thing.

"Do you think I failed your mother? Do you think she ever loved me?" The shade was almost pleading. His hands reached out as if to grasp something that constantly eluded him.

"What I think doesn't matter," Faustus told him. How much difference did it really make, how bad his best had been if it was all he had to give? "I expect you did the best you knew with her too."

"Did she love me?"

Faustus sighed. "I don't think so."

The old man nodded. "I needed to know." He reached out a hand again and this time his bath oil appeared in it. "There it is." His misty form thinned slowly until there was nothing left but the light from the oil lamp.

—

Marcus Silvius Valerianus did not come back.

"I expect that was what he needed to hear," Eirian said. "That you knew he did his best."

"His best was ghastly."

"He knows. But if he knows that *you* know it was all he had—"

"I don't know what I know. Will he rest now?"

"I told him our news the last time I had a sense of him, just before you saw him last. He seemed pleased. That might be enough. He must be longing to go."

"You didn't tell me you'd seen him."

"I wasn't sure I had."

Faustus didn't bother wondering why his wife even thought she had, since she talked to seals, although something there had changed since he had come back from Dinas Tomen. They had heard the seals crying on the shingle and he had asked her what they said, and she had told him she no longer knew. It was a bargain, she said. It was not his affair, and she hadn't told him more than that, but Faustus carried her other news with him everywhere, a small constant pleasure to warm him. Eirian was pregnant. *Three parts British*. That was what Iorwen had told him at the legate's banquet: "Your child will be three parts British."

Iorwen had also said, "You may wish to rule us, but we will absorb you," which came back to Faustus on the eve of Saturnalia as he stood on the north rampart looking out over the winter hillside and the remains of the old Silure fortress there, almost overtaken now by sapling trees and bindweed.

With his bonus and share of the spoil, Faustus had bought a piece of land not far from Isca. Now that West Britain was quiet, he might well be posted elsewhere before his term was up, but they would come back, he and Eirian and the child, and maybe more children, to plant a farm there, with sheep and pigs and grain to sell to the army. Gallia Narbonensis and the farm where he had been born held no lure for him, but it was strange how the idea of a farm in West Britain was different. Silvia had had a number of things to say about that, but not unkindly. She had also suggested that a shop in a *colonia* of the legions offered the chance to stay in Britain without the pigs, but Faustus found he wanted a piece of land, had wanted it since Eirian had told him there would be a child. He had recently had a letter from Tuathal, assuring him of the High King's unswerving devotion to Rome's interests as long as they did not include invasion or military levies and Faustus thought now of Tuathal's drive to claim the place in Hibernia that was part of his bones. It hadn't mattered that he had been raised in Britain.

Tomorrow would begin Saturnalia. Galerius had been given a long leave over the winter and was coming to visit, no doubt to see if Silvia looked like changing her mind. Faustus thought she wouldn't, although what Galerius proposed to do upon his own retirement might make a difference if it did not include pigs. A patrol went past him below, looking up to salute the primus pilus as they went, winter cloaks crimson splotches against the fields that supplied the Isca granaries. The tilled land stretched along the lower slope below the old Silure fortress like a sleeping cat and the stubble of its winter-shorn flanks might have been the fur of Cath Mawr himself. Faustus could almost see the great ribs rise and fall with his breath.

Cath Mawr, as old as the ancient barrows or the stone dances. Curlew had said, "We are only fleas in his fur." "Cath Mawr is the land's," Iorwen had said. "Old Cat *is* the land," his mother had said.

The wind picked up; it blew a clump of fallen aspen leaves into a bare hedgerow and scattered them a moment later as if the great sleeping form had opened one yellow eye and closed it again.

Faustus trotted down the stairs, half laughing at himself, but he went to the vicus anyway and bought a small fish. He saw Lucius at a jeweler's stall, inspecting a display of sigillaria, the little figures that friends exchanged as Saturnalia gifts. He called to him that dinner would be soon. That Lucius was still with them was another source of joy. On his way back to the fort, he laid the fish on the altar below the whiskered face and imagined that the tufted ears twitched. "From your fleas," he told it.

—

Lucius considered a small stone magpie and a clay otter. The otter brought a memory that slid away as soon as it came. The span of time between the day he had ridden along the headland and the day he had walked back through the gates of Isca Fortress had grown to seem shorter and shorter until sometimes he thought they had been the same day, although he knew they hadn't. He had had another name in that misty time between, but it was gone too. He was Lucius Manlius again and he was going to have a career in the army. Some other child had been made king of the Silures, for which Lucius who had known more than he let on, gave thanks to Minerva. The goddess of strategy and wisdom had no doubt known a very bad idea when she saw it. He paid for the otter and the magpie and went home to dinner.

—

The boy sat with his dark head bent intently over the small desk. Slowly the letters formed under his pen, with many splotches and oversetting of the ink bottle.

"That is very good," Llamrei said. "You will be as skilled as a scribe soon."

"What does a scribe do?" The boy lifted his head.

"He writes out important things for the king, but you will write your own." And speak Latin, and read the histories the Romans wrote about themselves, and thus know how to manage them. And not hear the hungry prideful voice that spoke out of the wind and the dark and ever always wanted only blood, no matter the odds.

"I will write out my own things," the child said firmly. A sandy furred cat came and curled around his ankles, and he scratched its ears with an inky hand.

A note on names, place names, language, and geography

Listed below are the Roman names for places mentioned in this book and their modern equivalents. In some cases where the Roman name is not known I have used a form of the current name, particularly for places in Wales. Other names I have invented since their ancient ones are not known. These are marked with *

Place Names and Their Modern Equivalents

Abona Sea Mills, Bristol
Aquae Sulis Bath
Ariconium Weston Under Penyard
Blaidd Llwyd* Tinkinswood
Blestium Monmouth
Bodotria Firth of Forth
Bryn Epona* fictional hillfort of the Ordovices
Burrium Usk
Caer Gai name still in use today
Calleva Silchester
Carn Goch name still in use
Castra Borea* Cawdor
Castra Pinnata Inchtuthil
Clota Mouth Firth of Clyde
Coed-y-Caerau name still in use today
Cow's Inlet* Brean Down
Deva Chester

Deva, the River Dee
Dinas Head name still in use
Dinas Tomen Castell Dinas
Dolaucothi (Luentinum) Pumpsaint, Wales
Dragon's Head* Braich-y-Pwll
Drumanagh name in modern use
Dun Mori/Moridunum Carmarthen
Eburacum York
Gallia Narbonensis Languedoc and Provence, southern France.
Glevum Gloucester
Gobannium Abergavenny
Hibernia (Inis Fáil) Ireland
High Isle Hoy Island, the Orkneys
Inber Domnann Malahide Bay
Inis Fáil (Hibernia) Ireland
Isca, the River Usk
Isca Silurum Caerleon
Laigin Leinster
Llanmelin name still in use today
Lleu's Well* Dol-y-Coed Spring, Llanwrtyd Wells
Luentinum (Dolaucothi) Pumpsaint, Wales
Magnis Kenchester
Mona Anglesey
Moridunum/Dun Mori Carmarthen
Narbo Martius Narbonne, France
Octapitarum St. David's Head
Orcades The Orkneys
Pen-y-Gaer name still in use
Pen-y-Lan name still in use as a suburb of Cardiff
Porth Cerrig Porthkerry
Sabrina, the River Severn
Tara Hill of Tara
Ty Isaf Ty Isaf Long Barrow
Uxella, the River Axe, Somerset

Vaga, the River Wye
Venta Silurum Caerwent
Viroconium Wroxeter

Glossary

amicus a particular friend, especially a crony of the emperor

angusticlavius literally "narrow stripe" from the narrow purple band on his tunic

Annwn Celtic underworld

aquilifer soldier who carries the legionary Eagle

as base unit of Roman coinage, 1/16 of a denarius

basilisk fabulous North African serpent with a deadly touch and poisonous breath

bean-sidhe woman of Celtic myth whose voice foretells death

Beltane Spring festival, May 1

bonasus bull-like monster believed to defend itself by ejecting caustic excrement

carnyx Celtic war horn

cognomen Roman final name (pl. cognomina)

colonia settlement of retired legionaries established in Roman provinces

cornicen Roman army trumpeter

corvus "raven", the spiked boarding ramp of a roman warship

dextra right hand

denarius silver coin worth about a day's pay for a skilled worker

Dis Manibus Roman tombstone inscription: "To the spirits of the dead"

Druids ancient Celtic priesthood

the Eagles the Roman army; from the eagle standards of the legions

Epona Celtic goddess of horses and guide to the afterlife
fian, pl. fianna band of young fighting men in Ireland
Furies Roman goddesses of vengeance and retribution
garum fish sauce ubiquitous in the Roman empire
genius loci the spirit or god of a place
the Goddess the Mother
haruspex official trained in divination
hypocaust underfloor hot-air heating system
Jupiter the great god, Roman equivalent of Zeus; Jupiter Capitolinus is the patron of Rome
Juno wife of Jupiter, goddess of women and childbirth
Lares household gods
laticlavius literally "broad-stripe" for the wide purple band on his tunic
latrunculi Roman board game of strategy
legate commander of a legion or other high office
libra Roman unit of weight, .722 lb
lorica armor made of segmented plates
Lugh/Lleu Celtic god of the sun and harvest
Lughnasa Midsummer festival of Lugh, August 1
Llyr Celtic sea god
Mars Ultor Roman god of war in his role as Avenger
Minerva Roman goddess of wisdom and strategy
Mithras Persian savior god popular in the Roman army
the Mother Earth Mother in any of her many forms
Neptune Roman god of the sea and earthquakes
nymphaeum a grotto dedicated to the spirits of water
Ocelus Romano-British god
onager a stone-throwing catapult; literally "wild ass"
optio second in command to an officer; a general might have several
Orcus god of the Underworld who punishes broken oaths; an aspect of Pluto
pilum (pl. pila) legionary's javelin
Pluto Roman god of the Underworld

poppy tears painkiller made from the opium poppy
portoria taxes paid on the import and export of goods
Praetorium commander's house in a fort or camp
Principia headquarters in a fort or camp
Prometheus god who stole fire from Olympus to give to humankind. As punishment, an eagle ate his liver every day and the next day the liver regenerated to be eaten again
pullarius soldier in charge of the sacred chickens used for divination before battles
procurator chief financial officer of a province
rota simple board game resembling tic-tac-toe
Samhain Fall destival when the Celtic dead may return to earth, October 31,
scilla urginea maritima, sea squill, used as an emetic
sidhe in Celtic legend, the hollow hills of faery; here a dwelling of an older race
signifer soldier who carries a cohort or century standard
sinistra left-hand
Tartarus in Roman mythology, region of Hades where the wicked dead are punished
terret harness ring through which the reins pass
Tullianum Roman prison where condemned were kept prior to execution; now known as the Mamertine
Typhon monstrous god and personification of volcanic forces
vexillum (pl. vexilla) Romans military banner
Via Lactea the Milky Way
vicus civilian village surrounding a Roman fort

Author's Note

Little is known of what went on in the years between Sallustius Lucullus's execution in approximately 89 CE and the arrival of a new governor, Aulus Vicirius Proculus, in approximately 93. The events in *Birds of Prey* are entirely fictional.

The various signs and portents that appear do exist. Wales has been prone to earthquakes in the past, the Northern Lights are sometimes seen as far south as the Black Mountains, and the vision seen by Loarn on the sky is a phenomenon known as the Brocken Spectre, a magnified shadow cast in midair on clouds opposite the sun. No statue of a cat-faced deity has been unearthed in Wales as far as I know, but some of the clay antefixes – roof terminals – that adorned the Roman buildings in Isca Silurum feature a particularly catlike whiskered face with pointed ears. At least one historian, Ray Howell in *Silures: Resistance, Resilience, Revival*, has speculated that they might represent a local cat cult or feline deity. Guesswork based on possibility is the work of the historical novelist.

Where I cross most definitely into the territory of myth is with the Old Ones, the little dark people of the hills. There was indeed a small, dark, probably blue-eyed, race who lived in Britain before the tall, fair Celts. "Cheddar Man," the Mesolithic body dated to 7150 BCE and found in Somerset, provided the DNA evidence for dark skin and pale eyes. These dark folk flourished even before the Neolithic farmers who built the long barrows and the great stone rings, and at least 6,000 years before the Celts first came. Their descendants were no doubt absorbed into the dominant populace long before the date of this novel, even if they did not entirely vanish, making their continued presence as a distinct people unlikely.

Mythologically speaking, however, they are still a presence and their echoes may be heard in folklore, in tales of the small ones who inhabit the hollow hills, the neolithic burial chambers that dot the land. They are seldom encountered and often vengeful and dangerous when they are. As each new wave of invaders flowed across Britain these old ones would have faded ever farther into the background, living on the edges of the newcomers' settlements, hunting with the flint and bronze weapons that the newcomers' iron blades defeated so easily. Their remnants, or the collective memory of them, might eventually achieve the status of the fae, the magical beings of fireside stories, for whom it is still advisable to put out a saucer of milk now and then. For that reason they inhabit this series.

As always I owe grateful thanks to my husband, Tony Neuron, for general moral support and map-making, and to Kit Nevile, who is a peerless editor.